iOɔ

The Witches of Riegersburg

by Julie Anne Stratton

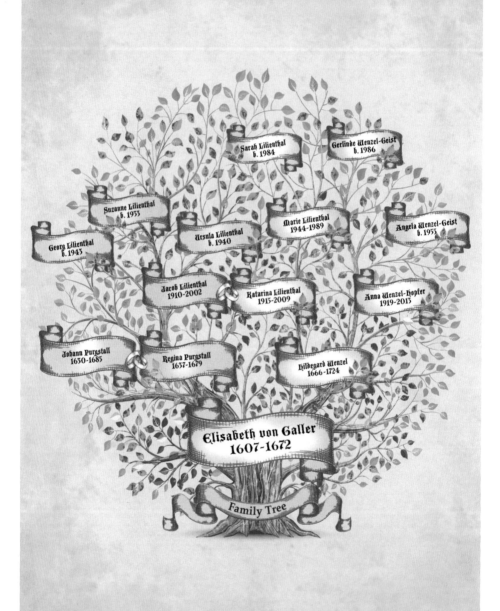

Sarah Lilienthal
b. 1984

Gerlinde Wenzel-Geist
b. 1986

Suzanne Lilienthal
b. 1933

Marie Lilienthal
1944-1989

Angela Wenzel-Geist
b. 1955

Georg Lilienthal
b. 1943

Ursula Lilienthal
b. 1940

Jacob Lilienthal
1910-2002

Katarina Lilienthal
1915-2009

Anna Wenzel-Hopfer
1919-2013

Johann Purgstall
1630-1685

Regina Purgstall
1657-1679

Hildegard Wenzel
1666-1724

Elisabeth von Galler
1607-1672

Family Tree

The Witches of Riegersburg

a novel

by Julie Anne Stratton

ANANKE PRESS

The Witches of Riegersburg
Published by Ananke Press
Copyright © 2020 by Julie Anne Stratton
All rights reserved

Interior and cover design by Ananke Press

ISBN: 978-1-7341720-1-0 (paperback)

 ANANKE
PRESS

Ananke Press
178 Columbus Avenue, #230137, New York, NY 10023
anankepress.com
info@anankepress.com

for my daughters Carmen, Katarina and Amrita

Because a woman brought death
A bright Maiden overcame it,
And so the highest blessing
In all of creation
Lies in the form of a woman
Since God has become man
In a sweet and blessed Virgin.

—Hildegard of Bingen
Quia Ergo Femina

We are aware that the gods of patriarchy are pale derivatives and reversals of ancient yet always Present Goddess(es). We suspect that phallocentric writers and artists who have even a glimmer of insight are sometimes made uncomfortable by their own state of deception. Those who have any awareness of the heinous crime of reversal, which is patriarchy must be in a state of deep conflict and fear of ... Her."

—Mary Daly
Quintessence...Realizing the Archaic Future

Contents

Baroness
Elisabeth von Galler

1607–1672

Chapter One

Riegersburg Castle, Austria, June 1665

lisabeth surveyed the preparations for the night's festivities from her throne set on a wooden dais. The air was chilly. She shivered and felt her golden chain, the one with a small crimson stone: the color of blood, cold against her chest. In one hand, she held an apple, the other — a staff carved of birch. All day, her servants had gathered branches from the ancient forests of her dominion that reached from Feldbach in the south and as far as Furstenfeld in the north. Elisabeth watched them assemble two enormous piles of wood in the middle of the field, necessary for tonight's ritual. Her back ached, but then she caught a whiff of fresh spring plants: possibly nettle or dandelion and a feeling of gratitude swept away her exhaustion.

Thank you, Goddess, for year after year bringing us plentiful crops.

This was her role, her duty as Baroness to the land and populace every year, to be present here at this celebration, not far from her fortress. She favored this large clearing because of its beauty and the view of rolling hills in the distance.

Elisabeth looked over at the Maypole positioned across from her and remembered fondly how she used to dance around it as a young maiden. She saw herself laughing and how the young men back then desired her affections.

I am grateful the ways of old still remain steadfast here.

The trees whispered as if they were enchanted:

"You now have power, real power; of wealth and land, of position, of respect, and above all, of magic. It's the kind of power that runs deep through your veins, like the rivers that flow through your land, like the wind that blows through the trees, like the rich, brown, fertile fields, and last of all, like the great blazes of Walpurgisnacht — the festival of flowers and new life. Be wary and hold onto it. Don't disregard us or all will be lost!"

At last dusk arrived and Elisabeth roused herself by concentrating on the bonfires being lit. Each stack was set on fire by her four guardians disguised as animals. Would her people come this year, like they had for generations or had the church scared them away?

In the evening, Elisabeth took note of townspeople standing and waiting at the edges of the woods: families, and farmers arriving with their livestock. Cattle, goats and pigs were to be purified on this sacred night. Every May, her subjects came to cleanse their souls by walking between the bonfires. She sighed with relief, seeing they hadn't deserted her this year. The women and maidens displayed wreaths of flowers and vines in their hair.

Her face, veiled with a long white cloth, was hidden for her safety. She felt her golden circlet, the one flaunting a large ruby, resting on top of her head. Elisabeth sat straight-backed, proud. Against her skin the silver-white fabric of the gown felt silky and her gray cloak — her special one with golden threads — sewn with care by Katl. It kept her warm. She loved wearing it and hoped all could see the sizable emblem of the crescent moon on its back. Elisabeth was honored to be their mistress of the rituals, which she knew were embedded in their very land.

A cloud passed in front of the moon, and as it did, she remembered her nightmares of late. Elisabeth shuddered. She'd dreamt of fires: no, burning and screaming women, men and even children.

I fear the plague and witch-burnings will visit us. Tonight, I need to push away my anxieties and focus on the task at hand. I am the White Goddess who will walk among them to re-unite with my love on sacred ground.

Darkness set in. The fires towered above their heads, burning and lighting up the huge crowd. Her people had come in anticipation of cures, miracles and healing. Looking straight ahead, she was fully aware the chair next to her was empty. He would come as he did every year. But, what if he didn't; he was a priest, a Catholic, no less! Maybe, he's changed his mind. They've spoken little this past year.

She scrutinized the four corners of the field where the masked helpers stood in guises of creatures, guardians of the festivities; a raven, a goat, a fox and a fish. Everyone stared back at her, waiting. She was uneasy, but mustered her courage.

"Welcome, sisters and brothers!" Elisabeth rose and raised her staff upwards. Above her, the stars sparkled in the dark sky; the moon was full and resplendent.

"We are gathered here on this night, at this hour, to set our fires against the darkness and to welcome the return of the Light. Tonight, is our time to celebrate!"

A roar of approval came from the crowd.

"It is time for the Goddess and her beloved Consort — earth and sky, the moon and sun — to wed. You have traveled here to be purified and healed. And I promise you all that this will be done. Herald the spring! It is our time! This is the season of joy and fertility to all. Call in the Elements!" Elisabeth cried, summoning the quarter callers, then turned to the east.

"We call the East," the masked figure of the raven said with a booming voice and stepped forward. "Come to us, element of air. Bring the winds to carry the seeds of wisdom and new growth. Hail and welcome."

The crowd cheered.

"We call to the South," cried the fox-figure, wearing a pointed mask. His tail waved around behind him as he ran forward and grabbed a branch. He lit its dried leaves with fire and sped around the fires, holding up the flame for all to see.

"Element of fire, come to us and cleanse our souls, purge our sins, and keep us warm through-out the night. Hail and welcome."

The people howled and waved their hands around, watching the fox's movements.

A fish-masked figure swayed and darted around the spectators, its dark clothes blending in the night. He yelled, "We call the West; may our streams and lakes be ever plentiful of fish. May rain keep our fields moist and rich. Welcome element of water!"

"We call in the North!" The goat figure jumped forward, displaying spiral horns on its head. It stomped its feet on the ground and spun with large leaps and bounds, bringing roars of laughter and hollering from the crowd. People started dancing and grabbing each other. "Element of earth, stay fertile that we have enough food to feed our people, your children. Welcome, Mother!"

Afterwards, the four beings walked to the dais and bowed down in front of Elisabeth. Everyone turned to her.

She put the apple and staff down and raised her arms once more to the night sky. The people stood quietly around the fires. Elisabeth could hear the crackling of the burning wood.

"I call down the Moon Goddess, Goddess of Light. Come upon me, your humble servant, that your will be done on this earth. May your healing powers flow through me for all to see and touch," Elisabeth cried and fell down onto her knees and hands, dramatically crying out in pain. Overwhelmed, she felt as though the power of the Goddess had entered her very soul and being. At once, the four animal-like individuals ran to her side and helped her up.

Turning to the townspeople, they yelled in unison: "Our Lady walks among us, blessed be!"

The people cried out and held their hands in prayer as the four callers escorted her off the podium and guided her around the populace. Passing her people, Elisabeth put her hands onto babies and small children, cradling their heads gently and assuring their mothers of the child's good health. Others, she prayed for and placed the palms of her hands onto the sick and disabled, bestowing well wishes and consecrations to all.

People cried out in gratitude.

An older man, walking with a cane, came to her. He stood in front of her, bowed, then turned to the crowd.

"Hear me, brethren, last year on this very night, I had

terrible pain in my knees and because of the grace of *Milady*, I walk again!"

He shuffling around, lifting up his knees. Shouts of approval spread through the crowd, people nodded, clapped and called out praises to Elisabeth as she walked past them, veiled, and led by her helpers.

'Thanks to the Goddess, who saves us. Blessings to Her!'

After an hour of moving around the circumference of the large fires, Elisabeth was worn out. The fox, who held her right arm, whispered into her ear. "We're grateful, *Milady*, just wanted you to know. If I may say so, my farm is doing well, thanks to your support, that is, to buy the new plow."

"Of course, Master Scheibelhofer. Your success is in our favor. Now, bring me back to my chair, for I am weary," Elisabeth said.

A horn echoed in the distance. Elisabeth hurried back to her throne and sat down.

Finally, he is here. I want to get on with this. He took his time as he usually does. I don't want to lay with him again, but…

The gathered crowd stirred and parted, revealing two men clad in green and brown walking out of the woods from behind the Maypole holding torches. They were followed by a tall, muscular man dressed in dark emerald trousers. A stag's mask covered his face, save for the beard that poked out from under it, and a pair of deer antlers rested on his large head. The three men sauntered through the center of the two fires until they reached the dais and halted before her.

The people shouted and chanted as he passed them by, "He's here. He's here, the God of the Hunt!"

The big man turned to the crowd, placed his hands on his hips and raised a curved horn to his lips, blowing it twice. Silence reined after.

"I'm here to claim my Queen. Does anyone challenge me? If not, my friends, let this be a time full of joy. Winter is banished and the growing season is upon us. Let us be merry and dance the night away," the man bellowed, then laughed before turning and lowering down upon one knee in front of her.

Elisabeth stood, picked up the apple and placed it into his outstretched hand. "I accept your offer. You are all my witness!" she called. "Let the music begin."

The man took his seat next to her and gazed back from behind his mask. "You're as beautiful as ever."

"Yes, yes," she said, dismissing his adoration. "Let us watch the dancing; we'll speak later."

They watched the young women stepping around the Maypole before them. Dressed in white, yellows, pinks and greens and wearing circlets of wild flowers on their heads, they brought joy to Elisabeth's troubled heart. She drank in the lovely vision of their hair flowing loosely down their backs and lively faces as they danced. A group of musicians played a hurdy-gurdy: fiddles, recorders and lutes accompanying them. The girls lifted up multi-colored ribbons tied to the top of the pole and danced, weaving the cords in and out, laughing and flirting with the young men who stood by watching. Older people walked between the fires. Though she was tired, Elisabeth loved this part of the revelries. Dance and mirth were all around. The drums pounded louder and louder as the night wore on.

She turned to her masked consort. "We need to talk, Georg," she finally said, leaning over to the man sitting next to her. "It is time again. This year, with the help of the Gods, we must conceive a child. The old ways must not be abandoned and I'm not the youngest anymore."

"Are we not here? And you are still strong and able," Georg answered, slapping her knee and chuckling. "You've never disappointed me in the plucking of your rose."

"Desist, man, lest you hit me again. Be warned. You know, I do this only for the better of my people and the land," she retorted.

"Baroness, that is *Milady*, I beg your pardon. The festivities carry me…" He touched his fist to his heart, then took her hand and kissed it.

"That they do. Do I need to remind you, I care for you now only as a brother? We've changed, I hope we are older and wiser," Elisabeth said, smiling. She took a breath and relaxed. "I believe the child we've waited for so long will be conceived tonight."

"The Faith-Keeper?" Georg said, drinking the wine that was served to him by a servant.

"Yes, she'll be born at Christmas-tide," she answered, and looked out at the dancing multitude.

"You're worried, *Milady*?" Georg said. "Is it that son-in-law of yours? Mark my words, he hungers for your castle and riches."

"True, he would rob me of Riegersburg and steal what's rightfully mine if I let him. He's treacherous and Regina is a great disappointment. She's weak and slow-witted." Elisabeth shook her head. She hated her son-in-law and on top of it, the Turkish army threatened her borders of Riegersburg. She could handle them, but was more frightened of the other danger.

How much longer could she protect her land and people from the impending calamities? This burden made her heart heavy with worry. "You've heard, I know, of the burnings elsewhere. I fear the Inquisition will come to Riegersburg. I've had nightmares of late. Can you trust the church to protect you from the burnings?"

"Don't fret, I'm safe. Not one of our followers would dènounce me," he answered, pointing to the celebration. "The old faith is strong here. Look, your people rejoice with us," he continued and jumped up. "Come. Let us walk the fires together."

They stood; the Goddess and her consort to move between the flames, holding hands. As they progressed past the Maypole where two torchbearers were waiting for them, the crowd cheered them on. Soon afterward they were on a path under a gentle moonlight that cast elegant shadows as it streamed through the trees. They followed the two men into the deepening woods to a small clearing in a sacred grove of birch, ash and oak trees.

Elisabeth eyed the seven torches spaced around the clearing and the bed of flowers, furs and sweet grass had been arranged for them in the center. The guides stayed behind at the grove entrance to guard against the curious and intruders.

Elisabeth knew this was her last chance at conceiving a child. Her fertile years were coming to an end and her faith was losing ground against Christianity. Its significance weighed on her. The deed was vital to placate the spirits of the land.

I need to make Georg feel honored and arouse his pleasure. Though he is the high priest of our coven he's also just a man and I've done this in the past with him. There was a time when I found him attractive and enjoyed being held by him. I don't dislike him. It's just my heart has changed and I desire Katl, my beloved maid.

Yet, she knew her sacrifice shouldn't be a chore. Mayhap that was why she hadn't conceived over the last few years, she thought remembering the son she'd conceived years ago. She'd spent her pregnancy over the border with a cousin in Italy. Regina or Johann must never find out about the boy or the child yet to come. Katarina needed to keep this secret hidden at all costs.

I hated to leave him. She looked upward. *Moon Goddess, I need a girl, hear my wish.*

She put her need for Katl aside for the good of all and began to dance and hum to the music coming through the trees. She prided herself as a skillful dancer as she circled around him.

"Come, my God, dance with me," she said picking up her gown and showing him her comely legs. Laughing, she was determined to feel young again.

"This is the Elisabeth I know of old," Georg answered, catching her arm. His eyes gleamed.

"Not so fast, let us enjoy the night," Elisabeth said, and gently pried herself from his grip. "Look at the moon. It is almost the very moment that our desires…"

"The occasion is now," Georg said. He lifted her up, carried her to the makeshift bed and laid her gently down on it.

As he pulled his trousers down to expose the extent of his awakening, Elisabeth grasped his hand. "Wait, we need to…"

But Georg removed her veil and kneeling beside her, spoke the words of ritual they knew so well. "Altar of mysteries unfold, the sacred Circles secret point, thus do I sign thee as of old, with kisses of my lips anoint." He bent over and kissed her.

Elisabeth sat up and reached for the chalice, which was filled with wine and her athame left there by her servants. She held the goblet, and Georg, the athame; her precious ritual knife made of gold and silver.

He lowered its point into the wine, and said, "Beyond the bonds of time and sense, Behold the mystery alright—"

Then putting both of his hands on hers as she held the chalice, he kissed her again. She took a sip of the wine and kissed him back.

After he drank from the cup, she sprang up, untied her cape, and drew her shift up over her head, leaving her naked body to shimmer in the moonlight. "Here," she said, "where the Lance and Grail unite, and feet, and knees. And breast and lip…"

She took his rough face into her hands, though his breath smelled of wine, kissed him fiercely on the mouth once more. Elisabeth nibbled his lower lip; his beard felt scratchy on her chin. He pulled her to him and fervently kissed her back until her neck tingled with delight. They moved from one position to the other. She ran her hands over his taut body, giving him pleasure, fueling their passion, until she felt the time was ripe. She cried out and he moved over her quickening, his pace until his head flung back in ecstasy.

Later on, she lay next to the sleeping man, warm and sweaty, wrapped in fur blankets. The music had stopped a while ago and the forest was quiet.

Elisabeth clasped her hands together over her heart and looked up at the night sky. Clouds passed under the starlit dome and she prayed to the moon, her trusted companion.

"Goddess, I beg you yet again, give me a girl child."

Yet, she dreaded the future of the Goddess and her worship, hidden now from the church but still alive. She thought she heard the wind whispering through the trees,

"Times are changing. Beware!"

Were the longstanding ways to be lost forever? Maybe this point in time demanded more of her. As she lay there troubled, an idea took shape in her mind. When all else failed, there was a way to keep the faith from disappearing. Unlike her people, she had learned to read and write. *What if?*

She yearned to be with Katl. So, not wanting to wake Georg, she quietly dressed and walked over and tapped one of the guards on the shoulder.

"Take me back to my castle."

Chapter Two

It was a grey morning and raining heavily outside the fortress. Pelting hard staccato sounds pummeled against the leaden glass panes. Elisabeth paced back and forth in her spacious bedchamber. Her four-posted bed with its gold and red brocade canopy was still unmade. On the floor, intricate handwoven rugs covered the cold wooden boards. A long, slender table covered with a pearl-colored damask cloth stood in the middle of the room. An opened bottle of wine, two golden cups and a plate of half-eaten bread and cheeses were on it.

Katarina sat on a small bench next to the fireplace where Elisabeth's coat of arms hung above. A pair of doves and two crossed swords painted in red, white and silver were born in the crest. The fire crackled, warming the room and a hint of burned candle wax and smoke tickled Elisabeth's nose.

"They'll need someone to blame for this relentless foul weather," Elisabeth said stopping to look out of the window. She placed her hands on either side of the jamb. "The crops are ruined. People will starve this winter; they'll look to evil doings." She pressed her forehead against the window then turned to Katarina, worried.

Katarina said, "*Milady*, the people of Riegersburg like you well and cannot be such as those in Linz. Your generosity is well known."

Elisabeth turned to Katarina and smiled. "After all these years, you still call me your lady."

"Habit, *Milady*, Lizzie, I mean. I don't want to slip in front of the others." Katarina warmed her hands against the flickering flames.

"Oh dear, Katl, how naïve of you, always believing in the good." Elisabeth came over to the woman and rested her fingers on her shoulders.

Katarina looked up. "You should be dressed, *Milady*. And I need to do your hair."

Elisabeth looked down at her woolen night robe, then bent over and kissed Katarina on the cheek. *Her concerns are always for me, despite the lingering danger to herself.* "My beloved, you've been my trusted servant and lover for many years. Do not fuss so over me. Rather, it is I who am concerned for your welfare. There've been burnings in Feldbach. You're not safe."

"Why? There is no need, lest your son-in-law is up to something. Pardon, *Milady*, but I don't like him, he covets your wealth and the castle. That's the only reason he married Regina."

"I know this to be true," Elisabeth said.

"He's out to ruin you. All those court processes he's put you through trying to snatch the *Burg* for himself." Katarina said with some heat in her voice and stood, putting her arms on her waist.

But Elisabeth waved her to sit back down. "At ease, my beloved." She paused. "My stupid daughter hasn't the wits to stand up to him. Thank my ancestors, my barrister and the spirits I won against his last suit."

"Regina was such a sweet child," Katarina said, gazing at the fire.

Elisabeth sat down on the floor next to her taking her hands and kissing them. "True, she was before she met him." She looked up into the woman's eyes. "I swear Johann will not get the Burg as long as I live. Yet, Siegfried's told me Johann plots to try Georg for sorcery. Not even the priests are safe, I fear."

"The Goddess will protect us," Katarina said, and jumped up again. "Let's look to the book for some workings to help. Thanks to your good judgment, we have all we need in there. Our ways are held safe in it."

Elisabeth watched her with rapt attention. Katarina went to the bedside cabinet, unlocking a drawer with a key she took from behind the coat of arms. Pulling out a heavy leather -bound book and placing it on the table, she leafed through the pages. "We'll cast a spell for our protection. Poor Georg, he may be lost, but we need to safeguard ourselves and the castle."

Elisabeth chuckled and got up to sit on one of the two chairs by the table. For the last three months, she'd spent long hours at night writing down every spell, every calling, every chant she and Katl could remember being taught from their teacher, old Wife Kietchelbach, along with ones they'd created. Kietchelbach died years ago, passing on the leadership to Elisabeth. Daily, Katl collected herbs, laying them out and drawing detailed pictures of them, meticulously labeling them and which ailments they cured.

Midwifery and tips on love potions were added along with the secret names of the Goddess and the spirits of the land. Elisabeth was proud of their work, although its very survival demanded utter secrecy.

"Here!" Katarina cried her eyes sparkling and arms waving. She pointed to the floor. "It'll be done tonight at midnight by full moon. We'll summon *Reudwyn*, the spirit of the rowan tree. There's one down in the orchard by the vineyard. I'll collect the berries this afternoon to make a red juice."

"And I'll draw a pentagram here at night with the juice and light the corners with five white candles. We've done our work in the past for the good; no one has suffered or known our workings," Elisabeth said, and hugged her.

"What would I do without your love, dearest?" Elisabeth said, laughing and playfully shoving Katarina. She looked out the window again where a dark cloud passed above and suddenly worried about her other daughter, the one kept secret from all, the girl conceived to carry on the faith. Her heart ached. She couldn't visit Hilde for fear someone would discover her and report back to Johann. A child committed in adultery was a grave sin.

She sobered and turned back to Katarina. "Is my child doing well with the farmer Wenzel and his wife?"

"Yes, your little girl is growing into a fine young lady: headstrong as you are, healthy and smart," Katarina answered with a gleam in her eyes and a good-humored grin. "They're good folk and will, surely as I speak, not deceive your good benefits and grace. The money you give them each month will hold their tongues.

Katarina bustled over and took one of Elisabeth's gowns out from a tall closet. She laid the soft green and brown dress with its white lacy collar on the bed and went about dressing her mistress. First the petticoat, then the corset was tied and pulled at the cords; then at last, the elegant gown.

Elisabeth loved the feeling of Katl dressing her. Was she being selfish not giving Katl more: possibly some land? But Elisabeth couldn't bear not having her close by and what better way to hide their true relationship than by having her as her personal handmaiden?

"I must get to your hair. Shall I put it up?"

"Yes," Elisabeth sat down. When Katarina finished the final pleating of Elisabeth's long hair, she went to the vanity and brought back a fiery ruby necklace and fastened it around Elisabeth's neck.

"You are still beautiful to me," Katarina said, putting in Elisabeth's matching earrings.

Elisabeth cocked a brow. "Still you say, was I not always?" She said as Katarina brought her silver glass over and held it up. Elisabeth eyed herself critically and judging herself quite presentable, rang the bell to be accompanied down to breakfast. A minute later the door opened and out she walked with Katarina following a few steps behind.

When she approached the dining hall, a manservant opened a large, thick oak paneled door for her to pass through into the expansive room. The towering stone cut walls displayed woven wall-tapestries depicting hunting scenes and landscapes dwarfed her as she drifted toward her chair at the end of a long, stately table. Candle-lit sconces on iron holdings flickered, casting wild shadows on the walls and between them narrow arch-topped windows looking out over the vast countryside let in bright sunshine.

Johann stood, but she waved him down as she took her seat. Someone cleared their throat and the sound pierced the silence.

She smiled, and after she laid her napkin over her waist, looked up and stared down the length of the long table at her son-in-law and her daughter, Regina. The three servants standing nearby waiting to serve the morning meal were ignored.

"Madam, we have been waiting as patiently as one can for almost an hour," Johann said with some heat in his voice, and waved one of the servants to bring him his breakfast of polenta and meats.

"Yes, Mother, whatever took you so long this morning?" Regina said. Her daughter looked worn and tired. Was she sick again? Elisabeth thought, noting her daughter's pallid complexion. Regina had light brown hair which was pleated on top of her head. She wore a blue velvet gown along with her favorite pearl earrings. It irked Elisabeth that her daughter was often ill.

"Dear, you do not have leave to question my actions."

Elisabeth glared at her daughter. She called to one of the servants. "Frederick, bring me my morning brew at once." To Katarina, she said, "You're dismissed for now."

After Katarina left the room, Elisabeth straightened her back and smiled at Johann. "So, tell me, Johann, what is this nonsense I hear about witches?" The servant brought her tea to her and she drank a sip, delighting in the herbal brew of nettles and peppermint. She wasn't going to let Johann intimidate her. Frederick brought her a bowl of barley porridge covered with crème and honey. She was starving and the smell was pleasant. The food warmed her manner and she savored each spoonful.

"Mother, don't be concerned," Johann answered as he ate. "It is really a small matter."

"A small matter?" Elisabeth put down her utensil, clasping her hands in front of her bowl. "This could affect the prosperity of my people...and the *Burg*! I've heard some are saying the weather is from sorcery. Surely you don't believe that rubbish?"

"It's come to my attention Father Agricola has had secret meetings at the *Hubershof*. There are rumors of womanizing, debauchery and even dancing naked. This is really nothing for your ears or Regina's, for that matter." Johann eagerly slurped dollops of gruel. At length, he sat back patting his rounded belly then nodding toward the servant, pointed at his bowl. "More, I'll have another."

"Mama, Gretchen, my maid, has told me of horrible things." Regina looked over at her husband nodding, appearing truly upset.

"Father Agricola? I cannot and will not believe such gossip! This talk is unfounded and dangerous. Heavens man, listen to yourself: he's a priest," Elisabeth said fixing her eyes on Johann. But behind her sharp gaze was fear. *He knows something. I need to avert his attention and deflect the rumors. The trials must not come to Riegersburg! I must do everything in my power to stop this madness.*

"So, he would have you believe, perhaps," Johann said.

"Do not talk to me of debauchery, Johann. We both know there are things better left unsaid," Elisabeth said, knowing he knew about her finding out about his wild nights with some of the wenches in town. She cleared her throat and let out a hearty laugh. *That should put him in his place. He'll not see me frightened. How dare he instigate without my permission?*

Regina, who was nibbling her oat cake, glanced at her husband and frowned.

The servants fidgeted as the hall became silent except for the wind blowing against the windows.

"Well, yes, you are quite right." Johann said. His face flushed red in agitation. "What then of other wrong-doings and the hail that has ruined our crops? Can you explain it?"

Elisabeth scrambled for an answer, but nothing seemed plausible.

Johann pounced on her silence. "What I thought, Madam. Thus, I've taken the liberty and have written the *Kaiser* for permission to run a trial here. Myself the judge. He gave me leave because of my barrister training."

Elisabeth's eyes widened. Regina looked up startled.

"Liberty?" Elisabeth said, finding her voice. "I say brazen insolence! You wrote Leopold behind my back on this matter? This is my castle, these are my lands, my people," Elisabeth yelled, pounding her hands onto the table. She stood, her chest heaving in fury. "You think overmuch of yourself, Johann. Have a care, I warn lest I disown you and Regina."

But Johann was unmoved. "It has been done. If the *Kaiser* and the Pope agree to my proposal, there is naught you can do," he said, raising his brow and tilting his chin in an ugly smirk.

Katarina is right, you are evil. I don't think you know of our coven nor have you ever attended Walburgisnacht. You believe the seasonal festivities of the farmers to be beneath you. Thank the Goddess for your stupid pride. My people are loyal to me not you. You insolent dog! And I need to get in touch with Count Esterhazy immediately. He's close to the Kaiser, he'll set things right.

Steeling herself, she drew a deep breath. "I will not have trials here in Riegersburg!" she shouted. "You're dismissed. I'll not have my breakfast ruined by your insolence."

Johann threw his napkin onto the table and stood. "As you wish," he said and marched out of the room. Regina began crying, holding her hands in front of her face.

"He has overstepped himself this time, daughter. You need to divorce him. I am still Baroness here," Elisabeth said and sat back down. Her legs shook under the table. She had heard of the torture methods used by the inquisitors on witches. None of them were pleasant, all of them fatal. She'd call for her barrister today and pray it wasn't too late to stop Johann.

Regina stood, avoiding her mother's gaze, leaving her meal unfinished.

"May I have your leave, Mother?"

"Fine! Go run after your husband." She watched her daughter scamper out of the room, then turned to her servant. "Frederick, bring me my quill and a piece of parchment at once."

Elisabeth finished her breakfast alone.

Chapter Three

Hubersdorf farm Austria, June 1665

A few days later, two hooded figures slipped past the walnut tree next to *Hubersdorf* farm along the stone wall encircling the place. Elisabeth could hear the wind rustling through the branches and leaves of the trees. She pulled in her cloak tightly against the dark and rainy night. She peered up at the waxing moon peeking through the clouds and shivered. They came to a wooden side door of the home and rapped. The door swung open before they could finish. Light from the fire within revealed her cape of a rich maroon, and one dark brown of her companion, Katarina.

"Come inside," a male voice called from within. "Quickly, before you are seen." They entered and closed the door behind them. Elisabeth pulled her hood back and observed the room she knew so well. There was a large table near the kitchen hearth, a few wooden chairs, a flask of red wine, and cups. A roughly hewn bed made out of cherry wood was pushed back into a corner. Tallow candles lit the room, casting shadows eerily on the white-washed room. "Take my mantle." She undid the clasp and handed it to Katarina, who had already taken off her cloak.

"Yes, *Milady.*"

"What is the meaning of this meeting?" Georg moved towards the women and embraced one after the other. "I got your note from Siegfried to meet, yet no reason written. Why the haste? Our monthly meeting is only three days hence." He motioned to Katarina and Elisabeth to take a seat at the table. She sat close to the fire and immediately felt its warmth. Georg handed them each a tin cup and poured out some wine. He sat down and took a swig, regarding each woman.

Elisabeth tapped her foot on the straw-covered dirt floor and raised an eyebrow.

"Now, don't give me that look, woman." Georg said with a smug smile. Katarina looked down at her hands, blinking nervously.

Elisabeth smoothed her dress, cleared her throat, and said, "Georg, Johann has obtained dispensation from the Kaiser to hold and investigate people on the accusations of witchcraft in Riegersburg. And there is nothing I can do about it for now. I've written to my friend Count Ezterhazy for help. He has an ear with Leopold and I hope to gain audience at court very soon. Johann will have his way until I can stop him. I know you believe you're safe because of the Church and your position. But I'm warning you, he has wind of our gatherings." Elisabeth lowered her voice to a whisper and leaning in closer, she continued. "Someone has betrayed us."

Elisabeth felt her knees weaken and the sensation of events moving too rapidly. Katarina reached over to take her hand, but she pulled it away, shaking her head.

Georg crossed his arms and frowned.

"Who would do that? Surely, not one of my brothers?" He frowned and rubbed his hair, then shook his head softly. "What can we do?" Georg studied them for a while, then averted his gaze toward the fire.

Elisabeth stared as well at the flames. The wind howled outside as if it were spirits calling out a warning to her. The crackling of the blaze couldn't calm her. Her muscles quivered and heat flushed through her body. After a few minutes, she pounded her fists on the table and with a raised voice said, "I will not let this weakling of a son-in-law rule my fortress or put fear into my people. I will fight him on this. I'm don't know who disclosed information to Johann but I assure you both I will uncover the truth. Though it's hard to imagine anyone did since our people have supported us for years in our doings. No one has ever questioned my authority."

Katarina put her hands over her face then drew a deep breath, and looked up again and over to Elisabeth. "Elisabeth, please. I've told you before he wants Riegersburg for himself and the child would be in his way. I overheard Johann and Regina speaking and worrying about their inheritance. And maybe he is using the weather to further his case and actually knows nothing. I'm certain Johann would do anything to ruin you even if it means killing. And he knows how you care for your people. He'll use your love against you!"

Georg stood up and paced slowly around the room wrapping his arms around his chest. "How much does he actually know about our faith and our child?" he said with a grave expression.

Elisabeth chose her words deliberately. "I do not believe he is informed about much more than there are meetings here. And I don't know if he really believes of our daughter's existence or who said anything. Siegfried has been investigating the servants and discovered naught. Or for the matter, Johann doesn't have a clue about our Lady, the Goddess and her magic." Elisabeth drew a sharp breath as she noticed a candle blow out. She glanced over to Katarina, then over at Georg. A sense of gloom rose up in her belly. "We all know the methods of priests looking for witches or pagans. Who of us would not confess to them under such barbaric torture or even survive?" Elisabeth's throat developed a painful lump and her voice cracked as she continued. "I've seen the burnings in other towns and know of their practices. It's horrible. We have been blessed by my people's faithfulness to me and by your church hiding our secrets all these years."

"Then I must burn all I have here that could incriminate us."

"Yes, and we need to inform the others to do the same and to be watchful. There will be no rituals until the storm has passed." Katarina said with her hands clutched together on the table. Elisabeth felt a deep sense of gratitude for her maid's unerring loyalty and devotion.

"I have decided the best place to hide our book of faith should be in St. Martins." Elisabeth said with a set jaw. "You need to make preparations such that Goddess' room is sealed off so no one can find it and the book must be kept there for now." She leaned in toward Georg and rested her hands on her knees.

Georg's mouth fell open and he let out a bark of laughter.

"So, I should put myself and the brothers in danger? Is this your plan?" He sprang up and walked over to the hearth with his back facing them, his large muscular frame silhouetted by the fire. Elisabeth's chest ached as she witnessed her one-time lover's despair. He'd always supported her and was her high priest, the father of her child; the future Faith-Keeper who was hidden safely away at the Wenzel farm. How could she convince him this was the only way? She knew instinctively priests from out of town would not find the book if it was right under their noses.

Uncertain of what to say, she rose and walked over to him, placing her hand lightly onto his shoulder. He turned, obviously gulping, exhibiting a smile which came on too quickly. He held his hand up, stuttering, "I've sworn to serve you, *Milady*, my love in the best and the worst of times. And I shall keep my promise to you and the faith."

Elisabeth wished with all her heart she could alleviate his pain and his duty. Yet, she knew he was to be her shield. She pulled him into a gentle embrace, stroking his curly brown hair.

"I will use my power to protect you, my love. This is my prayer and my promise to you and the others as the Faith-Keeper of The Lady of Light's wisdom and grace. Am I not the Baroness of Riegersburg?" she said gently.

She let go of Georg and sat down back at the table, close to her maid. With a sigh she let her head rest on Katarina's shoulder.

"What now?" Katarina asked.

"There is not much we can do other than warn the others. And stay calm." Elisabeth said looking up into her face. "Until I visit the court with my lawyers, we should not come here."

Georg sat back down and raised his cup. "To us, may we stay vigilant." Elisabeth straightened her sore back, lifting her cup high as did Katarina. The tangy wine tasted good and warmed her soul.

"We must be off before we're missed." Elisabeth swallowed the whole amount and sprang up. Katarina copied her and clad her mistress with her cape before putting her own on. The two women rushed to the door. Georg followed. Elisabeth reached

over and stroked his bearded cheek with her fingers. He opened
the heavy door and she left without a word.

As they walked past the farm and the trees, she
contemplated the moon again. A dark cloud moved across it
and she couldn't help feeling a dreadful sacrifice would happen
and she was powerless to avoid its reckoning. Her chest tingled
and her mouth soured. Elisabeth halted and raised her hands in
supplication to the sky. *Goddess, please help me protect my loved ones and
my people. I beseech you with my truest of hearts and intention. What can I
do? Give me a sign.*

"Come, *Milady*," Katarina grabbed Elisabeth's hand,
pulling her along. Nothing, No one answered Elisabeth's plea.
The night remained silent.

Chapter Four

Riegersburg, September 1665

amn them all. Feeble old Martha, they put her on the Hexenstuhl. Poor dear, I don't blame her for naming me. What else could she do? And then they killed her anyway.

Katarina shivered. She was hungry and terribly afraid. She tried to adjust her eyes to the darkness of the prison cell. The dungeon room was small, suffocating and filthy. Wet rotting hay covered the cold stone floor and the only light that shone in came from two narrow slits above her head. She needed to stay strong and prepare her mind with her teachings: the knowledge of the inner labyrinth. She knew she was in for an ordeal. She and Elisabeth had learned these workings together in the past from their teacher, Eleanor Kietchelbach. Only, Katarina never imagined she would have to use them one day. She'll not name her Lady and love, or anyone else for that matter. Johann won't break her. She'd heard of the trials, the tortures and the very thought of what was to come made her tremble.

She hugged herself. It had been four days with hope dwindling anyone was coming to deliver her from certain suffering and death. "Goddess, help me," she prayed over and over again as the sliver of light rained down over her. *Save me, Elisabeth, if you can.*

"Give me fortitude, Great Mother of us all, to stay strong, to not lose faith," she cried bitterly, thinking of her beloved Elisabeth's dark hair and loving eyes.

Nobody was safe in these times, especially the husband of an accused witch. She held Marcus no grudge for not visiting her, and was grateful to Elisabeth for sending her two children far away to **Kärnten** long before the trials began. Elisabeth had seen the signs of what was coming. They both knew Johann had convinced the emperor that the devil resided in Riegersburg. *Stupid man! May your soul rot in Hell.*

Behind the locked door, she heard footsteps echoing in the hallway. The door to her cell creaked opened and in came Siegfried and Thomas each carrying a lantern. She put her hands to her face, shading her eyes from the stark bright light and stood.

The older man, Siegfried, coughed and said quietly, "Time has come. Come along peacefully now."

"Thomas and Siegfried, to think you actually believe all this hearsay!" She eyed the tall young man on the left. "Thomas, I've known you since you were a wee lad. And Siegfried, how many times have we supped together?" Katarina spoke, looking the men up and down.

Siegfried fidgeted under her gaze, then turned his kind round face away. She knew the portly old man, who wore tattered gray jacket and trousers, didn't want to be here doing this deed any more than she wanted to be dragged in front of Johann. And Thomas? She walked up to the tall lad, maybe all of fifteen he was, and put her hands on her hips.

Looking at the uncertain thin face with a crop of uneven dirty blond hair that hung loosely on his shirt— she balled her hands into fists.

"You wouldn't be alive if not for me. To think, I helped your poor mother deliver you into this world only to see you betray me so."

Thomas stepped back, ashamed, and looked down at the floor.

"Now Katl, know that we're only following the lord's wishes. Come along with us upstairs, woman," Siegfried interrupted, reaching over to grab her arm. But she yanked it away from the old man.

Siegfried shook his head. "It's no fault of ours. You know we don't believe in this, but what can we do?"

Katarina snorted. "Where's your pride, man? He, the son-in-law, treats you no better than a dog. Shame on the both of you! Haven't we worked together well for our Mistress all these years?"

She spat at their feet and walked past them through the cell's doorway with her head held high.

After a few steps, she turned to face them again. Both men crossed themselves.

"I've a mind to curse the both of you," she said and her voice rang down the long stone corridor.

"Katl, we need to go," Siegfried begged. "Now, come along…"

"All right," Katarina said, turned, and marched ahead with them scurrying after her.

They climbed the narrow stairway leading up from the dank dungeons to the castle's spacious rooms reserved for the Baroness' family. Siegfried opened the door to a cavernous hall and gestured her in toward a long wooden gate which stood opposite the judge's lofty bench. Placed in the center of the back wall, the bench gave the presiding judge a view of the entire room with its towering book stacks and more importantly, the inquisitor's table with its abundance of rolled parchments.

Thomas and Siegfried quietly left her alone to face her enemy. The judge, Johann Purgstall, sat behind the bench looking at a document and talking in whispers to two strange men, not of Riegersburg, sitting beside him dressed in long black robes. Johann wore a white ruffled shirt collar making him appear apart and special.

Katarina felt a warm trickle of urine run down her thigh and pressed her legs together to stop the flow.

They mustn't see my fear.

"What say you, Frau Pauldauf, to the charges by the *Alte Vaitlin*? One Martha Peurin, accusing you of weather sorcery, debauchery and sleeping with the devil," Johann said, looking up from his reading and rolling a quill between his fingers. Why was he being so formal? She's known him for at least ten years.

"I was not aware of these sayings, Master Johann," Katarina answered, keeping her voice calm and steady.

"Did you not get the papers served to you two days prior to this hearing?" Johann said and dipped his pen into an ink well to write down some more letters. His head was adorned with a fake colorless wig. The two other priests beside him looked on her like vultures waiting for the kill, ready to pick and tear her apart.

"You know that I cannot read, sir," she answered. But she had seen the papers and had chosen to ignore it. Johann looked smug.

Thank the Goddess; the special book was well-hidden with her mistress.

"But I swear, all are lies. I've never wished anyone or thing ill will. You know that, my lord." This at least, was true. She glanced at the Iron Maiden, which stood partially open in the corner of the room. Its spikes reminded her of knives and daggers, feeling her heart pound and another warm trickle run down her leg. Johann saw her gaze at the device and smiled. One of the two men whispered into Johann's ear.

"Frau Pauldauf, we want to spare you pain. However, the evidence of Martha's confession along with the failed crops and the testimony of others has sealed your fate, I'm afraid."

"What testimony?" Katarina cried. "I've heard none against me."

"Oh, come now. It is no secret you were observed at Father Agricola's place on several occasions, participating in sexual orgies with the devil," Johann said. He stood, raised his arms as if calling on God then pointed his finger at her.

"Do you declare here before God and this court what others are saying are falsehoods? You did none of these evil doings? I say, confess to these crimes and save your soul or you will burn in hell, woman," he continued then sat back down. The other two men nodded in agreement, folding their arms in front of them.

"Master, I beg you, I've served the Lady, your Baroness and mother-in-law, for twenty years truly and well. Why do you fault me of these terrible things? All lies, hearsay. Sleeping with the devil? Why would I do that? I'm too busy for such devilry. Doing wrong by my neighbors? As I stand here before you, what was said is untrue," Katarina responded as her body burned with rage.

"Be quiet. Do you deny the charges made by one Martha Peurin?" Johann repeated. He sprang up and came from behind his desk, then leaned back onto its edge. For a moment, he stroked his chin with his pale fingers then his tone softened, "I could help you, Katarina, if you would just name the other witches. They are poisoning our crops and our lands."

He's trying to trick me and I'll have none of it. I won't confess the names of my friends and neighbors.

When she didn't answer, he walked towards her and put his hands on the wooden rail in front of her. She could smell his foul breath and see his yellowed teeth.

"Now Katarina, we may spare your children and husband if you confide in us," Johann said dropping his voice into a malevolent tone. "The servants say you bring the plants to flower in winter. I've witnessed this with my own eyes. How do you do this, if not with magic?"

"That's a trifle, as all good gardeners know," Katarina said. "Put the bulbs by a good lit window. And my children are far away from you and your murderous lot. Your real cause here is to ruin the Baroness and steal the *Burg* from her." Katarina raised her hand, shaking and pointing her forefinger back at her accuser almost touching his nose. "I say as God is my witness, if anyone has a pact with the devil it's you! Not me or poor Martha nor Father Agricola. He's innocent! You're the wicked one!"

"Du störes Weibstück!" Enough. Remove her to the chamber," Johann roared. He shook his fist at her, as he strode out of the room through the wooden door with the other two men following him. Shortly afterwards, Siegfried and Thomas came in and shackled her wrists and ankles.

"Quiet, woman," Siegfried said as she kicked and bit them. "Settle down."

"I won't go!" Katarina yelled as they dragged her out of the room. When she saw the futility of her resistance, she acquiesced, "Wait. I'll walk on my own."

Katarina's heart pounded as Thomas helped her stand. She tried to breathe, but with each step closer to the chamber at the end of the hallway, every breath became a labor. "Don't, please," she whimpered as Siegfried opened the door and pushed her in.

The servant's room was bare save for a large rack, a wooden stove, and a chair with short piercing nails on its seat and back. Various tools of torture she had no name for, and prods and sticks hung on the walls. Katarina's limbs shook uncontrollably. Although it was only a few moments later when Johann came in with one of the priests, it felt like forever. He eyed her with a talon-like gaze, then motioned to Siegfried and Thomas to leave the room.

"Katarina, save yourself from all this," he said, sweetening his tone, and waving his hands around the room. He came up to her and squinted. He wasn't much taller than her. Johann was a man of medium build, with pale blue eyes and a chin receding into his neck. His reddened nose with its aristocratic hook, shaped like one of the tools hanging on the walls, gave him an impish appearance.

What an ugly thing you are.

She tried to spit at him. When nothing came out, he laughed.

Why me? What could I say to appease him? Elisabeth, where are you? Katarina thought, turning her head toward the narrow-slotted window beside her. The sun was shining outside in her garden.

"I know you helped my mother–in–law hide her bastard child from us all. I have a servant to attest to your actions. Illegal, I say. Did she partake in your devilries as well?" Johann said, grabbing her chin and turning her face back to him.

"There is no child, Lord Johann," Katarina answered defiantly. "You wouldn't have me here, if you had proof of all these untruths. The Lady has only your wife Regina as her child and legal heir to the *Burg*."

"You are a sinner and a liar," Johann hissed, then backed away and paced back and forth.

He turned to the priest. "Take off her dress."

The man stepped forward and unceremoniously pulled down her shift so that it lay on the floor around her feet.

Katarina closed her eyes in shame.

"Whip her ten times across her back and legs for her impertinence. Maybe that will loosen her tongue," Johann commanded.

Katarina heard the priest walk over to a wall and take something from it, then felt the bite of the whip as it slashed across her legs, back and arms. Such pain she had never known and she screamed breathless howls with each lash.

Help me, Goddess! Help me endure this, she prayed as she felt the warmth of her blood run down the back of her legs

When finally, the last lash had been given, she slumped over, sobbing.

Johan was suddenly beside her. "No one need know anything you tell me, especially the Baroness," Johann whispered into her ear. "I cannot accuse her of sorcery, but," and his voice grew harsh and loud, "I can try you for witchcraft. She cannot save you here or help you, I've made sure of that."

"Even so, she cares not for you, believe me, silly woman. You're only a pawn in her schemes. Rest assured, I will get Riegersburg in the end, no matter, so save yourself!" He lowered his voice again. "Where is the child?"

Her body hurt, but he would not get her to reveal her secrets. She would not forsake her faith, the child and Elisabeth. The book will survive her and one day the truth will be told. "There is no child."

"What say you?" he repeated.

"I'll say no more to you," she answered and spat at him.

"So be it!" he yelled. "Put her on the rack," he barked. "We will see if you'll not speak."

The priest took her shackles off and tied her, naked, to the wheel. The wood was hard and cold. The ropes bit into her raw skin. Johann stood back gloating as the priest pulled on the lever, stretching her body, pulling her apart with each notch of the wheel. Blinded in agony, she cried out in desperation. Then everything went black.

The next thing she knew, cold water was being thrown over her face and body. She batted her dazed eyes open, feeling confused, the pain returned with a vengeance. Vomit threatened to overtake her as she tried to focus on the Goddess and Elisabeth's face.

This is all just a nightmare. Please let this be a horrible dream.

"Confess, Katarina," Johann was standing next to her ear, condemning her. Katarina shook her head and prayed. Johann motioned to the priest to move the lever another notch. As the rope pulled, she heard the pop of her arms dislocating at the shoulders and elbows. All went black again.

When at last she came to, she found herself alone with her agony and her broken body. She turned her head and looked around. The room was empty.

Siegfried came in.

"Drink this," he said and gave her a bitter tasting broth. Little by little, it warmed her throat. She was thirsty, parched.

"Help me, please," she whimpered. "Get me out of here or kill me. I can't take any more."

"This tea will help," he answered. "Remember for what you sacrifice." And then he hurried out the door.

"Lady, put me out of my misery," she lamented as tears streamed down her cheeks. "Spare me." Her body drifted into numbness and some of the aching receded.

"I've served you well. Goddess, why, must I suffer so?"

It seemed like an eternity until the door opened and Johann came into the room with the priest. Not again, she couldn't bear anymore torture. "So, Mistress Pauldauf, I ask you again for the names of those who danced at Father Agricola's gatherings?"

"I know nothing," she answered with a faltering voice.

"My patience is running thin." He walked around the rack, rubbing his hands. She looked away again. "Do you wish to suffer more?"

She shook her head and whispered, "No, my lord."

"Then tell me, what of my mother-in-law and the child?" He motioned to the priest to take a tool off the wall. It looked like large metal talons. "That can rip off your breast. Have you seen it before? A handy thing it is, really."

Katarina eyes widened. The thought of her breast being torn from her was unbearable. Finally, she wailed, "No, no, I will confess, Lord, I will tell you…"

The priest hung the torture device back on the wall, and grabbed a book and pen from the table in the corner. Sitting down beside her on a stool, he readied himself to write down her declaration.

Forgive me, Goddess, I am weak and can suffer no more.

"I name Father Michael Zirkulius, Magdalene Steslin," Katarina muttered and went on to name twenty-five people she knew from around Riegersburg; priests, widows, midwives and poor beggars. "They met at Father Agricola's farm; *Hubershof* at the dark moon. We did the dance with the devil, which came dressed in black feathers…like a raven. We wore black and yellow clothes in his honor." She was hysterical.

"And yes, we called on the Gods of old to make bad weather, to hail and spoil the crops. We did it for him, Satan," she confessed.

Johann and the priest crossed themselves. Johann nodded and the priest continued to write.

"In a circle, we danced around a large cauldron; black demons rose from the vapors and visited our neighbors, causing illness. Georg drank the blood of a cock we sacrificed. Then he fornicated with all us women and some men. He is the devil's apprentice," she said, feeling broken and lost. She couldn't help from telling her perpetrators about the others. Although she knew her friends would suffer the same outcome, she would say anything to get them to stop.

"What of the Baroness and the child?" Johann said.

"No, child. My mistress never partook in our Sabbaths. It's a rumor. She's innocent and as good a Christian as you are," Katarina lied.

The priest spoke for the first time. "This is enough evidence for her burning."

"No, I need to know of the child," Johann persisted and pointed to the lever. "Turn it until she confesses."

Katarina woke in a cloud of delirium and shadows in the dungeon where rats ran freely in and out alongside the cell's walls. She observed them having no idea of how long she'd lain on the floor. She was wrapped in a blanket, and felt like her mind was separated from her body. She tried to sit up but couldn't get her arms to move without unbearable pain shooting into her mind almost causing her to pass out.

At that moment, a door opened and a beacon of light flooded into the dark chamber. "Katarina, Katarina." A voice called to her as if from miles away.

"Oh, my Goddess, forgive me, my love," Elisabeth said. Katarina slowly turned her head to see the Baroness looking down at her.

Elisabeth dropped to her knees and gently took Katarina's head onto her lap. She placed another woolen blanket over her lover's battered and injured body.

"My love, what has that beast done to you?" Elisabeth wept. Tears ran freely down her cheeks. For a long time, Elisabeth just held her and wailed softly. Katarina couldn't answer any more because in the end, they'd ripped out her tongue.

"Please, can you ever forgive me? You've been faithful to our love and the Goddess. I tried to save you. They're mad. It's a dangerous time, not even my friends would step in to help. Johann is sanctioned by the Pope, no less, and the *Kaiser*.

"Believe me, Katl, this to be true," Elisabeth whispered and caressed Katarina's forehead, then bent down to kiss her cheek. "I do love you," Elisabeth wailed, rocking her back and forth.

A few minutes later, Elisabeth went on, "Siegfried has been my faithful servant this whole time and secretly giving you belladonna and willow in your tea to help relieve the pain. Johann, that brute, and his evil priests are outrageous. They've arrested over fifty townspeople; some farmers, all innocent, even Father Zirkulius. No one blames you, my love. Some died under torture. I wish I could've saved them and Georg, the poor man, was executed two days ago. They burned him at the stake. I shudder thinking of it. But I need to stay strong for the *Burg* and the others.

"They're planning to bring you to the stake tomorrow, my dearest. I can't bear it," Elisabeth said and lifted Katarina gently to her breast, holding her close to her heart.

"Your husband and children are safe. They're far away from danger, hidden. I made good on my promise to you. He cannot reach them or find them. I've hidden the book right under their noses with one of Georg's followers. He will be true to our faith. Johann will never think to look in the church! And my dearest daughter, born of the Goddess, is safe because of you. She is our only hope; our future. And when the time is right, she will receive teachings from our book. How will I live without you?"

Katarina wanted to console her and pushed her head against Elisabeth.

"Katl, I promise you: I will get my revenge on him. He'll be made to suffer for what he did to you. Mark my words. I pray to the Goddess that we'll walk together again and meet in the next life. Be strong and drink this."

Elisabeth raised a flask of warm draught to Katharina's parched lips. She drank it willingly. It tasted sweet, and as it went down, she knew it would be the last time they'd see each other in this life.

"I brewed this myself this morning, opium and honey, and hemlock to assist you in your passing. You'll have no pain."

Elisabeth took a silver athame from under her cloak and raised it straight up, chanting:

"I call upon She of the Crossroads,
Gatherer and guide of the souls,
She who aides all witchery,
Peace and release are wished for you, Katarina.
It is time to pass from this mortal world.
You will be remembered,
You must go now,
I call for the gathering of light to open,
So, my beloved sister, may pass through,
Pass now to the care of your guardians and the Lady of Light."

The words calmed Katarina, her body felt warm and she gazed one last time at her beloved before falling into a gentle abyss.

Chapter Five

Feldbach, Austria 1672 – seven years later

The coach stopped along the side of a deserted road. The trees of the forest were all shades of vibrant colors. Elisabeth used to love autumn with its leaves of yellow, red and brown. Now, years after the burnings, her heart felt like the decaying foliage scattered along the dirt road, dead. The years had come and gone like the seasons. *Has it been seven years since Katl's death?* Today, the ordeal of the trials felt like yesterday.

So many died.

Johann had not anticipated her cleverness. At first, she disowned Regina and him. She was Baroness and determined not to lose what was rightly hers. Elisabeth frowned and thanked the Goddess that her friend, Prince Eugene, had an ear with the Kaiser. She had successfully petitioned to end all the burnings in her town. Of course, Johann had been angry. She smiled, thinking of his frustration.

Later, Regina pleaded with her to forgive him. She gave them her Viennese residence and her *Landgut* in Burgenland, which finally appeased his greediness.

Elisabeth breathed in the fresh country air as her coachman opened the door. She stepped out, feeling a spark of anticipation.

"Wait here. Speak to no one," she commanded and headed into the woods several miles away from her castle. Until today, she hadn't dared visit her daughter, terrified of exposing the child's whereabouts. Besides, she'd been busy defeating the Turks as well as ruling her estates.

Although she took pride of her abilities, her duty of running the *Burg* was exhausting. In the last few months, peace settled back in Riegersburg. Her people were safe again, and Elisabeth could risk a visit.

She loved to walk and went on daily treks around the castle, visiting her farmers, workers and servants. These outings helped her keep sane and healthy. No one would question her this time. The birds chirped and trees cast shadows of light through the branches. This calmed her as she strode towards the farm, the place where her special child lived; protected and concealed from the church and Johann.

What does Hilde look like? Did she favor me or Georg?

Twenty minutes later, she walked through fields of barley, pumpkin and spelt then spotted a small farm nestled against a wooded hill. Chickens ran freely throughout the yard. The farmhouse had a thatched roof made of reeds. Next to it were pens filled with pigs, and a dark horse. A pair of geese came waddling aggressively towards her, honking displeasure. She stopped in her tracks, hands on her hips, and frowned.

"Mistress, call off your guards!" she demanded.

The farmer's wife, who was sitting on an uneven bench outside weaving a basket of willow twigs, stood. Alongside her was a girl of ten years.

There she is!

It was the first joy she'd felt in a very long time.

"Shoo, shoo, leave the Lady alone!" the woman yelled, and waved her arms at the goose and gander running toward Elisabeth.

"*Milady*, forgive me. I didn't know of your visit today. Hilde, go and fetch Papa from the fields. Now hurry up, be quick."

"Yes, Mama," the girl answered, staring at the stately woman before them with a wide smile. Elisabeth noticed Hilde's locks of gleaming black hair escaping from under her grey bonnet. A tattered grey apron covered a long, brown dress of rough linen. Her heart ached as she watched her daughter run towards the farmer's fields.

"Welcome, *Milady*. Please come inside away from wandering eyes," the woman said, and beckoned Elisabeth to follow her into the house.

Mistress Wenzel who was stouter and a good head shorter than Elisabeth was dressed humbly next to Elisabeth's traveling attire of maroon velvet.

Elisabeth watched the girl scamper into the field as she followed the woman inside. "How is she, Mistress Wenzel?"

"She's very well, *Milady*. Hilde's a fine young lady, though head-strong, mind you. And she can eat." The farmer's wife motioned to Elisabeth to have a seat on a bench then sat herself on a three-legged stool in front of an open hearth.

The aroma of rosemary and thyme permeated the space. Soup was cooking in a large cast iron pot hanging on a linked chain over the fire. The hearth's walls were black with soot. The woman picked up a wooden spoon and stirred the soup.

Opposite the hearth, Elisabeth sat on the edge of an L-shaped bench that hugged a crudely carved table. On the wall above the mantel was a single shelf with clay plates and mugs. A Virgin Mary statue sat amidst them leaning against the stone wall along with a wooden cross. Two small vases on each side of the cross held dried flowers.

Elisabeth fidgeted and cleared her throat. It was abominable that Hilde had to live in such poverty, but she was alive and that was all that mattered.

"It's not much, but she's safe with us," Mistress Wenzel said, whisking the spoon around inside the pot while avoiding Elisabeth's gaze.

Elisabeth nodded, but she was more interested in the living conditions her daughter was in. She peered past the open archway to a sparse room adjacent the kitchen. There were two narrow wooden beds, and a dresser, nothing more in it.

Am I doing the right thing keeping the child here? She could have so much more at my castle. Maybe I could have her as a maid. No, there's too many prying eyes and gossip there.

Farmer Wenzel walked into the room, a little out of breath. Hilde followed him watching Elisabeth suspiciously.

"Baroness, I had no idea," Farmer Wenzel said.

She waved her hand dismissively. "No need to worry. I need to tell you how to proceed in the care of my child." In truth, she just wanted to see her daughter to help alleviate her own aching soul. Her loved ones were all dead. It hurt her to know her daughter didn't know who she really was. She glanced over at

Hilde smiling. *How lovely she looks, Georg's eyes and my mouth and nose.*

She drew breath, fighting to keep her composure. "It's time the girl learned her letters and numbers."

The farmer looked at his wife in alarm. The girl's eyes widened and she put her hand over her mouth.

"Papa?" she said.

"Never ye mind," he answered. "We'll do as the Baroness asks, no questions. Go fetch some water from the well for our Lady," the farmer said.

Hilde's large dark eyes widened and she stiffened as if she might protest, then went and grabbed the water urn. Careful to curtsey to Elisabeth, she disappeared outside.

"She's a good child," Elisabeth said plainly, watching the girl leave.

"Yes! That she is, and a joy to us, not having any of our own. We're quite fond of her. But, *Milady* neither of us can read nor write," he said as his wife wrung her hands in her apron. "How are we to teach her in these things you demand?"

"I've arranged for a monk from St. Martin's to come twice a week to tutor her here. Do you think so little of me? All I ask of you is to continue the good care you have given her. As always, I will provide for her upkeep. The monk will have the same token as this one." She handed the farmer a silver piece engraved with a pentagram. "Hilde needs to be instructed in all I know and...."

"Yes, Baroness," he replied. "But if I may say so, won't that be suspicious?"

"It may, but the priest has been sworn to secrecy. I cannot tolerate or abide in our faith to die," Elisabeth said.

The man and wife nodded in agreement.

"In times like this, we have no choice. The monk will aid you with the farm as well, which will add to the appearance he is providing extra sustenance for the monastery." She narrowed her gaze on the old man and woman. "Lastly, and this is most important: when Hildegard comes of age, you are to inform her of her destiny as our Faith-Keeper."

"She is the one, our hope for a better future. After I'm gone, she will inherit my book and lead the community in the

ways of old faith, therefore, she'll need to be prepared by the both
of you in the ways of the *Lady* and our ancestors." She leaned
forward then, and with as much emphasis as she could muster,
added, "Heed me! The Lady of Light, needs be hidden from the
church, forever safe, therefore Hildegard must never lay claim to
the *Burg*. Though I have stopped his persecutions, Johann is still
too dangerous and, sure as day, he would do everything in his
power to have her killed."

"May we have a blessing, *Milady?*" Farmer Wenzel asked.
Elisabeth nodded.

The farmer and his wife came and knelt before Elisabeth.
As she placed her hands on their heads offering a thoughtful
expression, she wondered if her daughter would accept her role.

"I bless you both in the name of our Great Mother and the
God of the woods. May your lives be healthy, plentiful and long
for the Mother will not forsake you. You've done a great deed in
her service. Protect the child. Peace be to you and yours, brother
and sister."

Hilde walked into the kitchen as they stood. The girl
poured the water into a tin mug and offered it to Elisabeth. The
lady and the girl looked at each other in silence. Then Elisabeth
moved towards Hilde.

"Thank you, precious child. I must take my leave, now,"
Elisabeth said, grasping the mug. As she drank, the silence was
unbearable.

"Will we see you again?" the old farmer man said.

"I think not. Fare thee, child," Elisabeth said handing the
cup back to the girl and kissed her brow. Hildegard stepped back
in surprise. Elisabeth braced herself, pushing back the powerful
urge to wrap her arms around her child, and walked out of the
farm house, not looking back. She felt a heaviness and tightness
of her limbs. This would be the last time she'd lay eyes on her
beautiful daughter. As she went, escaping into the safety of the
woods, the tears she'd been holding back rolled down her cheeks.

Then from behind her, she heard, "Wait!"

She stopped and dared to look back at her daughter who

was standing at the edge of the woods. Before, she could move, the girl ran to her, and to her surprise hugged her.

"Thank you," Hildegard gushed looking up at her in adoration: so innocent and true. "You've been so good to my Papa and Mama, and now to me."

Elisabeth discreetly wiped away the hot tears. *Yes, all would be good. The girl IS connected to me!* She pressed her cheek against Hilde's and prying herself away from the girls' arms, Elisabeth felt a release of tension in her body.

As the girl turned and ran back home, Elisabeth whispered, "Go now and always remember you are loved."

Later, on her way back to Riegersburg, Elisabeth felt better and observed the light coming through the trees thinking it looked charming.

"Good-bye my daughter, May the Goddess keep you safe."

Katarina Lilienthal

1915-2009

Chapter Six
Feldbach, Austria 1927

Katarina hummed while banging her legs against the crate. Taking a break after helping all morning, she watched Oma working in her herbal garden, then blinked up at the sun shining in the sky. Oma's white hair, falling out of her bun, sparkled in the light. Everything was a dark and vibrant green. Bumblebees and small white and light-yellow butterflies flew circles around as Oma, bent over, pulled out weeds.

"Oma, tell me more about the different herbs," she said, jumping off her perch on the old wooden box next to the barn. She noticed Oma's floral-printed dress looked old and worn. *How does she work so hard? She's not well.*

The garden was vast, with a wide variety of herbs and vegetables. Red currant, raspberry and blackberry bushes grew along the sides in front of the woods. One of Katarina's favorite tasks in the fall was making jams and pies.

Oma stood up, arching her back and wiping her dirt-covered hands on her apron, then smiled down at Katarina and said, "Here, Kati, pluck some off now, smell and taste it." Oma reached down and pinched off some dark green leaves, rubbing them between her fingers. "See how the leave has points. Now smell it."

Katarina took a whiff.

"Smells really good."

"Then taste it."

Katarina took it and chewed. "I know this, it's parsley."

"Yes, and as you know, good for cooking. Now see this one, the leaves are longer, it has a lighter green and they are softer. Feel that." Oma moved over to a larger plant. Katarina touched the leaves. They were silkier.

"Pick it and taste it."

Katarina yanked off a leaf and stuffed it in her mouth only to quickly spit it out. "Yuck, it's bitter."

Oma laughed placing her hands on her hips. "That's sage. You can make a great tea for colds." She continued teaching Katarina the various herbs in her garden and what they were for until Katarina became sleepy in the warm sun and plopped down onto the grass, letting her lanky body fall back. "Oma, there's so much to remember!"

"That's enough for today. Now, take these chives to your mama in the kitchen, for lunch. Run along."

Katarina sprang up and clutched the long thin scapes. She brought them to her nose.

"They smell like onions!" she yelled, as she sprinted towards the house.

Hours later, in the evening, after Katarina's bath, Oma opened the door to her bedroom. "May I come in?" Oma placed a box she was carrying on the bed's blanket. Katarina wondered what was in it.

"Yes. Yes." Katarina, already in her favorite nightgown, sat up in bed combing her wet and tangled long brown hair. "Ouch," she cried as she pulled. Oma hurried over. Taking the comb, she carefully teased apart the knots. Cool air flowed through the slightly fluttering curtains. Katarina heard rain falling as Oma untangled her hair, sitting on the edge of her bed. Oma worked patiently until the comb ran smoothly through Katarina's still-damp hair. *What was in the box?* Her curiosity almost had the best of her.

"Thank you, Oma." Katarina leaned over and kissed Oma's cheek. She still loved to have her hair done, even though she'd just turned twelve years old.

Oma stroked Katarina's hair back from her face.

"It's time." Oma nodded solemnly, contemplating Katarina.

Katarina's eyes sparkled and she felt her senses tingle. She didn't know what was in the box, but she knew it was important. She bit back a smile.

Oma straightened up and took the box onto her lap.

"Child, what I'm going to tell you is going to be our secret because I know you have the gift." Katarina opened her mouth to respond, but Oma placed her forefinger in front of her mouth, continuing, "I know you love your mama and papa and sisters and brother, but they must not know any of what I'm going to reveal to you. There are things better not shared. You have to understand, the Catholic church condemns women like me. Do you understand?"

Katarina fidgeted on the bed, frowned and crinkled her nose. Not wanting to disappoint Oma, she clasped her hands on her lap, looking down.

"Yes, Oma. But, why can't our family know?"

Oma grasped both of Katarina's small hands, and narrowed her eyes. Katarina's stomach quivered and she wondered what Oma was going to say.

"In the past, women and men lost their lives for protecting the knowledge in this book. Even today there is still much prejudice. Trust me. You must swear to me and I know you're young. So was I when my mother taught me *the path*." Oma released her hands, closed her eyes and touched her own temple with her finger tips.

"I won't breathe a word. I promise. What's *the path*?" Katarina shifted closer to Oma, clinging to her and wrapping her arms around her. Oma hugged her in return and Katarina noticed tears in her eyes.

"Don't cry"

"I'm fine, though, I'm getting old and there's not much time. Now, don't you worry about me, you have much to learn. I will instruct you about it all in due time, but first-"

"What's in the box?" Katarina clapped her hands together and sat back onto her pillow.

"It's a book of magic." Oma opened the top of the box, lifting up a large book.

Katarina gasped and leaned in for she loved reading fairy tales.

"Settle down. It's not what you think. This is a book of real spells and real magic."

Katarina's eyes widened. She felt her hair lifting off her arms.

Should I be afraid of Oma?

"No need to be scared." Oma answered as if she could read her thoughts. Katarina remembered Oma often knew what she was thinking. She studied Oma carefully. Oma appeared serene as she placed the book on the blanket between them. Katarina wanted to touch it, as if it were calling her. She tilted her whole body closer and gawked at it. The book was leather with a large star on the front and a snake biting its own tail. It looked really old.

Katarina scowled. "Oma, the book has a snake." Katarina would scream and run when she saw a garden snake. Oma laughed and traced her fingertips on the star and snake.

"Snakes are good, as you know already, dear. They help the plants grow."

"I know, but I think they're slimy."

Oma laughed, then whispered. "How many points do you see on this star? Go ahead and touch the cover."

Katarina put the tip of her index finger on one of the points and counted, "One, two, three, four, five! Five. Does it mean anything?"

Oma nodded. Yes, it's a pentagram, the five-pointed star of protection. Come, sit right next to me." Katarina squiggled over and Oma wrapped one arm around her while opening the book.

"One day, you will use this book to heal others." She flipped a few pages over. "That is what the path is all about: helping others in their times of need and finding Her, the Goddess, in everything you see and hear."

"The Goddess, is she beautiful, Oma?" Katarina's lips parted and she felt giddy as she was on Christmas Eve. "And what about God?"

"Yes, she is, and much more." Oma tapped Katarina on her chest. "And more importantly, you find her right here in your heart. The Goddess' consort is God. That is a story for another time."

Katarina tilted her head, uncertain of what Oma meant. "In my heart?"

"You know how you love mama and papa, and how it feels when they hug you? So it is with the Goddess. She is in all the creatures, the rivers, the plants, everything. Even the fairies are a part of her." Oma opened the book to a page where there was a drawing of a plant with an explanation under it.

"That's parsley!" Katarina recognized it. "And faeries don't really exist."

"That depends on how you use your eyes to look. Listen, a long, long time ago, one of your ancestors, Elisabeth von Galler, drew this picture. And here you'll find out all about this plant and how it can help others." Oma explained. "And I'll teach you how to talk to the plants as well and even understand what the animals are telling us."

Katarina's jaw dropped and she batted her eyes in disbelief.

"No, really, honey. I will." Oma turned to pages, pointing out a few of the other plants and their uses. After a listening awhile, Katarina yawned and closed her eyes just for a second, only to fall into a deep sleep full of strange dreams of creatures and birds dancing around a fire.

When she woke early the next morning, she remembered Oma tucking her in and singing a song. It had strange words, pleasing to the ear, yet sounding very foreign.

She had never heard it before and wondered what it meant. Katarina knelt in front of her bed and clasped her hands together. "Dear God, I promise with all my heart to keep Oma's secret. Keep her safe. And me too." At the moment, she'd keep in touch with Him just in case.

Katarina sprang up and ran downstairs to breakfast.

Chapter Seven

In the late summer of '38, the non-Jewish patients of Katarina Lilienthal's husband Jacob stopped making appointments. This fact worried her a lot. She feared they should leave. Nights, she and Jacob discussed the political ramifications of the Nazi party spreading to Austria and possible outcomes if it did. Then, rumors of Hitler coming to Austria spread like wildfire. He was to speak in Graz in a few weeks. She knew something awful was going to happen because Katarina sensed certain things, like the day someone was going to die or when a storm was brewing. Her grandmother, Anna Maria, had taught her *the path*. Her namesake was "The Witch of The Flowers": Katarina Pauldauf.

She believed in her insights and dreams, one of them being the day a flock of black birds landed in her back-vegetable garden. This omen made her watchful. A week later, her calico cat *Mietzche* disappeared; a second bad portent! Afterwards, fear like a menacing demon, and visions of black tidal waves engulfing her tiny home visited her during the hours of darkness. Often, she startled awake in terror from her nightmares, only, she couldn't see exactly what would transpire. Katarina instinctively knew she needed to take precautions for an uncertain future. Jacob didn't agree with her, and called her irrational.

She hid her special book of secrets, the one he was unaware of, sewing it into the bottom lining of a large suitcase. On top of it, Katarina packed some of hers, Jacob's and Suzanne's toddler clothes along with family photographs and money. She kept it in the back closet.

Then, September Eighth came. Katarina would never forget the day.

The police, along with five other men they knew and called friends, came to evict them from their small home on the outskirts of Eisenstadt.

"Doctor Lilienthal. We insist you leave at once and take your dirty wife and brat with you," the men yelled. Their faces were grimaces of hatred.

When Jacob protested, they smashed his special medicine cabinet, which he built himself; then, trashed the chairs and desk in his office with large clubs and metal pipes. Katarina gasped, seeing the shards and broken pieces on the floor.

Katarina grabbed one of them by his jacket, trying to make them cease the destruction. "Wolfgang! And you, Reinhardt! You're our neighbors. Why are you doing this? Stop!"

She shook with fear and anger. Her daughter, Suzanne, who was holding onto her skirt, bawled beside her.

Wolfgang pushed her hard against the wall, causing her to fall forward, catching herself onto her arms. Ignoring her, he continued his rampage.

Standing back up and rubbing her wrist in shock, she looked over to her husband. Dumbfounded, Jacob just stood by, watching his livelihood being destroyed. Finally, he dropped to his knees and cried, "Alright. Stop. I'll leave. You can have everything I own, but I beg you, don't hurt my wife and child!"

It wounded Katarina deeply to see her husband so shamed. The men stopped and left, swearing and cursing, "We'll be back if you and your Jew bastard husband don't get out of our city!"

"They're barbarians," Katarina said, sitting down on the doorstep hugging Suzanne, who was crying hysterically. As she watched the men drive off on their motorcycles down the dirt road, she set her jaw. "How could they do this to us?"

"I have relatives in Vienna," Jacob said, looking at the eviction papers in his trembling hands. "I'll not stand by and see you or Suzanne hurt. We'll leave tonight."

"What about my garden, your work…my family?"

"Gather our things, dear," he said. "We can't risk it, they'll be back."

Two months later, Katarina, Jacob and Suzanne stepped off the city tram in Vienna. She was still in shock from her neighbor's cruelty, and worse yet, because her own mother wouldn't take her and Jacob in.

They walked through the once busy city under grey brooding skies toward the neighborhood of an old friend of Jacob's from the university. The tall majestic buildings loomed over them as they passed by a storefront boarded up with the Star of David painted eerily on its tainted window. They walked keeping close to each other, wary of watchful eyes behind darkened windows on either side of the street. Katarina never felt so naked and exposed. She drew Suzanne tighter to her with every step.

Finally, Jacob pulled out a slip of paper from his pocket, and after looking at it, said, "Here it is."

A minute later, they were standing outside a pair of double oak doors on the fourth floor of an old Viennese apartment building, anxiously wondering about their uncertain future. Jacob reached up, took the brass door-knocker in hand and rapped hard, three times. The banging reverberated in the ice-cold empty stairwell as he blew out small puffs of white breath. Katarina shivered with anticipation.

"Hurry," he muttered to the door, panting, exhausted from carrying Suzanne up the stairs. Katarina looked up into her husband's kind brown eyes and was reminded of how much she loved him. Then she reached over to her toddler daughter, who had her little legs in blue wool stockings wrapped around her father's waist. Suzanne's light brown hair was braided into two long strands.

Katarina stroked the girl's cold, ruddy cheek.

"Don't worry, *Liebchen*, everything will be fine," she said as Suzanne burrowed her head into her father's shoulder.

The door opened. Katarina grasped her husband's hand.

A tall blond-haired woman with two coiled braids wrapped around her head in the shape of a crown stood in front of them. She was maybe in her late twenties and her sky-blue eyes were soft. She wore a light brown linen dress with a thin belt fitted snuggly around her tiny waist. Katarina couldn't help from staring, finding her stunningly beautiful.

The woman smiled, and reached out to shake Jacob's hand. "Hello. You must be Dr. Lilienthal." She turned to Katarina. "And you must be Katarina. Please, come in," she said, pulling the door back. She put a flawless alabaster arm around Katarina's shoulder and guided her into the apartment. Jacob followed with Suzanne in his arms.

They exchanged pleasantries, and some details of Katarina and Jacob's exodus from Eisenstadt for a few minutes until the woman blinked. "Oh, where are my manners? Let me take your coats. And I almost forgot to introduce myself in all this excitement to meet you both. I'm Roswitha Stifter."

"Not to worry," Jacob said, putting Suzanne down, who quickly ran behind Katarina to hide. She handed the woman her long winter coat along with her daughter's crimson jacket and matching cap. Jacob hung his coat on the wooden rack, which stood in a spacious hallway with several lofty doors on each side.

"Thank you very much, Frau Stifter," he said. "We are indebted to you and Hans-Peter in our time of need. I'm sorry if we're causing you any inconvenience."

"Not at all, please, Dr. Lilienthal. Let's not be so formal. I assure you: a friend of my husband is a friend of mine. And you can call me Rita," she said. Her melodious and serene voice put Katarina instantly at ease. "It's the least we can do. Come into the parlor. My husband is anxious to see you and your family." She led them to the third door on the left, opened it and gestured them to go in.

Katarina took her daughter's hand and stepped into the large room with tall windows draped in lacy pearl-white curtains. A dark green velvet sofa and chairs covered with peach-colored, hand crocheted throws sat in the middle of the room around a mahogany coffee table. Persian rugs covered the lion's share of the floor and a towering grandfather clock sat at one end. Hans-Peter was leaning against a leather chair smoking a long cigarette. Katarina looked down at her worn brown loafers, feeling inadequate and embarrassed.

Roswitha went over to Hans-Peter and touched her husband's arm.

The man turned toward Katarina and her husband.

"Jacob, it's been years," he said, getting up and coming to them. As he clasped Jacob's arm, Katarina studied her husband's college friend. He was a polished man in every way, from his imported Italian shoes to the cream-colored jacket he wore. Yet it was his deep brown intelligent eyes and his aquiline nose that held her attention most.

Hans-Peter let go of Jacob's arm and stepped back to look at him. "It seems like yesterday we were studying anatomy with Dr. Florey at the Karl-Francis University. You haven't aged a bit. Can it be already ten years ago?"

Jacob nodded.

"You were the best in our class. How should I word this? It's quite unfortunate we have to meet under such horrible circumstances. Roswitha and I are very upset about this government. You know, we meet every week with several others who think as we do. You did the right thing to write to me for help."

Jacob sat on the sofa, pressed his hands onto his thighs. "I did not want to trouble you, but people are afraid and no one would help us," Jacob said, and glanced knowingly at Katarina, who had taken a seat beside him on the couch. "We had nowhere else to go."

Katarina pulled their daughter onto her lap, praying these people would help them. Could they save her and her family?

"Don't worry. You're innocent victims. We are so disgusted with the Nazi party. Shameful. It's a disgrace!" Hans-Peter walked over to one of the windows, peering out at *Wallnerstrasse*. He pulled the curtains slightly aside. "A group here at the university is working to end this madness and have been printing flyers. It is very dangerous, what they are doing, but something must be done, otherwise what will the Nazis do next?" He turned and faced her and Jacob. "I assume you'll keep this in highest confidence?"

Roswitha pressed her hand onto her husband's breast. "Dear, do stop. You'll distress the child."

Katarina sighed, stroking her daughter's hair. "She's fine."

"Yes, yes, of course," Hans-Peter said, and turned back to the group, smiling. "Where are my manners?" He broke away from his wife and came forward to join Katarina on the divan. "So, you're the beautiful Katarina who stole our serious Jacob's heart, and you, little girl, must be Suzanne." He tickled the child's belly, making Suzanne giggle with delight, then looked back at Roswitha and added, "Darling, please bring some coffee and cake for our guests."

Hans-Peter looked knowingly over at Jacob, and continued, "We gave our maid the day off." Roswitha hurried away, disappearing through the door to the kitchen.

"I understand your need to be careful," Jacob answered. "These days you can't be careful enough. There are Nazi informers everywhere."

While the men talked, Katarina remembered arguing with her husband and his relatives, since arriving in Vienna, about the need to leave Austria. All she had to support her argument was the recurring and immense foreboding, which visited her every night in her dreams. "I see a dark mass of clouds, blood and flooding waters," Katarina told them. Jacob and the others didn't want to leave their homes, businesses or country. Her husband wouldn't believe anything worse could happen to them than which already had.

In November, *Kristalnacht* ran through the streets of Vienna causing the Jewish community to quake with fear. From the window they watched and heard the Nazis roaming the streets, chanting, *"When Jewish blood drips from the knife, it's twice as good for us."*

That had been the deciding point for Jacob to leave their homeland. At her urging, he'd written his friend Hans-Peter, who was well connected. Now, they were here, and she wondered what the future held for them.

"Katarina, are you all right?" Jacob said, resting his hand on her arm as Roswitha walked back into the room. In her hands she held a tray with a blue and white porcelain coffee service.

"Oh, I'm sorry." Katarina glanced at the other woman hoping she didn't offend her.

Roswitha set the service down and poured their coffees. "It is so terrible what is happening, people turning against each other."

"Yes," Katarina said. "Our home was destroyed, and people we've known for years turned into monsters. I lost everything including my family in Feldbach. My father and mother support the Nazi party, and care nothing for their own grandchildren or us."

"Oh my God, how awful," Roswitha said, giving a glass of milk to Suzanne. "You poor dear, losing your home. And Jacob, your doctor's practice to those brutes. I can't imagine. But, no more of this talk. We have sworn to help you. Don't worry, there is a strong Viennese Jewish community here and they are helping many families who've been expelled from Burgenland until they can find safe passage. Some have left for the borders of Hungary and Czechoslovakia."

"That will be a relief," Jacob said. "My cousin David, who lives here in Vienna, put us up these past two months, but he and his wife have little space, what with four children of their own." Hans-Peter nodded in agreement, frowning.

Katarina watched Roswitha pour steaming coffee into the cups and pass them around to the group. Katarina lifted up her cup, inhaling the rich nutty aroma of her favorite brew. It perked up her spirits, and she took a sip, while little Suzanne greedily gulped down half her glass of milk.

"Slow down," Katarina scolded.

Suzanne pulled the glass away from her lips and bowed her head, but not for long. When Roswitha lifted the cover over the dark chocolate cake waiting to be sliced, the girl's eyes widened. And so, did Katarina's. She hadn't had chocolate for weeks and her mouth suddenly watered.

"Mama, Mama. Do I get a piece of cake?" Suzanne cried, tugging on her mothers' sleeve.

"Here, take this," Roswitha said, cutting off a piece and handing it to Suzanne.

The little girl took a big bite that left a chocolate ring around her mouth. She looked up at Katarina, who just taken a bite herself, and said, "It's very good, isn't it, Mama?"

Katarina nodded, swallowed then answered, "Yes, honey. It's delicious." To Roswitha, she said, "I couldn't have made it better myself."

"Now to the task at hand," Hans-Peter said. "There is a foreign diplomat who has been working diligently on emigration papers for many families. We can't tell you his name, but he is very concerned about the political situation in Austria and the plight of our Jewish brothers and sisters. Through him, we were able to obtain travel documents for you. Now some have fled to Shanghai, Argentina and England. But you are one of the lucky families, as you will be traveling to America."

Hans-Peter stopped talking and looked at them as if he were waiting for a reaction. Katarina was speechless. Jacob looked astounded. Hans-Peter glanced over to his wife, smiled with satisfaction and added, "The train leaves next Friday at 6:30 p.m. from the central station downtown."

Katarina gasped, and wept with relief. She couldn't believe her ears. America? Was this really happening? Hans-Peter took a cloth handkerchief from his jacket pocket and gave it to her. The prospect of living in America, so far away from family, was exciting, and yet alarming. She couldn't speak a word of English, although she knew Jacob was proficient enough with it to get by. But he wouldn't be with her every single minute.

"I know it's hard to fathom," Hans-Peter said.

"America…" Katarina sounded out the word slowly. Jacob was quiet. *Had he known, and if so, what was he thinking?*

"What is America, Mama?" Suzanne asked.

Everyone laughed, yet for Katarina the tension remained. She smiled and said, "A place where they make movies, and dreams come true."

The answer seemed to satisfy her daughter's curiosity, as she ate another large bite of the cake, spilling crumbs on the floor. Katarina bent down to clean them up.

"Leave it. Don't worry about them. I'll take care of it later," Roswitha said.

Hans-Peter motioned to his wife then. "Get the papers and the envelope from my desk." To Jacob and Katarina, he said, "You will travel by train to France, then cross the English Channel to Britain. From Britain you have passage already booked on a ship to New York City. I know this sounds rushed, but you mustn't wait a second longer than is necessary. There are rumors."

"I agree," Jacob said. "And I don't want to put my cousin in danger either for taking us in."

"Good! Now, along with the tickets for the train is money for the passage overseas and food. You will disembark at Ellis Island, which is just outside New York City. There, you will be processed at the immigration office and both be given physical exams. Be careful not to come in contact with passengers who might look sick, as they could give you something. TB is rampant, we hear on these voyages, and if you get it, they will hold you at the island for quite some time, and maybe even send you back in certain circumstances."

Katarina gulped and squeezed her hands. And when Hans-Peter's glance fell her way, he said, "You will be okay as long as you are careful. Now, once you are processed, you will need to travel to a city called Syracuse. It is in what is called Central New York."

Roswitha came back with the envelope and handed it to Jacob, who held onto it tightly between both hands, and continued, "There are friends of ours there we've given your names to. In the envelope here is their address. When you get there, find them and they will help you."

Hans-Peter broke back in. "Again, I repeat, do not...under no circumstance... mention our names to anyone, not even to family. No one. I can't stress this enough."

Roswitha knelt before Katarina and took her hands into her own. "We think the situation for Jews will get worse before it gets better, and we want to continue helping the resistance."

"Of course, I swear not to say anything," Katarina replied, realizing the danger and the magnitude of what Hans-Peter and Roswitha had done for them.

"We will be silent, do not worry," Jacob said. He paused, and except for Suzanne's scraping her plate with her fork to get the last few crumbs of cake, silence filled the room. Finally, Jacob said, "We should be off so you can enjoy the rest of your evening. I'm sure you are tired."

"Rather, it is you who are tired, no?" Hans-Peter said and sprang up. "Take care and safe travels. Remember, talk to no one and time is of the essence."

"How can I ever thank you or repay you for this?" Jacob said embracing his comrade.

"No matter, that's what friends are for," Hans-Peter replied and patted Jacob on the back. "We will see each other again, dear friend."

Warmth ran through Katarina's body. "Come, Suzanne, it is time to go."

"Mama, I'm still hungry," Suzanne said.

Roswitha grinned and cut two more pieces of cake off and wrapped them in a white napkin.

"Here you go," Roswitha said, bending down and handing the treat to the girl. She kissed her forehead. "Listen to everything your parents tell you to do, promise me."

Suzanne nodded, took the bundle, and reached up for Katarina's hand.

"Thank you so much, I do hope to see you again," Katarina said, knowing there was a good chance she never would.

"At a different time, I'm sure we would've been best friends," Roswitha said, looking up from her kneeling position. Then she stood, and went to open the living room door.

"We need to hurry," Jacob said. Hans-Peter helped Katarina into her coat. As Katarina and her family walked out into the cold stairwell, she noticed Roswitha holding her husband's hand.

"*Auf Wiedersehen,*" Hans-Peter stood next to his wife.

"*Auf Wiedersehen,*" Katarina and Jacob replied in unison.

Katarina walked down a few steps and looked back up at the couple one last time, standing in the archway of their door. As she waved good-bye, they closed the door leaving her alone. Jacob and Suzanne were further down the stairs. They had just given her and her family a new life.

They're angels. Katarina thought. *But, what about my family? Will I ever be able to come back home? What will happen to us in America?* Her heart ached. She reached into her coat and fingered the silver pendant in the shape of a pentagram. This was her secret. So far, Jacob knew nothing of her actual beliefs. Katarina gripped it. *Goddess, please protect us. Keep us safe on our journey!* She let go of the amulet and hastened down the steps with her husband and daughter.

Chapter Eight

December 1938

uring Friday night and well into the next day, the train sped through Germany and France. Katarina and Jacob took shifts watching over Suzanne in their compartment, which they were lucky enough to have for themselves. The cars rocking back and forth along with the clickity-clack of wheels riding on the rails made her sleepy. Katarina dozed off occasionally, only to wake up anxious about how they were going to survive in America. Jacob didn't have a job and she didn't know a soul. This, and the cabin's isolation, which at first made her feel, safe and secure, had gripped her in a suffocating embrace.

She looked out the window at the distant French countryside, as the train took on new passengers. As she watched those disembarking hugging loved ones, she couldn't help feeling like an orphan.

"I can't help but wonder if we should've left our home," Jacob said as if he was reading her mind. "Maybe we acted rashly."

"I don't know." She said, glancing over at her sleeping daughter. "But we can't go back."

Jacob nodded. "My parents, my brother," he muttered. "I didn't get a chance to say goodbye to them."

She took his hand and looked back out the window, unable to bring herself to say a word: she was leaving her family and the only country she had ever known as well.

At long last, they arrived in Calais, France. Jacob hoisted Suzanne
up onto his shoulders, took their suitcase, the only possession they
had, and walked from the train station. Katarina followed him
through the snow, hungry and tired, to the port. Along the way,
they passed an outdoor market where Jacob bought two loaves of
bread, some cheese and apples. There at the edge of the world,
they waited to board a crowded trans-Atlantic steamship coming
from Norway through Calais on its way to America.

"Don't let go of me," Katarina cried, grabbing Jacob's
hand. Her toes were frozen. She was afraid to lose sight of her
husband in the throng of people waiting to escape Europe. A huge
ship with two red smokestacks, and a pair of masts — one at the
bow and the other at the stern — loomed above the crowd. Several
life-boats were suspended along its sides.

"Don't worry, honey," he said, "Follow me. I see the
entrance over there. See the line of people!" He pointed to a group
of doctors who were holding medical examinations. In front of the
ship, a long line of eager individuals stood around, anticipating
their turn. The wind blew icy, salty air in from the ocean. Katarina
worried Suzanne might fall ill even before they boarded.

"Wait," she called to Jacob. "Bend down, so I may wrap
this around her head."

"She has her cap on," Jacob answered.

"It's not enough!" Katarina said, pulling off her woolen
scarf. Standing on tip-toes, she wrapped the shawl around her
daughter's head.

"Mama," Suzanne whimpered. "I'm hungry."

Katarina broke off a hunk of bread and handed it up to
her daughter.

After passing inspection and a list of endless questions,
Katarina picked her daughter up and followed her husband up
the ramp with everyone else to the main deck. We're being herded
like cattle, she thought as a man led them down a steep stairway
to the lower decks. She went down holding Suzanne with one arm
and grasping the rail, worried she'd slip and fall.

When she finally reached the bottom, the stench of piss and vomit slammed into her as she was swallowed up in the waiting throng with Jacob. As the crowd muttered and babies bawled, a uniformed sailor announced everyone was to remain on the steerage deck for the entire journey. When she gazed back, puzzled, Jacob elaborated, "The *"tween-deck"* between second class and cargo."

"I'm not sure I can stay here," Katarina said, pinching her nose.

"We have no choice," Jacob said. "Come, we must go now."

She followed him and the throng of refugees down the narrow galley way until they found their cabin, such as it was. Jacob set their bag in the darkened room, and light flooded in behind him, there she saw folks sleeping under woolen blankets in their bunks. "Jacob," she whispered, and gripped her sleeping daughter tight to her breast. "There are people in here."

Jacob turned to her. "What do you want me to do? Throw them out?"

"No." She shuddered as she eyed six rickety bunk beds and a simple toilet and lavatory peeking out from behind a tattered curtain in the corner. "But…"

"But nothing, there is nothing to be done about it. Here, you take the lower bunk with Suzanne," Jacob said.

After Jacob climbed up to the top bunk, Katarina climbed in fully dressed, pulling a blanket around her and her daughter. She lay there in the darkness gently stroking her daughter's forehead and listening to the creaks of the ship and the snoring of their cabin mates, she wondered what was waiting for them across the ocean.

Four days later, they sat on long benches in a teeming mess hall.

"Mama, I'm not hungry," Suzanne said, refusing to eat a chowder consisting of lumpy potatoes, black beans, chunky carrots and specks of bacon floating around in it. Suzanne was sea-sick and couldn't keep anything down.

"OK, but you have to drink some water," Katarina said. She sat and gave her daughter tiny sips from a metal cup. "When you feel better, you can have some crackers and milk." Suzanne smiled, but lay her head down on Katarina's lap.

"How are you holding up?" Katarina said, watching her husband eating a spoonful of the chowder. "It's not too bad when you're hungry."

"I'm feeling nauseated, too," he answered and looked at his bowl, pushing it away.

"You should eat to keep up your strength," she encouraged him. "Do you recognize any of the languages?"

"Mainly Polish, some Italian and German," Jacob said, looking over to the man sitting next to him. He turned to the man. "Where are you from? Do you speak German?"

"Yes, I'm from Gorlitz," the man said. "After my wife and I heard of the resignation of Schushnigg and his imprisonment, we decided to leave. I don't think Hitler will stop with Austria. I believe he means to take over all of Europe. It wasn't safe for us to stay."

The man's wife, a pretty blonde woman of around twenty-five years, nodded. Katarina marveled how perfect strangers would openly talk. Yet she understood they were all closed up in these uncomfortable tight quarters and needed some distraction.

"I owned a tailor shop," the man continued. "My brother decided to stay, so I sold him my half. He wouldn't listen to me. He's so stubborn! I begged him, his wife, and my parents to come with us, but they wouldn't leave. Oh, forgive me, my name is Wolf and this is Rachel." He extended his hand to shake Jacob's. "Are you leaving Europe for the same reason?"

Jacob sat back and was quiet a minute, then recounted the events of the plight of the Jews in Vienna, the rantings and destruction of Jewish stores during *Kristalnacht* and his family's persecution. The couple were appalled, shaking their heads, and the woman put her hand on her mouth.

"They smashed everything in my office and demanded we leave." Jacob said.

"See, darling. What did I say?" Wolf said, putting his arm

around his wife. "I just knew the Nazi party was dangerous. My God, what will happen to my family and our Jewish friends?"

"We can only pray that the worst is over," Rachel answered. They finished the meal in silence while others chattered around them.

In the days that followed, Katarina made it a habit to go outside with Suzanne and get away from the stench. Even in stormy weather, massive amounts of weary and unwell people wandered out onto the promenade deck along with Katarina to escape the foul air. They had been on the boat for over three weeks now, and it helped her daughter to breath in fresh air. The smell of the ocean breeze invigorated Katarina and she gazed at it stretching off in every direction as far as she could see. Its enormity amazed her. Finally, she had adjusted to living on the ship and she was pleased Suzanne was eating again.

Today was a drab, breezy morning and she and Suzanne were standing at the railing looking out at the endless gray water. As the ship thrashed in the rolling waves, the wind knocked Suzanne's cap off and she ran after it, barely catching it. Katarina hurried after her and grabbed her daughter's arm.

"Don't run off like that," Katarina scolded.

"Sorry, Mama. When will we be there, Mama?" Suzanne said, and pouted. "It's taking so long."

"Soon, dear," Katarina answered, as she did every day. "You have to be patient."

"What is America like?" Suzanne said, tugging on her mother's coat. Katarina led her daughter back to the rail, holding her hand, and pointed up at the gray sky.

"It is wonderful, you'll see. There are skyscrapers, large buildings so tall they reach up to the clouds," she said, and bent down to look into her daughter's eager face. "And there are shops everywhere. We'll buy a new dress for you, and a doll when we get there. Let's go back down to your father."

While others slept, her husband Jacob spent many nights discussing theology with a Jesuit priest from Freiburg. Katarina knew it was one of his passions. As she listened to these long-drawn-out conversations, she kept quiet and knit a sweater for Suzanne.

Tonight, the priest was recalling the memory of friends he worried about, telling Jacob they'd gone ahead of him two weeks ago. "I hope they made it over the border to France," the man said, grimly and crossed himself. "God be with them."

"With all of us," Jacob said. "So, you were in the resistance?"

"Yes. I couldn't stand by and do nothing. Is it God's purpose to love one group of people and not another?"

"I can't answer for God," Jacob said. "But I can't believe it's his intention to allow for cruelty and violence. I'm sorry, Father, but I question if there is a God sometimes. If He is all-powerful, how could he allow such terrible things to happen? I've lost my faith. It deeply saddens me, but…"

"To quote Thomas Aquinas, "*It is on account neither of God's weakness nor ignorance that evil comes into the world, but rather it is due to the order of his wisdom and the greatness of his goodness that diverse grades of goodness occur in things, many of which would be lacking if no evil were permitted*"," the priest said. "Do you know of his writings?"

"No," Jacob said. "I like this thought of his. It gives me reason to perhaps re-think my beliefs. Hmm…I shall have to look his works up. Thank you for sharing and now if I may change the subject: you chose to be a part of the resistance so you knew the danger you were in if you didn't leave."

"This is true," the priest said. "I thought by working out of the church's protection within Germany, I could do the most good."

"What changed your mind?"

The Jesuit grasped the cross hanging around his neck and sighed. "The SS. A good friend tipped me off that they were coming to arrest me. I hid in the church attic for a week until one night my brothers-in-Christ came for me and helped me escape into the forest that backed up onto our land. There, I met a man who led me to a truck heading over the border."

Jacob patted the man on the shoulder.

"It's okay. But I worry for those who are left behind. Excuse me for a minute. I'll be right back."

The priest left and when he returned, he had a bottle of red wine and three cups. "I've been saving this, but I didn't know why until just now. Our conversations have been a savior to me, and to recite Aquinas, *"There is nothing on this earth more to be prized than a true friendship"*."

He passed the cups around, but Katarina politely declined.

"You are sure?" the priest said.

Katarina smiled as the priest eyed her curiously. *He thinks I'm with child. Well, let him think so.* "Yes, but thank you. Go ahead, you two drink up," she said and got to her feet. "I'm going to get some sleep."

She walked away and heard their mugs clunk together.

A few days later, the sound of the steamship's bellowing horn announced their arrival at the shores of America.

"Look, I see land," Jacob said, and waved at the approaching New York harbor. Katarina took Suzanne's hand and joined him, along with a large group of anxious people at the rail of the promenade deck. Katarina was happy at last to have arrived safe and sound and her spirits rose dramatically as she looked at the skyline coming into sight. She'd never seen anything like it before. The buildings were tall, uneven and awfully close together, like jagged teeth. Above them, the sky was crystal blue with a few white puffs of cloud.

When they docked, Katarina expected to leave, but inspectors came aboard to visit only the first and second-class passengers. Jacob asked why this was, and it was explained to him that only US citizens were free to depart without an examination.

"That's not fair," Katarina cried, looking around at the others standing next to her.

A woman next to her, who was looking at Suzanne's runny nose, shook her head dolefully and in German, said, "They won't let us off 'til they look us over at a place called Ellis Island, I heard. Hope your girl isn't sick because they'll send her and you back."

"Even after we came this whole way? That's horrible,"

Katarina said, appalled, and wiped off Suzanne's nose with a handkerchief.

"*Ja*, it is. Good luck to you," the woman replied and moved away.

Katarina gathered Suzanne to her side and held her tight. "Jacob. They wouldn't take Suzanne, would they?"

"Honey, don't worry," he answered. "She's not sick."

"Where are we going?" Suzanne asked.

"New York, dear," Katarina said holding her daughter close. The child was so excited that she was dancing around on her tip-toes.

At length, the ship moved north through the Narrows leading to Upper New York Bay and into the harbor. Slowly, the tip of Manhattan came into view. When the Statue of Liberty appeared, Katarina inhaled slowly and lifted her eyebrows in awe. The enormous robed woman holding a torch straight up into the air in one hand, a book in the other, with a crown of stars on her head like a Goddess. Something touched Katarina deep inside then, like the statue was speaking directly to her; 'You have found your home here.' Her eyes teared up and she let out a sigh of relief.

"Why are you crying, Mama?" Suzanne said, frowning.

"I'm happy... so happy," Katarina said, bending over and kissing her daughter's cheek. As the statue passed by them, the mass of people on deck around them broke out in song and embraced each other.

Jacob reached down and pulled her and Suzanne into his arms. "One of the seven wonders of the world," he said.

The ship docked and the upper cabin passengers were released to the freedom of America. But for her and Jacob, their daughter and those escaping the perils of Germany and the occupied Nazi regime, it was a ferryboat ride to Ellis Island. There, on the tiny island in New York Harbor, they were herded across the pier to holding areas, waiting their turn to be processed.

Katarina and her little family stood in front of the three-story drab metal building, unable to move forward or backward, until finally the mass of humanity progressed forward through the glass doors to a huge room called the Great Hall. In it there were immigrants in a long line from all over Europe, and she recognized many different languages. As the line plodded along to a winding staircase, she looked upward and saw a man sitting on a stool at the top of the stairs.

"The inspector," Jacob said. "He's asking questions before he lets them pass."

Katarina felt her heart thump. "What kinds of questions?"

"I don't know," Jacob answered.

The inspector picked up a piece of white chalk and wrote large white letters on a man's jacket sending him off in a different direction from everyone else.

"Where is he being sent?" Katarina whispered to Jacob.

"I think for further medical examinations," Jacob replied and said no more. For the next two hours they inched their way up the stairs towards the man who would have total dominion over their future and as they did so, Katarina prayed silently to the Goddess for protection and strength. And then, at last they were standing before the man, who wore a stoic frown on his face. Next to him stood another man in a tight-fitting blue uniform and hat. From what Katarina could tell, he was a translator.

"What language?" the inspector barked in English, as he looked down through his spectacles at the open book before him. The man beside him translated, though Jacob understood the language perfectly.

"German," Jacob answered and handed the man their passports. As he did so, he added, "I understand English."

The inspector glanced through them. "That's good. And your papers."

Jacob handed them over as the man glanced at his pocket watch, as if he had someplace to go to. "Where are you from?" the man continued. "What is your purpose to visit the States?"

Jacob explained their reason for fleeing Germany and then answered many more questions until the inspector finally turned to Katarina and Suzanne. "Your wife and child?"

"Yes," Jacob said.

The man eyed her and Suzanne, and for a second, she

felt like a bug under his dark gaze. At last, he nodded. "Good, hurry up."

Katarina took a deep breath and, tugging Suzanne along, joined her husband in yet another line to a room called the Registry Room. Here, foreign currency was exchanged as well as arrangements made for transportation. The ticket office was located on the far wall of the mammoth room, and after they exchanged their Austrian shillings for American dollars, they walked over to join a line at one of the small windows to buy tickets.

"Where you headed?" The ticket agent asked when it was their turn.

"Syracuse for me, my wife and child, one way," Jacob said. "How much, please?"

"That'll be twenty-two dollars and thirty-seven cents. The girl can ride on your lap," the agent answered kindly, handing them their tickets. "Next."

"We have one hundred seventy-four dollars left," Jacob said, pushing the bills into a tattered envelope after completing the transaction. "It's plenty for the start, but Katarina, I don't know what we'll do later."

"We're staying with the Rosenburgs in Syracuse for a few days, like we'd planned. We can decide what to do later. They'll help us get a job or know where we can go," Katarina said, and picked Suzanne up. She caressed her daughter's hair. "It's alright, honey," she cooed to her crying daughter, "We're almost there."

Katarina watched the shore of New York recede from the back of the ferry and smelled the air. It was fresh and made her feel hopeful. The ferry boat landed, and they walked up to a long institutional looking two-story brick building with a huge clock in front.

Inside the building's sprawling dreary interior, they saw a maze of red steel railings with scores of travelers lined up behind them. The noise and buzz of the crowd was overwhelming, so she took Jacob's and Suzanne's hands as they walked through the modern-looking building.

"Look over there." Jacob pointed to the back doors. "That's where we need to go."

They fell in behind the departing travelers and soon they were standing on the platform overlooking twelve sets of tracks.

"Our train is on track one. Hurry, it's leaving in a few minutes." Jacob said. He corralled her and Suzanne and rushed ahead through the throng of waiting passengers to their car. Katarina stepped up first, then Jacob handed Suzanne to her and climbed up after them.

At long last, they were nearing the end of their long journey to Central New York. As the train advanced from the station, Katarina stared out the window, relieved to be alone in the compartment. She thought back to their train ride through France, remembering how isolated she felt and wondered if it would settle in on her again. But for now, the privacy felt good after the long ocean trip.

"The buildings are so tall," she said more to herself than her husband, who had since fallen asleep with their daughter in his lap. Katarina took off her jacket and placed it over her daughter's curled up legs. An hour later, the train had left the city behind them. As it sped north alongside the Hudson River, through long green pastures and forests she had no name for, the scenes reminded her of Austria. Would she see home again?

Chapter Nine

The Berkshires, 1945

Upstate New York reminded Katarina of Burgenland with its rolling hills and farmlands. At first, they'd rented a small room in Stockbridge. A year later, Jacob secured a loan from his boss for an old house on Amherst Road two streets down from Main Street. He worked tirelessly to fix it up, putting in a new cast-iron stove that heated the home in winter, repairing windows and painting the interior and exterior of the house. Jacob fixed up the home's electricity and installed indoor plumbing, a toilet and bath. Sometimes Katarina still used the water from the outside well because she felt like she was at her parent's farm in Austria.

The silver maple outside her front window dropped its leaves six times and during that time two more children came into the world. Luckily, both births — home delivered — were without complications. Katarina's days were filled with motherhood. She looked into her precious book of shadows to create spells and salves for the children's health. Its very existence gave her the courage to face each day with renewed vigor. Katarina promised herself to study it more when the children were grown.

Later, they bought a freezer, which made life easier on Katarina. She and her children harvested blackberries, raspberries and wild blueberries from the surrounding forest. Then she froze the berries to later make jellies and jams at night while the children slept.

Katarina supplemented their income by selling breads, pies, cookies and cakes to the local bakery. The owners were glad to work with her because they came from northern Italy and trusted Austrians.

"Come and keep your eyes closed," Jacob said, one morning covering her eyes with his hands. Suzanne grabbed Katarina's hand and led her into the living room from the kitchen.

"Surprise," he cried along with the three children. She opened her eyes and gazed at a new sewing machine, shiny black with bronze designs. It stood next to the window on its very own table.

"Oh my! It's a Singer. Can we afford it?" she said, clapping her hands together in joy. Katarina was ecstatic. She could finally sew decent clothes for the children. "Is it electrical?"

"Yes, it is. Nothing but the best for our wedding anniversary," Jacob said, and walked over to the machine. "Come and try it out."

Katarina pulled up a chair. This was the best gift she'd ever received. She sighed, remembering the years had been hard on Jacob. Many obstacles stood in his way: lack of money, scarcity of work, anti-German sentiment, and the language barrier to top it all off. The Americans didn't allow him to practice medicine so he worked long hours at a local lumber yard, Kriebels' Lumber Company, to make ends meet.

Later that day, Katarina kneeled in her garden and tenderly took each tomato seedling from an egg carton. Behind her, on the lawn, her three children played croquet with different colored wooden balls and bats. She felt content listening to their voices and turned her head, glancing at them running happily around.

The last frost was over, and the rich earth was tilled and ready. She planted twelve tomato plants in all, each two feet apart. Next to the tomatoes were numerous vegetables such as bell peppers, squash, and zucchini. Her garden took up a third of the back yard that was walled in with a tall wooden fence built to keep the deer from ravaging her plants. How she loved digging her fingers into the dark earth, even though her very pregnant body was in the way.

She sat back and considered the chives, rhubarb, and oregano. They were coming along nicely. Medical herbs like calendula, motherwort and valerian were at the end of the patch, which she used to make tinctures and salves from recipes found in her secret book.

Katarina was excited about two new sorts she was experimenting with: *Celebrity* and *Better Boy*. These varieties were said to be disease resistant and ripened in mid-summer.

"Kati, come quick," Jacob called from the kitchen's back door, waving his hands around with urgency.

What does he want? Katarina struggled getting onto her feet and wiped the loose dirt from her hands onto her apron before rinsing them off at the well's pump.

"I hope this one comes sooner rather than later," she muttered and rubbed her sore back.

"What did you say?" Suzanne said, a tall girl now of twelve years.

"Never mind, watch your sister and brother. I'll be inside," Katarina answered, and eyed her two younger children. Georg was six already, fast and wiry. Ursula carried long blonde curls and was born only fourteen months after her brother. Ursula was arguing with Georg as she tugged at one of the croquet bats he was holding.

"Yes, Mama," Suzanne replied, and ran over to discipline her siblings as Katarina hurried to the back steps and labored up to the door.

After walking into the kitchen, she stopped to catch her breath and put her hands to her stomach. She could feel the baby kicking. This one was active. Passing through the tidy kitchen, she walked, with its large cast- iron range. She glanced at the white ceramic sink with running water and plenty of counter space which stood to her right, and over the sink were built-in cupboards painted in daffodil yellow with a border of little flowers. Right next to the stove was a door leading to the pantry. *I love my kitchen Jacob made for me.*

She ambled over to the door leading to the living room. There her husband was sitting on his rocking chair next to his Regentone AW44 radio. The room was sparse, one old couch on the right with another wood stove next to it. The rectangular dining room table with two benches stood on her left and a round hand-woven rug filled the center of the wooden floor.

"The war is over! The Western Allies and the Soviets have captured Berlin. The Germans have surrendered!" cried a deep rumbling voice from the radio along with a lot of crackling. Jacob reached over to adjust the volume. "...Hitler is presumed to be dead..." The radio hissed for a minute, and Jacob tried to find better reception, but finally gave up. He sat back and gazed at the wall in front of him.

"It's done," Katarina whispered going to him. She put her hands on his shoulders and felt the tension in his muscles. They'd both heard the rumors of the death camps over the last few years and wondered about the family members who were left behind.

"Do you think they survived?" Jacob asked, looking up at her at last. They had discussed this many a time over the years, hoping for some sign of life; a letter or card from their loved ones.

She wrapped her arms around him tight, pressing her stomach against his head. She wasn't sure how she felt. "We won't know for sure until things settle," she answered and went quiet. In the silence, save for the ticking of the wall clock, her thoughts drifted. *I'm still angry at you, Papa, for disowning me. Are you even alive? I'm not sure I can forgive you. And Marie will I ever get to see you again? I hear the Russians have occupied Austria.*

"Let's not lose hope," Katarina finally said. "Your Papa was resourceful. Maybe they made it through enemy lines to Switzerland. Let's not forget, we're the lucky ones. We have a lot to be grateful for."

"Yes, but I need to find out what happened," Jacob insisted.

"Of course," Katarina said, feeling guilty because she suspected worse news was yet to come. She looked at him, remembering how much she adored him, and bent over to kiss him in his neck. He had sacrificed so much for her and the kids.

"There you go again," Jacob said. "Lost in thought and you're probably right as usual. Just like your insistence we leave Vienna. I wonder whatever happened to Hans-Peter and his wife. Do you remember her name?"

"Roswitha. Really, Jacob?" Katarina answered.

"Sorry, Katarina, you know me. I can't remember names. What do you think, another boy?" Jacob said, patting her stomach.

"No, it's a girl again. See the way it sets low," Katarina said, taking his hand and placing it on her flank. "I want to name her after my sister, Marie. Are you good with the choice?"

"Yes, of course. I love you and just want the child to be healthy like our other three. Oh, look, it's kicking!" he said.

She smiled. "Yes, she's a feisty one."

Jacob grinned and as he did so, the enormity of Germany's defeat seemed to well up in him. He gazed at her, and she noticed he hadn't aged much in the last six years, just some gray hairs around his temples. For everything they'd gone through since coming over from Europe, he was still as attractive as the first time she'd laid eyes on him, tall and lean, a full head of curly hair and kind brown eyes.

"It's time for celebration, I think," he said. "Go round up the children. We're going to town. *L'chaim!*" He swung her around in his arms then kissed her passionately.

"Careful, the baby," Katarina said, happy to see her husband's enthusiasm return after so long.

"I'm taking us all to dinner. What say you to Schrafft's?" Jacob said.

Katarina clapped her hands. They had never been able to afford going out to eat. She went to the kitchen's back door and called out to the children. "Ursula, Georg, Suzanne…come in and wash up. We have a special day. The war is over! We're all going to town to celebrate."

Chapter Ten

Berkshires

The next morning, Katarina and Suzanne walked — they had no automobile — to town to shop for groceries. It was a light, breezy Saturday, and Jacob offered to stay home with the younger ones, giving her time alone with Suzanne. Katarina cherished every moment walking with her older daughter. The previous night still lingered in her mind. It had been the happiest she could remember in a long, long time. Jacob was laughing, delighting the children with little magical slights of hand, pulling nickels and dimes from behind their ears. But it was when they got home, and after the children had been put to bed, that was foremost on her mind. Making love with Jacob was always special, but last night had been more than that. The way he'd looked at her, touched her, and kissed her had reminded her how good it was to be alive and free.

"Mama, the hamburger was so good. I wish we could go out every night," Suzanne said, twirling and spinning back and forth, making her skirt float around her skinny legs.

"Me too," Katarina answered. She eyed Kriebel's Lumber and Hardware Store across the street. It was where Jacob began his workday at the crack of dawn. Next to it was a tiny brick post office and two ordinary restaurants. Ahead, people were going into O'Leary's, a small general store that stood beside Metzler's Butcher.

As a rule, Katarina had felt conspicuous walking the streets here, knowing folks were suspicious of a German in their midst, but not today. She greeted people with a smile, even though she expected nothing more than a nod back.

"Mama, where are we going first?" Suzanne said, hooking her arm with Katarina's.

"I need flour, sugar, coffee, and of course baking chocolate for the cookies tonight," Katarina answered in a bubbly tone as they turned into O'Leary's. She grabbed a wicker basket by the door and pulled the shopping list out of her pocket. To Suzanne, she said, "Go get a tub of lard and some butter while I pick out some fruit and vegetables."

"You forgot we also need frozen orange juice," Suzanne said. "I love juice."

"Yes, I will, now off with you," Katarina said.

Suzanne took a couple steps, passing a large jar of candy, then turned around. "Can I have a toffee bar?"

"If there's some change left over, yes you can pick out one."

"Thanks, Mama." Suzanne ran past Katarina to open the store's glass door.

"Good afternoon, Mrs. Lilienthal," Janice O'Leary called out from behind the counter across the room. "How can I help you ladies?"

Mrs. O'Leary was a woman in her mid-thirties, Katarina guessed, and wore a plain blue dress with a white collar and green buttons. Her red lipstick matched the roses on her spring frock.

Katarina pulled out her list of dry goods and gave it to the woman. Mrs. O'Leary busied herself getting the items while Katarina collected her fruit and produce into her wicker basket and wandered over to the newly showcased toiletry items.

"The lipstick just came in from Max Factor, and doesn't Ella Raines look fabulous?" Janice said over her shoulder. "Normally, I don't buy make-up for the store, but it was on special. Will you be buying one?"

"No, no thank you." Katarina said, shaking her head as Mrs. O'Leary placed the groceries on the counter.

As the woman tallied the items along with Katarina's fruit and vegetables, she said, "So, Mrs. Lilienthal, how long has it been since you moved to town? We've never had the opportunity to formally introduce ourselves."

Katarina thought it was rather funny that it took the defeat of Germany to open the woman's mouth regarding introductions. She arched her pregnant body backward and winced. "I think coming up on six years now."

"Oh, my goodness, how time flies," Mrs. O'Leary said, as Suzanne came running back with the butter and lard.

She added them to the tally and smiled down on the girl. She turned back to Katarina. "Well, I think it's about time we fix that, don't you?" She paused; eyed Katarina then came around the counter. "Do you need to sit?"

Katarina nodded.

"How far are you along?"

"Going on eight months," Katarina said as she was led to a chair in the front of the store.

"You know, I see your husband and kids at church. Beautiful children, they are. I take it you're a Lutheran — I haven't seen you with him — anyway, we'd love to have you attend, that is if you have a mind for it. In fact, we're having a bake sale this Sunday to raise money for the wives who lost their husbands in the war. Perhaps you'd like to contribute. I heard you make a fine apple pie or what do you call it?"

"Strudel. I'm sorry but I not good in English," Katarina said. The woman's comment about attending church evoked an unwanted recollection. One Sunday morning, two years ago, her husband woke up and declared he was attending the church services at St. Mary's. She closed her eyes as the memory unfolded before her. Jacob and she had been arguing for some time about the children's education concerning God and it had come to a head that morning.

"I'm going and so are the children," Jacob said adamantly. "This is the one time; you may not question me.

"But you're not Catholic," Katarina argued, sitting up in bed. She watched him dress in his only good clothes, a pair of grey trousers and a jacket.

"I've made my decision, Liebchen. You're Catholic! Although you never go to church, do you? Don't you think I know you don't believe in God? All these years we've been together, I don't question you, do I?"

"No."

"You could come along with us, you know."

"No, I don't want to," Katarina said, and jumped out of bed to look into her husband's face. Suddenly, she wondered if he knew about her secret book and it frightened her. "As I remember, we were going to let them decide later. Right? That's what we agreed to, as far as I know."

"That's true, but I've been thinking this over lately. Ever since those nights on the ship," Jacob said as he continued to dress, "I've been contemplating what the priest said about Christ and baptism. It'd be easier for us and our children."

Was he serious? Katarina couldn't believe it. Why hadn't he consulted her? He must have known she'd argue with him. Over the course of their marriage, they sidestepped the issue of religion, by agreeing to wait. He was Jewish, and she was what? She was raised a Christian, but she wasn't sure she believed any of what they taught. And then there was the book. As far what she really believed, that was something she never confided in him for fear of being judged or even worse, him leaving her

"Did you ever think of letting me know?" Katarina demanded, putting her hands on her hips.

"That's what I'm doing now," Jacob said, and marched out of the room.

"Jacob, wait," Katarina cried and to her surprise, found the children were dressed and downstairs.

"Are you coming, Mama?" Georg asked.

"No, honey, not this time. I've work to do here at home," Katarina said, bending down to kiss his forehead. For weeks, she barely spoke to him. Jacob never apologized and shortly afterwards, Jacob and her children were baptized. But, what could she do, divorce him? That was out of the question. Katarina bit her tongue and accepted the fact.

Mrs. O'Leary tapped her arm. "Are you okay?"

"Oh, yes," Katarina said, and shivered as the memory evaporated and looked at Janice O'Leary's concerned face.

They were both quiet a moment, until Janice finally said, "Well, if you decide to join us, we'd love to have you. My mom,

God rest her soul, was German. It's been hard for them, us, I mean my family the last few years. Folks say unkind things, anti-German, but that damn war is over, isn't it?"

"You're German," Katarina said, brightening.

"Oh, yes," Mrs. O'Leary said. "Gruenwald was my mother's maiden name. Speaking of which, do you have a name for the baby?"

Katarina patted her stomach, smiling happily. "Marie if it's a girl and Hans for a boy."

A few minutes later, they were drinking iced teas and nibbling on cookies.

"Cheers to finally getting you to talk to you," Mrs. O'Leary said, who was insisting Katarina call her Janice. She raised her glass in salute and Katarina smiled, seeing that Janice was relentless in her pursuit of making her acquaintance. She raised her glass along with Suzanne and sipped the cold tan-colored beverage. It tasted slightly bitter and lemony.

"I'm Katarina, but you can call me Kati," Katarina said.

"You know, I could introduce you to some of the other women at church." Janice said as her soft brown eyes lit up. "You could sit next to me, my boys and my husband, if you'd like."

Is Janice someone I could confide in, Katarina wondered. Her gut told her *yes*. She wanted friends. Maybe, Janice was the first step. "Let me think about it. I do like the idea of getting some time alone from the children."

"I feel the same way as you on that one," Janice said, chortling. "This place, my kids and Mr. O'Leary keep me hopping. That is when he's home. He likes to spend a little too much time at the tavern, if you know what I mean."

Katarina recollected she saw Mr. O'Leary frequently grumpy and red-faced.

"But, he's a good man," Janice said, then leaned toward her and whispered, "This very Sunday, we're having a birthday party for Randy's eighteenth after the bake sale. You're invited, bring your whole family."

"Mama, please can we go?" Suzanne said, perking up suddenly.

"Maybe, I'll have to discuss it with your Papa," Katarina replied and stood up to leave. How could she say 'no' to a bake sale and a birthday party?

"I believe, that's a yes," Janice said as another customer walked into the store. She turned toward the customer. "Well, hello, Maggie, what brings you in today?" And before Katarina could blink an eye, Janice was off helping the woman.

She's a lively one, and a little nosey. I need to get home to cook.

"Yes, Mama." Suzanne ran past her, then turned and cut Katarina off. "Can we go?" She put down the basket and pressed her hands together as if she were praying. Suzanne tilted her head sideways. "Please." Katarina couldn't break her daughter's heart.

"Alright. I'll consider it," Katarina answered, watching Suzanne grab the basket crying "Yippie" and skipping ahead of her all the way home.

Chapter Eleven

Katarina loved to watch *I Love Lucy* on her RCA black & white console. Every day, she made coffee and sat down in her favorite chair at 4:00 p.m. Jacob would be at work, and the kids were either doing homework or at a friend's home. Suzanne was married and out of the house. This was Katarina's time. She earned it after doing her housework every day.

Leaning back, she propped her legs up on the reclining chair's extension and laughed at Lucy's antics on the TV while sipping her coffee.

"Mama, where are you?" Marie said, her voice calling in from the kitchen.

"I'm in the living room," Katarina yelled back.

Marie hurried into the room wearing a yellow skirt just above the knees, with a tailored button-down shirt with a matching print. White knee-high socks and loafers accented her long legs. *I did a good job of sewing her outfit.* Marie looked pretty with her hair in pigtails.

"I need to talk to you desperately," Marie said, sitting down next to Katarina on the coach. She tapped her fingers on her legs. "Can you turn off the TV?"

Annoyed, Katarina went over and switched off the show. Crossing her arms, she faced her daughter. "Now what's so important you can't wait until my show is over?"

"I think I'm pregnant."

Katarina's mind swirled in ten different directions at once. "What? How can you be sure?"

Marie covered her face with her hands. "Well, I didn't get my period, and I feel sick." She broke into racking sobs. "Mama, I'm so sorry. I didn't mean…"

"You shameless girl," Katarina bellowed, and walked over and slapped her daughter hard across the face. She stood there afterward, shocked at her reaction. This wasn't who she was and she immediately regretted what she did. She bent down before her daughter and pulled her into her arms. Maria stiffened. "I'm sorry. I didn't mean to…" She was at a loss of what to say. She didn't even know her youngest daughter was seeing boys.

Marie pulled away, her face red and marked from where she'd felt her mother's wrath. Touching her cheek with her fingers, she turned a grimace toward her mother. "I hate you. You're the worst mother in the world," she said and ran upstairs.

Katarina watched her go. Her little Marie had always been a lively child, headstrong and uncompromising. As a teenager, she argued about everything but she had always been responsible in the end. But pregnant? Katarina was horrified. She'd need to call Dr. Jamison, but first Jacob needed to be told. She picked up the phone and rang him at work.

When Jacob came home, he was bristling. "This is your fault, Katarina. You weren't strict enough with her. Always letting her get her way with this or that. Now see what happened?"

"It wasn't me who spoiled her," Katarina rebuked, emphasizing each word. "She was your little angel."

"No, you gave her too much freedom," Jacob shouted, pointing his finger at her. "Now what are we going to do?"

Katarina shook her head. "I don't know. Maybe adopt it out."

Marie was standing at the archway into the kitchen with her hands balled and planted on her hips. "What do you mean? It's my baby and I decide, right, Papa?"

Before Jacob could answer, Katarina said, "You're fifteen! You know nothing of raising a child, and we haven't the means to do so," Katarina said as her son, Georg, walked in through the back door wearing his black leather jacket and rolled up jeans. He popped the refrigerator door and grabbed a soda. Over his shoulder, he said, "I was going to get tickets to the Frankie Avalon Show. He's coming to Syracuse and I can't wait to see him. Dad, can I borrow your car?"

When there was no reply, he turned around and eyed his sister, then his mother and father. Wrinkling his brow, he said, "What's going on?"

Jacob glanced at Katarina then walked over and placed his hand on Georg's shoulder. "Could you go upstairs for a moment?"

"Sure, dad," Georg said, trailing off. He glanced over at Marie, who turned her head away, and left the room.

Jacob waited a moment then went over to Marie and put his arm around her. "Honey, your mother's right. Unwed mothers don't have a chance for happiness in this world."

"I don't believe you. I won't…I won't, it's mine!" She tore herself away from him. "You can't make me, either of you," she cried, and ran out of the house, banging the screen door shut behind her.

"Should we call the police?" Katarina asked Jacob when Georg came back later that night without his sister.

"She'll be back," Jacob answered. "Don't worry. She'll be back."

"How do you know?" Katarina said, and sat opposite him at the kitchen table. Marie was his little angel, and she knew he understood Marie better than anyone, herself included. At one time, the closeness Jacob enjoyed with his daughter bothered her, but not anymore. She decided to listen to him this time. He went into the living room and turned on the Huntley and Brinkley report.

As the newsmen reported on the beginning of Vietnam war and President-elect Kennedy's win in the other room, she tried to put her daughter's pregnancy out of her mind and make dinner. Something simple and easy, spaghetti and meatballs; comfort food. She set the table, called to Jacob and Georg and sat down. But Georg took his plate upstairs and Jacob said he wasn't hungry. She'd lost her own appetite as well. Dinner sat in the pot and turned cold.

Marie didn't come home until after dark. She walked in through the back door, past her mother and scrambled up the stairs to her room. Katarina glanced at her husband, wondering whether someone should go up and talk to her. In the end, she consoled herself Marie would come to them on her own accord. Later, her decision turned out to be the right one. Her daughter crept down the stairs, her eyes red and puffy, and sat next to her father, who was still watching TV, Katarina got up and went into the kitchen, knowing Marie would never open up with her sitting in the same room as them.

After a time, she heard muffled crying in the other room, and she crept quietly over to the archway and listened as her daughter repeated over and over, "He doesn't care... he doesn't love me."

While Katarina's heart broke for her daughter, all she wanted was to hold Marie and make it all go away, she knew there was no making it better. The question paramount to her was how it would all look to her neighbors and friends. People would talk and rumors would spread. She would be judged by people no matter what. No, there was no fixing this, save for sending her away, and even that would lead to curious questions which posed difficult answers.

She eavesdropped and listened to Marie tell Jacob between the tears that the father of her baby was a local boy of seventeen. Could the boy hold his tongue? She wasn't sure; all she could do was hope.

"Jacob, we need to send her away to a boarding school," Katarina said, whispering to him after Marie went upstairs to bed. She had heard from the kitchen that her husband had convinced their daughter to give the child up.

"What, so no one will know about the baby?" he said, frowning.

"Yes," Katarina said. "I'm not without heart, Jacob, but her remaining here will only make things harder for everyone, Marie especially."

Jacob nodded. "You're probably right." he said, as he walked over and pulled her into his arms.

Katarina buried her head in his shoulder. "I hate this," she said, and was quiet a moment before adding, "I don't think we should tell Georg or Suzanne anything."

"Are you sure?" he stepped back, looking down at her.

"Yes. Promise me you won't tell them."

Jacob shrugged and stroked her hair. "Of course, whatever you say."

Eight months later the baby was born. The nurse ferried the baby away, denying Marie even a peek at her child, who turned her head away as it was being washed and swaddled.

The only consolation Katarina had for her daughter was saying it was for the best as she sat with her after the birth. Marie held the baby once before it was brought to a room at the hospital where the adoptive parents were waiting. Katarina's resolve wavered for a second seeing her grandson, but pushed this feeling, of deep sadness and never holding him or seeing him grow up, far aside. Marie refused her mother's overtures of affection and didn't speak to anyone for days.

After that, any hope Katarina had for re-establishing a relationship with her daughter was over. Marie wanted nothing to do with learning about herbs or healing like she'd done earlier. She barely finished high school and spent most of her time alone in her room, brooding. And when Georg left for college, she didn't get out of bed for two weeks. She was drinking, too. In a last-ditch effort, Jacob got her a job at the lumber company where he worked. It was part time in the office — something to occupy her thoughts — but it didn't help. Often, he was called to pick her up from local bars where she'd passed out. And when he wasn't rescuing her, she was picking up men and spending the night with them. Sometimes, she'd hook up for a month or so, but it wasn't long before they shipped her home.

Years went by. The other children grew up and moved into their own houses. Yet, Marie's life stayed the same; she lived with her parents as a stranger. Katarina had given up on any change. Marie's future appeared bleak and destined for a sad ending until one day Father Peter Holden came to town. Marie, now thirty-nine, began to attend church and had started to take care of herself. Her drinking stopped and she even smiled at Katarina off and on.

So it wasn't a complete shock when Marie announced one day that she was thinking of moving into a place of her own. And for weeks, she would hum and dance to her favorite songs of The Beatles.

Katarina was hopeful and thought, maybe, just maybe, there was hope again, as she ironed Jacob's shirt while Marie watched TV in the other room. Then, without preamble, Marie called to her and the world crashed around Katarina all over again. "I'm keeping this one, mother, and there's nothing you or papa can do about it."

"Excuse me," Katarina said looking up from Jacob's shirt. She blinked, wondering what her daughter was talking about.

"I'm pregnant, and I'm a grown woman," Marie said, jumping up and walking to the staircase.

Katarina drew breath, fought through her first reaction, and said, "I'm happy for you, if that's what you want."

"It is."

"Does Father Holden know?" Katarina suspected the two might be having an affair.

"No, and no, he's not the father, if that's what you're wondering," Marie said, defiantly. "He's someone you don't know, and frankly I'm not seeing him anymore. He was, well…"

"Well what?" Katarina put down the iron and walked over to her daughter. "Is he married?"

Marie backed away. "Just like you to think the worst of me. No, he's not married," she said and strutted upstairs to her bedroom, slamming the door behind her.

Katarina never found out who the real father was, although despite Marie's insisting Father Holden was just a friend, she suspected it was him. Soon, rumors spread, and Janice, whom Katarina had become good friends with, dropped by to talk with her.

"There's speculation Jamie Goodman's the father," Janice whispered conspiratorially as they sat in the living room sipping tea. "He's a drunk, but a decent guy, I guess."

"So, where does this Jamie live?" Katarina said.

"Hmm…good question. Rumor has it he's left town with no apparent forwarding address."

Just great, Katarina thought. "Does he have family here?"

"Not that I know of," Janice said. "Oh, Kat. I'm so sorry. What are you, I mean, what is Marie going to do?"

There it was the question she knew was coming. She eyed her friend, discerning her posture and expectant expression then pushed her shoulders back and said, "She's keeping the child, and we'll help, of course."

Nine months later, Sarah Lilienthal was born to Marie, surrounded by family and friends.

As Katarina held her granddaughter in her arms, cooing and sniffing her, she felt possessiveness creep into her heart and whispered into the baby's ear, "Oma's gonna take good care of you."

Chapter Twelve

1984

The room was black except for two long tapered candles flickering on the mantelpiece. Katarina could barely make out the faces of the four women standing around a table in Maggie's living room. She smelled the remnants of burned sage and adjusted her robe. Taking a deep breath, she fetched a box of matches from the pocket of her green cape as the room filled with anticipation.

Katarina struck a match and bent down to light a stick of incense. Picking the stick up, she blew on it saying the following words: "By the power of the witches' breath I do create a new element holy onto itself." Earlier in the evening, Maggie and Janice smudged the room with sage, blessed and consecrated the four elements; air, fire, water and earth.

Janice, now in her sixties, was still a pretty woman with wavy brown hair swept away from her eyes. She picked up a bowl of salt. Dropping a few granules into the bowl of water on the table, she stirred it with her finger saying, "By the witches' hand, I do create a new element holy onto itself."

Katarina and Janice lifted up the new elements and walked around the circumference of the room deosil three times chanting, "By the powers of earth, and water, fire and air, we do consecrate and purify this space."

"The elements are blessed and consecrated. Now it's time to cast the circle," Louise said, appearing almost faceless with the dark hood of her black cape hiding her features.

This part of the ritual always gave Katarina chills. She

reached down to the table for her athame, the one with a small blue stone on its hilt. Down inside, she was anxious, but found her power as a well-trained priestess and raised the knife up to the ceiling. Focused on her actions, she held the tool straight up and walked purposefully around the circle three times drawing an imaginary boundary.

"The circle is cast, and we are now between the worlds. Let's call in the directions." She made her voice deep and guttural and laid the athame back on the table before taking her place again.

All was silent save for the soft breathing of the participants.

At last, Janice turned to the left and raised her arms. "Hail and welcome to the guardians of the watchtowers of the east. Power of air, welcome and blessed be." She drew a pentagram in the air with her finger then bent over and lit a yellow candle on the center table. Katarina beheld the table draped with an off-white cloth fondly. On it were five candles: four representing the four directions and their associated elements and one long white taper in a silver holder in the middle, representing the center.

There also lay a painted pentagram, a feather, an apple, Katarina's athame, an array of beautiful semi-precious stones and Louise's hand-made chalice. Around the base of the cup, wound a depiction of a snake working itself up to the rim. Since it was Imolg there was a straw representation of Brigid, the Irish Goddess of midwifery and fertility, lying next to the center candle.

Next, the women completed calling the other three directions and lit the three corresponding candles. Katarina turned to the center again, and the others followed suit. Weaving her wrists and hands around as if she were stirring an imaginary cauldron, she said, "I call to center, that which connects us all, that which binds us. To the spirits of the center, come and bear witness to our work tonight. Hail and welcome and blessed be."

Katarina lit the center candle and gazed around at the women in her coven: Louise, who always had a kind word, gentle Helen, her best friend Janice, and Maggie, who exuded confidence and fortitude. Each of them had developed a friendship with

Katarina over her years of living here. She recruited, convinced and eventually taught all of them *the path*. Her dedication to her religion required her to do it. Now, they gathered to celebrate together in complete secrecy several times a year at Maggie's home.

She placed her hand on her chest, felt tingling warmth in her limbs. Yet, she couldn't shake her worries about Marie's future - visualizing the worst. Katarina prayed tonight's ritual would help, hoping the Goddess would heal her daughter.

Helen fell down to one knee in front of the table. Her head was covered with white lace, and she raised her hands in supplication.

"Oh, great Goddess, Brigid, we call on, and invite you here tonight to aid us in our work. You, who are the Goddess of the forge and of the hearth, you have the power to heal and bring knowledge, light and inspiration, you, who helps all mothers in child birth, and in labor; we honor you tonight on Imolg and ask you to help our sister's daughter, to heal. Hail and Welcome Brigid." She stood back up and the rest all echoed her greeting, "Welcome Brigid."

Katarina held her breath then clasped her hands under her chin in a prayer gesture, whispering. "Please, please Goddess, help Marie."

Maggie, a thin woman in her late fifties with a long face, surveyed them and said, "The circle is cast. The directions and Goddess have been invoked. Please be seated."

Afterward, she went to another table in the corner of the room beside an unlit hearth. Two candles in golden holders stood on each corner of the pedestal table made of ash. She lit them, picked up each item on the table and said. "In the middle are two glass bowls," she said, "one filled with red wine and scented oil and the other pure water melted from the snow. There is also lamb's wool, red yarn and white lacy squares of cloth to put the wool in later. Tonight we create a charm for healing. Our intention is to focus on people or things in our lives which need attention." She turned to Katarina. "I need your athame, may I use it?"

Katarina nodded and handed it to the woman.

Holding up the knife, Maggie pointed its tip to the surface

of the water in one of the bowls. "Write which afflicts you or someone you love on the surface of the water." Then, she picked up the cream-colored wool, rubbing it between her fingers. "Then drop the wool into the red wine and let it soak.

"When you deem it has been completely doused, pick it back up, wrap it with the cloth and tie it together with red twine. Finally, drop the bag into the clear water here, saying the following incantation, 'The dark be lighted. The hard be softened. The rank be sweetened. By the power of the athame and by the power of the water.' Once done, we'll leave them all night until sunrise where I'll take them out to dry. Then, I'll give them back to you to sew onto your clothes and wear for a month."

"What will you do with the water?" Janice asked. "And how will I know which one is mine?"

Maggie narrowed her eyes, and her voice rose ever so slightly. "I will pour it back to the earth in my garden." She looked over to Katarina for help but Katarina shrugged, having no knowledge of this particular spell.

"It probably doesn't make a difference which one we get," Helen intervened.

"Alright." Janice said. "It's the intention that counts, I guess."

Katarina sat in one of the winged-backed chairs and noticed two books. One of them by Janet and Stewart Farrer was called, "Eight Sabbats for Witches" and the other was Gardner's book. Katarina's book was on the center altar in its place of honor. She touched the Stewart book, mindlessly, opening it to the front page to examine the chapter titles, but decided to close it again.

I'll ask Maggie if I can borrow it later. I know she's using some of their work to create our rituals and her charm today.

Katarina looked up at the others, observing they were waiting for her to start. "I can't start. You all go first."

She watched the women go to the table one by one as she twisted her marriage ring around her finger. Finally, it was her turn.

She walked over to the table. The candles lit the water bowl, making it shine and reflect the light. She picked up her athame and drew Marie's name on the water saying the words of the spell in a low voice. Picking up the wool, she put it in the piece of cloth, tied it with the twine and dropped it in the red bowl. The wine was dark, and it looked like blood to her. Trembling, she put her bag into the water and watched the red spread into the pinkish fluid. Dropping to her knees, she rocked back and forth sobbing, "Goddess, hear my prayer, hear my call. Please heal my daughter!"

Helen rushed to her and helped her up, guiding her back to the others who were in a circle around the table. "Dear, it'll be OK."

Louise drew breath and broke into humming. The rest joined in until the sound rang in Katarina's ears. She calmed herself, spread her feet on the ground to steady herself and sang a loud sonorous, 'Om' along with her sisters, which they answered with more intensity. As the women raised their hands to the ceiling singing, their pitch rose higher and higher until they were all shouting in unison "So mote it be."

Katarina dropped her arms to her sides and stared at the center candle. Crossing her hands over her heart, she continued praying silently.

Later, after the directions, Goddess, and spirits were thanked and devoked, the magical circle was opened. Katarina reached for Louise and Janice's hands. A final hand to hand circle was formed and they sang; "Merry meet and merry meet again. The circle is open but unbroken. May the love of the Goddess be forever in our hearts."

Katarina's heart warmed looking at the other four women.

"Let's eat," Maggie clapped her hands together. Katarina followed her into the kitchen, which was adjacent the living room. It had wood cabinets, a tan fridge, and matching range. Everything was spotless. There was a round table with four chairs around it to the far side next to a door leading to Maggie's backyard.

On the table, were Louise's tuna fish sandwich squares, a green Jell-O salad from Maggie with fruit in it, and whipped cream on top. Maggie was putting a kettle on the stove for tea. There was also Helen's crumble coffee cake and Katarina's homemade cookies, the ones she's learned how to bake from her Austrian

Oma so many years ago called *'Vanille Kiperl'*. They were dunked in powdered sugar, and were in the shape of crescent moons.

Katarina grabbed a plate, loaded it up with food, then headed back to the living room. She could hear the others laughing and joking from the kitchen. Her gaze flitted around the place, but couldn't settle on any one object. It was in the same room she'd been doing rituals with her friends the last twenty years. She eyed the familiar sofa, the two large different colored chairs, the vase with silk flowers on the mantelpiece. "The Lady of Shalott" by John Waterhouse hung over the fireplace. It was a copy, but one of her favorite art pieces.

Goddess, I've known them for so long. Over the years I've taught them all they know. I never believed I'd have such good friends and coven sisters.

She put her plate down and walked over to the spell table. Although the room was comfortable and orderly like Maggie, she felt suddenly out of place, even though she'd always felt calm and safe here.

Janice stepped beside her and smiled. She had a plate heaped with food. "There goes my figure," she said and laughed, until their eyes met. Frowning, she drew Katarina over to the couch. "Here, come and sit next to me."

"You know, you can call me anytime," she said in a soothing tone. "My mother used to say; "Things always work out for the better.""

Katarina gazed at her friend and felt her throat tighten. "I don't know, Janice…it's really hard," she said, fighting her urge to break down crying. "Marie sleeps 'til eleven, doesn't change her clothes, and seldom bathes. And the worst of it all is that she wanders around the house saying she's Mary Magdalena. When I correct her, she screams at me. She won't take care of the baby, leaving it all to me." She took a deep breath and looked over blankly at the altar. "I don't know what to do. Jacob says I should commit her to a mental institution." Her chest constricted and she felt a sharp pain in her heart.

Janice reached over and hugged her. "I don't know what to tell you, dear" she answered. "But, I'm….we're here for you anytime you need."

Helen, Maggie and Louise came back into the living room. Katarina looked over at Maggie, who'd cleared her throat as she sat down opposite them on a chair. "Well, if you want my opinion," she said in her teacher's voice, "I'd—"

"I don't think she does," Helen interrupted, and put her hands onto Katarina's shoulder.

How dare she judge me!

"No. No, go ahead." Katarina said, glaring back at Maggie. She knew Maggie hadn't approved of the way she'd raised her four children, always having something to say about her discipline style, or lack thereof.

"Well, it's too late anyway," Maggie said, tapping her foot a few times and tilting her head sideways. "You should've listened to Jacob years ago."

"Too late? What do you mean?" Katarina said, bristling. "Who are you to tell me what to do with my daughter? You don't have any children of your own, let alone a husband."

Maggie looked over her glasses at Katarina, then averted her gaze down to her plate. There was a strained moment of silence. The tension was palpable.

"Girls," Helen cried. "Please stop fighting. It's not going to help Katarina or Marie."

Janice and Louise nodded in agreement.

Katarina jumped up, slamming her plate onto the side table next to her.

"I'm going home."

"So soon?" Janice said.

Katarina glared at Maggie who avoided her gaze. "I don't feel welcome here," she answered.

Janice took Katarina's hands in hers and said. "Katarina, we've been doing rituals together ever since Helen's John died. We're sisters, remember? Don't go. Let us be there for you like you've been there for us," Janice said, dropping a hand and waving it around the room at the three women.

Katarina trembled. She hadn't been sleeping well, having to get up nights with Sarah, who was terrified about Marie's condition.

"I'm sorry but I have to get home," Katarina said. "The baby…"

"You never did like my Jell-O salad," Maggie blurted out.

No one laughed and Maggie averted her gaze. Suddenly she jumped up and moved toward Katarina, who backed away and pulled her hand from Janice. But Maggie wouldn't be deterred and hugged Katarina awkwardly. "I'm sorry," she said and rambled on, "I didn't mean it's too late. I don't know. Things just come out of my mouth wrong. I'll bring over the charm tomorrow. Am I forgiven?"

Katarina nodded then leaned her head on the tall woman's boney shoulder. "I hate your Jell-O salad," she said as a smiled forced its way across her face.

Suddenly, all four women were hugging her. "You'll get through this. Marie will be fine. Count on us."

Katarina extracted herself, wiped her face with her robe and kissed them all on the cheek. "Thank you." she said. "I don't know what I would do without you all." She picked up her book, dropped the athame into her purse, and took off her robe and stuffed it into a bag. At the front door, she waved good-bye and stepped into the cold night.

Maggie's house was a few blocks from hers. The air was crisp and fresh. Snow covered the lawns and roofs sparkled in the moonlight. She walked quickly along the road, wanting to get home.

It was after 9:30 p.m. when she unlocked her back door to the kitchen. The dishes were clean and stacked next to the sink. All was quiet. She hung her coat in the closet and tip-toed up the wooden stairs. Before she went to bed, she carefully placed the book of shadows into the back of the linen closet.

Once she had it tucked safely away, Katarina slipped into the room, undressed quietly and pulled her night-dress over her naked body. The moonlight lit the room with a gentle stream of silver light and she could make out her husband's form under the covers. Tired, she slid into bed next to him.

He rolled over and opened his eyes. "How was the card game?" he asked, rubbing his eyes.

"Same as usual," she lied, and leaned over to kiss his cheek.

"Marie was good tonight and helped with Sarah," he said. "She bathed the baby and put her to bed."

"Oh, that's good," she said, patting his arm. "You need to get some sleep. You have to work early."

Jacob laughed. "That I do. Good night." And he rolled over.

"Good night, honey." Katarina lay back and stared at the ceiling, then turned to the window and watched the moon sneaking in and out between the darkened clouds. Maybe the spell was already working. She hoped so. She closed her eyes, tossed and turned a few times before finally falling asleep.

Chapter Thirteen

1989

Sarah screamed and Katarina sprinted upstairs to find her petrified next to Marie in the bathroom. Katarina yelled, "Jacob! Jacob, call 911", as she ran to the linen closet and yanked out towels. Rushing back, she desperately tried to stop the rush of blood pouring out from her daughter's wrists by tying towels around them.

"Marie. Marie, don't leave me!" she howled, lifted her daughter's head, and placed a large towel under it. She put her ear to Marie's mouth to see if she was breathing. She couldn't hear anything. More than that, Marie's face felt icy cold. She gasped, looking over to Sarah, who was whimpering next to the sink. A shudder ran through her. Her daughter was dead! She rocked back and forth on her knees and tried to make sense of it, then crawled over to her granddaughter, hugging her protectively.

Jacob came into the room. "Oh, my God". He jammed a clenched fist into his mouth. Katarina shook her head, her eyes wide with warning.

"It's OK, honey," Katarina said to Sarah holding her away and looking into the little girls eyes. "Don't look. You need to go downstairs with Opa and wait for the doctor. Can you do this for Oma?"

Sarah shook her head.

"Oma, no! I don't wanna leave Mommy," Sarah bawled and tried to pry her way out of Katarina's grip.

"Sarah, dear," Jacob said soothingly. He walked over, gently lifting her up and whisked her out of the room before Sarah could protest. "Come with Opa…come with Opa." Katarina heard him say as he carried Sarah down the stairs singing softly to the little girl.

But Sarah was hysterical. "Mommy. Mommy," echoed all the way downstairs.

Disoriented, Katarina finally stood up to let the reddened water drain out. She felt like her legs were made of stone, but compelled her body to move into the bedroom and pull a sheet off the bed. She stumbled back into the bathroom, blinking nervously. Covering Marie's naked body, she went and sat on the toilet, stunned. She drew her arms over her chest, speechless, and unable to look at Marie. She stared blankly at the wall, never hearing the sirens or her husband coming back into the bathroom.

"Come," Jacob whispered helping her up from the seat. "They're here to take her. Ursula is downstairs with Sarah."

"She can't be dead. Jacob, bring her back… bring her back", Katarina sobbed as Jacob wrapped his arms tightly around her while the attendants took Marie away. After they were gone, Jacob stayed with her for a long time until she finally let him lead her down the stairs to where the police were waiting for a statement.

"I want to go to the hospital," she muttered as she sat on the couch in the living room.

"I do too," Jacob said, joining her. "But we can't help her any more. Let's talk to the investigators. We'll go later."

Katarina nodded, too numb to argue.

Two months later, Katarina looked up at the night sky from her back yard and wailed silently again while she paced aimlessly around her garden. She hadn't slept but a few hours each night since Marie died. Her heart ached and there was a constant tightness in her chest.

I don't care what the neighbors think. Why, Goddess? Why did you take her from me? I followed you with all my heart and soul. And I've healed so many others. Why couldn't I help her? You're cruel. She pounded her fists on the fence.

"Kati, stop!" Jacob yelled from the upstairs window. "You'll wake everyone up. Come to bed."

"I don't care," she cried, muttering more to herself than him. She staggered to the steps leading to the back door, collapsing onto one hand. The pain of her daughter's death was unbearable. Every time she tried falling asleep, she'd see Marie's slit wrists and Sarah's terrified little face. And then there was the grisly splatter of blood all over the bathroom and Marie's blank stare etched into her mind, haunting her every moment of every day.

She took a deep breath, straining to calm herself down and to sit down on the top rung. This wasn't how things were supposed to be. Marie had "the gift" as Katarina's Grandmother used to call it. She pressed her lips together. Her daughter's state of mind was a curse not a blessing, and it killed her.

Jacob had told her time and time again their daughter needed to be in a hospital. Only, she couldn't bear thinking of her daughter in a mental institution. Just the thought of Marie being locked up broke her heart. Instead, she gave Marie every herbal remedy she knew, creating healing charms which she hung around Marie's neck. But her daughter would just yank them off. Nothing helped.

I should've listened to Jacob. It's my fault she's dead."

She rapidly rubbed her upper arms and felt sick to her stomach then looked upward at the black sky. Katarina clasped her hands together. "Goddess, why didn't you take me instead?" she muttered then broke into sobbing. "Bring her back, bring her back."

And then there was Sarah, who was living at Ursula's now. It had been decided that since Ursula couldn't conceive it was the best solution for the child. Katarina couldn't argue with the decision because seeing Sarah every day reminded her of Marie. She was the spitting image of her mother.

Katarina's thoughts whirled. *It wasn't supposed to be like this.* It was as if she was watching the same movie over and over again. She was unable to stop the awful images of her daughter's suicide, which came unbidden and unwelcome in her visions.

She searched her mind for something to hold onto, stop the guilt, but nothing helped, not her love for Jacob, her religion or the rest of her family. She was lost.

The screen door opened and there was Jacob in his night robe. "This can't go on like this. We have three other children and two grandbabies. It's been two months. She's not coming back. You need to try and move on for their sake," he said, then sat next to her on the steps. He placed his large gnarled hand onto her knee.

Katarina pushed his hand away. "Move on?" *How could he be so callous?*

"She's gone. I see her face every day. You don't understand…"

"She was my daughter, too." His face twisted with anger and grief as he turned, grabbing her shoulders. "I could've taken her to the hospital. I didn't have to listen to you. I'm sick and tired of you always believing you're the only one suffering here. There are others, too. Ursula says Sarah wakes nights screaming for her mother."

Katarina balled her hands into fists, digging her fingernails into her skin. What was wrong with him? "You're a selfish, man Jacob Lilienthal. Like it was all my fault!" she spat. "Even if it is, who are you to tell me, blame me? I left my country for you. Leave me alone," she said prying herself from his grip. She glared at him, then stood and turned to walk away.

"I'm selfish? Damn it, woman," Jacob said, calling after her. "Well, I'm not alone. It was both of us. And just so you know…. I know of your book and those meetings at Maggie's. I'm not as stupid as you think." He caught her hand from behind.

"You're hurting me," she said, and the warning in her tone surprised her. Jacob pulled her toward him and embraced her. She struggled against him, but he didn't let her go.

"You know I would never hurt you," he said and looked at her searchingly.

She froze, and for a moment didn't know how to respond. Finally, she said, "I'm sorry, too," and melted into his arms. As she did so, she mulled over his knowing about her book all along and hadn't said anything. What did that mean?

Jacob's voice was hoarse. "Katarina, we need you. Sarah needs you. I need you."

"I know," she said. She hadn't been intimate with him in months, but she couldn't help it. She felt dead inside.

"I need you to come back to me," he said, pulling back and looking at her with pleading eyes. "Without you, I'm not the same man."

"I know."

"Then what?" Jacob said and when she didn't answer, his hopeful expression shattered. Katarina couldn't help but notice his speckled grey hair pointing out in every direction, making him look like a clown. This softened her heart. She knew he wanted her back, the Katarina who was full of life and spirit, the woman who was vivacious, had a sense of humor, the woman he married. She wasn't sure where that woman had gone or whether she could get her back. But looking at Jacob's distraught face, she knew she needed to try and find her.

At last, she said, "I'll try," then kissed him on the cheek and took his hand. Following him back to the steps, they stopped and regarded the stars for a few minutes. Her breath quieted and she felt a little better.

Jacob was quiet for a moment then said, "I know you don't agree with my choices in this matter, but would you consider coming to church with me?"

She thought about it and shrugged. After all this and what had happened, what did it matter? "I guess, after all these years, I could."

Jacob smiled.

She felt a smile on her face as well then said, "Why didn't you tell me you knew about my book?"

"I don't know. I trusted… well, I still trust…," he said squeezing her hand gently. "that I married my soulmate; the woman of my life, so I believe you do what you think is right."

"I'm not sure any more what is right or wrong," she said.

It's time for me to join Jacob at the Sunday services. Though on the other hand, I won't forsake my coven. And the Goddess can be said to be found in the image of the Mother of Christ. Why not? There wasn't a rule in my belief about not attending church. Maybe I'll find the healing I desperately need with God. Jacob laughed and pulled her tight to him.

As they walked into their kitchen, Jacob patted her on the bottom, and instead of complaining, she chose a timid giggle. Although it tortured her to think of Marie, she knew she needed Jacob's love and he hers. They'd been through so much together, and she didn't want to lose him.

"I'm off to bed. Are you coming?" Jacob said, putting his arm around her waist.

"I'm going to make some tea," she said, deftly extricating herself from his embrace. "I promise I'll be up in a few minutes." She'd find a way back to him no matter how hard it was. And she needed to visit Sarah. Her granddaughter lost a mother. Pushing up the sleeves of her robe, she put the kettle on the stove knowing in her heart she needed to find the strength to be there for Sarah.

"I love you," Jacob said as he left the kitchen.

"I love you, too," she called after him as the kitchen door swung shut.

Sarah Lilienthal
1984-present day

Chapter Fourteen

May 2009

Sarah trembled as she stood behind her camera tripod. She'd stopped to do a spontaneous shoot on the road back from Glendaruel and through the lens she observed a large dark cloud, a conspiracy of ravens landing on a hill to the right of Dunan's castle. A cold breeze whipped her hair into her face. She pushed the strands out of her eyes as she decided to try different angles of the scarlet red keep with its burnt ramparts standing in front of dense woods. Taking her Nikon B800 off, and using her hand strap to help move around freely, she took more photos of the deserted fortress and the dark grey sky. Natural light is the best way to set the mood, she thought. Apparently, a fire left it unoccupied, looking haunted. *There's a story here.*

Wrapping her raincoat tightly around her, she couldn't shake the feeling that something awful must have occurred.

Since she was a child, she possessed an uncanny intuition, and she battled this gift, if that was what it could be called, for fear of losing her mind as her mother had. Sarah rarely stopped a shoot when she found a subject that interested her, because photography was her life and ran through her blood. Yet this feeling overwhelmed her, so she climbed into her rental car and drove back to her bed and breakfast.

When she got back to the hotel, she hoofed it to her room and phoned her grandmother, Oma. It was what she always did when she was worried or upset. When Oma didn't answer, she called her Aunt Ursula.

"Oma's not answering," Sarah said, breathless when the woman answered. "Is everything OK?"

"Sarah, I've been trying to get ahold of you," her aunt said.

The tone in Ursula's voice unnerved her and she blinked nervously. "There's something wrong, isn't there?"

There was a long pause. Finally, her aunt went on, "Are you sitting down?"

Sarah swallowed hard and wound a long strand of her hair around her finger. *Oh, no!* "I am." Which was a lie. Sitting was impossible.

"Sarah, she died last night in her sleep," her aunt whispered. "She wasn't in any pain. It was peaceful."

Sarah felt a stabbing pain around her heart while pulling her iPhone away from her ear. She stared at its screen, numb and in shock.

"Sarah. Are you there?"

"Yes, yes I'm here." She tried to think of what to say. She knew her grandmother was sick, but she thought she was going to be fine, not…. She put her hand to her mouth and stifled a sob which was welling up from her gut.

"Can you fly home?" Ursula said in an even tone. "The funeral is this Saturday."

"Of course," Sarah answered. "I'll take the next flight to New York." She said her good-byes, hung up and paced around the room. Oma had been everything to her. Yes, it was true her grandmother had been diagnosed with cancer last year, but she believed with all her heart the old matriarch would beat it. *You couldn't have died! Not now. You love life You're tough!*

She closed her ears and as tears leaked out, she remembered the last phone conversation she'd had with her. 'Everything's fine," Oma said, "Don't worry about me. You just go and shoot those pictures I love so much.'

Why wasn't I there for her?

"Oh Oma," Sarah cried, dropping onto her knees. "You're the only one who ever understood me." As the reality of her grandmother passing galvanized her heart, her breath constricted and great whooping sobs racked her.

That night, Sarah paid her bill, packed her suitcase and headed for Edinburgh to catch the first flight to the States. As she blended in with traffic, memories of her childhood overwhelmed her, making it increasingly more difficult to drive.

She'd always tried to get up before Oma and race downstairs only to find Oma already in the kitchen dressed in her apron. The old woman would be bustling back and forth around the room singing her old Austrian folk songs while preparing breakfast. Sarah remembered loving the melodious sound of them.

And when Opa was there, he'd try to sneak up behind Oma and kiss her on the cheek, which would earn him a swift rebuke, telling him to go get the paper. She pretended she was surprised and annoyed, but Sarah knew she really adored the attention he gave her. Then Opa would laugh and go off and get the paper from the front porch.

She heard Oma's voice echoing down through the years. "Come, child, sit next to Opa for breakfast. Here are your favorite pancakes with berries from the garden and maple syrup."

"Mornin', thanks." Sarah would slip into her chair next to Opa, watching him read the latest news while drinking his coffee. Even now, she could almost smell the nutty fresh aroma of it. And when he was done, he'd lean toward her and smile, asking her how she slept.

"Great, Opa," she answered, picking up her fork to start eating.

"Don't start eating until your Mommy gets here," Oma reprimanded her.

Sarah opened her mouth to say something, but bit her bottom lip instead, frowning. Opa winked at her behind Oma's back, putting down his paper.

Soon afterwards, Mommy shuffled into the room. Her eyes had ugly dark rings under them and her raven hair hung loose and unkempt over the bathrobe. She'd sit and look at her empty plate without a word, never seeming to notice Sarah. Finally, at Oma's insistence, she'd mutter, 'Morning'.

"How many would you like?" Oma said, coming over from the stove to serve her.

Mommy looked up at Oma listlessly. "I guess two will do. Hi, honey," Mommy gazed over at Sarah, her eyes devoid of emotion.

Sarah squirmed even now as she thought about how her mother cut her food into small, measured pieces.

At length, Sarah forced the memory away and tried to focus on the road. She'd been driving for a while in and out of the rain pelting the countryside. A sign for Edinburgh said 200 kilometers. She checked her speed and did the math. With any luck she'd be there in a little under two hours.

As she pushed the pedal down, her phone chirped. She checked the name on the incoming call and went to hands-free. "Hey, Brian."

"What's doing with you tonight?"

"I'm on my way to Edinburgh," Sarah said. "My grandmother died…I'm going home…"

"Oh, I'm really sorry to hear that," Brian answered. "Are you OK?"

"No, but I'm managing. Anyway, I finished the work and I never had a chance to connect with Vanderhoost before I left. We were supposed to meet up before I left. Could you call him?"

"Sure. Hey, call me when you get in the States, okay?"

"Yeah, sure."

Brian hung up. Sarah liked him. He was always a very understanding boss. She prayed she could catch a stand-by seat and be in the Berkshires soon.

Two days later, Sarah walked down the middle aisle of the vast, cut gray-stone cathedral. As she walked the royal red carpet, guests murmured amongst themselves in the pews. Ahead, on the carpeted steps leading up to the apse, were large vases of flowering white lilies putting out a heavy perfumed scent. Combined with the varied perfumes and colognes of all the people around her, she felt nauseated. Taking a deep breath, she tried to swallow it down as the sonorous notes of "How Great Thou Art" floated from an organ in the great nave.

She was late, through no fault of her own: the traffic had been horrendous on the highway. And with the fact she hadn't been in church in years, she felt small under the critical stares of those around her. She tried to ignore them and avert her gaze to the towering arch-topped stain glassed windows and vaulted plaster ceilings as she slipped into her seat. But still her heart pounded and so out of habit, she played with the long strand of her braided black hair that hid the long line of red Chinese characters trailing down from her neck to the arch of her back. She'd gotten the tattoo as soon as she was old enough, in reverence to her mantra: *"You only live once, but if you do it right, once is enough."*

At last the organ went silent and the door at the side of the apse opened. As the middle-aged man in his vestments strode out, Sarah felt her body stiffen. Father Peter Holden stood looking out over the assembled mourners. She glared at the priest. *Of all people: him?* He was the reason she'd moved so far away from the peaceful, quaint town of her childhood. A place where kids rode bikes out in the streets, where doors were left unlocked, and your neighbors knew you by your first name. Her stomach twisted with anger and she wanted to scream as he stepped to the pulpit.

He adjusted the pulpit microphone and lamp, rustled papers and looked up with an air of grave propriety. "Katharina Lilienthal was a remarkable woman. She was a long -standing member of our community here at the Church of the Immaculate Conception," he said with a commanding voice.

"She was a kind and generous woman. She was devoted to her husband Jacob and their four children, Susanne, Ursula, Georg and Maria." Father Holden continued. He paused and looked out over his congregation. Sarah looked at the floor between the wooden benches.

"We all know of the church's flower arrangements she devoted her time for, and her work at the garden club. Katharina Lilienthal was always there for her neighbors. You could call on her any time," the priest said.

A murmur of agreement came from the people in the church.

"She was a good Christian woman who suffered in her last few years like a saint," Father Holden said and held his arms up. "We ask our Savoir and God to take Katharina up into his arms into Heaven. May she rest in peace. And now, her daughter Ursula will read from the Scriptures."

Ursula lifted her rotund body, draped in a black dress, and walked to the pulpit. Fumbling, she put her reading glasses on and turned to the microphone. At first, she didn't look out at the crowd and there was an uncomfortable silence as people looked around the room. At last she looked over to the casket and took a deep breath.

"I'll be reading from Psalm 2 and 1st Corinthians 4:16 - 15:8," she said holding the papers in front of her. "Hear the word of our Lord: Do not lose heart. Though outwardly we are wasting away, yet inwardly we are being renewed day by day. For our light and momentary troubles are achieving for us an eternal glory that far outweighs them all." Sarah felt her eyelids getting heavy and she stretched her spine, forcing herself to stay awake. Minutes later, Ursula looked up at the spire and at last finished the reading, "So we fix our eyes not on what is seen, but on what is unseen. For what is seen is temporary, but what is unseen is eternal."

Sarah looked down at her hands. Tears rolled down her cheeks as Ursula stepped down, moving back to her seat. In her place, Father Holden called for the Gospel and responses from the congregation. "Let us stand, sisters and brothers, for the Prayer of Our Lord"

For the rest of the Mass, Sarah endured the festering anger in her gut. And when it was over, she followed the family behind the casket, which was led down the aisle by the man she hated, with his altar boys holding up the tall golden crucifix. When they reached the narthex, her aunt Ursula tapped the funeral director and had them stop. Motioning to Sarah, she had her stand beside her and the casket so she could have a moment with her grandmother.

"I had her put in her favorite olive green dress and had her long white hair put into a French braid."

"And my request?" Sarah whispered as she put her hand on the cool metal surface of the casket.

"Yes, the red amaryllis is in her hands," Ursula said.

Sarah bent over and kissed the casket, visualizing the vivid red blooms on the amaryllis' which unerringly bloomed every year with its large deep red petals on Oma's front porch. Here, Oma would sit and read to Sarah on the porch swing Opa had hung from the rafters. Tales of Winnie the Pooh and Peter Rabbit helped fill the unbearable hole her mother had left in her life when Sarah was five year's old.

Over the years, the veranda became Sarah's favorite place to be in the summer. All the types and sizes of plants were displayed in clay pots. Large green ferns, philodendrons, rubber trees, and tiny evergreens lined up and down the steps like warriors ready to trip unwelcome intruders. Suspended from an overhead beam, baskets of ivy and spider plants adorning the view out to the fields.

Now, twenty years later, Oma was gone, too.

Dead!

Sarah stood watching the casket slowly being rolled away toward the hearse as neighbors and relatives came up from behind. A comforting arm wrapped around her. Aunt Ursula, to the rescue. She was led forward toward the line of cars as people spoke in whispers as they milled around in front of the church.

"Shame… after the thing with Marie…" said someone.

Sarah trembled.

"Don't listen, they're all old gossips," Suzanne said, pulling her aside.

Aunt Suzanne joined them. "We took care of everything," she whispered. "We're just happy you're here."

"Yes," Ursula echoed. "And I have something for you from Oma."

Sarah looked up, interested to know. "What is it?" she said in a rush.

"I can't tell you now," Ursula whispered, averting her gaze. She looked off ahead past the murmuring crowd, obviously not wanting to share more. "Later, and not a word to anyone else."

Now Sarah was really curious, but she refrained from pressing her aunt and instead looked around, recognizing people she knew from her childhood. She smiled over at Janice and Oma's good friend Maggie who were watching her with curious expressions as if they knew something about her no one else did.

Suzanne nudged Sarah. "Are you daydreaming?"

"No, I was just thinking about Oma."

"Oh," Suzanne said. "Sorry."

"It's all right."

Suzanne was quiet a moment then said, "You know, I'm surprised she lived as long as she did. Mama refused every modern treatment."

Sarah knew about her aunt's battles with Oma and the rest of the family over the old matriarch's healthcare. But Oma was a stubborn woman, refusing all the doctor's treatments and Suzanne's advice.

"I tried to get you involved. David tried to talk some sense into your grandmother as well but Mama was obstinate, as you know. Damn her!" Suzanne said and made the sign of the cross. "She should've tried chemo…maybe she'd still be alive."

Sarah really didn't want to go there with her aunt right then, but she couldn't help defending her grandmother's choices. "Maybe, but Oma's herbal concoctions helped her live longer than the doctor's prognosis, no?" Sarah put in, taking out her iPhone and turning it back on.

Suzanne frowned. "That's debatable."

"I'm sorry. I didn't mean to dismiss your input. I know you mean well."

At that very moment, Aunt Suzanne squeezed her hand and smiled up at the pulpit. Sarah zoned out and believed she could hear her Oma's gentle voice calling again from the past.

Time heals all wounds.

She remembered the time she fell off her bike and came

crying and limping toward the front steps of the porch. Oma was waiting.

"Come, let me have a look at that knee."

Oma sat down on the top step pulling her onto her lap. Oma stroked Sarah's raven black hair that hung wild and tangled down her back.

"It's not bad," Oma declared and she wiped the gravel and dirt off of Sarah's knee with a cold wet rag. Then she gently applied a greasy mixture from a small jar she pulled out of her apron pocket.

"Remember all things come to pass. Even the pain will stop if you don't pay too much attention to it."

An hour later, Sarah stood by a pair of giant gray weeping willows standing like guardians over the stones of the century old graveyard. The pastures unfolding up the hill lent the place a sense of timelessness, which she knew would suit Oma just fine. At length, the people gathered around the gravesite under a canopy and listened to the Father preside over Oma's internment next to her husband, Jacob David Lilienthal.

Once the brief service was over, the immediate family grouped around the casket. "I can't believe Opa died seven years ago," Sarah said and looked at Aunt Ursula, and Uncle John.

"Where does the time go?" Aunt Ursula said.

Suzanne spoke up. "We should be getting back to the house for the reception."

"Yes," Ursula said, "and I made your old room up for you. I hope you'll be staying with us. We've missed having you around."

"I'm so grateful to be home again," Sarah said to her aunt Ursula, then made her way around, greeting well-wishers, friends, and family she hadn't seen in years.

"There you are," Father Holden called, walking towards her. "The long-lost granddaughter back from her travels."

Sarah regarded the old bald priest, who was mopping a bead of sweat from his forehead with a handkerchief. He'd aged poorly, though his sky blue eyes remained as evil and enduring as ever. He gave her a wide, crooked grin, which contorted one side of his hatchet face. He was supposing to be the nice, jovial town priest, full of concern doing his duty. Sarah knew better.

She spied her cousin David, standing off at a distance and leaning against the large silver maple at the edge of the cemetery. He was Suzanne's son, and she liked him well. She turned to her aunt Ursula. "Excuse me. I want to say hi to someone." To the Father, she said nothing and swept passed him as if he wasn't there.

"David, there you are!" she said, glad to be away from the ugly and patronizing priest.

Her cousin turned to her and smiled. As usual, he was dressed impeccably in a dark suit that fit his tall, lithe body like a glove. His expensive looking shirt was open at the neck and his black Italian-made shoes were spotless. Why did he always look so smart and poised? And she wasn't. She looked up into his angular face with raven black hair which was much like her own. "It's so good to see you."

"And you as well," he said, hugging her.

Sarah loved him like a brother, grabbing his hand.

"How you holding up?"

She felt his grip tighten around her.

"David, I know you miss her. You were her favorite," she joked trying to ease the tension.

"No, you were!" he said finally pulling away. "What about you? You're   shaking."

"Don't worry, I'll be all right," Sarah lied.

"You sure there's nothing wrong?" David said, eyeing her critically.

"Yes, I'm just tired, is all. I've had a long couple of days."

"Oh, that's right. You were on assignment," he said.

"Yes over in Scotland for the magazine.

My plane came in late… and oh well, you know me, never one for a dress," Sarah said, and shrugged. "So, here I am, trying to wrap my head around all this. I just keep seeing her face and I want to…"

"I know. Let's get out of here." David frowned, worried and picked up her overnight case. His other arm went over her shoulder, and guided her to his Fiat.

Soon, they were driving on narrow and winding roads with no destination at all. They sped by farms, orchards, and the lush green Appalachian countryside.

Chapter Fifteen

Aunt Ursula's home

In the early evening, David's sports car pulled alongside the picket fence surrounding the front yard of Aunt Ursula's place, Sarah's childhood home. She felt a surge of warmth looking at the timeworn, periwinkle blue Victorian house with its white gingerbread trimmings. The sun created a blood-orange halo over the purplish hills behind it. Sarah stretched her arms over her head then reached over and hugged her cousin.

"I'm so happy we talked. You always know what's best for me," Sarah said, feeling better and more relaxed than she had at the church.

"Anything for my little cousin," he answered, ruffling her hair.

She cuffed him on the arm, laughing, before stepping out of the car. "I'm tired and jet-lagged. Hopefully, I can sneak past everyone on up to my room," she said, looking at the vehicles parked along the driveway and up the road.

"Hey, you haven't seen any of us since you moved out west," David said. "You can't expect to get out of this. Come on, Mom made *Apfelstrudel,* your favorite."

"I guess I can't argue with a lawyer from New York," she said, feeling guilty she hadn't been back to visit family for the last couple of years... especially Oma. That bothered her most. She grasped David's arm as they walked up the front steps and stopped just before entering the house. She suppressed a grimace, knowing Father Holden would most likely be there.

David stopped and looked her square in the face, like he did when they were children wrestling on the living room floor.

"What's wrong?"

She remembered how he used to tickle her until she'd tell him what he wanted to hear. Only now, this was one confidence she didn't want to discuss with him.

"It's just, we're never going to see Oma again," she said, leveling a gaze on him. This was at least partially true.

"I know what you mean. We'll get through this. Remember, Oma was one hell of a courageous woman. She outsmarted the Nazis. If she can do that, then you can face our family and all those nosey old friends of hers," he jested, then laughed and put his arm around her shoulders, guiding her through the door.

Sarah stepped into the spacious living room and set her bags next to the staircase. It was just like she remembered: the heather-blue couch, worn on the edges to the right, across from two large unmatched cushioned chairs. A small glass coffee table sat in the middle. She eyed the pictures of herself and family members along with the porcelain knick-knacks on the mantelpiece. Aunt Ursula's watercolor painting of a farmstead and red barn still hung over the hearth. Small groups of people engaged in quiet conversations stood in the living room. Uncle Georg, her mother's only brother, was making his way over to them with his wife, Julia.

"Sarah! David!" Georg hugged each of them.

"Nice to see you both again," Julia said, embracing Sarah affectionately.

Sarah hadn't seen either of them in years. She knew they lived in Santa Barbara, California. Georg looked almost identical to her grandpa; Opa. He was tall and lanky with mischievous brown eyes and a prominent nose, though he looked older than she remembered. Julia was ten years his junior and very pretty when she was younger. Sarah observed Julia was a little plump, yet still attractive.

"Great to see you both, too," David said, smiling over at Julia.

"Where are the boys?" David asked.

Sarah blinked. That's right, she had other cousins. She did the math. They must be in their early teens by now.

"They're out back, up to something," Georg replied. "They'll never get to know my mother as well as you two did…"

Sarah saw her uncle swallow hard before he turned away.

Julia reached over and took her husband's hand. "We all loved her, honey," she said and kissed his cheek. "Come, let's get some of your sister's cake."

As Julia led her husband to the kitchen, Sarah drifted to the family room and looked out the sliding glass door to the back yard where at least fifty more guests were milling around. Aunt Ursula came out of the kitchen wearing a flower printed apron over her black dress and carrying a fresh pot of tea.

"Sarah, good, you're finally here," she said. "David, you two are really just like teen-agers not telling us where you went. Where have you been for so long?"

"Just driving around," Sarah said and giggled for being scolded. She was home, and even if Father Holden was here, she wasn't going to let him get to her.

"Here, can you take this tea pot outside?" she said to her as Sarah took the pot.

"Come, David," Ursula said, taking him by the arm. "I need you to carry more ice and drinks to the patio." David looked back at Sarah and grinned as Ursula kidnapped him, shrugging his shoulders as he disappeared into the kitchen.

Sarah chuckled as she went out the door into the cool afternoon breeze that buffeted her hair. The tall, red-stained wooden fence enclosing the backyard had weathered a bit since she was last home and a few slats needed repairing. Extending out from the back door was a broad, rectangular slate stone patio. She dropped the teapot off at one of the many white plastic outdoor tables, grabbed a ham sandwich and walked over to the herb and vegetable garden on the far right. Farther on, there was a small goldfish pond with four white slender birch trees leaning over its stone apron. She peered down at the dark water and saw large goldfish swimming around. She loved this pond and the antique heirloom rose bushes that were just starting to bloom in a variety of colors. In the past, she would watch the small birds frolic between the roses before splashing around and ruffling their feathers in the pedestal bird bath shaped like a concave-faced sunflower. Today, the bath was dry.

An unwelcome familiar voice called from behind her.

"Sarah, you ran away so quickly this morning," it said.

She caught her breath. *Shit, how am I going to get away?* She eyeballed the guests around the patio area regretfully. They were too far away. She drew breath and decided to stand her ground. Father Holden rushed forward, blocking her passage. Sarah braced herself, and faced her nemesis.

Father Holden was a little taller than her, old and bland. Blotched scarlet patches covered his face as if he'd been drinking heavily the night before.

"Hi there," he said, crossing his arms over his hefty belly.

"You don't deserve to be here," Sarah snapped, scowling.

He rolled his eyes and at the same time raised up his thick, puffy fingers as if he was going to give a sermon. But she cut him off. "I know everyone here thinks you're a man of faith, but they don't know you for who you really are. I saw! I remember what you did to my mother. She was sick, and you cast her out, you heartless monster. You're lucky this is my grandmother's wake or else..."

Father Holden held her with a level gaze as if he was enjoying her discomfort. He stroked his chin with his fingers for a few seconds, then puzzlingly, let his arms drop to his sides.

"What do you mean? I had nothing to do with your mother's death," he said in a menacing tone. "You should not be so quick to judge without knowing the whole story. There is much I'm sure that has been left out by your grandmother."

"Really?" Sarah growled and shifted her gaze toward the house. Were it not for the friends and relatives who had come to pay their respects, she would've struck him in the face. She closed her eyes, remembering the day she was in his office at the parish with her mother.

Sitting across from him, her mother pleaded with him about something Sarah couldn't understand at the time. She was only four years old, after all, playing with her Barbie doll on a couch behind them. Yet, she knew enough to know her mother was upset.

"Peter, you can't just throw me away like this," her mother cried bringing her hands to her face.

"Marie, this is your fault. I forbid you or the child to come visit me. How many times need I tell you? It's over," Father Holden declared, and stood up from behind his large mahogany desk. "Leave! Right now! There's nothing more to say."

"But, Peter, you can't mean it!" Her mother had shrieked.

Sarah saw herself getting up from the couch and running to her mother.

"Mommy, Mommy," she called, wrapping her small arms around her mother's hunched shoulders.

"Now, see what you've done. You've upset the child," Father Holden admonished. "Go home, or need I call your mother?"

"No, no, don't call. I'll go," her mother said, her tone flat as she rose from her chair. Taking Sarah's hand, she walked reluctantly out of the room.

After that day, her mother lay in bed for days not talking to anyone, not even Oma, nor did she ever go back to church. Oma would help her mother bathe, bring her tea, give her herbal remedies and even sing at her bedside.

Nothing seemed to wake her from her lethargy. Except sometimes, Marie became agitated and walked around the house in her night gown, ranting, "I'm Mary, mother of God, where's my son?"

Once, her mother even hit Opa with his cane while he was trying to calm her down.

"She needs to go to a hospital," Opa said one night to Oma at the dinner table. Sarah could still remember Oma staring at him, then grasping the edges of the table so tight that Sarah could see the veins of her hands popping out.

"My daughter is not going to be put in a place for crazy people!" she shouted. "She's going to get better! I will cure her!"

Only Sarah's mother didn't get better.

"Is everything okay?" Father Holden said as he reached to take her arm.

"Don't... don't touch me," Sarah stammered and jerked away. "Never speak of my mother again to me or anyone else. Not you. Never. You'll get your punishment in your God-forsaken Hell, you monster," Sarah said.

"Why, Sarah. Why so irrational? Hmm, seems like your mother passed on her neurotic ways to you," Father Holden said and looked to see if anyone was paying attention to their conversation.

Sarah shuddered, hurrying past him to a table encircled with Oma's best friends.

For as long as she could remember, these five women met on Tuesday evenings at Maggie's stone residence on the outskirts of town. Maggie had the reputation of being eccentric and odd, not the marrying type, as her Oma would say. She had been Sarah's fourth grade teacher at the local elementary school.

When Sarah was younger, she and her friends were terrified of Maggie or Mrs. Davidson as they called her. The neighborhood kids believed she was crazy, often ringing her doorbell then darting away as fast as they could. Maggie would fly out the front door dressed in a bathrobe with her hair in curlers, yelling at them to keep off her lawn. Sarah regretted her childhood pranks and observed Maggie's wrinkled face. *I hope she's forgiven me.*

"Sarah, darling, whatever were you discussing with Father Holden? You look upset. Come, sit with us," Janice said, waving Sarah over.

"Nothing important," Sarah replied. Thank God she'd escaped from him. "How are you, Janice?" Sarah said, pulling a chair over. Janice had been a frequent guest of Oma's over the years, and was a woman who quite concerned herself with appearances. Sarah sat next to the thin woman with wavy brown hair that fell neatly onto her delicate shoulders. Vanity was alive and kicking in the octogenarian. Janice still owned the town store along with her son, John and his wife.

"As good as one can be at this age, dear. My, you look so much like your mother. She was a beauty. Such a pity," Janice said and the other women nodded in agreement. Only Helen, the town's seamstress, looked away as if she were embarrassed by Janice's candor.

"We'll all miss Katarina at the club. She was so good with the plants and the church garden," Louise said and took a tissue from her handbag, dabbing her eyes. She was a large-framed woman with tight, short red curls whose white roots were just visible.

"Now, Louise, you know Katarina wouldn't want us to cry. Your grandmother, Sarah, was a fighter. Right up to the end. She would still come and play bridge with us on Tuesdays, you know," Janice said and took Sarah's hand.

"And she was so good with herbs and the like," Maggie said. "She took good care of herself. I know for a fact she cured Henry Jamison of his prostate problems. And let me see, young Mr. Knight's wife, Jennifer, when she was in labor. Katarina got there quick before the doctor came, saved that poor woman and the baby. I believe he's about fifteen now."

"Yes, and we were just planting some spring bulbs at the clubhouse three weeks ago. God bless her soul, some daylilies," Helen said, the fifth member, the quiet one. "She always told us of your adventures and how good you were at photography."

As Sarah listened to them chitchat, she noticed something she'd never paid attention to in the past. Each woman was wearing a small silver-star pendant with semi-precious stones at each point pinned to their dresses. "That's a pretty pendant you're wearing," Sarah said. When Helen glanced at Janice and started fidgeting, Sarah wondered why.

Janice jumped in. "Oh, these. They're Eastern Star pins. You know, from the Masonic lodge?" She paused and smiled. "The chapter…they allowed us, Catholics, to join years ago."

Sarah thought about their explanation, not sure she went along with it, until she saw Father Holden saying his farewells out of the corner of her eye. Sudden relief poured through every vein of her body.

"Well, it's so nice to see all of you again," she said, making her excuses and went around the table to give them each a hug. "And thanks for all the food you cooked for us. Oma would have appreciated it."

"It was the least we could do for Katarina," Maggie said. "Sarah, do come over for a visit. Don't forget. And remember, we're here for you if you ever need anything."

The grandfather clock in the living room struck nine. The dishes were cleared, food wrapped and stored or given away, trash gathered and put out, and the tables and chairs in the backyard folded against the back wall of the house. Sarah noticed Suzanne conversing with David in the living room and holding his hand on her lap. Walking into the kitchen to drop off the last items from outside, she joined her aunt Ursula, uncle John, Julia and Georg who were immersed in a lively conversation about politics and the housing bubble as they washed the dishes. In the den, her young cousins were sprawled on the floor playing a video game. Jake, the youngest, was asleep on the couch. Robert and Michael sat on the floor with their backs against the sofa, battling each other with their remotes. Tim, the oldest, was watching.

"Hey, come here," Tim said, waving to her. Earlier, Sarah and David had played badminton with them in the back yard. She shook her head, deciding instead to head back out to the garden and wander among the birch trees and maybe sit on the stone bench next to the fish pond.

Oma was dead.

She felt empty, lost and alone.

Something was pulling her away from her family, a sense of disconnect. *My mother never really loved me or she wouldn't have killed herself.* She cried into the palms of her hands, stifling down wet gulps. As she sat there in her grief, she felt an arm wrap around her shoulder and smelled the familiar scent of baby powder. Aunt

Ursula was sitting next to her on the bench.

"I brought you some *Apfelstrudel,*" the woman said, and handed Sarah the dessert and a tissue. "It'll be alright. I'm glad to see you finally crying."

Sarah studied her aunt's sympathetic face and rested her head on her shoulder, sniffling and wiping her nose. They both sat hushed for a while, looking at the wooded hills in the distance. Finally, Sarah took a bite of the strudel.

"Thanks," Sarah said, and licked her lips. "Just like Oma's."

Ursula pulled her tight.

"I always thought of you as my own daughter, honey," Ursula said. "And I've never regretted raising you after your mommy died. Remember that. I'm so proud of you. You're a beautiful young woman, and so good at what you do. A great photographer, wow! But more than that, you are so strong, more like Mama than my sister."

"I could get sick like her." Sarah said, and they both knew what Sarah was driving at.

Ursula faced her and shook her head. "Don't you ever worry about that. You won't. I know it. Your mother was very different from the woman you've become," She took Sarah's face and kissed her on the forehead.

"I hope so." Sarah sighed and embraced her aunt.

"Believe it!" Ursula said, squeezing her tighter.

Sarah nodded. "You've always been there for me, you and Uncle John. I was just thinking of my mother. I'm sorry I don't come home more often to visit. Can you forgive me?" Sarah said.

"For what?"

"You know. After my mom…" she shrugged, and went on "you became my mom and John my father."

"Are you feeling guilty because we never had any children of our own?

Don't you worry, we are quite all right," her aunt said.

Sarah looked up at her aunt. There was a question she'd had for years, but had never had the courage to ask. "It bothers me, I don't know who my father is, whether he's alive or dead or whatever. Oma told me she didn't know and to let it go. But I just can't believe no one knows."

"Your mother never told any of us, though we tried to pry it out of her. Later, maybe, Mama might've known, but she never told me." She patted Sarah's shoulder. "Sarah, let's please not talk about that today. Come, I have something to give you. Something Mama gave me."

Ursula led her into the house and up to her old bedroom. As Sarah opened the squeaky door to her childhood room, she saw it was just as she had left it before going away to college nine years ago. Even the same lace curtains still adorned the windows. Posters of her favorite pop groups were plastered on the walls, along with pictures of school friends and her first attempts at photography. A bulletin board and high school sport team's plaques hung over her writing desk. Her favorite brown teddy bear lay on the pillows that were covered by the pink quilt Ursula had made her for her thirteenth birthday.

"I can't believe you still have this." Sarah said, plopping on the bed and picking up the stuffed bear, which smelled a little dusty.

"We wanted to keep everything the way you left it, so you'd always have a home to come back to," Ursula said. She walked over to the oak chest of drawers, pulling something out of the top one. It was big and wrapped in a maroon silk cloth.

"What is it?" Sarah asked, setting the stuffed bear down.

"Honestly, I really don't know, Mama wanted you to have it," Ursula said. "All I do know is a few weeks before she passed, Mama called me to come over. She said to be sure you got this."

She put the bundle on the bed between them and nodded to Sarah.

"Well, let's open it," Sarah said, clapping her hands together.

"No. Mama was clear. This is only for you: no one else. She made me swear no one except you would ever see what it is. She said, *"Sarah is the only one who has the gift."* Those were her exact words," Ursula answered, drifting to the window and looking out over the countryside.

"Your grandmother had an uncanny ability of knowing

things, like the weather or who was calling on the phone before it'd ring. When we were kids, we got used to her sensitivities. Suzanne and I don't agree on this, but I know, there were occurrences I couldn't explain," Ursula ran her fingers through her hair, turned back, and headed toward the bedroom door.

"Anyway, your grandmother wanted you to have this. I'll be downstairs with the others. No one else needs to know about this, okay?"

When Sarah nodded, Ursula closed the door behind her. In the silence left by her aunt's wake, Sarah pondered the dreams she had time and again of bees swarming before thunderstorms and the ravens flitting on the cliffs in Scotland. Was this the gift Oma was talking about, and would it lead her to losing her mind like her mother did?

At last, she untied the black cord around the large object on her lap. The silky cloth fell open, revealing a russet brown leather book, worn and stained, black on some spots of the binding. It appeared to be very old. A silver metal clasp held it closed. She lifted the heavy book up and sniffed it. It smelled of lavender and old musty bookstores. In the middle of the front cover, a large five-pointed star encircled by a serpent biting its own tail, along with strange imprinted symbols. The edges of the pages were jagged and looked as if they'd been charred by fire.

Isn't a pentagram a symbol for witches? Or does this have something to do with the Masons and the pins Oma's friends were wearing? Why would Oma, a devout Catholic, give me a book about devil worshippers?

Chapter Sixteen

Sarah opened the metal clasp of the old book Oma had left her and turned to the front page. At the top corner of the yellowed leaf was the year 1659 written in neat small, slanted letters. *This book must be over 300 years old!* In the middle of the page was a sun depicting a face and other symbols she didn't recognize. Under it were a few lines written in what looked like German. The characters were similar to the English alphabet but angular and hard to decipher. Carefully, she opened the pages of the book. One leaf fell out onto the bed. She put it back and noticed two distinct names on the bottom right corner of it. One name was *Katharina Pauldauf* and the other, *Elisabeth Freifrau von Galler*. Who were these women?

She examined more pages of what appeared to be astrological charts, moon phases, drawings of plants and animals. Strange looking verses were interspersed between painted pictures of flowers and herbs. Sarah recognized the drawings of nettle and lavender. Oma had taught her a little about herbs. Then, the handwriting changed.

There was a new name, *Hildegard Wenzel*, written on the bottom of the pages and dated 1692. Other names followed as she flipped to the end of the book where she found just blank pages. She discovered the last fifty pages were written by Oma herself, some of it in German with the later passages in English. One drawing of a naked woman caught her eye. She was kneeling by herself with a cup in her hands, raising it up as if in supplication to the moon. Her head was draped with a cloth, partially hiding her face, otherwise she was naked. A table stood next to her, and on it rested a lighted candle, feather, pentagram and dagger.

Oma had written under the picture; *"Whenever you are of need, come to Me when the moon is full and I will, Hecate, Queen of all witches and heaven guide you, my daughter, to your heart's desire."*

Sarah dropped the book next to her onto the bed. Had Oma been a witch or something like that? No, that couldn't be. She'd sat next to Oma every Sunday in church. Oma was a Catholic! Sarah stood and went to the window. Looking out over the pastures, she tried to make sense of what she just uncovered. What was the legacy of the book that Oma had passed on to her? Sarah didn't believe in religion— not God anyways— and certainly not in witches. She was an atheist. Why did Oma keep this secret from everyone? She remembered a funny scene from her childhood. She was thirteen at the time and had just started her period.

At the time, she was living permanently with her aunt and uncle. They were out of town on an anniversary trip to Montreal, so she was spending the night at her grandparents. She'd woken up with cramps and went downstairs to the kitchen.

Outside, she'd heard humming coming from the back yard so she stepped out onto the back patio. Her grandmother was stark naked and taking a shower with the garden hose. With her back turned to Sarah, Oma had to be oblivious to not being alone, but she called to Sarah over her shoulder.

"Come, it's refreshing, nothing like a cold shower to wake you up," Oma said, and turned to beckon her to join. Sarah was utterly astonished. How did she know she was there?

"Oma, someone could see you," Sarah had scoffed at her, embarrassed because her grandmother was well into her seventies. Sarah folded her arms in rebellion.

"Don't look so shocked, it's only a woman's body." Oma had laughed and walked over to shut the water off. Grabbing a towel from the patio chair, she began to dry out her dripping grey hair.

"Someone might see you," Sarah insisted, looking away.

"I'm not harming any one. Plus, everyone's asleep. Go inside and put a kettle of water on the stove. Also, set the table for breakfast. And don't forget to get coffee started for Opa." She waved Sarah briskly away then.

Afterward, Oma came in wearing her bathrobe with a towel wrapped around her head, turban style.

"That's just what the doctor ordered," she said with a flourish and got a pan out from the kitchen cupboard. To Sarah's bewilderment, her grandmother acted as if nothing had happened as she cracked egg after egg on the side of a ceramic mixing bowl and scrambled them up with fresh herbs, onions and tomatoes. Up until this day, she'd never understood why her grandmother had acted this way, but now with the book in her hands, she began to understand.

She turned through the rest of the blank pages, wondering if there were anything else, but found nothing more until she came to the back cover and there discovered a letter taped and addressed to her!

She felt her heart quicken as she carefully pulled the tape away and took the letter into her hands. For a moment she stared at it, almost afraid to open it. With a trembling hand, she slipped her finger under the flap and took out the letter.

December 6th, 2010- Today is St. Nikolas day.

Dearest Sarah,

If you get this letter, then I have passed on to be with your Opa and my ancestors. I so wanted to see you one more time. Don't cry, because I am with you in spirit, my little bright one. I've missed you these past few years since you moved to Seattle. But you were always one for adventure. Do you remember the time you walked all the way to the grocery store with your tiny basket to buy candy when you were only five years old? You gave me quite a scare. It was lucky that Mr. O'Leary, Janice's deceased husband, called Opa to come and pick you up. I should have scolded you but I could never stay mad at you very long. There are so many stories about you, which have made my life the happier for it. I am so proud of your success as a photographer.

And now, for I wanted to always tell you. I entrusted your aunt Ursula to give you this book. Please don't be shocked, it's not what you think it is. All my life, it's been my guide, helper and source of light.

I was going to give it to your mother, but as you know, she was very ill. Her death is my greatest regret. The gift, her insight and magical abilities, was a burden for her.

You know you look like her, the same hair and face, but you're different and strong. I know you don't want anyone to know about your hunches. But I've recognized the gift in you. You have "the sight". It's important you learn to use this gift or it might cause destruction in your life.

This book will teach you the path. You must believe me when I tell you all that I did was in the name of love with no harm to others. This book survived the time of the burnings which raged throughout Europe. My mother passed it down to me from her mother and so on from the 1600's. Take great care of it. There are secrets in this book I should have taught you, but now you're going to have to find them out for yourself. Some things may stay a mystery; others will be revealed in time.

One last favor I would ask of you: I wanted to get back to my homeland in Austria but couldn't because Opas' family was murdered in the Holocaust. I never forgave my family for what happened. I loved your Opa— he was the love of my life— and I knew how much it hurt him to never see them again.

Did I ever tell you I met with him in secret because my father didn't tolerate mixed marriages and warned me not to marry Jacob? But I did nevertheless, and to cut a long story short, he disowned me. That will seem strange to you in today's world. Some things change for the better. I hope, Sarah, you find someone to love like I did your Opa. We were so happy until the Fuhrer arrived in Austria.

It was the eleventh hour, and we barely escaped with our lives. The Stifters, friends of Opa, saved our lives. But after the war, we lost contact with them. Could you find them or their children? Go to their graves if they've died, and put flowers there for me?

You're a different generation than I, and I've come to realize with time, I want to forgive my family. Unfortunately, my parents are most likely dead by now. If you can, please find my sisters and brothers. Their names are listed on the back of this letter. My deepest wish for you is to travel back to the country where I was born. This book's journey began in Reigersburg. Go there and may the Goddess protect you.

Carry me in your heart,
Oma

Sarah set the letter down. When her Opa was alive, she saw how he hated the Nazis because they murdered his family at

Dachau. Could she travel to Austria knowing this? She wrapped the book back in its cloth and hid it under the bed, sensing the need to respect Oma's wishes but having so many reservations.

I'll Google the women listed in the book tomorrow.

She picked up the photograph of her and Oma from her dresser, and kissed it. Closing the bedroom door, she overheard laughter creeping up from below. David and Uncle Georg's family were exchanging old family stories. As for the story of this book, that would remain with her for the time being. Certainly, she couldn't let David know about it.

Chapter Seventeen

Seattle, July 2009

The moon was splendidly full outside the apartment's large window. The Space Needle's point poked right up into its belly. A clear night was unusual in Seattle. Sarah squeezed Oma's letter in her hand and looked out at the lights of the city. They reminded her of stars. The real ones were hidden by the city's unnatural brightness. There'd be a glorious dome of sparkling lights in the Berkshires or on a deserted ocean beach in Hawaii, not merely grey sky. One bright beacon of light solely held her place in the dark sky, as if challenging modern technology. The North Star shone bright and obstinate tonight.

Sarah smoothed the piece of paper and folded it, then placed it on her dresser next to her grey futon. She felt restless as she wandered aimlessly into her living room where a counter split the space in two. The red rectangular sofa stood along with two leather chairs on one side, a spotless Ikea kitchen on the other. A half-eaten piece of toast and a tall cup of cold green tea were left on the Formica top, forgotten.

Gazing over at one of her favorite pieces from her trip to New Zealand hanging on the wall, she went to the apartment's clerestory; floor to ceiling window. In her opinion, the picture told a tale of the island nation and its storied people. She'd waited at the beach that day to get just the right light and exposure to capture the magnificence of Mount Maunganui. Even the meaning of its name was significant: *Caught by the Morning Light*. Looking back at it brightened her feelings for a moment.

Her grandmother had always told her she had a knack of taking photographs of places and capturing the fleeting expressions of strangers. And to this, she couldn't argue. Traveling on photo shoots was when she came alive and rediscovered the magic she'd had as a child in the Berkshires.

She turned back and looked out over the buildings. The vista before her gave her the feeling of living on a ship and riding over a deep rolling sea. She sighed. She hadn't been sleeping well the last few days. So much was on her mind, chief among them was not being there when Oma passed. She felt guilty. Every time she closed her eyes, she saw the old matriarch and then the memories of home and the woods behind her Oma's house. As a child, she roamed them, escaping the harsh world that had crashed all around her. And it was here she'd discovered a small overhang carved out from a rocky outcropping in the forest. Her special place, her cave: a magical dwelling. The sheltered grotto gave her protection from the rain and offered a haven when the memories of her mother threatened to overcome her. Here, she would sit looking out at the world with her wool blanket wrapped around her and her favorite doll held tight to her breast.

Sarah wanted desperately to feel the safety of her special place again, to be among the precious trinkets of broken glass and stones she'd placed in a half circle around it, marking it as her space. More than that, she longed for the comfort of being cocooned in the forest, with its symphony of song that made her happy and peaceful. She gave names like *"Old Man Tree"* or *"Young Silver"* to the surrounding trees. And when Oma would ring the back porch's iron kettle bell calling her home, dirty with tangled hair, she'd hide her doll and blanket and pull a curtain of brush over the opening to the cave so no one would see it, and go running to the only person that could make the world right.

She was a wild thing, as Oma would say to her Opa. Wild things were fearful. Nights were the hardest for Sarah, and Oma knew this and would bathe her in songs steeped in German folklore to soothe her. She begged to know the meanings of these wonderful enchanting songs sang in the old language, but Oma would only tap her fingertips on Sarah's chest and say, "Listen to the melody and you'll get the meaning in your heart."

And now, the plea from her Oma to go to Austria had

taken hold, and with it a deep yearning had sprung up to go to the old land. In ways, she felt like Bilbo from *The Hobbit* being called away from her comfortable, modern life to an adventure where she didn't know the outcome.

The book's references to Katarina Pauldauf and Elisabeth von Galler nagged her.

She researched the names of the two women and found Katarina Pauldauf was burned at the stake as a witch in the late 1600's. Her nickname had been the Witch of the Flowers, and the other woman a baroness of a castle, who turned out to be the witch's employer. As she perused websites in her search for information, she came upon pages talking about Riegersburg's ongoing exhibitions. One of them had an exhibit on witchcraft, no less. Intrigued, she poured through all the literature, reading as much as she could about the region and the castle's history.

However, as strong as the urge was welling up inside her to go to Austria, she couldn't help feeling afraid. It was like walking into an abandoned house where the ghosts of its past moved around in the dark, lurking and waiting to kidnap her like the world did with her mother. The darkness calling her was primordial, messy, and enticing all at once.

She got up and crossed her arms, went to the window again and stared out over the dense urban sprawl, then rushed to her bedroom and pulled the large book out from under the bed. To her surprise, she had become obsessed with it, inspecting it many times a day, as if the book itself was asking her to unlock its mysteries.

Should she hand it over to historians at a museum? It had to be worth something. She flipped through pages to a place in the book showing a table with different phases of the moon. It frustrated her that she couldn't decipher the German script. She screamed out loud. "Damn. Fuck!"

What knowledge was it hiding? She examined the back cover, feeling the inside. Something felt hard under the glued paper.

She drew back, surprised and curious then took the book with her to the kitchen. Rifling through the drawers, she found a knife and used it to carefully make an incision along the edge of the book. Shaking it sideways, a silver pendant tumbled onto the top of the counter. A silver pentagram! She picked up the antique handcrafted pendant and examined the white stone in the middle with its two opposite-facing crescent moons. A circle encased the five points of the star.

She took it with her into the living room and grabbed her laptop. Typing "pentagram" into the Google search bar, she waited as the page loaded on the screen.

The pentagram was used in ancient times as a Christian symbol for the five senses. Each point represented the five wounds of Christ. An unknown poet of the fourteenth century England credited the symbol's origin to King Solomon. The symbol was key to understanding a secret mystery.

The page explained each of the five points is aligned to a virtue. However, further down, she found that the reversed pentagram was called the flaming star. When turned upside down it formed the hieroglyphic of black magic. A goat's head could be superimposed over the star, two horns at the top with its ears to the right and left, the beard at the bottom symbolizing antagonism and evil.

Sarah examined the silver pendant with Oma foremost on her mind as she did so, wondering what this all meant. If Oma had used magic, Sarah was certain it was only for the good.

The woman didn't have a malevolent bone in her body. Reading further, she saw the article mentioned the practice of the five star symbol in the modern day Wicca movement and Free Masons. What did all this mean? Her head throbbed, so she closed the laptop's screen and sat back onto the couch.

Earlier that week, she'd spoken with her boss and convinced him to let her do an article on Riegersburg and the southern part of Austria. It would be a compelling topic for the magazine, she'd argued, something different. Europe was in vogue again. Next, she'd asked Vanderhoost, a Dane who was married to an American, if he'd tag along. The diminutive and kindly man with little round-wired spectacles was an excellent reporter who worked regularly with her.

She dragged the photocopies she'd made of the book from

the coffee table to take with her to Europe. Why was all the text and pictures a jumbled mess? And why had some pages refused to even be copied? She didn't understand it. It was if the book was asking her to take it to Europe.

Her iPhone rang. She reached over to check the caller ID. It was her cousin, David. She admonished herself, having not called him since the funeral.

"Hi, David."

"Hey, stranger, haven't heard from you since Oma died," David said, sounding hurt. "What's up? Do you have some time to talk?"

"For my favorite guy? Always time for you," she replied. "I've been so busy with work…can you forgive me?"

"Sarah, please, well, let me think, David said. "The time you were in China, and I didn't hear from you for two months or when you let me know—after the fact—you'd been lost in New Zealand because of — what's his name, that guy you work with—Vandepoop?"

"That's Vanderhoost, and you know he's terrible with directions. He got lost using a GPS for God's sake," Sarah said and laughed. "So, am I off the hook again?"

"Yes, darling. That is, if I can talk to you about Jenny," David said. "She broke up with me yesterday for the third time. She just moved out with some of her stuff. Said she's moving in with Kate, her best friend. Kate hates me and I don't know why. I think she has the hots for Jenny. She's been in her ear for some time now and has got her believing I cheated on her."

Sarah knew her handsome cousin had been unfaithful to other women in the past, but she loved him anyway. "Well, did you?"

"I haven't much as looked at another woman since I met her five years ago. I love her," David said, and his voice broke.

"Give it a couple of days, then, call her, David. And really, am I the one to be asking about relationships? I haven't had one in years." Sarah said, knowing she hadn't ever kept a relationship longer than six months.

"OK. You're right, I guess. I'll wait. How've you been? Any

new loves? A boyfriend or a woman, my free-spirited little cousin?'"

"No, I don't have time for romance. You know me — difficult, hard headed, like to do things my way," Sarah said. "I haven't been sleeping well since Oma's funeral. Say, I need to ask you a question."

"Okay."

"Oma asked me a while ago if I'd go to see her relatives in Austria."

"Really?"

"Yes. I never told you. Anyway, I've been thinking of going to visit them. What do you think?"

"You're not serious!" David cried. "They let Opa's family die! They're all Nazis. You remember Opa's horrible accounts of 'Kristalnacht'. How their neighbors plundered the stores and beat Jews. How the local police came and forced them to leave their home. Everything Opa worked for ...destroyed. They left Austria just in time, before the Nazis started rounding up people for the death camps. So, to answer your question: no, I don't think you should go. Personally, I don't want anything to do with them."

"But, David, remember Oma wasn't Jewish. She loved Opa and those friends of Opa's, I can't remember their names, the ones from Vienna. What about them? They helped Opa and Oma escape to America. Your mom would know. They were good." Sarah argued.

"The name was Stifter," David said, some heat in his tone.

"Calm down, I get it," Sarah said. "But Oma believed in the good of people. I want to find that couple, that is, if they're still alive, and also our cousins."

"Sarah, I know when you get something in your head, you won't listen to reason, to me or anyone else for that matter, but think again on this. Anyway, when were you thinking of going?"

"At the end of August," Sarah uttered. "I talked to Brian, my boss, into doing a piece on Riegersburg." She smiled and hoping to lighten things up, added, "And I've asked Vanderpoop to join me."

"So soon? When were you going to tell me? Let me guess, you already have your ticket. Why do you even bother asking?"

"Because you're my best friend, my only brother — well almost — and we tell each other everything," Sarah said. "David, I'm really sorry I didn't tell you earlier. Please, forgive me. I knew you'd be mad, but I'm doing this for Oma. Her death made me think of her life and where she came from."

"Right again, I'm not happy, but it's your life, dear. Just don't make me have to fly over and save you from the gas chambers."

"That's not funny, David."

"Sorry, but you know what I mean."

"I do, and don't worry. Vanderhoost will take good care of me. Even if he gets lost sometimes." She wanted out of this awkward conversation so she switched gears and said, "And with Jenny, it'll get better, you'll see. She'll be back in no time. You're irresistible."

"I hope so," he said. "Well, I've got to check out and get some sleep. Call me from the old country as Opa would say. You know me; I can't stay angry with you for long. I love you. Take care, kiddo."

"Love ya, too." Sarah answered and ended the call leaving out the part about the three-hundred-year-old book.

Chapter Eighteen

Two Weeks Later

Sarah nudged the short thin man in his middle thirties next to her. His head rested on a tiny pillow by the side of the airplane window. "Vanderhoost," she whispered.

He opened his eyes, sat up and rubbed the stubble on his pointy chin. Reaching for his black-framed glasses, in the seat pocket in front of him, he said in a heavy Danish accent, "Are we there yet?"

The sound of his rolling his R's, made Sarah laugh because it reminded her of someone speaking with a golf ball in their mouth.

"What?" he said, frowning.

Sarah knew he was sensitive about his accent and her humor maddened him. "Nothing. Just that you're cute." This brought about a scowl. "Oh, come on now. You know how I feel about you. You're my friend, and friends know it's just playing."

He eyed her skeptically.

"And just so you know, I'm so grateful we're working together on this. Your thoughtfulness as a skillful journalist, coaxing stories out of the most pig-headed people, is invaluable."

"You're buttering me up, but okay," he said. "So, let's go over again what we're here for."

She pulled a file from her briefcase and opened it. As they went over the shoot, she thought about the last four days. She'd sent off last-minute emails, corresponding with the owners of the castle, along with the local parish of St. Martin. They'd responded that the church had an extensive library, including primary documents pertaining to the witch trials.

And there was a website dedicated to saving Jewish lives during World War II. One page was dedicated to Roswitha Stifter for her efforts that sadly led to her and her husband being arrested by the Nazis shortly after they'd helped her grandparents escape. Miraculously, both Roswitha and her husband had survived the horrors of the Nazi death camps, only to divorce after the war. Roswitha had recently passed away at ninety-four, leaving one grandson, Michael Stifter, in Vienna. His contact information was on the website. Sarah planned to call him as soon as she arrived.

Sarah's ears popped. "I think we're descending."

Vanderhoost peered out the window as the pilot's voice came over the speakers in German. She'd tried to learn some German the past two months but she still scarcely understood the basics.

"What did the pilot just say?" Sarah asked.

"Fasten your seat belt," he said, closing the folder. Patting her on the knee, he added, "We're going to be in one of the most spectacular cities in Europe."

"I can't wait!"

He smiled. "I was here, in Vienna, as a college student. It's the most beautiful city in the world.

She put the folder in her bag and took out a travel brochure. "It says here; 'Austria Classic Hotel' located in beautiful Vienna's center, only four minutes to *Stephansdom*. I want to visit the Hapsburg summer castle; *Schönbrunn*, and the cathedral before we leave for Riegersburg." Sarah rattled on as she felt the wheels of the plane fall out.

"All are very nice places. What I'm looking for right now is a cup of real coffee, not that swill they sell you in the States. Did you know Vienna is the city of coffee houses?"

"No, I didn't."

"Well, be prepared for a taste of ambrosia. By the way, where are we staying again?"

"Remember, I told you about visiting the son of that couple that saved my grandparents?"

"Yes, I look forward to meet him. I'm sure he has some very interesting stories to share," Vanderhoost said and smiled back, not looking in the least piqued. "You, I want to thank you for convincing Brian about this assignment. And to think, he's giving us two days in Vienna. Now, if only my boyfriend wasn't so scared of me traveling overseas, I could enjoy it so much more. Can't wait to drink some good beer as well and eat the food! You Americans don't understand cuisine."

"I know," Sarah answered, rolling her eyes. Pete had been Vanderhoost companion and lover for a long time, and Sarah was sure that if anything happened to Vanderhoost, the man would shrivel up and die.

The plane veered right and as it did so, she felt a thunk from the landing gear dropping into position. She put the brochure away as the stewards came around to tell people to close their window shutters. A moment later, the pilot came over the intercom and issued one last command as the lights dimmed in the cabin.

Excitement raced through Sarah's body. She was landing in the very country her grandparents had fled over seventy years ago, a place steeped in tradition and immersed with mystery. One of them was in her suitcase, in a book wrapped between her clothes. She wondered where it would lead her, as the bump of wheels met the surface of macadam runway.

"That wasn't too bad, was it?" Vanderhoost said, after the plane came to a full stop at their gate. He tapped her on the shoulder and they both jumped out of their seats to get to their bags. His chirpy behavior riled her because she was a nervous flyer and couldn't wait to escape the crowded plane.

After they dropped their bags off at the hotel, Vanderhoost suggested a walk around downtown. "We need to adjust to the time difference," he said as they strolled through the narrow pedestrian alleys.

Sarah looked up, gawking at the impressive old 'Art Noveau' buildings on either side of her. Jetlag often made daylight look surreal to her, muting the colors of everything into odd shades. With its Gothic, bleak and darkened towers grazing the sky, *Stephansdom*, the city's large cathedral, rose up majestically at the heart of Vienna. She bent her neck back to look up at the parapets and took out her camera to get a few shots.

"There you go again. Put the camera away," Vanderhoost said tagging her on the shoulder. "Stop being a tourist and let yourself enjoy the moment. There'll be time enough for that later."

She supposed he was right, and put her camera away. They walked amongst the vibrant people under a clear blue sky and listened to their banter back and forth. Vienna was like a fairy tale city she had seen in books when she was a child. Its varied architectural buildings were thick with artistic history. Vanderhoost pointed out places he'd been, telling her about the site and how it came to be. At last, he came to a stop and said, "Now, let's visit the catacombs."

"The what?" Sarah said. She followed him through a maze of narrow streets until they came to a towering cathedral. Vanderhoost strode through one of the tall oak doors standing open in front of them. Sarah followed. She immediately felt a cold dampness on her forearms. The vast space echoed their footsteps as they strode across its polished marble stones. The reek of incense was everywhere.

"*Stephansdom* is over nine hundred years old when the stonemasons began building it," Vanderhoost said. He bought tickets from a cashier's booth in the narthex and handed her a brochure in English. "Come, let's get to the tour guide waiting at the back of the building."

They joined two other couples and a minute later they were at a metal fence with an iron door. "This leads down into the catacombs," Vanderhoost said as they passed through. As they went single file down a long stairway, clammy air wrapped itself around her bare arms. At the bottom, Sarah hesitated, not really wanting to see the skeletons or the gloomy places beneath the city, but the rest of the tourists followed the attendant eagerly down a narrow corridor, leaving her alone. Vanderhoost came back. "Come on. You'll not want to miss this."

"I'm sure," Sarah said and started off with him into the gloom.

The electric candle-lit passageway ended directly under the cathedral. She passed walls with rows of tombs on each side, marble tablets with inscriptions of former bishops gleamed under bright lights. Shadows flickered on the side-walls, and farther along there was an opening to a large dirt room filled with skeletons. Sarah imagined she heard the dead whispering, "*There is only today. Life is short and miserable. Be wary and flee while you can!*"

An icy rush of air brushed past her, bringing goose pimples on her bare skin. She suddenly wanted to run, but she mastered herself.

"Plague victims," Vanderhoost whispered into her ear before following the rest of the tour through the catacombs.

"I don't know about you, but I could've skipped this tour." Sarah said. "Where do we go from here? No more weird locations, okay?"

Vanderhoost frowned, looking at her as if she had no appreciation for history. "Fine. May I suggest one of the celebrated cafes along Vienna's main center plaza called the *Stephansplatz Cafe?*"

That sounded great to Sarah, and she followed him to a café with plush red velvet lined benches and chairs. The place was busy; but they found a spot next to a large window with a perfect view of *Stephansdom*. Sarah took her seat at a polished black and grey stone table and picked up the menu, written in German and English.

"You should try a *Verlängerte* and a piece of *Sachertorte*, Vanderhoost recommended, looking up from his menu.

"What's that?" Sarah said as a waiter dressed in a white shirt, bow tie and black slacks approached their table.

"*Verlängerte* is like a latte, only better and richer. The *Sachertorte* is a chocolate cake and a Viennese specialty."

"Sounds good to me," Sarah agreed, handing her menu to the waiter. As Vanderhoost ordered for them, Sarah looked out at the pedestrians. There were a lot of people out shopping.

"The Europeans like to walk and window shop," Vanderhoost said. They watched the coming and goings of people for some time, each in their own thoughts until the waiter returned with their order. As the man set their lattes and dessert in front of them, Vanderhoost said, "By the way, I changed my mind about tomorrow. I picked up a notice about a Mandelbrot exhibition at the *Museum Hundertwasser*. I love his work."

"You're kidding," Sarah said with her fork full of moist cake halfway to her mouth. She set it down and flopped back against her chair. "Remember, I don't speak German!"

Vanderhoost sipped his latte and waved a hand. "Not to worry. Everyone here speaks English."

"And you were going to tell this when?" Sarah said, crossing her arms over her chest.

Vanderhoost shrugged. "I thought I had."

Her iPhone chimed. She pulled it out and looked on the screen. The number looked familiar. "I think it's the son, I forgot to tell you I reached him earlier in my room. Hold on."

"Well, answer it," Vanderhoost said.

"No need to get bitchy," Sarah said and answered the call.

After the long day in the city, Sarah was exhausted and happy to be back in her hotel room. She flung off her shoes and jumped onto the bed.

Tomorrow morning, she was meeting up with Michael Stifter. He'd generously offered to accompany her to *Schönbrunn*. Moreover, she wanted to go over some of the notes she'd pieced together about Riegersburg, Katharina Pauldauf and the baroness. Sarah regarded the picture she had of the alleged witch holding a flower. The woman brought flowers to bloom in the middle of winter. Katarina had been married to the baroness' keeper of the castle. Why wasn't the Baroness burned along with her maid? She Googled which population was persecuted and learned discrimination against the working class was commonplace, according to the experts.

After fifteen minutes in front of her laptop, she took out the letter from the local parish. She looked down at Bishop Baumgartner's last statement.

'It was a very unfortunate time for women'. *Unfortunate, indeed.* It was a dangerous time. She was glad that she didn't live in the late 1600s. *Maybe they would've burned me too, as a feminist.*

As she read, her eyelids drooped and she fought to stay awake. How did Oma get the book? The answer would have to wait until she could research more. Sarah's gut feeling told her to heed her Oma's warnings even if it was the twenty-first century, and not tell anyone her real reason for coming.

Sarah dressed in something comfortable, a T-shirt and soft cotton shorts. After closing her laptop, she pulled back the fluffy comforter and lied down on the bed. No air conditioners here. Soon she was in deep sleep.

She didn't know where she was, and it was pitch black. She heard a cry and began to walk toward the sound. Lights blinded her, and then there was a loud screeching noise.

Sarah woke, startled. It was three a.m. Although she knew she was dreaming, she couldn't shake off the notion something bad was about to happen. She stood and looked out the hotel window at the sleeping city, then hugged herself and went back to bed to read up on Empress Marie Theresa and *Schönbrunn*.

The next morning, Michael Stifter stood waiting in the hotel lobby. He was of medium build, mid-thirties, with dirty blonde hair and red-rimmed glasses. Euro-Schick, as they said in Austrian slang.

"Hi, I'm Sarah Lilienthal," she said, reaching her hand out to him. "You're Michael, right?" His hand felt sweaty.

"Yes, it's crazy. You're actually here," Michael said. His English was excellent. "Oma spoke about your grandparents not long before she passed. Our grandfathers were best friends apparently at the university, before the war. Did you know that?" He wasn't letting go of her hand. Sarah gently pulled her hand away.

"Sorry, I get carried away. And I forget how Americans are with touching. I spent a year traveling in the States. Sorry, again," Michael said earnestly. A moment of awkward silence followed.

"You know, my Oma wanted me to find you and thank you," Sarah said as people walked past them in the hotel. "And I'm really sorry that I couldn't meet her, I mean, your Oma."

"Oma was ninety-four," he said. "She was amazing, I'm sure you would have loved her. Opa died a while ago. I still can't believe how they survived the concentration camps. You know, she was in Auschwitz. The Nazis found out they were helping Jews escape." He looked at his watch.

"I'm sorry; we should be finding a tram. You only have the morning, right?"

"No, please tell me more; I wouldn't be here if it wasn't for her and your Opa!" Sarah said. "I read all about them on the website. Their story touched me deeply. But, I do kind of need to get going if I want to see the castle. We sent our suitcases ahead to the train station via the hotel service. That should give me more leeway."

"What time does it leave?" Michael asked.

"Five-thirty, so I have loads of time to explore."

"I know a quick way to get there," he said. "Follow me."

They made their way outside the hotel, through the cars, throngs of people rushing to work, and bikes to the tram station. A small crowd was standing around the clear plastic enclosure. Sarah felt tense and looked at the approaching tram when a young man next to her stumbled out onto the tracks.

In a split second, she jumped forward, grabbed his arm, yanked him up and pulled him back. They fell onto the concrete pavement just as the tram came to a screeching halt next to their feet. People ran to them screaming. There was some confusion as Michael helped her up. The tram's conductor jumped out from inside the tram. The young man stood with the help of others, calling something over to Sarah.

"She doesn't speak German," Michael shouted back in English. The man rushed over and grabbed her hands.

"Thank you, thank you," he said. Sarah, still shocked, could only nod. Michael and another woman were talking with the conductor. "You saved my life." The young man cried and embraced her.

"You're welcome." Sarah found her voice but couldn't help remembering the dream from last night. The young man thanked her again.

Thirty-five minutes later, Sarah and Michael were riding to the royal Hapsburgs' family summer residence. Sarah felt uneasy and tried to shake off what had just happened.

"Look, there it is!" Michael pointed to an enormous yellow building from the tram as they approached. "Built by Marie Therese, who was Marie Antoinette's mother, the one who lost her head in Paris. Oh my God, look at that line. We'll have to wait for an hour."

"Do you mind? I really want to see how the royals used to live,'" Sarah said and stepped off the tram.

"Of course, you'll love it," he said.

Sarah pulled out her Nikon. "Can I take some pictures?" she said.

"Yes. Will you send me copies?"

Sarah nodded.

They walked through the outer gates towards the line extending toward them on the huge courtyard. To her right was a large carriage drawn by two grand, white Lipizzaner horses. Waiting for whom? Sarah had never seen such opulence and splendor in any of her travels. At the entrance booth of the castle, they were given a brochure. She opted for the live tour because it was in English and listening to German all day had given her a headache.

The tour presenting the wealth of the Hapsburgs with rooms after rooms for all occasions lasted for hours. They had a quick lunch in between with Michael filling her in on fun facts of the royals.

When it was over, they made it out back to the immense sculptured gardens. It was hot by then. She took out her water bottle and drank, then took more images of the fountain depicting a larger than life Poseidon holding his trident triumphantly up in the air. Encircling the statue was a pod of dolphins with naked women.

"I wanted to put some flowers on your Oma's grave, but I'm afraid I won't have any time," she said as Michael and her sat down on a bench overlooking the grounds and tourists.

"Don't worry, I can do it. I've wanted to visit the cemetery. You gave me a reason. She always said to me, 'Michael, things happen for a reason.'

"Our grandmothers would've been so happy we met today," Sarah said. "Times have changed for the better. Thanks for meeting me. I'm really touched," Sarah said, wanting to somehow repay him in the future for his kindness. She leaned forward and gently squeezed the top of his hand.

"Me, too." Michael looked at his watch. "We need to hurry to the train station, it's getting late. The train will be leaving in an hour."

Sarah misjudged the time. In the end, she was running down the aisles dragging her luggage between the trains, with Michael behind her. She hopped on just as the train began to move while he raised her bags up to her. The doors closed and she looked out the window to wave goodbye. With a sigh, she headed to her coach. She hadn't contacted Vanderhoost and hoped he was on the train. Taking out her ticket, she scanned it to look for the seat number while pulling her stuff behind her.

Vanderhoost was three coaches away. She opened the glass door and fell forward onto a blue sofa-like seat.

"There you are. I thought you missed the train," Vanderhoost said, dropping his newspaper to his lap.

"Really, you would've left without me?" Sarah said, pulling herself upright. Sometimes he infuriated her.

"No, I knew you'd make it," he answered. He got up and hoisted her bags onto the racks over the seats. As he did so, she noticed a man in his early thirties sitting by the window reading a magazine. They exchanged glances. *Damn, I sure made an entrance, didn't I?* Embarrassed, she sat opposite Vanderhoost.

"I can't believe the train was already pulling out," she said, still feeling the stranger's eyes on her. She tried to ignore him. "Are they crazy? It just turned 5:30. I had to run. Talk about punctual."

"Austrians have some of the German precision," Vanderhoost said, and there was a hint of a smile that said it was her own fault. "That's how things run over here."

"I guess, but you could've warned me," Sarah said. She glanced over at the man. He had returned to his reading. *Good!*

Vanderhoost picked his paper up and opened it. "I thought I did, back in Seattle."

"Yea, you did, but not enough," Sarah answered. "Sorry, I should've called or texted."

Vanderhoost went back to reading his paper and they both fell silent for some time. With nothing to do but look out the window, she dug out her brochure of the castle and examined it, but as she did so, she found herself darting looks at the man beside them. He had brown hair, slightly unkempt and a handsome face. A short–sleeved shirt and a brown vest clung to a lean athletic body. His grey trousers had seen a lot of wear, along with his brown scuffed shoes.

Who wears vests in summer?

Suddenly, the man looked up and caught her staring at him. "Excuse me, but where are you from?" he asked.

"I'm, we're from Seattle, Washington, you know, America," Sarah said, quickly correcting herself.

"Felix Greundlar." He offered his hand.

Since they were going to be traveling for two hours with the man, she supposed they should be friendly. Sarah slipped her hand into his, and felt her body stir. "Pleased to meet you. Sarah Lilienthal and this is my colleague, Arnborn Vanderhoost."

"Very nice to meet you," the young man replied as Vanderhoost looked up. The two men acknowledged each other and everyone fell quiet for a minute. Finally, Felix said, "Lilienthal, that's a Jewish name, right?"

Sarah smiled and baring a toothy smile, said, "Why yes, yes it is." With her chin in the air, she leaned forward saying, "My grandfather was born here and left just in time before the Nazis murdered the rest of his family.'"

The man looked down, his cheeks reddening. Obviously, he knew he had stepped in it and was at loss for words. Finally, he looked up. "Oh, I'm sorry. I didn't mean that the way it came out."

"Let's not interrupt your reading," Vanderhoost said to the man, ending the uncomfortable conversation. He gave Sarah one of his signature looks: 'What the hell?'

For once, Sarah was glad for his abrupt manner. She folded her brochure, stuck it in her bag and went back to looking out of the window. They were heading out the city now and the industrial buildings that passed by were covered in soot; ugly compared to the rest of the city. *Probably built by the Nazis.*

An hour later, they were speeding by pastures and an occasional riotous field of wild flowers.

Here and there, hedgerows of ash and poplar sprung up along with a rangy willow. It was like moving postcards; quaint towns, farmhouses, vineyards and churches everywhere. It all looked like a Norman Rockwell painting - kept up, clean and perfect.

The pace of the train with its rocking back and forth made her sleepy. She looked over at Vanderhoost who was already dozing. Felix was reading his magazine, and hadn't engaged in any way with them since Vanderhoost cut him off. She closed her eyes and let sleep overtake her again.

She was alone in a church, crying into her hands. The wooden bench she was kneeling on hurt her knees. Why her? Why did God take her mommy away? She was so angry at God. And then she felt a hand on her shoulder. She looked up and there he was; Father Holden smiling — no, smirking- down at her.

She opened her eyes with a start and caught Felix looking

at her. They locked eyes before he quickly averted his glance out the window.

"We're almost in Graz," he said, not looking back.

There was something in the way he said it that made her anxious. She tucked her hands behind her elbows, then drew her bag up into her lap as she watched him fold his magazine in half and stand. Taking down his small suitcase, he said, "*Wiedersehen.*"

"Bye," she mumbled as he hurried past her out of the partition, wondering if he meant good-bye for good or see you around. She didn't know hardly any German but she knew *Wiedersehen* could go either way. She turned to Vanderhoost. "Wake up. We need to get ready, we're in Graz."

Vanderhoost stirred, straightened his glasses, which had slid down his nose, and got up. Grabbing their bags, he led the way off the train with Sarah following behind. As they went through the terminal, she looked down at her sleek black EcoWatch, noting that they had plenty of time to make their connection to the tram into the city.

"There's the tram we need," Vanderhoost said, ten minutes later.

The narrow streets of Graz were swarming with bicyclists and cars interweaving with the tram. People sat outside at restaurants eating and drinking. Flowers hung from boxes in almost every window of the four-and five-story stone buildings.

"What were you talking about?" Sarah said to Vanderhoost. He was talking in German with a woman beside them.

"The tram is running a little behind schedule, so I asked her if we'll be able to make the bus transfer to Riegersburg on time. She assures me we will." Vanderhoost said. The tram stopped every two blocks, letting a constant flow of passengers in and out.

"Are you sure?" Sarah asked.

"Yes, she is very sure."

Sarah's body buzzed with anticipation and she let out a whoop.

When passengers looked back at her, Vanderhoost frowned. "Shush. You'll make us look like idiot Americans." He pointed out the window ahead. "See, it's right across from the tram stop. We'll be fine."

"This city is so alive. Look at all those people over there," Sarah said as the tram sped by a huge outdoor farmers' market. "I wonder if I can talk Brian into letting us stay a few days more after Riegersburg, to check out this city."

"Good luck with that," Vanderhoost said as the tram slowed down.

People got off at a huge plaza with a large stone building on one side.

"This is the city's central square. That big building over there is city hall; *Rathaus*," Vanderhoost said, and looked up from the city guide map he'd bought at the train station. "Look back and up to your left as we leave. You'll see the *Uhrturm*." He pointed through the window to what looked like a huge clock.

Sarah gasped in delight, punching his arm. "Mr. Know-It–All. What would I do without you?" She giggled as he shrugged.

Vanderhoost moved towards the exit door. "Come. Next stop is where we need to get off."

She followed him, trying not to bump into people as she went. "Excuse me. Sorry. I'm so excited! When did you get so good at directions?" she joked.

"Well, it's obvious; we're traveling in a country where I understand the language," he answered with a smile.

The tram came to another town square where trams were coming in from all four directions. When it came to a stop, the doors swung open and Vanderhoost sprang ahead into a crowd. She ran after him with her camera bag bouncing, dragging her suitcase by the handle. Looking both ways at the corner, she darted to the bus with Riegersburg in bold letters on the front. She stepped up into it behind Vanderhoost, who was paying the conductor for their ride. Chest heaving and out of breath, she put her luggage on the seats behind them and sat, hardly believing she'd be at the fortress in an hour.

Chapter Nineteen

The road to Riegersburg Castle

Sarah rubbed the moisture off the foggy windows, disappointed not being able to glimpse more. What she could see through the rain looked like a moving painting of neatly set apart stucco farm houses, fruit orchards and dense forests with dark green deciduous trees. The landscape reminded her of upstate New York. The bus rocked back and forth on a small, winding road, which was so narrow at times she worried they wouldn't make the curve without hitting oncoming traffic. A few older women and a couple of teen-age boys who didn't seem perturbed, were texting on their phones or sleeping. The bus stopped at every little town along the way, annoying Sarah because she wanted to be in Riegersburg already.

"Did you know Riegersburg was never conquered in all its eight hundred and fifty years? Not even by the Turks," Vanderhoost said while reading his guidebook. "It's considered to have the strongest fortification of the Occident."

The bus jolted to one side during a sharp bend and he accidently bumped into her shoulder. "Sorry," Vanderhoost said.

Sarah groaned as he closed his book and fiddled with his glasses. She reached over and picked up the book on his lap.

"What would we do without this? It's you who always helps us out of sticky situations. Remember the time we got lost in Thailand on the train and got off at the wrong station. You had the map memorized."

"Exactly. One should be informed about every assignment," Vanderhoost said, defensively grabbing his book back. "I accept your apology, despite your bitchiness, because I know you like dragging me around the world."

"Let's talk more about the castle over dinner when we get there, OK?" Sarah opened her backpack. Reaching in, she pulled out a few balls wrapped in golden foil and offered him one. "Want one? I bought them in Vienna."

"Of course! You know I love chocolate, especially Mozart kugels," Vanderhoost said and plopped one into his mouth.

The sun peaked out from behind the clouds. Mist spiraled up around the bases of trees. Twenty minutes later, it'd stopped raining, leaving the tall grasses wet. She closed her eyes for what seemed a minute until Vanderhoost tapped her arm.

"Look. There it is!"

In the distance, a small castle atop a steep, craggy stone hill rose like a ship riding a large wave. It towered over the surrounding smaller slopes and valleys. The fortress looked as if it was on stage with its own light crew, encircled in a hue of pink and purple haze. Sarah couldn't keep her eyes off it. One side of the fortress rose directly up from a completely vertical drop. Her skin tingled as she watched the orange sunset behind it. She reached over the seat to get her camera, but around the next curve the castle disappeared altogether.

Damn. I'll get opportunities later.

This is where the book's journey began, or so she believed. What was her connection to this castle? She looked at her iPhone anxiously, checking the time and crossed her arms over her chest, squeezing herself tightly. Elisabeth von Galler and Katarina Pauldauf had lived and died here. Why did these two women write the book? Would she be able to find answers about the book's origin, and them? Vanderhoost didn't seem to notice her fidgeting and was reading his guide again.

The bus passed a Marian shrine set back on the roadside leading into a forest path. Its white paint was chipped and cracked. A rosebush wrapped itself around the grate protecting the Mother Mary statue. Next to it was a blue ceramic vase holding dried flowers. A raven was perched on top of it. She shivered, hearing once that ravens were omens for bad luck.

Winding its way up the hill to the town's entrance, the bus pulled up into a big public parking lot behind a stone church.

They were here at last. She stepped out into the warm air with her camera equipment and small rolling suitcase and threw her backpack over her shoulder. She was tired but excited as she waited for Vanderhoost.

"I asked the bus driver about the hotel," he said, marching toward her. "It's only five minutes up the road.

Sarah followed him while he struggled with his luggage through the tightly woven streets of Riegersburg. As they walked, he complained about packing too much stuff. She was busy watching people milling around shop windows and gazing at the trinkets and goods behind the glass.

Finally, they came to *Riegersburgerhof*, located in the center of town and across the street from the foot of a cobblestone road. A gift shop to the left of their lodgings, which showcased wines and liquors in its window, was closed for the day.

Vanderhoost pointed to a sign in the shape of an arrow with *Riegersburger Burg* written in black letters. "Look! That's the road leading up to the castle."

Sarah glanced up the steep road that led to the first gate of the fortress, hoping to catch a glimpse of it. But the castle was obscured by the landscape. "That looks like a long climb," she said.

"The guide here says it's a forty-five minute hike," Vanderhoost said, massaging his right wrist. He nodded toward their hotel. "Let's get inside, I'm starving."

The receptionist showed them to their rooms and let them know dinner was underway. After dropping off her luggage, Sarah made her way back downstairs to the bar. In the adjoining room were many tables covered in white and green-checkered table clothes. Oil paintings of landscapes and farms hung on the rich paneled walls, giving the place a feeling of being time-worn and deep-rooted. A mixture of locals and tourists were dispersed throughout several rooms. Sarah spied Vanderhoost already seated at a rectangular tabletop next to a massive green tiled fixture of some sort. It looked like a very large oven.

Sarah slid in onto a bench next to him and tapped the fixture. "What's this?"

"It's called a *Kacheloffen,*" Vanderhoost said without looking up from his menu. "They use it to heat the rooms, and it's used as a stove, also. Back before electricity they'd bake breads in it as well as use it for heating."

"What would I do without you?" Sarah said and picked up her menu, which was written in German and English. "Anything look good?"

"It's all good."

"Okay, then can you recommend something?" she said as a pretty waitress came to their table. Vanderhoost rolled his eyes and recommended the trout with potatoes and a green salad.

Ten minutes later the food was served.

"What's the black stuff on my salad?" Sarah took a bite of the fish. It was flaky and melted in her mouth. "Yum."

"Oh, pumpkin seed oil; a Styrian specialty. Try it, you'll like it," Vanderhoost said. "We have an appointment with the castle's manager at 8:30 a.m. tomorrow. After that we'll get to see the exhibitions and rooms of the castle. The owners, the Hohenburgs, are out of town."

"Great, I can't wait," Sarah said and tried a tomato dripping with oil that tasted nutty and rich.

"He's a busy man, but we're lucky," Vanderhoost continued. "I need to ask him for some extra time for an interview and see if we can look at the dungeons. They're generally closed to the public."

"After that, we meet the bishop, right?" Sarah said and yawned. "I think I need to get to bed. I'm exhausted."

"Yes, remind me to ask them, tomorrow. We'll also want to look at their records of the witch-hunts." Vanderhoost said, and called the waitress over to pay the bill.

Sarah tossed and turned, only to wake up at 4:30 a.m. She pulled herself out of bed and took a warm shower. After dressing for the day, she lay back down to think about the day ahead, trying to visualize the castle. As she did so, her jet lag caught up with her and she finally fell asleep.

A loud knock at the door woke her up.

Vanderhoost's raised voice came through the door, "Sarah, I've been waiting at breakfast for thirty minutes. Hurry up or we'll be late."

Sarah lurched forward, dazed, then shuddered. She glanced at the clock and jumped out of bed, grabbed her camera bag, jacket and opened the door.

"Sorry, I dozed off. Anyway, I'm ready," she said, following him downstairs to the breakfast room. After a strong cup of coffee and wolfing down a couple pastries, cheeses and meats, she felt better.

"Come on, let's go," Vanderhoost said.

Outside, it was drizzling again. Sarah wore her hiking boots and a dark blue rain-coat. Vanderhoost had his long black umbrella under his arm as they made their way across the street to the road leading up to Riegersburg.

The road was steep, but Sarah was used to hiking and kept a fast pace. Vanderhoost panted behind her. By the time they reached the first archway leading to castle, Vanderhoost was almost wheezing. Sarah stopped to give him a rest and to take a few shots of the surrounding countryside as he caught his breath.

"This impressive piece is called the *Wenzeltor*, after the Baroness's maiden name," he said, placing a hand on his hip. Sarah looked up at the imposing stone building with its entrance arch in the middle.

Elisabeth von Galler must have been full of herself, Sarah thought, and started off again. Soon after, they were marching alongside a shoulder-high barricade with thin gaps on their right and a stone wall on the left. Sarah stopped and peered through the slits of the barricade, observing snippets of the surrounding hilly land.

"That's how they kept the Turkish army at bay," Vanderhoost said, joining her. He put his hand through one of the spaces giving her a run-down on how the men of the fortress used the openings to not only fire their arrows at the enemy but also use them as a shield.

Before long, they arrived at an algae-covered pond with a sickly lime color, giving off a pungent odor. Small hawthorn trees hung over its banks. She pinched her nose. "It smells putrid."

"It's probably used as a wastewater pond," Vanderhoost put in.

Sarah waved her hand, and turning away, strode ahead toward a large gnarled oak to the right of the next gate, which Vanderhoost called the *Pyramidentor.* "Oh, look, a monarch butterfly!" She watched it flutter around one of the branches of the tree and took a picture. "When I was a little girl, there was a field behind our house. Every summer the Monarchs would return and I'd go out to watch them." She sat on the bench encircling the tree. Vanderhoost joined her and they spent a few minutes in silence, looking around and gathering their strength for the last of the uphill climb.

Awhile later, Sarah started off and discovered an extensive oval field surrounded by yet another stone wall far above the smelly pool. This one was barely three feet tall.

"Let's check this out," Sarah said and ran through an opening onto the mowed grass. It was a huge field under the full view of the castle. She reached the edge of an outlying barrier and looked down. "Come look, my god, it's a straight drop," Sarah cried. Vanderhoost puffed his way over to her and wiped the sweat from his brow with a handkerchief.

"Spectacular! Look at the view. You can see for miles," he said. His chest was heaving as he tried to catch his breath. She turned to look at a vineyard farther up beyond the field. Clumps of light green grapes hung abundantly on the vines. The vineyard spread past the wall and up a gentler incline to the fortress itself. It was magnificent. The sun was peeking through the clouds and it had stopped sprinkling a little while ago.

She took out her camera— the eye to her world—and zoomed in and out all around the castle taking shots. She loved the way it fit into her hands.

"Hey, we're late," Vanderhoost said. "Take pictures later."

Sarah turned to him as he went about adjusting his eyeglasses and then took off again, not slowing down her pace toward the looming castle ahead. She came up to the outer wall of the keep where giant wooden double doors stood open and entered the outer section of the castle. She turned back to Vanderhoost with her hands on her hips as he came puffing up behind her.

"Hold on, Sarah. Before we can visit the castle we need to find the office," he said and pointed. "There it is, to the left on the second floor."

A sign hung outside a green door. They went inside to inquire about the manager, and found out Mr. Hammer was already in the inner courtyard next to the well, waiting for them. They just needed to walk over the drawbridge located above the keep's moat to find him. She followed Vanderhoost over the wooden overpass and looked down at the moat. To her surprise, she saw it was filled with grass. The walls of the castle extended straight up to the lofty tower.

Vanderhoost took off his jacket, drank from his water bottle and marched through yet another door into an inner courtyard with Sarah following him.

"*Grüss Gott.*" A man said, who was standing next to an ornately fashioned metal structure, came forward with an outstretched hand. "I'm Mr. Hammer."

The Austrian's accent was thick, and his long nose was sharp in his angular face. He wore a dark green and grey jacket on his medium built body, and a white shirt - ironed meticulously. The thin red tie he wore contrasted sharply with his green pants and matching jacket. The jacket buttons were made of what looked like bone.

"Nice to meet you. I'm Arnborn Vanderhoost, and this is Sarah Lilienthal from the "The Seattle Times," Vanderhoost said and shook the other man's hand. Mr. Hammer reached for Sarah's hand. Hesitating, Sarah complied but found his grip too firm for her liking.

"We're very pleased the Hohenburgs agreed to let us do a piece on their castle and the witch trials," Vanderhoost said.

Sarah nodded, then wandered off a few steps away to take more pictures of the complex metalwork over the well.

"The Hohenburgs are out of town as you know. They extend their apologies to you both and have placed you under my care. They were very pleased to have your magazine do an article about our castle.

While we're well known here in Austria, we're not known so much around the world. I hope I can answer your questions about the *Burg*. However, Mr. Vanderhoost, just curious, how did your magazine decide upon us?" he said as he glanced at Sarah who had stopped her picture-taking and was watching the men talk.

"Well, Sarah stumbled on the theme, and she's generally good at finding interesting stories," Vanderhoost answered.

"I see. We're excited about the coverage. Let's start with our new exhibition. I'm sure you'll both find it of great interest. It's called "Witches and Sorcerers," Mr. Hammer said, motioning them to follow him through a small door and up three flights of steps into a room set up for a witch's trial.

The room was divided into two parts by a long wooden barrier. There was a long row of shelves with books at the back. A mannequin of a man was seated at a wooden desk, his wig a bit lop-sided. Another man standing at his side with a life-sized statue of a woman in shackles who was leaning on the railing in front of them. The unsettling part for Sarah was that the figures didn't have faces. Then she saw why. In the corner of the room was a large metal casket behind the woman with spikes inside its walls. There, a face of a woman had been pounded into it.

Sarah put her hand to her mouth in disgust and looked away.

"That's the iron maiden, a torture device," Mr. Hammer said eyeing her and guessing her unsaid question. "The inquisitors used it to force confessions." Sarah shuddered at the thought of sitting in it.

"The man seated at the table would be Johann Purgstall, who presided as the judge. He was also the Elisabeth von Galler's son-in-law.

The accused woman behind the fence is the *Blumenhexe,* Katharina Pauldauf. They said she could bring flowers to bloom in winter. Sad to say, they executed her... well, burned her at the stake," Mr. Hammer said as a matter of course as he stared at Sarah.

Why was he staring at her? Sarah wondered. She recoiled from the very thought of living back then when situations were so dangerous for women. And the fact that Katharina Pauldauf, who wrote her book, was executed made Sarah's stomach turn. Despite her discomfort, she forced herself to pay close attention as Mr. Hammer continued with the details of the trials, and of the witch craze that had plagued central Europe, while Vanderhoost quietly took notes on his iPad. When it was all said and done with, it disturbed her that the castle's owners charged people money to see an exhibition about these atrocious crimes of the past.

"No worries, Miss Lilienthal, we do not support such barbaric ways for a long time here in Austria," Mr. Hammer said, and smiled, motioning them to follow him into the next room.

Is he trying to be funny?

They went through a few more chambers showing pictures of the trials, facts on the history of the witch-hunts, and an original portrait of Katharina Pauldauf. Although it was warm outside, the castle was cold inside. Sarah developed goose bumps on her arms. She gazed at the painting, mesmerized. The maid was holding a delicate bouquet of flowers and was wearing a black and white lacy dress with a head covering of the same colors. The woman, in repose with her hand on a marble topped table, was perhaps middle-aged. Not a stunning beauty by any means, but what she lacked in looks was made up by her eyes, which gave the impression she was someone who knew her mind.

As Sarah stared at the woman's steely blue eyes, she felt a warning in her heart. A chill ran down her back so she pulled herself away and caught up to the men in the next room.

"This is the Knight's Hall." Hammer said, waving his hand over his head.

The voluminous room had an armory, shields and weapons hung on the walls that drew up to a towering coffered wood ceiling. A pair of large carved oak doors was at the far end beyond the long dinner table. Life-size figures were seated at it and were in the process of merry-making and eating. Sarah snapped a few pictures of as many objects as she could as they moved through the hall and headed for the Baroness' chamber room.

When they pushed back the door into the woman's bedroom, Sarah studied the large canopy bed and a long table draped with a red cloth. Over the mantelpiece, hung a shield with two doves and two swords. Opposite the bed was an open window. Curious, she ran over to peer out of it, and to her surprise, she looked straight down at a rocky cliff. She flinched and stepped backwards.

"Be careful. That shouldn't have been open," Mr. Hammer said, raising his voice. He walked over and promptly shut it by turning the latch securely into place.

"No wonder this castle was never taken," Sarah said.

Vanderhoost came beside her and looked out the closed window then scribbled into his notebook.

"We're very proud of that fact," Mr. Hammer said, and went on to explain about the Baroness, whom they called *Schlimme Liesel*, "Bad Lizzie."

"She was head-strong and opinionated for her time, which is probably why she was married three times." He laughed. "She battled the Turkish army and won!"

Vanderhoost nodded at Sarah.

Afterwards, he showed them an enormous empty hall influenced by the Baroque style of the time. On one of its vast white walls was a life-sized portrait of the Baroness.

So, this is Elisabeth von Galler. I wonder what kind of woman she really was? Sarah thought, scrutinizing the daunting facial expression looking back at her. She wasn't a very attractive woman even though the woman wore a welcoming smile. But it was her attire that made Sarah even more curious. It didn't seem all that different than Katarina's, which she'd seen earlier.

Mr. Hammer walked towards a small door on the far side of the room. As they followed him, their footsteps echoed on the polish floors. "This is the dance hall where Elisabeth von Galler entertained lavish social gatherings," he said.

Sarah felt chilly in her shorts and T-shirt, wondering how much longer the tour would last.

"Miss Lilienthal and Mr. Vanderhoost, the Hohenburgs will need to review the photographs and, of course, the article before they go to print," Mr. Hammer said when they came to the end of their tour. "You understand, I'm sure, seeing that Riegersburg is a private estate. Your office's lawyers have already looked over the documents our lawyer drew up, giving your magazine the rights to publish. Please come this way to my office where you both can sign some waivers."

Mr. Hammer led them outside to the courtyard and over the drawbridge to another smaller courtyard. "My office is up on the second floor of what used to be the Watch House, or Guard's rooms," he said.

They followed him a flight of stairs into a small cramped room where he beckoned them to have a seat. He pulled a folder off the stack of papers on his old wooden desk and slid the waiver document in front of her. "Your signature is required near the bottom. It's marked with a red sticky."

Sarah perused the document, and satisfied she wasn't putting the magazine in a libelous situation, signed the paper. Looking up, she caught Mr. Hammer looking at her strangely again.

Sarah and Vanderhoost made their way down the road, passing under the broad archways. As they went past the large grassy field, she wondered if the Lords of Riegersburg had conducted medieval tournaments on it and she half expected Vanderhoost to be launching into a long lecture in his continuing effort to educate her. But he was quiet. This was unlike him, and while she liked it, it left her uneasy.

They made it back to the hotel, passing two-storied homes and conjoined storefronts in a rainbow of pastel colors. Almost every window was decorated with boxes full of pretty, colorful flowers. Tourists milled about in khaki designer shorts and polo shirts or sat casually eating outside at tables under large sun umbrellas. But Sarah was still fighting jet lag and the sun beating down on her in full force wasn't helping. She told Vanderhoost she was going to skip lunch and take a short nap.

Sarah sipped the strong bitter expresso; feeling refreshed after her nap, and said, "What did you think of the castle?"

Vanderhoost, sitting across from her on the hotel's terrace, said, "The fortress is splendid and the mystery of the place intriguing. Mr. Hammer was very gracious, I thought, today." He nibbled on a small pie oozing with cherry filling.

"I thought he was a jerk! Condescending, I didn't like him." Sarah wished she'd ordered a tart as well. "I felt like he was looking down on us because we're Americans and we're stupid or something." She swatted at a fly buzzing around her food. "And he stared at me all the time."

"Really? He's just stiff and they don't avoid gazes here. That's European, well, German, I mean Austrian. Don't worry; I'll handle him in the future. What are you up to this afternoon?" Vanderhoost said, and finished his pastry with a smack of his lips, looking pleased with himself.

"I think I'm going to wander around the town, take some more pictures," Sarah said. She couldn't wait to get out on her own and explore. "What about you?"

"Well, I was hoping to interview the family, but that's not going to happen. There are other employees, however, that I could get together with. Also, I'm going to look over the agreement this afternoon and call Brian." Vanderhoost said. He took a sip of his cappuccino.

Sarah nodded. "Well, I'm off. Have fun!" She jumped up, snatched her camera case from the back of her chair, and ran down the steps towards the road.

Later, after taking pictures of specialty shops, tiny alleyways and quaint houses, Sarah found herself on the outskirts of town. There was a building across the street with two giant lion-faced door-knockers on its iron gate. Feeling a compulsion to find out what was behind the gated door, she went to it and heaved on one of the door's metal rings. Yanking it open, she discovered a garden behind the entranceway. She lingered on the threshold for a moment.

A statue of Mary stood in the center of an otherwise empty garden, save for a stone bench directly opposite the statue. Mary's lovely face was humble and peaceful and her arms were spread apart, palms open as if welcoming her to come in. At the statue's feet were the figures of a dove, lion and a deer. A ring of multi-colored roses was positioned around the statue, giving the impression of protection, as if the roses were keeping people away. Sarah pulled the camera strap up over her head and set her heavy camera on the bench and sat. The air was still here, bees and insects were buzzing in the roses. She leaned back and closed her eyes, enjoying the peace.

"Miss Lilienthal, it's you, isn't it?"

She looked up startled to see a man coming from behind

the bench. To her surprise, it was the man on the train-ride from Vienna to Graz. Only now he wore a brown robe which blended with his full head of curly brown hair. He stood in front of her, looking down. He was better looking than she remembered.

"You remembered my name," Sarah said to him with a forced laugh, feeling awkward around him. She got up, intending to leave, but didn't want to appear rude or give him the impression she was anxious. "I'm sorry, but I don't remember yours."

"Felix, Felix Gruendlar," he said. His voice was pleasant and reassuring. "Please don't go. I don't want to scare you away from our garden. What are you doing in Riegersburg?"

"I'm here on assignment from my magazine taking pictures. I'm a photographer, as if you couldn't tell," she said, dragging her camera off the bench. "Anyway, I'm traveling with my colleague, Vanderhoost, the short guy you met on the train. He's a journalist." She considered him, wondering if he was a monk. "So, are you a priest or something?" she said, crossing her arms in front of her, legs apart.

"Not yet. And I live here, actually. I'm studying at the seminary." Felix said quietly as his warm dark brown eyes swept over her. Her body tingled uncomfortably.

Sarah smiled, covering her mouth with her hand. "I never would've guessed that on the train."

Felix sat on the bench then looked away from her, bending forward with his hands on his knees as if he were unhappy, then turned back to her. "Well, that's easy to understand," he said. "I was a gymnasium teacher, English, actually, so old habits die hard. Anyway, I wanted to do something more meaningful with my life, so here I am."

"And so, you are. I don't meet very many guys who want to be priests back home," Sarah said, shoving her hands in her pockets. She wondered how to politely excuse herself as he went on telling her about his aspirations of working with the less fortunate. Finally, she said, "Well, I should be getting back to the hotel. Vanderhoost will have a fit if I don't show up for dinner on time."

"It was very nice to see you again." Felix said and reached his hand out toward her.

She hesitated at first, but shook his hand because this seemed to be the customary thing to do. His hand felt warm and soft in hers and a strong sensation of attraction ran through her again. She felt herself flush and hoped he didn't realize her reaction. *I've got to get out of here.* "Well, good-bye," she said, and left him sitting on the bench.

Back in her hotel room, Sarah flopped onto the bed. She was confused about the attraction she felt to this man. *A priest, no less.* She hadn't been in a relationship with a man for close to three years. Her therapist attributed the lack of staying connected to a lover or a partner to the trauma of her mother's death. She left relationships before she could be hurt, often hurting the people she loved and who had loved her back.

She sighed and tried to put Felix out of her mind. Besides, she had work to do. She took Oma's book out of her suitcase and flipped it open to the beginning. Grabbing a dictionary, she went about deciphering the words using a reference book that showed her the equivalent letters to *Kurent* in modern German. Translating each word to English using Google Translate, she wrote them into her spiral notebook. But the sentences didn't make sense. After struggling with it for the better part of an hour, she slammed her pen on the desk and pushed back in her chair. *This is ridiculous. It's going to take me forever to learn the meanings hidden in this book. Oma, why do you really want me to learn all this?* She sighed. *Maybe I should enlist Vanderhoost's help.*

She wrapped the book up hastily, and left it on the night table. Locking the door behind her, she rushed downstairs to dinner.

Chapter Twenty
The Next Day —

Sarah and Vanderhoost walked to St. Martin's Church. Its origins went back to the 1400's, where it was originally a Magdalena Chapel. Actually, the place was even older than the Middle Ages, with the new structure built right on top of an ancient ruin.

Its doors were open, letting in the warmth from the outside, and Father Baumgartner stood at the end of the polished stone aisle by the central altar depicting the tale of St. Martin and the goose. The colorful, lead-glass windows from the 1950s were in stark contrast to the stone reliefs of Christ's Stations of the Cross.

"Fräulein Lilienthal and Mr. Vanderhoost, welcome," the bishop said as he strode toward them. He was dressed in a long black cassock robe. A tall man in his mid-fifties, he had aquiline features and a square jaw line. Sarah found him rather attractive.

"Thanks for meeting with us, Father. I'm Arnborn, and this is Sarah, my associate," Vanderhoost said, shaking Baumgartner's hand.

Sarah decided to stand back from the men and wait her turn. After Vanderhoost stepped back, she came forward and after greeting him, said, "May I take picture of you in front of the altar?" Sarah asked, noting the light was perfectly cast through the windows.

"Sure," the priest replied. Sarah snapped a few quick shots of the bishop who held himself rigid, which was usual for subjects who were unused to having a professional photographing them.

"Relax, Father," she said. "We don't want you to look scared."

Baumgartner smiled. "No, we don't. How's this?" He let his shoulder down, rested a hand on the altar and faced the camera.

"That's great," she said, and snapped a few more shots.

"I'm not used to being the man of the hour," Baumgartner said after she lowered her camera. "Anyway, shall we?" He waved his hand toward the side door of the apse and down a long corridor with tall arched windows. On her right she saw the garden where she'd sat the day before and, on the left, she spied a large, overgrown herb garden. At the end of the corridor was his office.

"I noticed you were looking at our garden. It's fallen into an untidy mess, I'm afraid," he said, taking a seat behind his large wooden desk piled high with papers and more than a few books. "But with the dwindling staff and fewer men seeking the way of the cloth these days, we don't have the time to devote to the upkeep of the seminary as we used to."

Sarah pieced together what he said in his thick Austrian accent as he leaned back into his leather chair. He glanced back at the wooden cross behind him on a wall between two long windows, then looked at them with his head tilted.

"How can I be of service to you?"

"We would like to ask your permission to have a look at the church records dealing with the witch trials of Riegersburg." Vanderhoost asked.

"Of course," the bishop answered. He leaned forward, folding his hands in front of him. "Do you speak German? It would be much easier for me if I didn't have to use English."

Vanderhoost nodded and switched to German. Sarah observed a small figurine of the Virgin Mary on the bishop's desk. Beside it was a miniature golden chalice.

As the two men spoke, Baumgartner glanced at Sarah, who was checking her cell phone, more than a few times. By the time they were finished, Sarah felt uncomfortable on top of growing impatient; she tapped her finger tips on her thigh. At last, she spoke up. "Excuse me, but could you tell me what you're talking about?"

Both men looked at her in surprise.

"Fräulien Lilienthal, Mr. Vanderhoost was telling me you have relatives in Feldbach?" Baumgartner said. "Perhaps I know them."

"Yes, I do, and I plan on visiting them later this week," she said. "My grandparents were from Burgenland, but had to escape to America during World War II. My Opa was Jewish."

"I see," Baumgartner said, leaning back again. He seemed to be contemplating that in his head, "Well, no matter. Anyway, I'm intrigued about your article. As you know, the theme of it skirts a dark part of our history."

"Well, I hope it's not a problem," Sarah said.

"No, no, not at all," the bishop said and got up. "Anyway, as you can see, I have a lot of work in front of me and I'm sure you're anxious to get to yours. Let me take you to the library where we have the original documents of the trials." As Sarah got up, he eyed her intently. "It's a shame you don't speak German, Miss Lilienthal. It would be so much easier. But I'm sure you will manage just fine, I trust. Follow me," he said, lowering his voice. Did she hear something strange in his voice? He moved quickly ahead of them to the door and ceremoniously held it open for them.

"Not to worry," Sarah said as they entered the hall. "I have Vanderhoost." She patted her partner on the shoulder as the bishop locked the door behind him.

"Of course, you do," he said, and strode ahead of them, making a sharp turn to the right into a sheltered alcove where he stopped in front of an opened door. "This is our library, such as it is."

Sarah stepped into the high-ceilinged room with towering wooden stacks whose shelves were laden with what must have been thousands upon thousands of books. As Sarah canvased the room, she saw a small desk in a far corner of the shadowy library. Behind it sat a man studying a book under a brass lamp that cast a soft golden light. She caught her breath.

"Felix, come. I've some people to introduce you to," Baumgartner said.

The man got up and shuffled over to them. When he came near, his eyes widened with recognition. The bishop darted a glance between Sarah and Felix. At last, he went on, "Felix, this is Fräulein Lilienthal and Mr. Vanderhoost. They're here to do an article on the castle. Please assist them with whatever they need."

Baumgartner looked at his watch, turned to Sarah and smiled graciously again. "And now, if you'll excuse me, I need to attend to a pressing matter."

Sarah's heart raced. *Well Felix, we seem to run into each other a lot. I wonder if that's a sign I should get to know you better?*

"Didn't we meet on the train?" Vanderhoost asked.

"Yes, I was coming from Linz back here to the seminary," Felix said, and cleared his throat.

"What a coincidence, seeing you again! We're researching the witch trials of the 1600's. Can you show us any records the church has?" Sarah said, noticing the acolyte seemed to be deliberately avoiding looking at her. She suppressed the urge to laugh, a habit she had when she was nervous, and willed herself to remain calm.

"Yes, of course Fräulein Lilienthal or is it Frau Lilienthal?" Felix said, and blinked. "I wasn't aware I'd be seeing you again so soon."

"It's Fräulein," Sarah answered, noticing Vanderhoost scrutinizing her. She rubbed the back of her neck, irritated by Felix's question.

"Why so formal? I'm Arnborn, and this is Sarah," Vanderhoost said, and reached out to shake the younger man's hand.

Felix smiled. "Okay, Arnborn and Sarah. Follow me. The records are in the back down this aisle."

They trailed after him into a section of the library that had obviously been unused for years. Sarah caught a faint whiff of vanilla in the air. Felix climbed a rolling ladder and reached for a leather-bound book, and as he did so, dust particles exploded off the shelf and danced in the thin beams of light pouring in from the windows. Over his shoulder, he added, "We have a new temperature control system and a de-humidifier, but these books should really be in a museum."

"How old is this section?" Vanderhoost said calling up.

Felix braced himself on the ladder, opened the book and started leafing through it. Without looking down, he said, "The library, itself, is about two hundred and fifty years old." He came to a page that stopped him. "Ah, I think this is what you're looking for right here. Let's take this ledger back to the front."

Felix descended the ladder and his brown robe swished back and forth. Sarah had to suppress a giggle, but couldn't. They looked funny next to each other; one man short, a bit squat and the other tall and thin.

Vanderhoost frowned.

"She does that when she's nervous," Vanderhoost said in a sharp tone and pinched expression. Ignoring her, the two men strode ahead out of the stacks to broad wooden table piled with books and papers. As they went through the ledgers Felix retrieved, Vanderhoost broke into German, as if to spite her.

But Sarah was having none of it and said, "Care to share?" as she looked over their shoulders.

Vanderhoost scowled a little, and backed away so she could see the book, whose author's handwriting looked just like that in her Oma's book.

"I've a Google translate here, and being proficient in German myself, I'm confident we can make some sense out of this, although, it will take some time," Vanderhoost said taking a dictionary out of his leather bag along with his laptop and a small book.

"Will you be needing any more help?" Felix said, eyeing Sarah.

"Vanderhoost is on top of this, I'm sure." Sarah answered.

"Well then, I'll check in later. I've read up some on the trials, they even executed some priests," Felix said and left the room.

Sarah sat down opposite Vanderhoost at the table as he read, searched the internet and took notes for a few minutes until he looked up at her.

"What's up with him?" he asked, regarding her over his glasses.

Sarah shrugged. "Nothing."

"Really? It looks like something to me, the way he looked at you," he said, rolling his eyes with his shoulder's back.

"Stop, I don't like him, if that's what you mean?" Sarah retorted and sprang up from her chair. "It's none of your business, anyway."

"No need to get huffy," Vanderhoost said. "Someone likes someone."

"No, I don't," Sarah said and decided to explore the rest of the books in the library. She wandered up and down the aisles until she calmed down. What was getting into her lately? She wasn't going to admit she was attracted to Felix. At last she returned to the table.

She pulled a chair up beside him and sat. "Sorry, I'm a little rattled. Do they mention Katharina Pauldauf?"

"Apology accepted, for now, though it's about time you..."

Sarah made a 'cut your throat motion' with her hand.

"OK, I'll stop," he continued and inspected the next page. He rubbed his hands together and said, "They do right there, look. Can you believe they executed over sixty people on grounds of witchcraft in two years? And within the circumference of only fifty miles?" He took off his glasses and sat back in his chair, sighing. "It's not pleasant to read, because it goes into to detail how they tortured the poor accused people, who were mainly women." He leaned forward and pointed out a passage. "For example, here it says they ripped women's breasts off with an iron prong. Truly barbaric!"

"Oh, my God, that's disgusting." Sarah said, feeling sick. "How could they get away with that?"

"The law was different back then. It required a confession of guilt in order to convict the accused, which is illogical to me because anyone would admit to crimes after being tortured like that." Clearly, Vanderhoost was just warming up.

Sarah needed some air. "I think I'm going to take some pictures of the church and garden. I'll be back later."

"And leave me to your dirty work," Vanderhoost said with a snort.

Later that afternoon, when Sarah came to pick him up, he was showing signs of exhaustion, which was apparent in his grumpiness. Sarah knew to keep her mouth shut when he was in a mood, so she waited for him to make the first move. He pushed back from his chair. "I've had enough for one day."

Sarah nodded and they left the documents and ledgers on the table with a note thanking the seminary. Back at the hotel, they had an early dinner, and shortly after, Vanderhoost excused himself, —mumbling about how they would've burned him at the stake back then, too—, and went up to his room to call his partner, Peter. This left Sarah alone and feeling restless, so she went into the inn's tavern.

The bar was empty except for a few local men in Styrian jackets, jeans and wrinkled dress shirts. As she entered the room, they eyed her suspiciously. An awkward silence followed Sarah as she found a seat at the opposite end of the bar. She ordered a glass of wine from the pretty young woman who was tending the place.

"This is a specialty wine of Riegersburg," the woman said, setting her drink in front of Sarah. As she did so, the men standing at the other end of the bar looked away and resumed their conversation. That was good because she didn't feel like being hit on. She took a sip of flowery, light wine that had an herbal aftertaste, and sighed. She felt lonely, and she missed her friends from Seattle. But the thing foremost on her mind was Felix. She couldn't stop thinking of him.

As she pondered what to make of her sudden attraction to the young priest, the sound of a barstool scraping the floor next to her made her jump. "Miss Lilienthal, is this seat free?" Mr. Hammer said, and sat down next to her reeking of cologne. To her chagrin he assumed she wanted company. He ordered a drink and eyed her wine glass. "I see you're a wine connoisseur."

"Not really," Sarah said, keeping her eyes forward.

"Well, we take our wines very seriously in Austria. Our

whites, especially. They are quite unique; you would have to agree?" he said as if there was no argument to be made otherwise.

"Really? I would have never guessed," Sarah said, taking a sip of her wine. She set her glass down and glanced at him. "I assume you come here often?"

"In the evening, after work, before going home to the wife." Mr. Hammer said as the bartender brought his glass of wine to him. He nodded to the men at the end of the bar and raised his glass saying *Broscht*. They replied in kind. "This one is from *Neusiedler See* and is particularly good. Do you drink much wine in America?"

"No, actually, I don't drink much at all." Sarah said.

He leaned towards her conspiratorially. "Lilienthal, that's an Austrian name, you know. Jewish, I believe."

Sarah pasted a smile on, wishing he would disappear. "Yes, my grandparents were from here."

"So, you speak German?" he said, raising his brow.

"No, not really," Sarah answered, shifting her weight on her chair. He made her feel stupid. "My mother spoke it, and I know a few phrases." Do you speak any other languages, Mr. Hammer?"

"I know some French and of course, I speak Hungarian fluently. I'm from Budapest, you know," he said, and looked down at his glass. They sat for a while in silence sipping their wines. The bartender asked if they wanted another round and he asked for another glass, much to Sarah's disappointment.

When they were alone again, Mr. Hammer said, "So, where in Austria were your grandparents from?"

"My grandmother actually grew up not very far from here in Feldbach." Sarah said as he watched her closely. "My grandfather was from Burgenland, and yes, he was Jewish, which was why they had to flee from here. They barely escaped with their lives, no thanks to your country's government at the time."

"My family had nothing to do with the Nazi party," Mr. Hammer said, and shook his head. "The Second World War was devastating on us all, not least of which for the Jews."

There it was, her Jewish descent entering the conversation,

which she half expected by now. She gritted her teeth and dug into her purse for her wallet. "Well, it was nice to see you again. It's been a long day for me, so I need to be getting back to my room."

He motioned to the bartender, said something in German and turned back to Sarah. "Let me pay, I insist."

Sarah considered the offer, wondering if there would be any *quid pro quo* expected in the future. "Well, thanks, much appreciated."

Leaving the tavern, she heard his deep baritone voice call after her. "*Auf wiedersehen*, Fräulein Lilienthal."

Chapter Twenty One

The Next Morning

The sun shone through Sarah's hotel room window, casting a warm glow on her bedspread. She woke with a start, recalling last night's dream of the statue of Mary, the one from the garden at the seminary of St. Martin's. It was alive and walking toward Sarah, with outstretched arms, crying 'Save the child, save the child.' The Mary figure had a beam of light streaming from its heart, with a black cloud trying to engulf it. The rest of the dream eluded her. Sarah fidgeted with the pentagram necklace around her neck, then got out of bed. A shower would help shake off her feeling of being on edge.

Half an hour later, she slid into a chair opposite Vanderhoost, who had two small pieces of white tissue stuck on his freshly shaven face.

"Good morning, I slept awfully, and guess who came to the bar last night?" she said.

"Mr. Hammer," Vanderhoost said without looking up from his newspaper; *Die Zeit.*

"I was going to come in and join you, but I got a call from Peter and went back upstairs. He's always sick when I'm doing overseas assignments. Do you think he's trying to hint to me that I need a desk job?" Vanderhoost said, looking up. Sarah had long stopped being surprised at Vanderhoost; he had a nose for finding things out.

"Yes, Peter told me once he'd like you closer to home but you're one of the best reporters we have," Sarah said, taking a large bite out of her breakfast roll before washing it down with coffee.

"I know I am. And jetlag is becoming a problem, if you know what I mean. No sleep can make a man grouchy," Vanderhoost said.

"I want to show you something after breakfast," she said. He looked up over his reading glasses questioningly. "I can't talk about it down here, but I desperately need your help and opinion. And you are the only person in the world who knows German that I trust completely."

Vanderhoost leaned towards her and crinkled his nose. "Now you have me curious." He tried to get her to tell him her secret over breakfast, but she crossed her arms and changed the subject to his notes about Riegersburg and their story for the magazine, then showed him some of the pictures she'd taken on her camera. "Don't you think the graininess of this image adds to the feel?" It was of the fortress up the hill in the distance and the entranceway surrounded by climbing roses in the foreground.

"Yes, you really caught an interesting angle on this one."

"I'll have to tweak and edit it back in Seattle, of course, but I think I'm onto something."

Back in her room, Sarah put her suitcase on a small table at the end of the bed and pulled out the book from under her clothes. Vanderhoost stood next to the window.

"What is it, why all the secrecy?" he said and sat down next to her. "You usually can't keep anything to yourself, always so transparent, at least to me."

Sarah hesitated. Yes, she was transparent, and it bothered her that she was. At last, she handed him the book.

"Wow, this is heavy and looks ancient." He opened it to the front page and took out his pocket magnifying glass. Moving over to the desk, he set it down and started examining it as she rubbed her palms on her legs.

"Spectacular! This is possibly of great historical significance." He looked back over his shoulder at her. "How did you get this?"

"Go to the end of the book and see whose name is written at the bottom of the page," she said.

He turned the back cover over and scanned the letter fastened to the back page then turned back toward her. "Your grandmother?"

She nodded.

"She gave you the book?" he said, astonished. "Was she a practitioner of the craft? A Wiccan? Really? I remember you telling me she was Catholic?"

"Well, yes, she was, or so I thought," Sarah said and told him the story of Aunt Ursula, and her Oma's premonitions.

He got up, walked back over to the bed and looked her in the eye. "This book, this is why we're here, isn't it?"

Sarah felt her cheeks burning and looked down at her feet, avoiding his gaze. "Yes, well... but Oma forbade me..."

Vanderhoost clapped his hands together. "I knew it! I told Peter, *"There's something more to it than Sarah wanting to come here."* Don't worry, your secret is safe with me. To think you might be like the Mayfair witches, a real Book of Shadows! I did a piece on *Pagans in America* in the early nineties. There are no actual historical Books of Shadows in existence that I know of, so this is amazing. I don't think you realize what you have here. We need to get experts to look this over," he said.

"No. Absolutely not!" Sarah said. "You saw what she said in the letter. I'm not to tell anyone, not even my Aunt Ursula. The only reason I'm showing you is because I can't read German and the *Kurent* is illegible to me. It would take me forever to decipher it. I need your help. Please? Could you translate the first chapter? And promise not to say anything, not even to Peter?" she said, taking his hand and studying his face. "My gut tells me there's something else in Riegersburg, and I need to find out what it is."

"Okay, calm down, you have my word. I can keep secrets, unlike someone I know," Vanderhoost said with a knowing smile and squeezed her hand.

"You're not funny. Swear!" she demanded.

"Okay. Cross my heart and hope to die." He got up and pressed his hands on his upper thighs. "We have to get going. Mr. Hammer is giving us a tour of the dungeons this morning." He moved to the room's door.

Sarah picked up the book and stowed it into her suitcase. "Can you translate some of the pages later this afternoon?" Sarah grabbed his shoulder as they walked out the room.

"Most certainly, Watson at your service. I'll begin decoding today" Vanderhoost smiled. "I can't wait."

An hour later, Mr. Hammer was waiting at the metal well where they had first met him, and was looking at his watch. They were late, and out of breath from the climb.

"No wonder no one could conquer this fortress. The climb up this hill alone would kill them before they got to the top," Sarah said, trying to catch her breath between the words.

Mr. Hammer didn't look amused.

"Come this way and I do not have very much time this morning so let us get started," Mr. Hammer said.

Vanderhoost said something in German which appeased the man, because he nodded and waved them on through a small door on the opposite wall.

"Careful. The steps are narrow and slippery," Mr. Hammer said as they made their way down two flights of stairs into a dark and wet cellar. The electric lights on the walls gave off a yellowish gleam, unnatural and haunting. Sarah touched the cold stones as he led them along the corridor, pointing out the cells and explaining how prisoners were kept in what would be considered atrocious conditions today.

"Here is the cell where they kept *Die Blumenhexe*; Katarina Paldauf. They say she died before they burned her at the stake." Sarah's interest perked up as she followed the two men into a small square room. Otherwise empty, it had a slit on one wall allowing air and sunlight through. Her chest constricted and her muscles tensed. She jumped as Vanderhoost walked past her over to the narrow opening in the wall.

"Very interesting, you can see over the entire countryside

from here," Vanderhoost said. "This dungeon is under the castle, but it must be on the cliff side."

"Yes, so it is. No way to escape as you can see. It's a straight drop outside the window," Mr. Hammer said. "Fräulein Lilienthal and Mr. Vanderhoost, I am so sorry, but I must be going. I have an appointment later this morning. Please follow me back upstairs."

Which was quite all right with Sarah. She couldn't wait to get out of here and she pushed her way past Mr. Hammer into the hallway.

"I'm feeling faint. I want to get out of here," she muttered. Vanderhoost rushed over and took her arm.

"This way," Mr. Hammer said, and he led them back up to the inner courtyard before bidding them a good day.

Sarah took a few minutes to collect herself before joining Vanderhoost to walk back down the castle's main path. With the main castle behind them, the fortress walls cast long shadows out over the surrounding landscape as they passed people walking up the hill.

Vanderhoost stopped at the second archway over the path. "Are you OK?"

"Yes, I think so," Sarah said. "I don't know what happened, but I don't really want to talk."

Vanderhoost nodded and they continued on down. After a time, they came to a wrought iron gate with a sign. "There's a "Bird of Prey" show at 11:00 a.m.," he said, pointing at the sign. "Why don't you go watch it while I go back to the hotel to translate your book?"

Sarah hesitated. "I'm not sure I'm comfortable with that."

But he insisted, saying he needed to be alone and that she'd be a distraction. At last, she reluctantly handed him her hotel room key. "Remember what I said about no one else seeing it."

With her time as her own, she opened the gate and headed toward the "Bird of Prey" show, down a dirt path past large outdoor cages. In one of them was a vulture. Another one had a large white owl, and a few were empty. She paid the entrance fee to a young man standing in front of an outside arena and strode toward a crowd of onlookers seated on semi-circular stones. She took the path to the farthest left side, and there she sat behind a metal guard rail protecting her from falling over the side. Peering over the edge, she saw tiny church steeples, farmsteads, and forests spreading out over the countryside far below, reminding her of a beautiful quilt.

The sound of shouting drew her attention back to the middle of the arena where two men stood dressed in what appeared to be hunting attire. One of them addressed the crowd in German and she wished she could understand what he was saying as the other man went and brought an eagle back with him on his gauntlet. The bird was sent off to fly above the heads of the crowd as the man brought out a falcon wearing a brown leather hood. When he carefully took the hood off the bird, it flew up into the sky.

The other man unleashed a length of coiled rope from his belt and tied a chunk of meat to the end of it. Tossing it in the air, with a broad swirling arc he swung it round and round. Out of nowhere, the falcon came swooping down for it. The falconer parried, and the bird darted back up, disappearing from sight bringing about excited applause from the crowd.

Sarah was mesmerized by the beauty and strength of the well-trained birds as they careened through the warm morning air. Their speed and grace called to something deep and eternal within her. In her childhood, Opa took her every August to the State Fair in Syracuse where there was a "Bird of Prey" show. It was her favorite part of the fair. She felt as though she wanted to fly with them, to be free and fearless. But they were caged like her. She was caught in the past— not able to shake off her mom's suicide— blaming herself though her therapist said otherwise. Now, she was torn between her love of independence and finding love. She wanted to find the balance, but didn't know how to.

The man called down the eagle and as it dove for the meat, she took out her camera. But the person next to her tapped her on the shoulder and told her she needed to put her camera away. They didn't allow free pictures. After the show, she had a picture taken of her with the white owl she liked so much. Perched on one of the trainer's arms next her, the bird tufted its wings and she leaned over to it, feeling the soft feathers on her cheek.

Sarah headed down the stone road back to the hotel, coming to the vineyard on her right, then decided to walk through it. The dark grapes were ripe and appealing. She plucked a few and ate them eagerly, watching to see if anyone saw her. No one stopped her, so she walked towards the huge vertical drop leading straight up to the castle. In the distance, she saw something along the wall, so she took out her camera, zoomed in and discovered there were rock climbers scaling the side. *What were they doing?*

She approached the cliff where she had a better view and saw three of them hanging on their lines. One of them was pointing up to a fourth man standing on a ledge.

Down at the base of the wall, a crowd was watching the whole endeavor, many of them pointing up to the men. Sarah again looked through her camera lens and this time saw a man standing in front of a cave. To the left of it was a narrow rocky trail leading away. She traced it with her lens and quickly discovered it was leading back to where she was standing. This cave was something she was determined to find out about later. Right now, she hastened back down the road, curious to find out what Vanderhoost might have deciphered from her Oma's book.

Sarah pushed the door open to her hotel room.

"Guess what I saw today? Some rock climbers were…" She frowned. Vanderhoost wasn't there.

Maybe he was napping again, so she went next door to his room. When she knocked on his door, it cracked open. "Vanderhoost, you in here?" she said, stepping into the darkened room. She panned the room, saw the made bed and his suitcase over by the window. Where could he have gone? And then it hit her. Did he have her book with him? She ran back to her room again. Her suitcase lay open on the floor beside the bed. *He took my book…without asking me! What the hell?* She balled her hands together nervously. He would never leave his room unlocked while he was away. Her heart thumped rapidly. Had someone interrupted him or worse?

She plopped down on her bed, trying to think about what to do next and as she did so, saw that her waste paper basket next to the desk was overturned. Vanderhoost's magnifying glass lay next to it on the floor. She jumped up and ran over to pick the lens up and as she bent down, saw a crumpled sheet of paper next to the basket with his handwriting. She snatched it up, pressed the wrinkles and creases out of it and started reading:

"To the Faith-Keepers of the future, there was a time when She, Our Mother, the Lady of Light, ruled along with her consort, the Green God of the Hunt. She had many names, Cerridwen, Astarte, Inanna, Artemis and many more. The Tree of Life was Her holy symbol as life itself her body. Beware truth-seeker for your knowledge of this may cost you your life and those you love. All acts of love and courage are in Her name. Be free of slavery of any kind. These secrets and wisdom of our ancient ways are passed down from the high priestess to her daughter. The circle of life is open to all initiated in her path and ways of the craft…"

Sarah stopped reading. She was absolutely dumbfounded, wondering what it all that meant. But right now, she had to find Vanderhoost, so she put the paper aside and ran downstairs to the receptionist to ask her if they'd seen him. They hadn't seen him since lunch.

"Call the police!" Sarah said in a rush. "Someone broke into our rooms and my associate is missing." She felt the rising panic threaten to overcome her and she ran back upstairs, calling Vanderhoost's cell phone only to hear it ringing from his room. She ran into his suite and followed the sound to his jacket hanging on the chair. As she did so, she heard a voice behind her.

"Hello, Miss Lilienthal? I'm Mr. Oberwald, the hotel

manager. Is there something wrong? Can we be of some help?" he said as she turned around to see him march into the room.

"Yes, there's something wrong. My colleague is missing!"

"For how long?" Mr. Oberwald said.

"I don't know. I was out and when I came back, he wasn't here and the door was ajar."

"The door does latch a bit hard," the man said. "Perhaps when he went out, it didn't pull shut all the way."

Sarah shook her head. "He'd never go anywhere without his jacket or his phone. You need to call the police," she said.

Mr. Oberwald arched his brow. "Surely, he is just out for a walk, Miss Lilienthal."

Sarah shook her head and then grabbed his forearm.

"No, you don't get it," Sarah snapped. "Look, if you don't call the police, I will."

"Very well, I'll see what I can do," he said, rolling his eyes. "I make no promises though. The police will want more than what you're telling me to open up a search." He bid her a curt good-bye and left the room.

Sarah raked her fingers through her hair, frustrated and worried about Vanderhoost. And if that wasn't bad enough, she'd lost a book that had been kept safe for centuries.

Chapter Twenty Two

An Hour Later

Sarah sat across from Police chief Gruendler with her arms crossed, biting her lower lip. He stood next to the large window of his sparsely furnished office looking out at an empty parking lot. A police officer dressed in a green and grey suit knocked on the door, came in and went over to whisper something into his commanding officer's ear. Chief Gruendler frowned and looked over at Sarah about to say something but decided instead to sit down on his grey metal chair.

"Apparently my son is here," Chief Gruendler stated. *I did recognize the last name. To think his father is a cop.* Felix hastened into the room and shook his father's hand. *Why were they so formal?* Her mind raced as the older man motioned Felix to take a chair next to Sarah. *How did he find out?* Sarah thought noticing the startling resemblance between father and son, each having the same thin nose and square jawline.

"Papa, I'm sorry to interrupt, but word travels quickly in a small town. I heard Mr. Vanderhoost went missing." Felix said, gazing over to her. "I wanted to be of some help to Fräulien Lilienthal."

"You never mentioned it to me." Chief Gruendler said, his face reddening. "I didn't know you knew her and the reporter,"

Sarah fidgeted with her fingers, getting impatient.

Felix looked past his father, avoiding eye contact. "We met on the train from Graz to Riegersburg," Felix said, his words tumbling out. "Then two days ago, they showed up at the cathedral library to do some research for their magazine."

"I see. Well, you can't help the police, and for that matter,

I've been trying to convince Fräulien Lilienthal it's too soon to search for a grown man who is, as far as I know, only went missing two hours ago. Please escort her back to the hotel because she is clearly upset," Chief Greundlar said.

Sarah jolted up. "My friend wouldn't go off without telling me. And for that matter, leave his iPhone behind. Never! And another thing: don't presume to tell me how I feel," Sarah snapped at them. *How rude of him to talk as if I wasn't there! What is it with these European men?*

"We have this matter under control. Two of my officers will be sent immediately to search for him if we find there is merit for it. Right now, we have to follow protocol."

"Meaning?" Sarah growled.

"Meaning: if your colleague doesn't show up at the hotel within twenty-four hours, come back and we'll file a missing person's report and contact your embassy. Call me tomorrow," Chief Greundlar said, and rang for his officer to take them away.

Sarah was beside herself and shook her head. "Really!" she said, after jumping out of her chair and marched out of the office with Felix clambering to follow her out.

"Wait," Felix called out from behind her, but she bounded down the stairway of the police station and out into the cool evening. She took a deep breath, trying to collect herself, then turned and walked briskly towards the hotel.

When Felix caught up to her, he grabbed her arm before she could climb the stairs of the hotel, and said, "I want to help," he insisted.

"Are you following me?" Sarah said, facing him and pulled her arm way. "How is it you always seem to turn up?"

Felix stared back and shook his head. "Of course not. Like I said it's a small town and I asked for you first at the hotel. The front clerk told me you were at the police station. You can trust me."

Sarah sighed and looked up at the flapping flags hanging from the rafters. One was the red and white Austrian flag, the other was a green one with a lion representing the *Steiermark*. She didn't know what to do and she was worried about Vanderhoost. Maybe they were right. Everything seemed picturesque and peaceful. Why did she feel such foreboding? Her stomach was in knots. She looked back at him, wrapping her arms around her torso.

He paused and as he stood there, she saw he wasn't the enemy, and right now she did need a friend. At last, he said, "Have you eaten?"

"No, I haven't," Sarah admitted, although she wasn't sure if she could force anything down.

"Then have something with me. I'm buying, of course," Felix said. When she hesitated, he added, "Don't worry. He'll show up, and if not, I'll help you look later."

"I guess you're right. I need to go up in my room, first."

"Good, then, I'll be in the restaurant."

"Where is he?" Sarah muttered as she freshened up in her bathroom. Looking in the mirror, she braided her long hair as she appraised the rings under her eyes. Oh well, she wasn't one for make-up. A few minutes later, Sarah went back downstairs to the restaurant where Felix was waiting for her.

He'd found them a seat at a table and had ordered two glasses of red wine, a plate of cold meats and sliced bread. When he saw her coming toward him, he got up and pulled out a chair for her.

She reached for a glass, took a long sip and sat down. "Thanks, I needed this. Thanks for listening to me. Your dad doesn't take me seriously at all," Sarah said, looking straight into his warm eyes and wondered if he found her attractive. He was a priest; what was she thinking of? She needed to stay focused on Vanderhoost's disappearance.

"My father's a stubborn man. Sorry," Felix said. "Though, waiting seems to be the reasonable thing to do. Don't worry, it'll all work out." His words sounded hollow to her, like those of an adult speaking down to an unruly child.

"Sorry, too, but I feel so agitated." Sarah took some of the cold cuts off the wooden serving board along with some of the freshly grated horseradish. She spread a large helping of it onto her bread and took a healthy bite. Instantly, her sinuses were stinging and tears came to her eyes.

"I was going to warn you that our *Kren* is really strong." Felix said and laughed as she coughed and grabbed her water glass. He patted her on the back as she drank.

Finally, she set the glass down and took a deep breath. "Wow," she said, and coughed again.

Felix took a piece of bread and handed it to her. "Here," he said. "This will help." As she took a bite, he sipped his wine, waiting for her to get her composure back. When she did, he went on, "So, tell me about your work."

She cleared her throat telling him stories of her adventures with Vanderhoost and their travels around the world working for her magazine, especially about her love of photography. This temporarily distracted her and amused him. He listened.

"… Like the time our luggage was lost on its way to India. Vanderhoost insisted on wearing traditional Indian garb, which were way too long. He looked really funny and had to roll up his pant legs to his knees or they wouldn't stay up. Then, he lost his glasses while riding an elephant."

Recounting the memories as they nibbled their meal seemed to relax Sarah and she leaned back in her chair.

"What about your family, though? Do they approve of you wandering around the world?" Felix said.

"When I was a little girl, my aunt and uncle encouraged me to follow my dreams. Oma was fantastic and so was Opa. She was a great cook and Opa was so kind and they really loved each other." She blinked and the corners of her mouth dropped. "They're both gone now. My Opa died a while ago. And my Oma passed this spring of cancer. I can't believe she's gone. We were very close."

"You must have really loved her," Felix said. She looked past the tables to the window where the late afternoon sun was giving the lush countryside a radiant orange glow.

"And your parents?" he continued.

Sarah caught her breath.

"I'm sorry, I don't mean to pry." He was quiet a moment, then said, "My father isn't happy about me wanting to become a priest."

"I thought I saw something between you two at the station," Sarah said.

Felix finished off his bread and wine and waved to the waiter for another round. "Ja, well, he told me a year ago he didn't approve of me joining the church. He wants me to continue teaching, then marry and have his grandchildren. I'm an only child and my Mama passed away a few years back."

"I lost my mom, too," Sarah said and looked to see how Felix would react.

"There are times when I miss my Mama as well. I'm sorry." He placed his hand over hers, but she pulled away and put it under the table onto her lap. Her palms felt tingly and sweaty. She felt blood rise to her cheeks. Did he notice her reaction? But the only thing she saw on his face was empathy and concern. *Why am I telling him all this? He'll make a great priest.*

"It's okay. It was a long time ago." She picked up her iPhone and glanced at the time. "

Sarah took another bite of food. They were quiet for a while until Sarah spoke up and turned the conversation to music, books and her limited German vocabulary.

"*Bitte, Danke* and *Tchüss*. And oh yeah, *Liebchen*. That's the extent of my vocabulary," she said. In the States, Spanish is the predominate second language, so that's what they teach in high school. It came in handy while I was doing a piece on the Mayan ruins in Central America.

Felix nodded. "It sounds like you're quite an adventurer."

"My job takes me to a lot of places; it's why I love it," she said. "So, tell me, does all your reading revolve around church and history or do you venture out into the world of fiction?"

Felix shrugged. "I like all kinds of books, really, but there are a few I like more than others," he said and went on to tell her about the history of the church. Their conversation stretched from late afternoon into early evening.

At last, she pushed her plate away from her and thanked him for the meal. "We really should be talking about finding Vanderhoost, so I'm off to my room to get a few things for the search."

"Perhaps I should come with you. I mean, if someone has broken into your room once, they might come back."

"Okay."

He followed her upstairs and stood close behind her as she turned the key to open the door. She tried to ignore the musky, sweet fragrance of his cologne that was driving her crazy. The last thing she needed right now was to fall into old habits and take him to bed.

"I won't be long," she said.

He grabbed her arm, and it was like she'd been zapped. "Let me go in first," he said.

"Oh!" She flashed a smile, felt heat come to her face and backed away. "I guess I should, or what was the point of you're coming up with me?"

He walked in ahead of her, checked the closet and peeked into the bathroom. Satisfied, he came back and stepped aside for her to pass. "I'll wait out here for you."

Again, she caught a whiff of his cologne as she brushed passed him. "I'll be right back, just need to grab something warm to wear."

"Take your time."

Sarah pulled the door shut behind her and went to her suitcase. Dragging out a hoodie, she pulled it over her head and noticed the last strands of daylight sliding over the roof-tops from her window.

"Where will you look for him?" Felix said as they marched through the hotel lobby. "You really should wait here in case he comes back or calls."

"He doesn't have his cell phone, remember?" Sarah said.

"I'm taking my phone. I have a picture of him on it. I'll show it around town."

Felix stopped and frowned.

"What?" Sarah said turning back.

"That reminds me. I left my phone at the abbey. Damn it," Felix said.

"Do you need it?" Sarah said, feeling impatient.

"Well…umm…"

"Look, it's getting late. If you need to get it, go, but I'm not waiting. I'm sorry we spent so much time talking, we shouldn't have." Sarah said and checked her knapsack to see if her flashlight was there. She pulled it out, clicked it on and off. "Good, it works." Then she flung the bag over her shoulder. "So, you coming or not?"

"I guess," he said and followed her to the door. When they were outside, he looked down the street and pointed. "Let's start at that pub down there." Felix tilted his head to the right and smiled.

"Alright, but I don't find this funny and don't say I didn't warn you, because I'm checking every place in this town."

Twenty minutes later, the street lights flickered on and the shop windows lit up giving the town a festive appearance. The tourists and locals strolled about in the balmy evening breeze that rippled the canvas canopies and outdoor table umbrellas. The outdoor cafés were busy. Couples were walking arm in arm. In the park across the street, giggling children could be heard playing some game.

Sarah stopped everyone they met and showed them the picture of Vanderhoost while Felix translated in German. They even knocked on doors near to the hotel. No one had seen or heard of Vanderhoost.

Above on the hill, with the moon a perfect crescent behind it, the illuminated castle presented a glorious yet frightening appearance to her. Sarah moved up the dark stone road towards it.

"I'm going to look up around the castle," she said and flicked on her flashlight.

Felix chased after her. "You said he was lazy. Would he have hiked up to it?"

"I don't know, but I'm going to look. If you're tired, go

home," she said. He was frustrating her.

"I'll come, *Heilend Sacrament,*" he swore.

Interesting, he used the same words her Opa used when he was mad, she thought, as they approached the first archway. She gazed up at the inky dome of twinkling stars. Except for the nonstop sound of crickets and the soughing of the grasses, all was silent. At the wrought iron gate to the vineyard, she saw a flickering light from the darkness of the stone wall on the side of the hill.

"Look over there!" she cried.

However, when Felix turned to look, the light disappeared. He turned back toward her. "What am I supposed to be seeing?"

"There was a flashing light over there on the wall, but it's gone now. Damn!" she sighed. "Come on, let's go," she said and strode into the vineyard. When she reached the other side, she panned her light over the ground, searching for the narrow stone pathway she'd discovered that afternoon. Felix followed her tentatively, wary of the one-hundred-and-fifty-meter drop to the twinkling yellow streetlights of the town below.

She strained her neck to look up at the castle looming above her, its ghostly black tower wrapped in pink and purple light. Sarah pointed to the small stony path ahead.

"I'm pretty sure this path will lead us over to where I just saw that light," she said. "I bet someone was in that cave over there."

"What cave?" Felix said. "And that is not a path! It's a ledge."

Sarah ignored the later comment. "There's a cave over there. I saw it today and there were climbers going up to it as well, and a crowd watching," she said and started toward the narrow cliff-side trail.

"Wait!" Felix said, grabbing her hand. "You don't know how stable that rock is and to make matters worse, it's dark out. One misstep and you'll end up dead."

She shook his hand off. "If you want to stay here, fine, but I'm going," she said. She knew he was right, though. It was dangerous — terrifying actually — but staying here and doing nothing wasn't an option. She screwed her courage up and turned away.

A minute later, she was ducking onto the ledge that dipped down along the towering rock on one side, and on the other, fell away to a dark void. She hugged the smooth granite wall beside her, playing her light over the perilous ledge leading to the cave. Behind her, Felix was muttering something in German.

"One foot in front of the other," Sarah called out as she picked her way along the treacherous rim. Occasionally, she felt stones run out under her feet and bounce over the edge, pinging against the wall as they dove into the black world below. She stopped and caught her breath then moved again until, at last, she saw a small opening in the granite wall ahead. "The flash light will help," Sarah said.

"There it is," she said to Felix, and headed for it.

They treaded, carefully for fifteen frightening minutes until they reached the opening to a small cave. The entrance was small. Sarah ducked into the drafty hole. She shined her light around the spacious dead-end chamber looking for an exit and felt along the walls, but found nothing.

Felix came up behind her. "Hmm… I never knew about this. It seems to be just a grotto though. See, nobody. You sure you saw a light coming from here?"

"Positive," Sarah said, and frowned. She played the light over the walls again, examining every nook and cranny then sighed. "I don't understand. I know what I saw!"

"I believe you," Felix said, "but there's nothing here. Let's go before your batteries burn out and we're walking that ledge blindly."

Sarah had to admit he was right. She took one last look, turned to leave and felt something knock against her foot. She aimed the light down and saw the tip of an iron ring poking through the hardscrabble stone.

"Wait," she said and kicked the rubble away with her foot. As she bent over to see what it was, Felix joined her.

"A trap door?" he said.

She braced her feet on the ground and yanked it open. Flashing a beam of light into the hole, she said, "There's another room down there, and a ladder. I wonder where it goes? I'm going down!" She left her backpack in the cave.

"Hold on, you don't know how old that ladder is. If it snaps, you'll be trapped down there. Let's get back. We can return tomorrow and…"

But Sarah was already climbing down with her flashlight in her mouth. When she hit bottom, she called up. "You coming?"

"Yes, I'm coming," Felix called back down to her with a huff.

As she waited for him to follow her down the rungs, she panned her light over the walls and down a wide stone passageway. She wondered how far it led into the heart of the mountain and whether it went right under the castle.

As Felix stepped off the last rung, he said, "I don't know about this."

"Stop worrying. There's no one here. I thought you wanted to help," Sarah said.

"I do!"

"Well then, stop fighting me," she said and struck off through the passage. After about a hundred feet they came to a fork. Sarah flashed her light back and forth between them.

"Now what?" Felix said.

"I'm not sure," Sarah answered. She silently debated what to do, when she heard the faint sounds of voices echoed from the passage on her right.

"Do you hear that?" Felix whispered.

Sarah put her hand up, focusing on what sounded like disembodied wailing. She put her finger up to her mouth and pointed to the right from where the voices were echoing. Felix moved quietly behind her as she crept down the cool, wet tunnel, keeping the beam of her flashlight on the earthen floor. It felt jagged and slimy. The air smelled dank and earthy.

As they progressed, the wailing got louder and with it came the drone of chanting voices. "We shouldn't be here," Felix whispered behind her."

She turned and shushed him. "Will you be quiet?"

He frowned and was about to say something when the chant came to a sudden crescendo and ended. They froze and looked at each other. Sarah flicked off her flashlight and pressed herself up against the wall. In pitch dark, she suddenly felt as if the tunnel was pressing in around her, sucking her breath away until at last the chanting started again. She let out a breath and flicked her light back on.

In the gloom, she saw Felix's dark, anxious eyes staring back and there were beads of sweat on his long, thin face. She turned toward the resonating chant, hesitated, then started inching her way forward until he grabbed her arm from behind. When she turned to see what was the matter was, she saw him shaking his head.

She turned and played her light down the tunnel then looked back at him again. Even though her heart was pounding, she hadn't come all this way to stop now. She pulled away from him, started off, and soon after saw a flickering light stretching back toward her from an opening ahead.

Slowly, she inched forward and soon afterward found herself peering into a broad cavern lit by burning torches that hung from metal sconces. Out of sight, the two of them looked down at a flat, round dais with a set of stairs leading to it. Hooded dark figures dressed in long black capes walked counter-clockwise around it and chanted words she couldn't understand. They stopped and when they did, Sarah saw Vanderhoost lying restrained, blindfolded and naked on a large upside-down pentacle made of white stones. His arms and legs were tied with small red rope to four opposite poles. Each limb extended towards a tip of the star. The flames sputtered and cast long shadows onto the floor. She put her hand to her mouth while her other hand clutched Felix's arm.

Vanderhoost was spread out, his arms and legs extended to the tips of the star. Struggling against his bindings, he cried out, "Let me go, let me go!"

The only response he got was the drone of the mantra coming from the hooded figures walking around him until there was a thud of a door shutting. Sarah jumped as a tall shadowy figure appeared near the opposite wall. Her friend's cries rang in the passageway.

The tall figure seemed to glide towards Vanderhoost, and

when it stood over him with its head dipped, Vanderhoost choked out the words, "I'm an American citizen!"

The individual looked up and around at the circle of people around him and said something in German then took an apple from his pocket and jammed it into Vanderhoost's mouth. Raising its arms, the man recited an incantation in a deep baritone.

Sarah shuddered for her friend and couldn't understand anything being said. She dared not ask Felix for fear they'd be discovered. Two members began pushing each other, clearly arguing. The leader moved in between them, then went back to his position. It was silent again.

Sarah's heart raced as an incantation began and more joined in. It was a horrible, high-pitched cacophony sounding like the cries of otherworldly beasts. All the while, Vanderhoost struggled and pulled on the ropes.

Felix tugged Sarah, motioning to her that they needed to leave. She shook her head, but this time he would not be denied and he dragged her back along the passageway where it was safe to whisper.

"We need to get out of here and go to the police, right now," he mouthed.

"I won't leave my friend," Sarah hissed. "You get the police, I'm staying."

"You're being stupid and stubborn. What are you going to do? Overpower them? We can call the police as soon as we're out of here. We should get reception outside. Sarah. I swear! I'm not leaving without you."

"You go. I can't leave him." Sarah said and pounded a fist against the rock wall.

Felix grabbed her shoulders and shook her. "Listen… calm down. We need to go. You're not helping him by wasting time here," he sighed quietly.

"Fine," she said, peering into the darkness. She shook her head, sucked a breath, and followed Felix back down the passage with her flashlight beam bouncing off the walls. When they came to the fork, her foot caught on something, and she tripped knocking the flashlight out of her hand. As it hit the ground, it made a pinging noise which reverberated back down the passageway. Abruptly, the drone of the mantra stopped. She felt her heart thud and groping for her light, she snatched it up.

"We better get out of here," Felix said, his whisper urgent. "Give me the flashlight."

They ran down the dark corridor sprinting, towards the ladder and as they did so, Sarah heard raised voices coming up behind them.

"The ladder, quick, you first," Felix said.

Sarah leapt onto it and scampered up into the small cave with Felix right behind her. She snatched her bag from the floor. Slamming the trap door after him, he grabbed her hand and they moved out onto the stone ledge. Pressing against the wall of the mountain, they moved as fast they could.

"Careful," he said.

Sarah nodded and the two of them skirted the side of the towering mound back to the vineyard. When they were on grass and level ground Sarah looked back and saw a light coming from the cave.

"Run!" she yelled, and took off through the vineyard, not daring to look behind her. When she came to the stone road, she rushed down it as fast as she could until she heard Felix cry out behind her. She stopped and turned around to see him lying on the ground with his hands around his ankle. "What happened?"

"I slipped and fell!" he grunted. "Shit, I think I sprained my ankle." As she ran back to him, he struggled to his feet. Sarah put her arm around his waist, steadied him and looked up the dark road stretching under the night sky. As far as she could see there was no one coming.

"Can you walk?"

Felix shook his head.

Sarah surveyed the road beside them. "There are thick bushes next to the wall next to the pond. If they're coming, they won't see us in there."

"You won't be able to lift me."

"Yes, I can." Sarah grabbed him, supporting him under his arm; she lifted and pulled him along. They hid behind one of the dense bushes, scratching their arms and legs. The sound of her heartbeat reverberated in her ears and she dug her fingernails into her arm. Crouching down next to him, she took out her iPhone from her pant pocket and dialed the police. As the phone rang her heart fluttered.

I don't believe in a Goddess but maybe this is the time to start. Goddess, please protect us.

Sarah recited the words over and over again in her head. Her eyes burned and her body tremored.

Finally, someone picked up. 'Hallo, Kann ich Ihnen helfen?' *Great!* She handed the phone to Felix and grimacing; he spoke to the person in German on the other end as three shadows came running down to the road. Felix hung up.

Two kept going, and one stayed behind, looking around. The man strode to the wall, peered over it down at the town, then walked back to the pond and bushes.

Sarah held her breath as a light flicked on the bush in front of them began to rustle. She braced herself. As the stranger moved closer and closer to them, a voice called out from below. The light diverted and a moment later they heard footsteps tromping away down the road.

Felix let out a breath. "Jesus, my ankle is killing me."

"I think it's safe now," Sarah said. She started getting to her feet, when Felix grabbed her arm.

"They might double back. We wait here for a little while longer."

They crouched in the bramble for what felt like forever until at last, sirens filled the night's quiet. She could hear shouting at the bottom of the hill. Cautiously, she parted the bushes and crept out onto the road and a moment later Felix joined her, limping. Down the road they saw two police cars. Chief Greundlar stepped out of one car with another officer. Two more officers climbed out of the other. Sarah put Felix's arm around her shoulder and they hobbled down the road toward them.

When Chief Greundlar saw them, he strode toward them. "What's the meaning of all this?"

Sarah turned and pointed back to the castle, willed herself to stay calm and inform the Police chief as best she could about what had just transpired, while Felix translated into German. "They have my missing friend captive below the castle, performing some satanic ritual or something. We need to go get him now before they get away," she said. "I'm afraid they're going to kill him."

"I can't believe this," Chief Greundlar said. "Is this really true, Felix?"

"Yes, Papa," Felix said.

Chief Greundlar glanced down at his son's leg. "You're hurt?"

"It's nothing, just a sprain," he said and winced. "Look, Sarah is telling the truth. I saw it with my own eyes."

Chief Greundlar turned to his officers and said something in German. Felix translated for Sarah as the officers ran up the road toward the castle, saying, "He just told them to go see what is going on and bring your friend down to safety."

Sarah let go of Felix and started after them.

Chief Greundlar rushed after her and grabbed her arm. "You can't go. I demand you stay here. It's not safe." Sarah stopped, warding him off. "Let go of me!"

"Fräulein Lilienthal, my men will make sure no harm comes to your friend. Right now, the most important thing is to let them do their job. Please, I must insist you come to the police station. That is where you will do the most good," Chief Greundlar said.

Sarah took a deep breath, glanced back up at the castle and reluctantly stopped trying to wrench free of the Police chief. "You'll let me know the minute they have my friend safe and sound?"

"I promise, now please, I need to get a statement from you and my son."

"I should be there for him," she stammered, then walked back with him towards Felix who was leaning against the squad car.

Chief Greundlar opened the back door for her to get in and as Felix climbed in beside her, the chief said, "I'll call Doctor Stein and have him come to the station to take a look at your ankle. These kinds of things don't happen in my town," he said. "Chanting, tying people up? I assure you, they'll be caught and brought to justice," he said in a heated tone,

"Don't worry, they'll find your friend," Felix said to her as the car raced along.

Sarah wasn't so sure about that and buried her face in her hands. Felix put his arm around her shoulder and drew her tight to him. Being held felt comforting and she melted into him. "Why did they take Vanderhoost?" she cried. "Who are they and what do they want?"

"I don't know," Felix said.

The book must have something to do with it, Sarah thought. It has to! Fear as black as night, smoldered in her stomach. She grasped Felix's hand for reassurance and wept.

Chapter Twenty Three

In The Town

Sarah stood outside the hotel tapping her foot. She'd skipped breakfast, having lost her appetite, and hadn't even showered. She should have never given the book to Vanderhoost. It was her fault he was in danger. Last night had been a long sleepless night for her. The interview at the station had gone on for hours. She decided not to tell them about the book, not knowing for sure who really was involved. It was a small town after all.

Later, the town's doctor came and examined Felix's ankle. It was sprained, not broken. Finally, she was escorted home. She thought about her phone call to Vanderhoost's companion, Peter. It had taken her the rest of the night to get the courage up to call him and tell him all that transpired with Vanderhoost's abduction. As she anticipated, Peter was not only hysterical, but livid.

"Oh my God," Peter had said, "Sarah. What the hell is going on over there? I knew something was wrong. Jesus Christ, they'd better find him alive or I'll shoot myself. I'm calling our embassy right now. They need to get off their German asses…no, their Austrian asses!'

"Peter, listen to me!" Sarah shouted back into her phone. She took a breath, tried to make her voice sound more convincing. "You don't need to come…the police are searching for him. I know they'll find him. I'll call as soon as I hear anything… yes, I promise."

Peter's words echoed in her head as she looked up at the

soaring blue sky. Not a single cloud was overhead. Why, of all days, was the world smiling down at her? Was it a sign Vanderhoost was alive? She switched her backpack to her other shoulder and started off towards St. Martin's from the front steps of the hotel. She wanted to see Felix and talk more about what happened last night. Along the way, she figured she ought to pick him up something to eat from a bakery; a box of cinnamon rolls, a couple coffees and on a whim, a sandwich.

When she arrived at the monastery, she found the doors wide open. She hesitated by the gateway. *Should I see him?* She eyed the inner courtyard and the gardens a moment, then regarded the walkway. She felt foolish. *Why am I so scared? It's just breakfast.* At last, she walked in and as she made her way around the gardens, she saw a turtle dove perched at the feet of the Mary Statue. For some reason, the appearance of the bird made her hopeful.

The seminary housing was on her right, and was a few stories high. She opened the side door into a small dim lobby looking for some kind of directory, mailboxes, anything to give her a clue as to where his room might be. But all she saw was a long spartan hallway. *I guess I'll have to go hunting.* She went down the long corridor and was met by a cleaning woman coming out of one of the rooms.

"I'm looking for Felix Greundlar. Do you know what room he's in?"

The woman just looked at her.

Great! She let out a breath. *Once again, you didn't think things through.*

The sound of a door opening behind her made her jump. "Can I help you?" said a man's voice.

She turned around and saw a young priest step out into the hallway. *Thank God, someone who speaks English.*

"Yes, I'm looking for Felix Greundlar."

"Ah, he's up on the third floor. Follow me, and I'll take you to him."

Sarah fell in behind the young man as he led her up through the old building. The floors creaked as they walked down

"He's in the last room on the left at the end of the hallway," the young man said, and pointed to his door down at the end of the corridor. He flashed a quirky sidelong smile that made her wonder what he was thinking of her. Whatever was going through his head, she didn't want to know. She thanked him and headed down the hall.

Before she knocked, she rehearsed what she was going to say to him. While it was true, she had sought comfort in his arms in the squad car last night, a woman just didn't go in a seminary dorm visiting a man about to take his vows of priesthood. She decided a simple *hi* to start would suffice, straightened her shoulders and knocked.

There was no answer, so she knocked again.

Finally, his voice called out from behind the door in German. She heard something fall over, and banging around. Her stomach tightened. Why was she reacting to him like the crushes she used to have in high school? *Breathe. You only want to talk.*

"It's me, Sarah."

The door swung open and he stood there in a T-shirt and sweat pants, looking tousled and pleasantly surprised. His brown hair was sticking up in several directions.

"Rough night?" Sarah said.

"Sorry, I just got up. Didn't sleep well with the ankle and all," he said. "The pain was bad. I fell asleep around five."

"Oh, I'm sorry to hear that. I brought you breakfast to cheer you up," Sarah said and extended one of the cups of coffee toward him.

He took it. "Thanks. Umm, well, come in," he said, hopping back to his unmade bed. Sarah closed the door behind her. Feeling awkward, she drifted over to a desk and set the bag of cinnamon rolls on it.

"Sit, sit, please." He motioned to the chair next to her.

She furtively took in his strong arms and lean muscular body as she sat.

"You didn't have to…" he said, and sipped his coffee.

"I know, I just need to talk to someone," she stammered. "You're the only person I know here, except for my relations I never met in Feldbach."

Felix sat down on his bed. "You have relatives here?"

"Yes, but that's a story for another time. Here, you choose." She handed him the bag, and he took the sandwich. They sat there in silence eating and drinking until at last, he said. "They'll find him."

"So, you haven't heard anything more?"

"No. Don't worry, my father will call you as soon as he has news."

"I hope so," Sarah said. She paused and added, "How can you be so sure? Those people were— I don't know how to describe it—"

"Crazy, mad?" He bit into his sandwich and set it down. "You know, what you did last night was dangerous. What were you thinking, going into the tunnel?"

"I don't know. I was worried about Vanderhoost's welfare." She averted her gaze to the small window. "I wanted to find him. It's my fault he came here in the first place and…" Sarah felt her throat tighten, and her mounting frustration was getting so she couldn't think straight.

"Don't blame yourself," he said and stood up. Hopping over to her, he put his arms around her. "You didn't do anything wrong. Bad people abducted him and we don't know why."

Sarah looked up at him and saw his tender compassionate gaze staring back.

He snatched a tissue from the desk and wiped a tear off her cheek. "Who could they be?" she asked. "I don't know what to do."

He bent over and kissed her forehead. "You can't do anything right now but wait." He looked at her, then drew her to him and kissed her softly on the lips.

When he pulled back, she wondered if history was repeating itself. Her mother had been lured into a priest's lair and look how that had ended. At last, she said, "You feel it too?"

"Yes," Felix whispered, and held her at a distance regarding her with a calm gaze. Sarah stood up and put her arms around his shoulders, then pressed her lips onto his warm neck. Felix let out a breath, as if he were holding back built up tension. Now, he kissed her in earnest with his tongue exploring every inch of her mouth. He wrapped his arms around her waist and they made their way backward to the bed, falling sideways onto it. Groping, clawing at her, tearing at her clothes; he couldn't seem to get enough of her, then suddenly he pushed back breathlessly.

"I can't do this," he said, pulling himself to the edge of the bed. She put her hand on his arm. He trembled and pulled his hands over his wavy brown hair.

"Yes, you can," Sarah whispered hoarsely. She wanted him and stood up to take off her jacket and shirt. She tossed them onto the bed, then reached behind her and unclasped her bra. Felix stared at her nipples, and groaned.

"You're catching me off guard." Felix stood and grabbed her shirt off the bed. "Please, put it back on."

"Really?" Sarah said, bristling. She snatched her shirt from him and pulled it on, stuffing her bra into her pant pocket. She wasn't used to being rejected. *Fuck you.* Embarrassed, she stalked toward the door.

"No, wait," Felix cried.

She flung the door open and was about to leave when she heard a loud thud behind her.

Turning back, she saw him sprawled on the floor and holding his ankle. She had a mind to leave him there, but that wasn't who she was. "Serves you right," she said, bending over to help him up.

He grimaced as he got to his feet. As she led him over to the bed, he said, "I know what that sounded like, but it's not what you think," he said. "I find you really attractive, and if I wasn't— "

"You mean like wanting to be a priest?" Sarah said, and looked up at the ceiling and sighed. "What was I thinking? A priest!"

"Not quite yet," Felix said.

"Doesn't matter. I seem to have a knack for picking the wrong ones. I'm real messed up when it comes to men."

Felix looked back at her. "What do you mean?"

Sarah tapped her hands on her thighs, not looking at him.

"I'm a good listener," Felix said taking one of her hands.

She peered over at him from under slit eyelids. He appeared genuinely concerned about her or was it he just felt sorry for her? She didn't share her personal feelings and thoughts with anyone except for her counselor. As for her sex addiction, one-night stands and inability to form meaningful relationships with men, well, that was locked up with the key thrown away.

"I don't do relationships… and even if I did, you can't… not that it makes a difference," Sarah shook her head gently. "Never mind."

"No, it's my fault," Felix replied. "I should never have kissed you." He paused. "Sarah, if it were a different time—"

Her iPhone rang. Sarah sprang off the bed to take it out of her jeans jacket. "Hello."

"Ms. Lilienthal. We have found your friend Mr. Vanderhoost," said the Police chief on the other end. He was wandering around in a forest outside of Riegersburg."

Sarah's heart jumped as she eyed Felix. "Is he okay?"

"He's a little shook up, very agitated and asking for you. Can you come to Feldbach? There's a clinic in town taking care of him."

"Yes, I'll be there as soon as I can," she answered and picked up her jacket from the floor and said, "They found him. He's alive!"

"Wait, I want to come with you," Felix said, hopping up onto one leg.

"No, sorry, you can't," Sarah said and ran to the door. She glanced back at him, something tugged in her belly seeing him so vulnerable yet, she was frustrated with her own feelings developing for him.

"Hey. Why not?"

"He's my best friend and I need to be alone with him now. I got to run. Catch you later," she said, yanking the door open before rushing down the hallway.

Chapter Twenty Four
Three Days Later

Sarah leaned against a wood paneled wall and scrutinized everyone in the great hall of the castle that was buzzing with reporters and curious bystanders.

As soon as they were back to Austria, the Hohenburgs organized a press conference, but requested no one take any pictures. Mr. Hammer had called her earlier in the morning mentioning concern about their property and bad publicity. Felix was seated on a chair uncomfortably close to her, catching her up on any new developments.

Sunlight poured in from the enormous windows behind the prince and princess who sat front and center on a broad mahogany table with microphones. The middle-aged pair was dressed modestly for their station in life, Sarah thought. Mr. Hammer sat on their left, with Bishop Baumgartner, Police chief Gruendlar and the Major of Riegersburg on the other side.

All the important players in town are present.

"Did you know about the existence of this cavern?" one reporter questioned. Felix translated for her and she sat down. She eyed him, wondering what, if anything, he thought about their encounter in his room.

"We had no knowledge of this cavern," the prince answered. "But we have heard of underground passages below the *Burg*."

"How is the investigation proceeding around the American's abduction?" another reporter queried. "Do you know anything more about the group? Who they are and what they're intentions are?"

"At this time, we cannot give out any information," Mr. Hammer jumped in. "The Hohenburgs are working with the police very closely on this."

"Excuse me. Should the people of Riegersburg be concerned for their safety? Can't you give us more information about who the American is and why he was kidnapped?"

"He is still in the hospital and doing well under the circumstances. We cannot tell you more because we don't want to jeopardize the investigation," Police chief Greundlar said, glancing over at Sarah and Felix. "There are witnesses, but for their safety, their identity is confidential for now. The Grazer police force has been called in to assist us in this matter. And I promise you, we will apprehend the villains. There is no need for the public to be worried. We are stationing extra police officers around the town and castle."

At this point, the Hohenburgs announced the meeting was over and the reporters were cleared from the room.

Sarah found it odd, listening to all that went on. She was standing right there, and suspected anyone of them could be involved. Was it the prince and his wife? They seemed innocent enough, and genuinely upset. She never liked Mr. Hammer; and he did have access to the *Burg*. Might he not be involved? She eyed him suspiciously as she sat next to Felix on a side bench against the far wall of the room.

"All traces of the ropes and tapers were gone when the police hiked up there last night," Felix whispered in her ear. "My father told me the assailants left nothing in the cave except a foul smell."

"I feel like I'm in a nightmare...kind of like *The Da Vinci Code*." Sarah said, studying him. Why was he jerking his knee up and down? "It's surreal. I can't get the awful chanting out of my head. By the way, when I saw Vanderhoost yesterday, he said he doesn't remember anything about his abduction. Just that he woke up naked and tied up on the stone floor. He didn't see anyone's face." Sarah tilted her head sideways.

"He can't recall anything?" Felix said, scanning the room, and then turning back to her.

"No, he has a large lump on his head and he wants to fly home as soon as possible. To quote his exact words, 'I'm not staying a minute longer than I have to in this town of lunatics!'"

"What about the investigation?" Felix said.

Sarah shrugged.

"What about you, are you leaving, too?"

"I don't know," she answered in truth while starring down at the polished wooden floor. She had a mind to ask him about his feelings for her, but things were moving too quickly to process. Should she stay or leave? Then, he leaned ever so slightly against her shoulder, and she recalled their encounter in his room. She flinched away from him and he lowered his head. Sarah pursed her lips, and to her relief saw Mr. Hammer walking over to them, followed by the owners of Riegersburg. Her heart raced in anticipation of meeting them.

"Miss Lilienthal... Felix," Mr. Hammer said.

Sarah sprang out of her chair and helped Felix to stand. She handed Felix his crutches, and smiled, though inwardly, felt being sized up by Mr. Hammer. His smile like a fox, sly, which his little mustache accentuated. She didn't like the way he moved; it was too slick.

"May I introduce His Highness, Prince Hohenberg and his wife, Princess Anna."

The prince extended his hand to Sarah. Prince Hohenburg was an attractive and tanned man in his early forties, with a full head of dark hair. Felix looked awkward as he shook the prince's hand.

"I don't want to inconvenience you. We are deeply concerned about the terrible occurrences in our castle," the prince said with a stern expression. His wife, dressed in a traditional Austrian dirndl, was slim with neatly blonde hair and pretty blue eyes. The princess nodded as she rested her manicured hand on his shoulder. "I assure you, we will stop at nothing to find the intruders, and they will be prosecuted. My lawyer and the police are investigating with my full cooperation."

"Dear, don't get any more upset, remember what the doctor said," the princess said.

"Yes, yes…well we will accommodate your stay as well as Mr. Vanderhoost's here in Riegersburg forthwith until more is discovered."

"Thank you, but I believe, my colleague wants to travel back to the States," Sarah said. "However, I'd be happy to take you up on your generous offer, should my boss grant me extra time here."

Mr. Hammer cleared his throat. "I'm sorry, but I regret to inform you Mr. Vanderhoost can't leave as yet." He bent a severe gaze on her, and added, "I do appreciate his eagerness to get home, but it's essential for the investigation that he stays until we resolve this matter."

He's not going to like that! She suppressed the urge to fire back and say, *Says who: he's an American citizen!* Drawing breath, she scowled at Mr. Hammer and said, "Well, I can't speak for him."

The Police chief piped in, "Unfortunately, Mr. Hammer is correct, Fräulein Lilienthal. Your partner was party to a crime, and so by our law, he required to stay until the matter is sufficiently settled. But do not to worry, I'll have one of my officers look after you while you're both here."

Everyone looked at her as if in anticipation.

"Felix and Fräulein Lilienthal, I must insist you don't speak to anyone about what you've seen or done. I know you understand. We don't want to jeopardize the investigation." The Police chief stared at his son, patting Felix on the shoulder.

Sarah looked down at her sneakers, wanting all this to go away and to get back researching her story, and more important, recovering her book. But who had it? "I'll see what I can do," she said, knowing that despite the authorities, Vanderhoost might fly home anyway. He'd already called his lawyer in the States.

"That should do. We must be taking off and get back to Monaco where we left our children," the prince said. "Our lawyer, Mr. Shanstien and Mr. Hammer will keep us updated daily. We shall be back within a week." The prince reached out again to shake her hand and Felix's.

"Well, we just met royalty," Felix said as he watched the couple leave the room. "Come on, let's get out of here." Sarah walked into the courtyard and over the moat, until she stood outside the *Burg*. Felix limped after her. "Can you hold one of the crutches?"

She took it and he hobbled down the road next to her under clear skies. The fresh air felt good on Sarah's skin. Despite the insistence everything was being done to find the culprits, she was still upset about what had transpired in the castle and was having a hard time not to rush down the road to her hotel room. In her opinion, the royals and the police were giving out platitudes.

"My father says the police couldn't find any leads. They've called in experts from Graz. Our little town never experiences anything like this," Felix said as if reading her mind. He stopped to catch his breath. "Please don't be upset with them. Everyone is shocked."

"I was surprised no one brought up the possibility of witchcraft. That was what we witnessed. Right?" Sarah answered and peered over the parapet on her right next to the road. "Riegersburg has a history of witch burnings."

"It looked like it but, surely don't you believe in those kinds of things?" Felix said, and uttered a theatrical groan. "They're concerned about the bad publicity. Our town depends on tourism."

"That's what they worry about? Really?! Those criminals were going to kill Vanderhoost! I have to get back," she snapped back and darted ahead.

"No, Sarah, please don't leave."

But she was really angry and worried about what to do next. "I'm sorry," she said, and, threw down his crutch, then quickly marched down the road. She'd gotten about halfway back to town, when her iPhone rang. It had Vanderhoost's name flash onto her screen. Accepting the call, she recited every detail of the press conference to him.

"Peter wants me home," Vanderhoost said in a resigned tone. "But I'll give it a few days, and only because there'll be a police officer outside my door. Remember, I'm the one who was abducted, book or no book. He'd better be carrying a gun. Are you coming to visit today?"

"Sorry, I can't. Remember my relatives in Feldbach? I called them when I first arrived. I'm supposed to meet them today. But I'll be up as soon as I can afterward though."

"Humph!"

"Please don't be upset. I really need to see them and…"

"Fine, leave me to these Nazi nurses," he said. "They order me around like I'm a dog. At least, the food is decent enough for a hospital. Go and find your long-lost family."

Sarah didn't like the joke about the Nazis, but let it pass. "I'll drop by as soon as I can, promise."

"You do that."

The line went dead and along with it any hope of researching the origins of her book, taking photographs for the magazine and visiting Austria. Then again, the enjoyment of discovery had ended much sooner than that. It just hadn't been driven home until now. Her iPhone rang again and she looked down thinking it was Vanderhoost wanting to apologize, but it was Felix. She debated whether to answer and decided to let it go to voice mail. She couldn't allow herself to get involved with him, yet she couldn't stop thinking of him either.

She'd woken up the last two nights, shaken. In her dream, she'd been kneeling in front of the Mary statue in St. Martin's garden. A golden light was bathing the stone figure. The light was enveloping her as well. Then the figure came alive and floated above her and as it did so, all went dark. There was something menacing there, something dangerous, but she wasn't able to see or understand what it was. Why did she keep dreaming of the statue? Did it have anything to do with the book?

Sarah avoided the journalists outside the hotel by going around to the rear entrance. Back in her room, she called room service. In the meantime, she pulled out her camera and gazed out the window.

The sky was a cerulean blue, not a cloud in it, and the rolling hills looked peaceful. How could everything seem so calm? She couldn't really blame Felix, but his excuses about the town's reputation irked her. Who was behind the abduction? It must be someone higher up, because how could they not know about the cavern? Wouldn't the castle's maintenance crew have found the cave and told the Hohenburgs? Someone was covering something up.

Yesterday, she'd rented a sporty VW Golf and drove it to Feldbach. Before she'd gone to bed, she'd went online and found the Wenzels were only a few miles past the hospital. She phoned them a second time, reaching her cousin. The conversation had been awkward, but they invited her to come today.

She checked her camera gear and its battery then went about cleaning her lenses. Keeping busy when she was restless helped her to think, and right now she was anxious as hell. In a matter of hours, she was going to her Oma's relatives, fulfilling her Oma's wishes to re-unite the family. She glanced at the room clock. Time felt leaden and heavy.

There was a knock at the door. Startled, she stood. "Who is it?"

"Sarah, it's me, Felix."

She sighed. "What do you want? And why are you here?"

"Don't be silly; you know why. Let me in."

She hesitated, then went and cracked the door open.

"I'm sorry if I offended you," he said.

She gazed at him forcing herself not to move.

"It's not that, Felix. It's just that I'm feeling confused about where we're heading," she explained, pointing to him and her. "I need to stay focused here. I'm going to see my relatives in Feldbach for the first time. It's nerve-wracking, especially after the last couple of days."

"Can I come in?"

Sarah shrugged and pulled the door back. He hopped in and she gestured toward the bed. "Have a seat, but don't get any ideas," she said as her lunch was delivered.

While she ate, she told him the abbreviated story of her grandparent's flight to America during the Nazi *Kristalnacht*. As Felix listened, he bowed his head putting his hand onto hers. "It was a dark time in my country, which we have not forgotten, I assure you. I am sorry for your Oma and Opa. To lose so much is beyond me to understand." He paused, looked away then turning back said, "I would like to come with you, if you would allow me: be your translator."

Her first reaction was to decline, but having a translator made sense. The question became: could she trust him to tell her exactly what they said, say nothing of keeping any confidence that might come out of it? But the fact was, she needed a friend in this foreign country, so she nodded.

Fifteen minutes later, they stood next to her rental car and she was having second thoughts about Felix coming along. Felix shoved his crutches over the back seat and pulled himself into the passenger seat, she said, "Felix, I've changed my mind about you coming along. I'm sorry. I just have to do this alone. I'll drop you off at the seminary." She glanced at him, he looked disappointed. *Sorry, Felix, but you weaken my ability to focus on what I'm really here for. I need some space.*

"Very well," he answered, sighing.

She ground the gears into first. He frowned. "Are you sure you can drive this kind of car?"

"You bet. Buckle up," She said and pulled away from the curb. The VW stalled. A car laid on the horn behind them.

"Damn it!" She cranked the engine on again, popped the clutch and flew ahead down the narrow streets, determined to show him, and all these stupid Austrians, she could drive standard.

"Slow down!" he said, grabbing hold of the door.

Sarah only laughed, liking the rush of speed. Sarah saw St. Martins ahead and came to an abrupt stop, throwing Felix forwards against the dashboard.

"Thanks. Promise me you'll drive safely to Feldbach," he said, opening the door and reaching for his crutches.

"I will." Sarah sped away, not looking back once.

Chapter Twenty Five

Thirty Minutes Later

Sarah arrived at Anna Wenzel's home and parked the car on the long flagstone driveway leading to the main building. It was at the foot of a small hill on the edge of the woods. The farmhouse and barn were painted in a neatly arranged blue framework around the newly whitewashed stucco walls. A small sign hung over the door with the numbers 1845. Two large oak barrels with bright pink flowers stood like sentinels on either side of an olive-green door.

To the right of the house, a large vegetable garden surrounded by a wire fence, reminded Sarah of Oma's garden in the Berkshires. Instantly, she was homesick. Farther away, fields of corn and pumpkins, and an apple orchard. Two small children were outside riding on their tricycles. When they saw Sarah, they ditched them on the pavement and ran up to the front door.

"Mama, Mama," they cried, running in and leaving the door wide open.

Sarah hovered outside near the front door, wondering how she would introduce herself and why she was there as she smelled an aroma of something baking.

It was reminiscent of sweet pastries or fresh bread. She rubbed her hands together and before long, heard someone calling out from inside. Sarah closed her eyes and took a deep breath. *Well, here goes!*

An old woman with silver white curly hair, and bright eyes appeared at the door wearing a printed cotton dress with an apron around her waist. She came out and grabbed Sarah's hands into her own wrinkled ones and was clearly excited.

"Grüsse, Grüess di' Gott. Du bist die Enklein von Katarina! Bitte Komms' rein."

"Anna?" Sarah said, feeling a fluttery empty feeling in her

stomach. *This is Oma's sister. She looks so much like her.* Anna nodded happily, gesturing for her to come into the house. A younger woman with loosely braided brown hair, dressed in jeans and a t-shirt, ran around from the back of the house.

"Sorry, but Oma is so excited to see you. I'm Gerlinde; we're cousins," the young woman said, hugging her.

Sarah stuttered, "I'm Sarah…" *Oh my God, I can't believe I'm actually here.*

Gerlinde gave her a friendly smile. "Me, too. Come. My mama and aunt are in the living room; everyone else is at work or school."

Anna and Gerlinde led Sarah into a spacious room with a large dining table on one side and leather sofa on the other. There sat two middle-aged women with the two younger kids she'd seen outside. One was on his mother's lap and the other peered out from behind a reclining chair. Gerlinde led over to the couch and had her sit on the other side of the women.

"We so happy have you here. Me, Angela," said Gerlinde's mother in broken English. She waved her hands excitedly around the room, gesturing to the women and children looking on. "This is my sister, Evelyn, her children; little Maria and there Daniel behind chair. You have coffee and strudel, no?"

"Thank you so much," Sarah murmured, touched by their kindness. She noticed their porcelain service already set up on the coffee table with a dessert.

"Oma made this *Topfenstrudel* this morning for you. She explained to me it was one of your Oma's favorites," Gerlinde said.

Sarah put her fingertips to her mouth.

If only Oma could be here.

Over the next hour and half, many questions were asked about her and America. Gerlinde translated while they sipped coffee and ate strudel.

"This is delicious," Sarah said biting into the delicate, flaky strudel with a hint of mint. Anna sighed and patted her knee.

The afternoon wore on with stories about the family Sarah's Oma left behind, and as it did, Sarah thought how much Anna reminded her of her Oma. And there were tears that came often. At length, Sarah pulled out two pictures and handed them to Anna.

"That one is of Oma and Opa in front of our home in the Berkshires with Aunt Suzanne. This was taken just after they bought it. See how young they are! The second one is of them with Georg, Ursula, Suzanne and my mother Marie," Sarah said as she pointed out people in the photograph. "You can keep them."

"Meine geliebte Schwesterchen, Vielen Dank," Anna said clearly touched. Gerlinde translated; "My dearest sister, all the time in America. I thought she'd been killed by the Nazis along with Jacob." Anna looked out the window, then back at the photos. "I'm so grateful to know she had a good life. Why didn't she contact us, do you know?"

"I don't know, other than she loved Opa, and she couldn't forgive what happened in the Holocaust. My Opa's relatives were either killed or well… we just don't know what happened to them." She paused. "She left me a letter after she died," Sarah said. "In it she asked me to come to her homeland and re-connect the family."

Gerlinde told her Oma what Sarah said.

Anna pulled out handkerchief and dabbed her eyes.

"You know, we didn't hate the Jews," Gerlinde translated for Anna. "We were all scared of speaking up. If I knew what I do today, I would've said something. I have carried that regret all my days. But I don't want to talk about those times, too painful. Please excuse me for a minute." The old woman appeared to struggle finding the right words to say. Finally, she got up and Gerlinde helped her out of the room.

Sarah hoped she hadn't offended her Oma's sister as she watched them leave. But the Nazis had killed Opa's relatives. Sarah ran her fingers through her hair, as David's reaction to her coming here, flashed before her.

"It was terrible part of our history. We very ashamed and sorry, but please to excuse us," the woman named Evelyn said in a quavering voice. "We need to fix dinner. You stay, no?"

Sarah nodded, worried, as the two women got up and shuffled to the kitchen. With the two younger cousins having already gone outside to play, Sarah was left alone on the couch. She pulled her knees together. The Black Forest wall clock ticked loudly. A bird came out on the hour, chirping. Sarah could hear the rattling of pots and pans in the kitchen where Evelyn and Angela were talking while cooking dinner. Had she come all this way to make them feel guilty? Had she blown her chance of reconnecting the family?

Gerlinde and Anna hurried back into the room carrying a jewelry box. Gerlinde sat next to Anna listening to her story then reciting it for Sarah.

Anna said, "My sister was headstrong even as a child. We grew up in this house, you know, same house. This place has been in our family for generations. Wenzel is a very old name. I loved Kati, but God forgive me, I have to tell you, I was jealous of her as a child. She was Oma's favorite. Oma took Kati to the woods to help collect her plants. They both loved gardening, and the animals. I did, too, but we all knew that Kati had the "gift", like Oma."

Anna sat back and seemingly waited to see if there was a reaction from Sarah.

"Gift, what do you mean?" Sarah said, feigning surprise, though Aunt Ursula had used the exact same words back home. Sarah wrinkled her brow, remembering one of the names in the book; Hildegard Wenzel. Her insides were vibrating. She swallowed. That was the connection! Hildegard must be an ancestor of theirs.

Anna recounted another long passage of German and crossed herself. Gerlinde translated. "She says, like Oma's home-made remedies that people from all over town came by for, Oma's garden was the envy of our neighbors. I wanted to be Oma's favorite. I was not so nice to Kati. I remember the day I stood behind the barn door as Kati came running by. I put my foot out and tripped Kati and she fell backwards and hit her head on the corner of a wagon. She was knocked out. I was so scared and I ran to Oma screaming for help.

Kati woke up later and she had to lie in bed for a week with Mama and Oma nursing her. I felt so guilty, but Kati never betrayed me. One day, she came to me and said, *"I forgive you, Anna. I know you really didn't mean it."* And she hugged me. After that, I swore to be the best sister to her. Years later, when she met Jacob, our father was against the marriage. She was so young. In those days, Catholics didn't marry Jews. Papa was so stubborn, God rest his soul. He cut Kati off from us. But I kept in touch with her secretly."

As Gerlinde finished, Anna jutted her chin and flattened her lips and leaned forward, sighing heavily. In broken English, she continued, "I never see her after she go to Vienna."

Gerlinde's eyes widened, and she waved her hands in disbelief as she said, "Oma, you never told me this."

"Something's better left unsaid," Anna said patting her granddaughter's leg with Gerlinde translating. To Sarah, Anna said, "We just stop talking about her and the war." Anna folded her hands, appearing sad. "I look for her and Jacob after war, but couldn't find them. I hope they safe, but in my heart I belief Nazi find them and…"

Anna looked out the window, lost in thought and continued, "I was married during war, but my husband didn't make it back from Russian Front. Later, I marry Gerlinde's Opa, Hans. He dead now too."

Anna was quiet a minute and Sarah waited to see if there was more, she would say. At last Anna came to herself and went on, "One more thing I will tell to you. Just before war ended, my Mama, she passed away.

"There wasn't much food for people. We were lucky because we had farm. I remember hiding with my sister in barn as Russian soldiers came one night. There were rumors, they rape women."

"Oma, that's terrible." Gerlinde gasped.

"Yes, very bad time. They come steal all our food. But they leave my father and brothers alive. Luckily, they didn't find us. Then, few days later young priest come by asking for Oma. Father told him she passed away. Priest looked very upset and ask about a book. He not say why he wanted to see her or what book. When he leave, he come to me and say, the Lady of Light need you. I not know what he mean so I tell him: go away. I never saw him again."

It took every ounce of restraint for Sarah to keep a straight face when Anna mentioned the book. *So, there's a connection to the church.* She needed to get back St. Martin's and do more looking around. Right now, she needed to play dumb and said, "The war must have been awful."

"It was," Anna said. "So, tell me. Your Mama and you were close?"

"Yes, we were very close."

"Where she living?"

Sarah stared down at her cup, not wanting to answer. "She was mentally ill," Sarah said as her voice faltered. She wondered if she should tell Anna about her mother's suicide. It wasn't something she wanted to talk about, but the old woman was waiting for an answer. Finally, she met the old woman's eyes and said, "She, umm... she killed herself."

"I so sorry," Anna said in a soft voice. She moved over next to Sarah and pulled her against her shoulder. "You here with us now..."

Anna whispered something in German to Gerlinde then that sent her granddaughter out of the room. When she was out of earshot, Anna pulled away from Sarah and said, "I say something for you, no Gerlinde. Right?" The old woman looked at Sarah solemnly and went on. "I don't know why I tell you," She pressed her lips together. "People say, my Oma was a witch."

Now that the words were out, things began to make sense to Sarah, but she didn't say anything just parted her lips and covered her mouth with her fingers.

Anna reached over beside her and took up the intricate wooden box she'd brought back with her. Gerlinde came back into the room. Handing it to Sarah, she said, "There is necklace inside."

Sarah opened the box and took out a hand-crafted necklace with a ruby pendant on it. Lifting it up to the light coming in from outside, the necklaces' dark red stone glittered within an intricate silver frame. "It's beautiful."

"See on back," Anna said with Gerlinde translating again. "There are initials of Elisabeth von Galler. She was Baroness from Riegersburg. My Papa say she give to our ancestors for important service they do for her. But no one remember what it was."

Did the book and the necklace have any connection? Sarah had a strong hunch they did. She needed to get the book back and have it translated to find out, and put the necklace back into the box.

A few minutes later, Angela came in with her husband who'd come home from work, and to invite them all outside to dine alfresco on a long wooden table that sat under a large hazelnut tree.

Sarah placed her hand on her chest when she saw all they had prepared for her. She looked at her extended family who were spread out around her, hardly knowing what to say. "Thank you so much, this is lovely."

Angela smiled and showed her to a place at the set table and before long sixteen Wenzels were digging into cured meats, breads, salads and cheeses.

"May I take a picture before we eat?" Sarah said to Gerlinde before everyone got down to business.

"Of course," Gerlinde said, and rounded everyone together to stand in front of the house. A chair was brought for Anna to sit in the middle with the smaller children gathered at her knees.

"Everyone say cheese," Sarah said, which was translated by Gerlinde. That brought on smiles and chortling as Sarah snapped away, taking as many shots as she could before everyone started moving again to get back to the dinner table.

Wine and beer flowed into mugs and glasses as her new extended family talked across the table, sharing their eventful days. That Sarah couldn't understand a lick of what they were saying didn't matter, because she was amongst family. She relaxed and pushed her worries away, enjoying the precious moments as the fiery orange sun dropped behind the tops of the trees.

Forty minutes later, on the road back to Riegersburg, Sarah cried out loud, "Shit. I'm lost." There were no streetlights or directional signs in the middle of the woods and the GPS wasn't working. She stopped the car, groaning out loud, she slapped both hands on the steering wheel. Should she call him? She hesitated, then grasped her iPhone.

Chapter Twenty Six

Twenty Minutes Later

After she gave Felix a detailed account of where she might be, he found her shaken and tired twenty minutes later. Apparently, she was just five minutes from Riegersburg in the woods and didn't know it. When they got back to the hotel, she asked him if he had some time to talk. She had a lot on her mind, specifically what if anything the church might know about her Oma being a witch or for that matter her ancestors before that. How far did it really go back?

"Let's go to the bar," he said.

Now that he was sitting opposite of her and enjoying a beer, she couldn't figure out where to begin. She watched him set the large *stein* down and wipe his mouth with the back of his hand and rolled her eyes.

"Hey, just because I'm a priest doesn't mean I can't appreciate a good beer," he said, sitting back in the booth. They were the last customers. "How was the visit?"

"It was great," she said. She sipped her wine and told him about all her long-lost relatives, especially Anna and her lineage to the Baroness of Riegersburg. But as far as the necklace and the book were concerned, those details she left out — at least for the time being — until she was sure of him.

"The Baroness from Riegersburg?" Felix said, raising his brow. He turned his head to look at the pretty bartender, who was staring at them from across the empty room while polishing glasses behind the bar.

Sarah wondered what that was all about. Did they know each other? If he wanted another beer, certainly he could have gotten up and went over and got one. "Something the matter?" she said, pointedly.

Felix looked back with a start. "What do you mean?"

"Well, the look you're giving the bartender

"Oh, I was thinking about getting another beer."

"Hmm…" Sarah said, not entirely believing him. "So, I assume you don't believe them."

"Believe whom?"

"My family…about the Baroness," Sarah said.

"It is a stretch," Felix said, "but not out of the realm of possibility, I suppose."

"Well, I believe them," Sarah put in and paused, mulling over her next comment. Finally, she said, "Have you ever heard a rumor of the Baroness being a witch?"

Felix blinked and knitted his brow. "No, why do you ask?"

"Just something I've been wondering," she said, trying to be nonchalant about it. *Well, I guess I'll have to find out what the church knows another way.* "You know me, my mind goes all sorts of places. Anyway, I'm tired and should get to bed." She took a last sip of her second glass of red wine.

With all the beer she'd had at the Wenzel's home, she was feeling a pretty good buzz. She collected her backpack and attempted to get out of the booth. But her legs weren't working very well, and she stumbled. Felix flew over, despite his ankle, and caught her arm.

"Let me take you upstairs," he said.

"No, I'm fine," she said, brushing off his hand. Calling over to the bartender, she told her to put their drinks on her tab then tottered out of the room. Against her wishes, Felix was following her up the stairs. "You really don't need to see me to my room. I'm good. And I can't believe they don't have elevators!"

"It's an old building," Felix said as they reached the second floor.

Sarah giggled nervously when they came to her room. "Well. Here I am, so…" She turned toward him, sending him her best *you-can-leave-now* look and searched in her backpack for her key for what seemed to be an eternity. But Felix remained put: standing just a little too close for her liking. As she opened the door, he reached for her arm causing every nerve in her body to tingle. It quite unsettled her and she moved into the room with him following.

"What are you doing?" she said, trying to keep her old habits in check. What she really wanted was to throw him on the bed and rip his clothes off.

"I know I shouldn't be here,' he stuttered, "but…"

"But what?" Sarah said looking into his shining brown eyes.

Despite the warning in her heart and the effort to avoid another mistake in the long list of bad judgments with men, the alcohol was winning out. He went over to her bed and sat down, relaxing his posture.

She went over and sat next to him and looking over, saw him swallow. "Well, I'm waiting," she said.

Felix pressed his lips together and came to her. When their lips met, her whole body shuddered. They rolled backwards onto the blanket, running their hands over each other. Her drunken state took hold and loosened her resolve. She bent her back as Felix nibbled at her ear and she moaned with desire. A sensation of warmth flooded her body.

He pulled back and looked at her, then drew her to his chest. Knotting her hair in his hand and he pressing his lips over hers, he was everywhere, squeezing, fondling, and licking. She wriggled out of her pants, and with a sharp tug, popped the buttons on her blouse. He sat back on his heels, pulled his shirt over his head and looked down at her like a starved animal. Sarah reached for his belt, looking up at him knew she wanted him now. She tugged at the buckle and unzipped his pants. When the front flaps parted, she saw the large bulge straining against his dark briefs.

She put her hand around it and heard Felix moan as she squeezed. Then, he gently pushed her onto her back and took one breast at a time into his mouth. She cried out in pleasure as they hardened with each nibble. Stroking her back with his fingers caused her whole body to shiver with delight. And she smelled his musty armpits.

She reached down and felt how his penis hardened under her touch.

"Sarah, are you sure?" His voice was hoarse, looking at her firmly.

She nodded and parted her legs ever so slightly.

He moved up and over her. Sarah held her breath, looking at him. He advanced his head to hers and parted her lips with his tongue. She moaned, arching her back to meet his movements and allow him to enter her. She cried out loud in pleasure.

The feeling she was experiencing was like gravity; no, as if fate was pulling the strings: this country, this place, the book, her heritage. Although she wasn't a virgin, she felt like she was moving through new and uncharted territory. She peeked at him; his eyes were closed. Sarah rubbed his back as he thrust himself deeper and faster into her. She held his face and called out, "Yes, yes. Felix!" She climaxed, feeling overpowered by her reactions. Sarah caressed his buttocks with her hands. He groaned with a deep guttural sound, not yet coming.

"You are the one," he whispered into her ear still moving in her, stroking her hair. Their movements slowed and became gentle. They went from one position to the other until Felix was on top of her again pushing with greater intensity. She lost all sense of time. There was only him, their love-making. All else disappeared, until she felt a burning sensation in her loins, a furnace of hunger which built itself with each thrust. She climaxed again calling out. "Yes, Yes!"

Seconds later, Felix's head moved up and down, his whole body shaking. She knew he was coming. At the very last moment, he pulled out and fell on top of her letting his passion spread all over her belly.

"Sarah," he murmured and rolled off, gathering her up into his arms. She rested her head on his chest. They lay still and relaxed.

Felix propped himself up onto his elbow.

"You okay?"

"Umm…yes. Understatement of the year," Sarah said, tracing her fingers over his hairy, muscular chest. "You are certainly a surprise."

Felix knitted his brow. "How so?"

"Well, I never would've guessed you'd be so gentle and good."

"Thanks," he smiled, brushing the hair out of her face.

"You are really beautiful, you know that," he said, gazing at her.

Sarah had heard those words so many times after sex with men in her past she'd normally cast them aside as BS. Yet, somehow, their coming from Felix felt different. She smiled up at him. "Do me a favor; lay back down so we can snuggle?"

He caressed her cheek and as he did so she molded her body around him, laying her head in the crook of his arm.

"I'm not on any birth control. So, it's good you pulled out, and I could still get pregnant. Hopefully not. Don't know what I was thinking, haven't had a boyfriend for a long time," Sarah said, knowing she should be upset with herself not using protection. Not under any circumstances did she ever want children, not with the history of mental illness in her family.

"I'm so attracted to you," Felix said, "but…"

"And?" Sarah said.

"I'm supposed to be celibate. Oh, God. Can you forgive me?" Felix's voice trailed off as he rubbed his forehead, seeming genuinely worried. "I'm going to be ordained next month," he said, and glanced out the window. "But…you." He faltered, pulling her close to him.

"Yeah, I'm not sure either…" she answered, feeling his palpable sudden remorse. Never had she felt this way before about a man. She'd experimented with women a time or two, but no one had ever reached her heart like this man. She'd never encountered anyone this ardent. *Is this the way you feel when you meet your soulmate?* A very deep feeling of emotion gushed from her heart and felt as if it were flowing over to him. Sarah was afraid to open her mouth, afraid of what might come out of it. None of her relationships ever worked out.

They lay there for some time, dozing on and off until at last, Felix sat up and stared down at his hands. "I've got to go." He reached for his pants.

"No, wait," Sarah said. She grabbed his arm, her mouth falling open. "We really need to talk about this."

Felix raised his brow, as he stood up to finish dressing. When he averted his gaze from her. Sarah's body went rigid. She wrapped her body with a sheet, crossing her legs, and watched him gaze out the window. He fingered his cross. At last, he turned back. "I need some time here. Can you give me some time?"

"Don't worry about me," Sarah said, pasting on a smile. But a small voice inside her couldn't help wondering if she was his swan song before his ordination. Then again, hadn't she started things? But she also reminded herself, she hadn't invited him up to her room. He had followed her, and even when she gave him an obvious look of goodnight, he had stayed put. And she was on a pretty good buzz from too much alcohol. For all intents and purposes, he had the most to bear for what had happened.

He started to say something, as if he was begging for her to act, eventually letting his shoulders slump forward.

"I know this is tough," she said and stood with the bedsheet wrapped around her and moved to the door. "We both have some thinking to do."

Felix nodded.

Sarah opened the door, "Well, it's getting on and I have a busy day ahead of me."

"Right," Felix said, as he passed her, he bent toward her to give her a kiss on the cheek, but she pulled away. "Yeah, I guess not."

He went out into the hall and left without looking back.

Sarah shut the door, clutching herself and leaned back against it. Sliding down onto the floor, she rocked back and forth. Then she looked around the empty hotel room and her lower lip trembled. "I shouldn't be getting this upset," Sarah whispered. "I need to calm down." But the fear she had since she was little settled in like an old friend. Her chest ached and she hyperventilated. Awful images of blood, water and her Oma inundated her mind. She jumped up and rushed over to her backpack and took out Oma's pentagram. Holding it and recalling Oma's face helped her calm down. *Breathe!*

Her throat felt thick as she lay back onto the bed. Picking up the pillow he used, she sniffed it. It smelled like him, triggering the memory of their love-making to replay over and over in her head. However, she was exhausted and ultimately fell asleep hugging the pillow.

Chapter Twenty Seven

St. Martin's Monastery

"Thank you, Goddess. You have answered my prayers." Arnulf reached over and brushed the top of the book with his fingertips. Their nerve endings tingled with delight as he closed his eyes, savoring the moment.

Destiny brought you back to me. You belong to me. I'm the rightful owner of your wisdom.

He laid his hand flat on the book's cover and one on his heart. "I swear to protect the faith, and she'll not take you away, ever again."

The book rested on an altar in front of him next to his opened Bible, a golden chalice and a wooden cross. Normally his knees would be aching, but on this chilly morning dressed only in his night robe, nothing fazed him. He salivated and he stroked his throat thinking of all the knowledge awaiting him inside the covers of Elisabeth's writings.

Stupid American girl doesn't even understand German.

Like an evil demon, his usual longing and aching rose with his need to touch it. Normally he'd suppress this craving, yet in light of his clear road to more authority, maybe he'd allow a reward this morning.

Why not? The urge was great; so intense, he reached down. His breath quickened as he stroked his erect shaft. In between the pages of his Bible was a picture of a naked woman. Looking at it stimulated him even more, until release came hard and quick. He jerked his hand away and swallowed uncomfortably.

I shouldn't follow my base instincts outside of the sanctity of ritual. It's sinful.

Feeling unclean and unworthy, he jumped up to grab a washcloth and wiped the evidence away then smoothed his robe out and looked in the mirror at his disheveled image.

Tapping his finger against his bottom lip, he grabbed a comb and carefully straightened his hair. Then, he shaved, making sure not to cut himself, and pulled off his nightshirt to observe his body. He was proud of his lean physique, and he turned sideways to observe it. His butt was solid and his stomach flat. He smiled.

She will learn to love me.

After applying deodorant, he meticulously dressed himself, then knelt on the small bench in the corner of his white-washed bedroom. He lit a tapered candle that cast long shadows over the perfectly made bed. His night robe lay neatly folded on top of the pillow and a pair of weights for training rested next to his shoes peeking out from under the bed. "Goddess, forgive me, for I have sinned," he said on bent knees. But his gaze fell back on the book again and he bent forward to kiss its leather musty, lavender scented cover.

"I've been vindicated for all the sacrifice and hard work. Lady of Light, you are here again. Your worship shall arise, and I shall be your champion" he muttered as warmth radiated throughout his body.

He was the chosen one.

But an image of the girl came again to him, and his muscles tightened. How could she be the Faith-Keeper? She was foolish and untaught in the ways. A desire for vengeance surfaced, and he growled ever so slightly. He clenched his fingers together, remembering his confession to Father Stainzel so many years ago as if it were yesterday. That was before he found Her, The Lady of Light.

"In the name of the Father, and the Son and of the Holy Spirit. My last confession was seven days ago." Arnulf muttered through the latticed opening between the wooden confessional boxes in St. Martin's Church. As he held his cross, his hands trembled. Arnulf drooped his head forward. *I want to escape. Do I need to tell Him everything? It's unfair.* His words were met with a long silence from the other side. The back of his throat ached, and he prayed for salvation.

"My son, what have you done?" Father Stainzel's voice dropped, and the man coughed. Arnulf jumped at the sound of the older priest's voice. He'd expected someone else, one of his brothers, not Stainzel!

He tried to maintain a steady tone of voice. "I have given myself to sexual gratification and denied my faith."

"Elaborate. Tell me more."

Arnulf's neck stiffened, and he sighed with exaggeration. "Do I really need to express all the details?"

"Yes, son."

Again, there was a long silence, save for the Father's heavy breathing.

"It was…" Arnulf's chest caved and he covered his face with his hands. "I can't tell you. I won't," he yelled, struggling to fight the overwhelming compulsion to flee.

"God knows all, and you can't run away from Him. This is for your salvation. Go on, son. Find the courage to confess!"

Arnulf pulled at his collar, feeling his rapid heartbeat. But words wouldn't come and his knees weakened. *God will not forgive me, and I'll be stripped of my vocation, banned from my brothers, and the church.* His resolve not to say anything left him, and he squirmed on the hard bench.

Father Stainzel's voice interrupted his thoughts. "Remember Son, Christ sacrificed himself for our sins, for your sins."

"It was Evelyn. Evelyn Mellacher," Arnulf stuttered. "We had sex, she wanted it. She made me do it."

Arnulf heard Father Stainzel hit the wall. "Dear God.

She's only fourteen years old! How could you?"

"I don't know. She was helping after Sunday school and…"

"I don't want to hear it. Just get on and repent. You are a great disappointment. I had hopes for you but, now…"

"Oh my God, I am heartily sorry for offending You, and I detest myself for this sin. I dread the loss of heaven, and the pains of hell," Arnulf said as his stomach was taut and painful. He bit down and forced himself to continue. "But most of all, because I have offended You, my God, who are all good and deserving of all my love. I firmly resolve, with help of your Grace, to confess my sins, to do penance and to amend my life."

Arnulf moved forward onto the edge of the bench and clutched his hands together.

Silence roared in his ears. *Say something!*

Finally, Father Stainzel's voice came back like a slithering snake through the lattice, coiling his throat. "You will rise every morning at five a.m. for six months and pray for an hour for forgiveness," he pronounced. "And you must never speak of or touch the girl again. And you had better pray she's not with child. Now make the Sign of the Cross with me." Stainzel said and cleared his throat. "Give thanks to the Lord for He is good."

Arnulf closed his eyes and let his head fall back. Drawing a deep breath, he responded. "For His mercy endures forever."

As the door of the confessional shut and footsteps tripped away, Arnulf hardened his heart. The man would make his life a living hell. *You never forgave me, did you, old man?*

Outside his leaded window, Arnulf studied the sunrise. The bright saffron globe was peaking over the tips of the multi-colored trees of the church's back garden. He appreciated beauty. What God would create suffering as his tool to salvation? What nonsense. How stupid he was as a young man to believe his old teacher, Stainzel. When the old man finally died, Arnulf found the true faith on his own. He smirked, and uttered dark words, "Ignorant old man. What did you know of the world? Its attraction, its richness, the Goddess or even of God." They rang eerily throughout his room.

Baring his teeth, Arnulf remembered how he'd supplemented Stainzel's medication with poison, causing him to die earlier than his natural time. Arnulf's mouth curled with dislike, so wanting to share his achievements with others. Of course, he couldn't. No one would understand or appreciate how he'd worked himself up the ladder from a poor farm boy to his current position.

Walking back to the mirror, he smiled with satisfaction. *The perfect murder.* Not long after Stainzel' s death he found letters in the old man's safe; a key, a hidden room and Her. As often as he could, Arnulf knelt in front of Her picture behind the library, and prayed for enlightenment. And in these prayers was born the foundation of his ultra-secret Order of the Guardians, Lady of the Light, and created rituals and celebrations according to his aspirations and beliefs of Her.

Long nights were spent reading and studying whatever he could find out about Goddess worship, and what he deemed Her faith to be. As the years passed, he recruited others from the town. They followed him unquestioningly.

And when the American girl came and started asking questions, he'd put two and two together. His curiosity came alive when he heard her relatives were from Feldbach. The Police chief's son confirmed Arnulf's suspicions when he discovered the girl's associate, Vanderhoost, with the book in the library, innocently reporting back to him. It was too easy. Arnulf walked into the library and found the man alone. Sneaking up from behind the unsuspecting man, he knocked Vanderhoost cold over the head. Later, Arnulf sent Wolfgang to the hotel to mess the man's room up, and throw suspicion away from the monastery.

Arnulf sorely wanted to kill the reporter, but the intruders at the castle had gotten in the way. He smiled, recalling the

American's pleas. Fear fed him, but he wouldn't let it jeopardize his ultimate goal. He craved power.

The Goddess delivered the book back to its true Faith-Keeper: him. His loins quickened, thinking of the girl as he strode out of his room. He brushed this feeling of eagerness aside and blew out the candles.

Chapter Twenty Eight

A Week Later

A week passed since Sarah had visited the Wenzel's home. On the patio in front of the hotel, Vanderhoost sat opposite her cleaning his glasses. It was one of those hot, humid, windless days where the air stuck to her skin like flies on flypaper. Sarah sipped her coffee, darting her gaze around at the tourists sitting at tables next to them.

"No one has come forward to talk to the police or give any information. If you want my opinion, this is typical for small towns," Vanderhoost said. His hands fluttered eventually pointing to the road leading up to the castle. "This could take months the way the police work here. I want to fly home."

Sarah said. "The police said—"

"The investigation is stalled," Vanderhoost cut in. "Do you really think you'll find out who stole the book?"

Sarah leaned over the table toward Vanderhoost and hardened her voice. "I need to find it. It was my Oma's,"

"Understood," Vanderhoost said, pressing back in his chair.

Sarah sat back as well and softened her voice. "Sorry. It's just all so frustrating." She paused, picking nervously at her breakfast of eggs and toast, and said, "Do you think the Hohenburgs have anything to do with it?"

"Probably not." Vanderhoost said, sipping his coffee. He tipped his head toward a couple sitting nearby and gave her a knowing look. "Our neighbors over there are talking about us."

Sarah furtively glanced their way. "Yes, I know. I heard them mention something in German about the Americans.

"It's more than that. They're saying we brought on all this drama to their quaint little town."

"Oh really? They're blaming us?" Sarah said, and glanced at them again. The woman made brief eye contact before the she looked away. Sarah undid her hair, tossing it around. *As if it was our fault other vacationers were staying away.*

Vanderhoost finished his coffee. "Well, I suppose it's to be expected. Anyway, I don't care what that Police chief says, I'm flying back home. I've already booked my ticket for next Monday out of Vienna."

It took a moment for the words to register in Sarah's brain before she leaned forward across the table, this time nearly knocking her glass of water over.

"What? And leaving me here all alone in this mess!" Sarah cried, her nostrils flaring. She grabbed her glass and swallowed a large gulp of water, almost choking. He was leaving her in a country where there were maniacs out somewhere in this town with her book, if it was even still in the town… and not sold off to some distant collector of old books… or who knows where?

Vanderhoost seemed not all affected by her outburst He took up his napkin, and in a restrained voice, said, "As I recall, you told me your cousin David wants you to fly back home, too, and if I remember correctly, we were supposed to be back in Seattle by now."

"I'm not going home without my Oma's book," Sarah said, emphatically. But how was she going to get it? And who could she trust to help her? Certainly not the police! And Felix's father was the Police chief? She was sure the man would be pumping his son for information. She had to figure out a way to keep Vanderhoost from leaving, but right now she hadn't any idea about how. One thing she did know. With Vanderhoost, the harder you pushed, the harder he resisted, so she decided to back off, and respond to his comment concerning her cousin. "You're right, David does want me to fly home, but he trusts my judgment."

Vanderhoost cocked his brow. "Does he?"

"Yes, he's just concerned about me is all. We phoned last night and he's worried about me."

"He should be. Listen, I'm sorry, really, Sarah. I knew you'd be upset, but Peter wants me home, and I'm tired, and I don't mind saying: damned frightened," he said as he tucked a credit card in the sleeve of the bill folder, then added, "I'll fly back when they catch the culprits. I've had enough drama for a lifetime. My ulcer is killing me."

"Then why are you drinking coffee?" she said, pointedly.

Vanderhoost tilted his head and rolled his eyes. "You have to ask?"

She shrugged. "Well, you do what you have to do." *And I'll do what I have to do to keep you here.* "By the way, you haven't forgotten there's a meeting scheduled with the Hohenburgs and Mr. Hammer on Friday."

"No, I haven't forgotten," Vanderhoost said, handing their bill to a passing waiter.

Sarah reached over the table and laid her hand on his arm. "We'll find out more about the investigation. I hate Mr. Hammer. He's creepy. I wouldn't be surprised if he wasn't one of the bad guys." *Please don't leave me here alone with them. I need you.* "Maybe something will turn up. If it does, would you stay on a couple more days? I promise I won't say another word about your leaving if nothing comes of anything."

Vanderhoost eyed her for a moment. Finally, he said, "I'll think about it."

Sarah smiled. "Oh, and I heard the royal family has come back with their children."

"Did they?"

Her dreams of impending doom were fading like a washed-out cotton t-shirt even though the book was still missing. Sarah bit her lower lip, looking at Vanderhoost to see what he was thinking. She desperately needed to find answers.

"And the priest, what about him?" Vanderhoost said, finishing off his croissant.

"You mean Felix?"

"Yes. By the way, I know you slept with him."

Sarah felt her face suddenly get warm. She opened her mouth to say something but nothing came out.

"Oh, come. You don't think I'm that blind, do you?"

Sarah stammered. "How—"

"The way he looks at you. It's so obvious." Vanderhoost said. He eyed her, and the expression on his face betrayed his disappointment. "You know, you used to tell me everything. I can't blame you though…"

"Alright, I did. But it's not going anywhere. He's too busy studying and preparing for his ordination this fall and the last thing I need is to get involved with someone halfway around the world." She lifted her chin and forced herself to keep eye contact with Vanderhoost. The truth was, Felix hadn't contacted her since they'd slept together, and she was hurt. History had repeated itself yet again, except this time she wasn't the one breaking it off. She felt her throat tighten.

"Maybe it's for the best," Vanderhoost said, his tone soft and caressing. He tapped his fingers on the table. "Like you said, you live in Seattle and he's going to be a priest, a Catholic one at that. You know what they say about sex and their guilt complex?"

Sarah gazed over at a young couple walking by holding hands. Her voice broke and she slumped back in her chair. "I don't know why, but I… there was a connection…" Then, she remembered Father Holden was the reason her mom was dead. Sarah was determined not to end up like her mother, pining after a man who didn't want her. Sarah stared at her empty coffee cup. *He'll see he's making a mistake.*

"Sarah, I'm sure your hormones were racing, and being here in this fairy tale land made you vulnerable," Vanderhoost said, twirling his fork around. "You'll be over him in a heartbeat once you're back on American soil."

He was right, yet her heart was heavy. Sarah needed a sign of what to do next. If she was supposed to have inherited "the gift", why wasn't it working?

"I think I'll take a morning stroll," she said. "You don't mind, do you?

"Not at all," Vanderhoost said.

Sarah backed her chair up and stood. "Thanks for breakfast. I'll catch you later."

Vanderhoost waved her off and took out a magazine from his bag to read.

The scent of fresh bread coming out of the oven in the kitchen made Sarah's mouth water as she walked past it to get her camera equipment upstairs. Unexpectedly, her appetite returned, but she shuttered it away for the time being. She had too much on her mind and she needed to think. The best way to do that was to grab her camera and go for a walk. She climbed the sweeping hotel staircase and walked to her room where she changed into a tank top and a pair of khaki shorts, and slipped on her tan sandals. Finding a Cliff Bar in her bag she gobbled it down, and proceeded outside the hotel with her camera bag flung over her shoulder.

She looked up and down the avenue, debating which way she should go, but it was really no contest, and a half hour later she was at the gate to St. Martin's garden. For some reason she couldn't quite understand this place pulled at her like a magnet. Perhaps, it was because Felix lived up in the rectory's dorm, or maybe it was something else.

She parked herself on the bench across from the Mary statue and tried to relax. As she stared at it, she realized the statue might be representing a point of reference, a guiding light. But what was it pointing to?

The scene in the cave under the castle played itself over and over again in her mind. The memory of Vanderhoost being bound to an altar with the cloaked figures chanting some ancient incantation made her shiver all over again. She closed her eyes, trying to shake the feeling off and breathed in the scent of lavender that was in full bloom all along the edge of the garden.

"Mary or Goddess, give me a clue. I need to find the book." She was not a praying woman and never had been, but she was getting desperate. She opened her eyes —*What the hell. Give it a shot.* She got up and walked over to the stone woman and knelt before her. Small white and yellow butterflies flitted about the statue. Chubby yellow and black-banded bumblebees buzzed around the flowers in the garden.

Dear God or Goddess, I know I'm not a religious person and that I don't go to church or whatever place to worship, but I'm a good person and I try to do what's right. And right now, I'm in desperate need. This book that my Oma gave me is very important to me and maybe it'll bring me closer to you —I don't know. Please help me. What should I do?

She took a deep breath and looked up.

The sun was blazing, then Sarah spotted something shiny catching the sunlight next to the rose bush. It lay on the ground peeking out from under the mulch, near the stone base. She picked it up, and to her astonishment, it was a silver amulet much like the one her Oma had left her. Strange, she'd never noticed it before on the other mornings she'd been here. *What was a pentagram doing in a church garden?* She turned it over and saw initials on it. G. A. Her pulse quickened and she bumped into the statue getting up. She dug into her pocket and took out Oma's pentagram and compared the two. She'd been carrying Oma's since coming from the States.

The amulets were identical, probably crafted by the same hand, except for the initials on the back. Oma's had the letters H.W. *Who were G. A. and H.W.? How did the amulet get here?*

Without warning, she sensed someone was watching her and she turned around just in time to catch a glimpse of a tall, dark figure through the church's window. Had someone been watching her in the garden? Felix! Who else would it be? And why didn't he come out and talk to her? She grabbed her camera bag, which lay on the garden bench, and slid the pentagrams into her pocket. *I'm going to give him a piece of my mind.*

She marched up the garden walkway to the rectory door, yanked it open and sprinted down the hall. She ran with her heels skidding on the polished marble floors. Fifty feet down, she made a left into another long hallway which ended at the library. The hairs on her arms stood up from the cold air in the church. She sneezed. Damn— no tissues—so she wiped her nose on her T-shirt. Ahead of her the heavy wooden door was ajar.

She tugged on the metal knob, pulled it back and walked into the shadowy room spattered with golden sunbeams coming through the upper windows. She stopped, and her leg muscles tightened. It was uncannily quiet, save for the thudding of her shoes on the floor.

"Felix? You in here?" she called out. She held her breath waiting for him to answer. "Felix, it's me Sarah. If you're in here, please say something." But her plea was only met with silence, which set her nerves on edge. She held her camera case in front of her as she crept along the towering stacks of books.

He wasn't there. I should go back, she thought and was about to turn around when she noticed a small door ahead. She hadn't noticed it before when she was here with Vanderhoost. She opened it, careful to make as little noise as possible. On the other side, she found a small, dark room with a dim light rising up from the floor below. The air smelled stale and musty. A railing circled the light and went downward. She looked behind her then stepped inside, tiptoeing toward a glow until she came up against a metal guard rail.

Hesitating, she peered over the edge. *It's a spiral staircase!* Lights were flickering in the shadows below. She gripped the handrail and started down the stairs. As she descended, her footsteps thudded in her ears and a chilly draft heralded the way. At the bottom, she came to an empty room with stone walls.

In front of her hung a life-sized painting of a woman, and on each side of it were large gold pedestal stands. Giant white candles flickered on them, casting a saffron patina over the woman who sat naked on a throne. Sarah stepped up to the painting and studied the woman. In one hand the woman held an apple, and in the other, a staff carved in the shape of a serpent. A crown of stars rested on her head. She had long auburn hair, which flowed over her shoulders and past her naked breasts to her thighs. Behind the throne was a great tree where an eagle sat regally on a branch. *Who is this and why is she here?*

On one side of the splendid woman stood a magnificent stag and at her feet lay a unicorn, a lion and a rabbit. Sarah forgot her fears for a moment and reached over to touch the frame.

"She is beautiful, don't you think?" Bishop Baumgartner's' voice echoed behind her. "I knew it was only a matter of time until you found your way here."

Sarah jumped, and held back a scream. Turning around she could barely see him because he was draped in a black robe. He must have been lurking in the darkness behind her all along. More important, though, why was he here?

Her heart drummed. Blinking rapidly, she watched him push back his hood. In the candlelight, his face had a spectral, menacing quality to it. But it was his glazed eyes that held her like talons. He advanced towards her and she backed up until she was inches away from the painting.

"We've been waiting. The Goddess spoke to me in my trances, telling me the Faith-Keeper would come back to me one day and help me in the old craft. And you came. I felt you were the one from the first moment we spoke in my office. Do you remember? I could hardly believe it at first, but when you said your relatives were from Feldbach, I was hopeful. And to my surprise, your partner Vanderhoost came to the library with the book. It was divine providence. He had no idea I was watching him. So naïve."

"He brought the book here?" Sarah said, hardly believing Vanderhoost would be so foolish. Her mouth went dry as she moved to the right, farther away from Baumgartner. "No, he wouldn't."

Baumgartner pressed ahead, trapping her. "Oh, I'm afraid he did. Obviously, he didn't remember that little detail."

"Because you whacked him on the head!" Sarah said, recoiling from his rotten breath. She darted her glance around the room for an escape. "You don't really want…"

He laughed. "I'm sorry but the stairwell is the only way out."

Sarah gauged the distance to it, debating if she could outrun him. She didn't know what the man had planned for her, but she guessed it wasn't anything good. And she was pretty sure she wasn't going to be able to talk her way around him. She could pepper him with questions and stall him long enough that an opportunity for escape might present itself. At last, she said, "So, what's so special about this book that you were willing to kidnap an innocent man?"

Baumgartner considered her with an ominous gaze. "Power, Faith-Keeper, power! Too long it has been kept away from the Brotherhood. We were entrusted with its safekeeping for centuries until your great grandmother, the old Wenzel bitch, stole it from us." He spat. His gaze drifted off as if he were remembering a past injury. "The church is corrupt. How dare she!"

Sarah saw a vein pop out on his neck. He stepped closer, narrowing the distance between them, his gaze intensifying.

"The book has come back to me now, no thanks to that old doddering Bishop Stainzel. He thought he was clever, locking that letter in his desk. He underestimated me."

"What letter?" Sarah said in haste, anything to distract him.

"The letter which told how the book was lost. Yes, I learned your heathen grandmother took it to America."

"My Oma was not a heathen!" Sarah yelled back. "And the only power books hold is in the mind."

Baumgartner snorted. "Do not lie to me, Faith-Keeper; you had the book. You know the power it carries and how it can be wielded.

Left to men of lesser minds, it is but a trinket, but to men who know the ways of the Divine, it is an oracle. Long we've kept the faith, since before World War II, even back to the burning times. Since Georg Agricola died protecting us all."

He pointed to the painting. "Our divine purpose is to guard the practices of *Her*."

"Who do you mean? The woman in the painting?" Sarah said.

Baumgartner ignored her question. "We've preserved her

worship right here under the church's nose." He chuckled again, pleased with himself. "This confirms how powerful *She* is or how else would you have found your way to *Her* sacred altar?"

He took another step toward Sarah until he towered over her.

She put her hand up, scrambling for words to buy time and said, "I saw you from the garden and followed you here. I thought you were Felix. If I am the chosen one, shouldn't you bow down to me?" She swallowed and tightened her fists, staring at him with all her resolve and defiantly squaring her shoulders. "The police are investigating, you know. They'll notice I'm gone. Let me pass."

"I'm afraid that won't be possible," he said, shaking his head. A thin smile curled his cracked lips. "You see, I need you. or I should say, we need you. The Great Rite needs to be consummated and it can only be done with the Faith-Keeper, you and me, the high priest. Our crops will flourish and the wealth of the Goddess will be bountiful. I knew you'd follow me. I planted the amulet in the garden." He rubbed his hands together, grinning.

He's delusional.

Sarah didn't know what he was talking about, but she did know, it was now or never, so she shoved him as hard as she could, and darted for the stairway.

"Du blödes Weibstuck," he hollered after her.

Not daring to look back, she leapt up the stairs. Sarah could hear him scrambling after her. Rounding to the top of the steps, she tripped over a tiny stack of books, falling down onto one knee. "Shit," she cried, and before she could get up, Baumgartner was on her, pushing her down again as she tried to get up. He strode to the door leading to the library. Shutting it, he turned the key while keeping her in sight.

"Don't fight me, Sarah. I don't want to do you any harm." Narrowing his eyes menacingly, he continued. "This is our destiny. You are the womb, the vessel of life. You'll understand in the future when you accept your role."

Baumgartner's words chilled her. She knew there was no way out now, but she swore to herself she'd find a way out later.

He took out some rope, a piece of cloth, and a hood from under his cloak.

"Be a smart girl. Nothing will happen to you if you cooperate."

Sarah stood and looked around, not answering him as she focused on keeping panic from overtaking her.

"Put your hands behind your back."

She did as he ordered and reluctantly let him bind her wrists together. He gagged her mouth with a cloth and slid a hood over her head. She heard him run down the stairs and come back.

"Here is your iPhone." She heard him rustling around in her backpack then smashing it on the floor. She'd dropped her camera bag in the stone room. She groaned.

Baumgartner guided her till her thighs hit what felt like a stack of books. His grip was tight, his fingernails digging into her upper arm as he thrust her into a chair. Her stomach felt sick. "Sit down and wait."

I have to wait, you asshole. Vanderhoost will call the police.

Sarah heard him creak the door open, slam it shut and turn the bolt. She was alone. Bending over, she shook her head until the hood fell off. The room didn't have any windows. What could she do? She tried kicking down the door, but it was massive and didn't budge. Her mouth hurt from the cloth cutting into her lips so she looked around for something to pull it off. She tried to get a pen from her bag, pulling against the railing until it hurt, but nothing worked.

The light still shimmered from the center of the space. He had left the candles burning. Carefully, she went down the stairs to the chamber below and searched along the stone walls for a possible hidden entrance, but didn't find one. There was no way out. She looked at the painting. Was this what this Goddess wanted of her? She fell onto her knees and wept. Completely exhausted with the ropes biting into her wrists, she climbed back up to the top room and waited.

Chapter Twenty Nine

In The Forest

When the door opened hours later, Sarah was on the floor shivering. She raised her head and saw two men come into the room. "*Scheisse*," one of them swore. She froze as they hurried in, grabbed her and threw the hood back over her head.

"You don't have to do this," Sarah pleaded in a low whisper threw the gag, but they only grunted and drew her up. Accompanying her on each side, they held onto her shoulders and prodded her out of the room. She stumbled. One of them helped her back up. They didn't speak as they pushed her along the aisles in the library and out into a hallway where she heard their footsteps echoing. She couldn't help wondering if this was how it must have felt for victims brought to the guillotine in Paris during the French revolution.

Moving stiffly, her muscles sore and aching, she became acutely aware of sounds around her. A door creaked open and she felt cool, fresh air on her skin. She was outside and it must be night because she heard the sounds of crickets as they dragged her along.

A few minutes later, her head was pushed down and she was shoved forcibly into a car. Sarah wanted to yell at them, "Who the hell are you, you can't do this. It's the 21st century!" But she was gagged.

The car door closed behind her and two more doors slammed shut. Her wrists were raw from the bindings. *I'll make a run of it when we stop again.* She heard the car radio playing music as it sped away. Voices yodeled and the pounding "Oompah-pah" beat was extremely unnerving. The men in front were talking quietly. She wished she'd learned some German so she'd know who they were and what they wanted.

Awhile later, the vehicle stopped. The back door opened and Sarah tried kicking at them, but to no avail. They pulled her out, and she fell hard onto her butt. As they yanked her back onto her feet, she could hear the crickets. The incessant noise ground away at her resolve to stay calm. An owl cooed and she flinched. She must be near the woods because she smelled the resin of pine trees.

Her abductors guided her forward. The ground was soft, and dried leaves crunched under her sandals as she shuffled forward, afraid of falling and wanting to kill some time. Twice, she tripped over what were probably tree roots, only to be caught by one of the men.

I need to figure out a plan to escape.

After several minutes, she heard men yelling. Her mind raced, trying to anticipate what was going on. Surely, they wouldn't kill her. It sounded as if a loud argument was underway. She couldn't be sure because of the language, but the tone and cadence told her it must be one. They brought her to a halt, and she could feel the heat of a fire. The yelling ceased and only the crackling of wood filled the otherwise silence.

Someone snatched the hood off her head. Bright flames temporarily blinded her and she desperately tried to prevent herself from shaking. A few feet away, hooded figures stood in a circle around a clearing. Their faces were covered. She squeezed her eyes shut and opened them again.

Who the hell are these people?

Her pulse raced madly and she clenched her jaw, determined to stay calm. Tremors flooded her body. They're the same group who abducted Vanderhoost! Across from her was a flat stone slab decorated with candles and flowers. She backed away, wanting to flee.

But two of the figures rushed over to her, grabbed her and began to undress her. She twisted and fought, falling backwards onto her tailbone. Kicking and screaming as hard as she could, they couldn't control her. More people came and restrained her legs and arms, all the while signaling and barking directions to each other.

Someone grabbed her blouse and with a sharp tug, ripped it off her. Moments later, she was stripped of her clothes and was being carried to an altar. Terrified, she shrieked through her gag and peed on one of them. She was rewarded with a slap to her face.

One of them grunted in German. A moment later, her body was spread-eagled on the altar with her hands and legs bound to wooden posts at each corners of the platform. She shivered against the icy cold granite that was hard against her skin. Her cheek ached.

Finally, they unknotted the gag. It fell from her mouth onto the stone surface under her head.

"You, assholes! You can't do this to me. My friend will tell the police. You'll all go to jail. Let me go!" Sarah shouted over and over again until her throat was sore. "You won't get away with this. I swear. You're crazy." She slumped her shoulders back onto the cold stone to take a break from struggling against the ropes. "I can't believe this is happening. Help me, help me," she whimpered, but they paid no attention to her.

Like dark specters the figures swayed and hummed around the fire. Minutes later, they removed their cowls, revealing animal masks carved out of wood. The masks were evil looking and hauntingly striking at the same time. There was a raven, owl, cat, fox, and many more. The people moved around, imitating beast-like sounds, hollering up into the night.

Doesn't anyone hear them?

Except no one did, and it wasn't long until Sarah was mesmerized by the macabre movements of the individuals who were turning and dancing around the central fire.

They're insane!

The chanting grew louder and louder until they raised their hands in unison and stopped moving. The droning came to a sudden end. She looked up at the full moon and an abundance of stars sprinkled through the tree branches and felt faint. She was a few feet away from the heat of the fire. Her arms and legs were becoming numb. She clenched her teeth trying to stop them from chattering.

What now? What are they going to do to me? There must be a way to reason with them. Are they going to kill me?

The mob around her parted, and a tall formidable man came from out of the dark forest. Except for his stag's mask, he was completely naked. The raven character fetched a chalice and handed it to the man, who raised it to the sky. Then they brought him a knife. This, too, was held up to the stars. Both items were laid on the altar on either side of her hips.

Using their distraction with the ritual to her advantage, Sarah struggled against the ropes, hoping they'd loosen. She felt her right hand might be able to slip out of the knot. Keeping an alert gaze on the proceedings, and ignoring the increasing pain of her wrist, she focused on twisting and pulling.

I'll get my hand free.

A fox figure brought her book and held it open for the stag-masked man to read. He read the passage using a slow cadence, his voice commanding the assembly's attention. It was Baumgartner's voice.

Shit!

She almost had her hand pulled through the binding ropes.

Immediately, Baumgartner stood over her. It was as if the devil himself materialized before her eyes. The light of the fire exposed the mask's pointed antlers, his protruding eyes were evil and dark. As he loomed over her, she gasped for air.

He's going to rape me!

He climbed up onto the stone on hands and knees, then turned his mask up and howled. Sarah yanked her hand free and grabbed the knife next to her. Clutching it, she extended it towards his hairy chest.

"I'm the Faith-Keeper!" Sarah screamed and he flew back in surprise at her courage. "The book was given to me. If you do this, you'll go to jail." She caught a glimpse of him watching her suspiciously. "I call upon all the women before me, Elisabeth von Galler and my Oma Katarina. I swear if you don't let me go, you'll suffer. Untie me or I'll curse you all!"

She tensed her arm, ignoring the pain running up and down her limb, and pointed the weapon at Baumgartner. Everyone stood still as if they didn't know what to do. The fire crackled ominously.

Baumgartner laughed, "You stupid girl. You think you can stop me?" He lunged at her and knocked the weapon from her hand, sending it flying over the side of the altar.

"You don't know the ways of the mystery. You can't even read German nor have you a clue of the old ways. How could you lead us? I'm the master here. You will obey," he said, contorting his face.

The crowd murmured approval.

Sarah cringed.

Baumgartner laid his stag mask on the altar, and pinned her freed arm down. Terrified, she looked up at his dreadful, cruel face, fighting to free her arm from his iron grip. Then from the corner of her eye, she glimpsed the fox figure running forward and snatching the knife from the ground and pointing it Baumgartner.

"No. You can't do this!" the fox cried out in English.

It was Felix!

He took off his mask and her heart went cold.

What the fuck is Felix doing here? He's a part of this? My God. No. He can't—

A wave of nausea overcame her and she tasted bile in her mouth.

"Get off her," he cried.

Baumgartner looked over at Felix, astonished at first, then his face twisted in rage.

"Felix, put it down!" Baumgartner roared, and got off the stone. He repositioned himself with a broad stance, threw his chest out and faced the younger man. But Felix stood his ground. They stared at each other. Baumgartner glanced over at her, then as if he were on stage, pulled his shoulders back and extended his hand to Felix.

"You're my best student, like a son to me. Come, give me the athame," Baumgartner said in broken English.

Was he trying to impress her by speaking English? He's fucking insane.

"No. Let her go," Felix cried, holding onto the weapon. He glanced over at Sarah and addressed the rest of the on-lookers, keeping his eyes on Baumgartner. "This can't be what the Goddess wants of us. Her word is love. This is rape. I know you all understand. *Vergewaltingung!*"

In an instant, Baumgartner lunged at Felix, who was quicker and parried to one side.

"You won't kill me. You're not man enough," Baumgartner cajoled, waving his hand in dismissal. "You don't have a chance against me. Everyone stand back."

The two men circled around each other with their arms outstretched, each man's expression determined and hard. The others gathered around them, watching and waiting.

Sarah unknotted her other wrist, and was working frantically to free her right ankle. She prayed she could liberate herself and run away as fast as she could while the rest were distracted by the combat. In the heat of the moment, they'd forgotten about her and no one was paying attention.

She glanced as Felix darted forward at the older man's belly. Baumgartner with his athletic body, for an older man, strong and muscled, sprang back. But Felix drew blood. Looking down at his lifeblood oozing from his abdomen, he roared, "Du Hund!" He leapt at Felix, both fell to the ground, rolling around. Quickly, Baumgartner was on top, holding down Felix's arm, which held the dagger. Felix punched him in the mouth with the other hand and wrestled himself on top.

The others called out in a frenzy, egging the two men on. Baumgartner and Felix struggled, punching and fighting in a deadlock until Baumgartner, now on the bottom, was able to roll back on top again. He twisted Felix's arm around and jammed the knife's deadly blade into the younger man. Felix screamed in pain. Baumgartner grabbed a fist-sized rock and hit Felix's skull with it. Felix lay there quiet with the dagger sticking out of his side. Baumgartner stood up, looking down with a frown on his face at the motionless body, still holding the stone in his hand. The others backed away.

"Felix, no!" Sarah let out an uncontrollable sob and covered her eyes. Then she frantically tried to free herself, shaking hysterically.

Baumgartner moved towards her.

She heard shots, shouting and dogs barking. Flashlight beams bounced off the trees and she froze, watching the hooded characters run off in panic. Some just stood there bewildered as if they knew it was over.

"Polizei. Stop, oder wir schiessen!" Police chief Gruendlar ran into the circle of the bonfire followed by two more police officers and a dog. He looked over at his son on the ground and yelled. "Mein Gott, Felix!"

He ran to his son, falling to the ground. One of the officers came with his weapon raised towards Baumgartner, yelling. Baumgartner dropped the rock and the officer kicked him to the ground. The other policeman rounded up the five people who hadn't disappeared into the forest.

"*Er lebt.*" Police chief Gruendler said, putting his ear to Felix's mouth.

He reached for his cell phone and called for help. The police chief stood up and changed places with the officer in front of Baumgartner. He faced the naked man, who was looking at the ground, slumped over.

"Arnulf, warum?" Police chief Gruendlar raised his gun to the man's temple. A moment passed; Sarah held her breath.

Before Baumgartner could answer, the police chief knocked him on the side of his head with the butt of his gun. Baumgartner fell over, moaning. During the commotion, Sarah still had one ankle tied to a post.

"Please free me," she cried. Police chief Gruendlar told his officer to cuff Baumgartner, then hastened over to her and untied her ankle, offering his jacket to cover herself.

"Are you hurt?" he asked.

"No, not really, but…" she said, and rushed over to Felix. She took a breath and knelt down next to him. Her heart fluttered. "Please don't die," she whispered, taking his hand. She rocked back and forth and noticed his chest rise and drop. He was breathing.

Hesitantly, she bent over and kissed his forehead, then jerked back and dropped his hand. Felix had betrayed her. She was crushed. How could he have done this? She looked at police chief Gruendlar questioningly, who was kneeling on the other side of Felix holding his son's hand, repeating over and over again, "*Warum?*"

Three more officers arrived on the scene. She heard sirens in the distance as she waited for the emergency squad. Shortly afterwards, they came running into the clearing. They gently pushed her away, placed Felix onto a stretcher, and carried him away. Police chief Greundlar followed them into the woods. Should she go with him to the hospital? No, she wouldn't. He'd lied to her.

The rest of the mob was being rounded up by the remaining officers. Baumgartner had already been hauled away. She stood there with her muscles quivering, wanting to punch something or someone. *I could kill him. He knew all along. That bastard!* She saw the book and rushed over to where it had been left on the ground, then searched for her shorts and underwear.

After putting on her tattered clothes, she picked the book up, and held it to her breast until she spotted Vanderhoost running onto the scene.

"Oh my God, Sarah. Are you alright?" Vanderhoost called, and hurried over to her.

Her lungs constricted and her chin trembled. She fell into his arms, opening her mouth, but was unable to form any words.

"I'm here. It's OK." Vanderhoost guided her over to a boulder to sit and took off his sweater to cover her legs.

"When you didn't come for dinner or answer your phone, I called the police chief and demanded they search for you. I wasn't going to take any chances after what had happened to me."

She lowered her head and swallowed hard. "Felix is one of them." She blinked up at her friend.

Vanderhoost didn't appear surprised. "I'm sorry, but I've had a hunch for some time. I knew somebody must have tipped them off to clean up after my abduction but I wasn't sure. Felix, what a fucking bastard, I should've let you know my suspicions."

"Yes, you should have. How did the police find me?"

"A farmer saw the fire and apparently went into the woods

to look then ran back, called the fire department who called the police. I was at the station when they called, coincidently. Since they blew me off on the phone, I decided to take matters into my own hands," Vanderhoost continued. "At first, they were standing around talking. Of course, I knew I had to step in, so I said, *"You're idiots. These guys are the same guys. I'm sure of it. Sarah is in danger!""*

"Of course, Gruendlar wasn't too happy, especially because I insisted on coming along. He agreed to go with a few men and dogs but refused to take me with him. Can you believe him? Fuck that. You know what I mean. I called a taxi and followed them. What else could I do?"

"He saved me," she muttered under her breath with her eyes tearing up. She avoided Vanderhoost's gaze and felt a release of tension in her body. Felix had protected her. If he hadn't fought Baumgartner, she would've been raped, maybe even killed.

He must care for me.

"At least I found the book." It was a poor consolation after the events of the evening. How could've she have been so blind to his real intentions? Sarah had a hard time accepting Felix was one of the bad guys.

"Don't feel sorry for him," Vanderhoost said with a quick, disgusted snort. "He's an asshole! He deceived you."

"I know. You don't need to rub it in. Why did he do this to me?"

Vanderhoost shrugged. "Do you really want me— "

"No. Just shut up for now," she said, knowing she'd never forgive Felix for what he did. How could she feel any kind of love towards him? Why had her heart fluttered, kneeling next to him? One thing was for sure; she desperately didn't want him to die.

"Sorry."

"Honey, it's OK. That's what friends are for."

Firemen ran into the clearing, bringing buckets of water and pouring it over the fire pit. The embers glowed for a few minutes, sizzling and sputtering until the flames were completely extinguished. Sarah's energy felt like the wet coals, drained and empty.

A police officer came over to where they were sitting. "Fräulein Lilienthal, please come." He helped her up and gave her a blanket. She wrapped it around her shoulders, handing Vanderhoost back his pullover. The young officer held a flashlight and guided them out of the woods, where a car was waiting for them.

The police car raced through the unlit curvy roads past darkened houses and farms. Sarah felt sore, shocked, and deeply wounded. She looked out the car window at the luminous full moon, then pulled the blanket tightly around herself, resting her head on Vanderhoost's shoulder. Her heart ached.

I'll never forgive him!

Chapter Thirty

Sarah sat on a tan leather divan touching the material which felt smooth, then repeatedly ran her fingers through her hair. The book lay next to her hidden in a canvas bag. It'd had been four days since her ordeal. Thick whitewashed walls kept the long hallway cool outside the Hoehenburg's private apartments. She shivered and watched the door next to her. The room behind it was where the meeting was going to take place.

Her arms had dark blue and green bruises. She lightly messaged her red swollen wrists. After crossing and re-crossing her legs several times, she stood to look at pictures of the Riegersburg showcased in modern plastic frames. It rose up out of the steep mountain, shot from different angles, set in all four seasons.

Her new iPhone rang and she pulled it out of her skirt pocket. It was David.

"How are you this morning, little cousin?" David asked. "Just checking in after your hysterical call. I knew you should've stayed here and not gone to Austria. I don't want to say I told you so, but…"

"Then don't. I'm fine. I'll be flying home in a few days."

"No need to get snippy," he admonished.

"No need!" Sarah snapped. She'd told him everything about the abduction, the book and about Felix, but left out the part about the sex, embarrassed about her bad choices. David and she had spent well over two hours on the hotel's phone three nights ago.

"I still don't know if I should hand over Oma's book to them. This is a tough decision, David. Oma entrusted the book to me …what should I do?" She weighed the pros and cons in her mind. She couldn't read it and probably wouldn't use it, whereas they'd exhibit it at the castle. Experts could research it. The book belonged here.

"Calm down. I don't know either, but it's probably the right thing to do," he said quietly. "It'll still belong to our family. And it will be there where the legacy all started. You know I love you, so take a deep breath. Do you want me to come over and kick what's his name's butt?"

"You mean Felix. And yes, could you?" Sarah said, grimacing. "Like you did when we were kids and Joe Cawthorn was picking on me. Do you remember when you gave him a bloody nose?" she said, gazing at the door to see if anyone opened it. The royal couple was running late. It was after 4:00 p.m.

"Yes, but it was you who punched him. And I had to pull you off him. Listen. Focus for a minute," David said, his voice deepening. "When you meet with the Hohenburgs, don't let them take the book without a contract. And have them draw one up in English. They're definitely going to gain from all this. Just think of the publicity! You declared on Monday you wanted no part of it. Remember? Do you really believe in witches and…?"

"No, but Oma did. You're right, as usual." She didn't tell him that a part of her really did believe in magic. Sarah suppressed "the gift" as Oma called it, and remembered bits and pieces of her mother's erratic behavior from her childhood. Her instinct told her the two were connected in some way and her posture went rigid.

The door opened and she jumped, startled. Mr. Hammer waved for her to come in. "I'll send you anything they provide me. I have to go."

"Promise me not to hand it to them before I look over the documents," David said.

"I promise. Bye." Sarah hung up and entered the room. The living room had tones of grey and black, and was elegant and modern. Behind a black leather sofa hung a large silver-lined mirror. A large deer head adorned the other wall and a white fluffy throw was draped over one of the chairs. Mr. Hammer motioned Sarah to sit. She fussed with her clothes wondering whether her outfit was appropriate.

"They'll be here shortly," he muttered, and sat on the other black chair. Photographs, of the Hohenburgs and their three children, in various sized frames stood on the matching silver side-tables. Sarah checked her EcoWatch.

A few minutes later, the Hohenburgs appeared from a side door along with their lawyer. Sarah stood, fearing she was going to screw something up. They greeted her and motioned her to sit again as they sat down opposite her on the couch. Sarah took the book out of the bag and placed in front of her on her lap. She folded her hands on top of it, tapping it nervously with her fingers.

The prince rubbed the back of his neck, avoiding eye contact with her and whispering with his lawyer. In comparison, the princess sat with a smile, her posture relaxed, her legs gracefully to one side.

Police chief Gruendlar hurried into the room and pulled up a chair. He apologized for being late. His face was unshaven and he looked like he was wearing a three-day old rumpled shirt. "I was at the hospital with my son."

"Of course. How is he?" Mr. Hammer said, and glanced at his watch as he fidgeted with a pen.

He's such a jerk. I guess you never know who the bad people really are.
She'd heard from the police that Mr. Hammer was blameless, and the royal couple was found to be completely innocent of any involvement in her kidnapping.

"He'll make it. Thank you for asking." Police chief Gruendlar's ears reddened and he coughed. Clearing his throat, he continued. "By the way, we've apprehended Bishop Baumgartner. And I am happy to report the members we caught in the woods confessed. They gave us the rest of the names we needed. Our town is safe again and the castle will be back to normal," Police chief Gruendlar said with a weakened voice as he studied the royal couple. "They will be prosecuted, I assure you."

The prince narrowed his eyes and forced a smile. "So, you

have taken care of this mess?" his voice sharp.

Greundlar blew out a noisy breath and looked over to Sarah for support, then put his hands up in defeat. "I have… though it's a great disappointment to me." He shook his head and dropped his hands limply onto his lap.

Sarah quivered, recalling the incident then attempted a weak smile. She hadn't had a good night's sleep since her abduction. She just wanted to get this meeting over with. She felt deserted and lonely because Vanderhoost had left for the States yesterday. Peter had demanded he fly home immediately. "I'll see you in Seattle," leaving her here by herself! Could she really blame him?

"Yes, yes. And we are, of course, very grateful for your diligence. Now what about the book?" Prince Hohenburg said while Sarah gazed out a window. She turned back toward him, noticing his smile looked like it was frozen on his face.

The lawyer leaned forward, and said, "Fräulein Lilienthal, the prince and his wife believe the book belongs to the castle and needs to stay in Austria as an important historical document."

"Yes, I understand," Sarah said, trying to remember his name. She turned the book upright and held it against her chest like a shield. "I just want to make sure…"

What she really wanted was to get her life back to normal. She didn't want to believe in a divine power or a pre-planned destiny. Last night, she'd decided not to follow "the path" her Oma wanted for her. Yet today, she wavered as she looked around the room. That was until her gaze rested on Princess Hohenburg who was quietly sitting next to her husband. She was so poised.

"We have no precedence for this kind of matter, so I called the Police chief in Graz, and our government inspectors of Styria," Police chief Gruendlar said, cutting in. "There's the unequivocal evidence of Fräulien Lilienthal's letter from her Oma. That alone proves Sarah is the sole owner of the book. We've concluded, for now, the Hohenburgs have no legal claim to it." He leaned back in his chair and folded his arms together.

"What? This is preposterous!" Prince Hohenburg said, and tilted his head backwards. He paused a moment. "This book is of great importance to our castle. I demand it stay here. I cannot believe something of such historical importance should be in the hands of an American!" The prince shifted his position on the sofa.

"Experts need to examine it. Is there nothing we can do?" He glared at his lawyer, but the lawyer shook his head.

The prince glared at Sarah, but she met his gaze defiantly. Finally, he turned and flicked a piece of lint off his suit. "I'm not going to sit here and listen to this absurdity. Please excuse me, I have business to attend to."

And then to Sarah's astonishment, the prince sprang up and stalked out of the room. As the door shut behind him, Sarah fought the urge to yell after him.

It's my book, you stupid prince!

"My dear, please forgive my husband's outburst. He's been overwrought by the recent happenings right under our home. It's been awful. I'm truly sorry and I know it doesn't excuse his behavior. You must be terribly upset and the bruises are well...I know you went through something very traumatizing," Princess Hohenburg said and looked over to their lawyer, who nodded in agreement while pulling at his necktie as if to loosen it.

Sarah frowned and looked directly at the princess.

He's overwrought! I'm the one who was abducted. Maybe I won't give it to them!

"So, dear, I want to afford you time to think about other options. Could we negotiate the idea of scanning the book or borrowing it from you for our museum as a special exhibition piece? That is, if you're still open to working with us? We would be very grateful and, of course, would compensate you handsomely. Our lawyer could write up a document to ensure the book stays in your legal possession."

The princess's kind demeanor soothed Sarah. Something in the cadence of her voice made Sarah believe her. "That sounds reasonable. My cousin David is a lawyer from New York. I spoke with him this morning, and he'll take care of any legal papers for me. Write up a draft, but please, in English, and email it to me," Sarah stammered and squeezed her eyebrows together. "I'll forward it to him and let you know my answer. I'm not sure how

I'm feeling about the future of the book. But, for now, it belongs here where Elisabeth wrote it."

"Thank goodness. Believe me. We have your best interest at heart." The princess said and reached over the table, taking Sarah's hand with her own.

Sarah gently pulled her hand away from the princess's soft, cool fingers. "I'm planning on staying a few more days." she said, placing the book on the silver-grey coffee table. The book looked large and out of place in the fancy room.

"May I?" said the princess. When Sarah nodded, the woman took it and opened it to the first page. "Oh, my dear, Elisabeth's name is right here. This is truly exciting." She carefully closed it again and eyed Sarah.

"I'll hand it over when the papers are signed," Sarah said, her voice cracking. She stared down at her sandals, feeling guilty giving it away, but on the other hand, the book almost cost her life. *Oma, forgive me.*

"Well, that is wise. We are happy to have your cooperation. We'll send off a draft to you tomorrow," the lawyer said.

"I'm staying with my relatives in Feldbach. You can reach me there. Here is my email address," Sarah said and wrote it down, her hand trembled. She picked the book back up and slid it into the bag. It felt heavy as if it was telling her to leave it on the table. She rubbed her nose nervously.

Everyone stood.

"Then it's settled. I'm glad we've come to an agreement. Thank you," Princess Hohenburg said, taking both of Sarah's hands again into her own. "It'll be safe here.".

A maid came in and escorted Sarah and Police chief Greundlar out of the room and down to the inner courtyard. As Sarah strode over the wooden moat with the Police chief after her, she wondered if it was it worth it? Were there still secrets she needed to learn from the book?

No. For now, this arrangement was for the best. In the future, she'll come back and maybe… She marched down the cobblestone road with the Police chief beside her.

"My son's been asking for you," Police chief Greundlar blurted out from beside her. They'd passed the vineyards, leaving the keep behind them. "I promised him to talk to you. I just can't believe he'd do such crazy, bad things."

Sarah didn't turn or stop moving. She knew Felix's arrest must have shocked the police chief to his core: he was the moral pillar of this town. She was furious and pressed her lips together. Her eyes teared up, and she didn't want Felix's father to see she cared.

"He's going to live," Police chief Gruendlar said. "He's in the intensive care ward in Feldbach. He almost died. Please stop."

Sarah turned to face him. That was too bad, because she felt like killing him herself. She was damned she'd was going to visit him, even if Felix had saved her from being raped or something worse. The fact he was a member of that evil circle made her churn inside.

Had Felix told him about our intimate encounter?

She rolled her eyes, shaking her head vigorously. "No." Sarah forced the word out, turning and picking up her pace.

Her thoughts raced while she worked her way down the stone road. Felix knew the whole time, all along, and hadn't warned her of Baumgartner. How could he have deceived her and been so nice at the same time? She'd slept with him, by God. How stupid. On top of everything, she'd developed feelings for him, even started to fall for him.

I won't forgive him. Never.

"Wait. He was a good boy, really." Police chief Gruendlar stuttered, coming alongside her. He took a handkerchief out of his jacket and wiped his forehead. "It was Arnulf who corrupted him. I can't believe it. Arnulf and I grew up together. And to think he baptized Felix as a boy."

Sarah let him vent. Felix almost died, lost a lot of blood saving her. Her throat constricted and went dry. She wasn't going to allow herself to think about the man who'd awoken stirrings in her heart then betrayed her.

Fifteen minutes later, they came to the main street in front of the hotel.

She turned to him, uncertain of what to say. "I'm sorry. At least he's alive," she said apologetically.

"It's for the best, then," Police chief Greundlar said, avoiding eye contact. *"Auf Wiedersehen."*

"…I'm so sorry, again, but I will never see him…ever," Sarah uttered to the Police chief, then ran up the stairs.

Chapter Thirty One

Sarah came out of the front double doors of the hotel. Gerlinde was waiting outside next to her car. Sarah felt the warm slight breeze against her skin and waved hello.

"Let me help you," Gerlinde said, and ran up to help Sarah carry her luggage to the car.

"Thanks for picking me up," Sarah said, and climbed into the front seat.

"No problem. Oma insisted you to stay with us. You're family!" Gerlinde looked over at her with a wrinkled brow as they drove out of the town. "Come, let's get out of here."

"I'm so happy to get away from it all," Sarah said, letting out a sigh of relief.

Gerlinde sped through the narrow streets. The car window was open and wisps of her blonde hair waved around her face.

She shook her head to get the strands out of her eyes, clutched the steering wheel then said, "I can't believe what happened. It's all over the news about the bishop of St. Martin's. You must have been terrified. That's why we called the hotel. How are you?"

Gerlinde's kind-hearted concern for her welfare made Sarah feel tender and vulnerable, so she looked away.

"I was terrified. Baumgartner was horrible," Sarah said. "If it wasn't for Felix risking his life for me, he would've raped me. I'm not a spiritual person, but I think the Goddess or some higher power was protecting me." She held her breath and licked her lips, contemplating the countryside's beauty passing by her window. She didn't want to believe in a Goddess, because if there was one, why did She allow her mother to die?

"So, you believe in a Divine Power?"

Should I mention Goddess?

"Yes. I do." Gerlinde leaned back, glancing at Sarah with a gleam in her eyes. "God brought us together again, didn't he?" She reached one hand over and brushed Sarah's arm. "Do you mind telling me how it all started?"

"No, of course not. It all started at the Mary statue," Sarah said. "You know the one at the garden at St. Martins… Well, actually on the train to Graz." She went on to tell all about the book, and of Oma, and how she met Felix, and of Vanderhoosts' abduction and the book's disappearance. Last of all was the painful memory of the secret room at St. Martins, and her abduction. The repulsive details of the attempted rape she kept to herself, at least for the time being.

Gerlinde stared back. "I can't believe people do these kinds of things in the 21st century," she said. "It's barbaric!"

"Neither can I." Sarah touched her throat, wiping her damp palms on her jean shorts.

Gerlinde pulled the car over to the side of the road next to a huge tree and embraced Sarah. "I'm so sorry you had to go through those awful things."

It was as if a dam broke inside. Sarah let out her feelings of sorrow and anger, sobbing onto her second cousin's shoulder. She wept until the recollections of the horrific creatures, the chanting around the fire, and the fight between Felix and Baumgartner, subsided. Her heartbeat steadied and she calmed down.

"Better?" Gerlinde said. She pulled back and reached into her purse. "Here's a tissue."

Sarah nodded, wiped her tears, and took a few slow and easy breaths, tipping her head back onto the headrest.

They sat there in silence for a few moments until Gerlinde sprang out of the car, and walked towards a hulking tree, which stood by itself in a field of wild grasses. Its bark was black and peeling and its trunk was at least six feet across. Sarah's jaw dropped open in awe. Its branches were as large as some tree's trunks and the crown spread majestically over the field. Sarah got out of the car and followed Gerlinde over to the tree.

Gerlinde patted the grand tree, looking up at its branches. "This is the oldest elm tree in all Austria. It's over five hundred years old. It stood here when our Omas were girls. Even in Elisabeth von Galler's time. The woman who wrote your book could've stood right where you are now. And now here we are. Maybe it's a coincidence."

Gerlinde took Sarah's hand. "I can't help believe it was God who brought you back here. Legend says a branch from this elm brings good fortune and health. But you must keep it under your bed for a year. Only take the ones you find around on the ground." Then she stretched her arms out in an easy-going manner.

The two women searched around on the ground.

"I have one," Sarah cried, and picked up a slender branch. "This better bring me better luck."

Gerlinde winked at Sarah who put the stick on the car's back seat then jumped back into the front. Her cousin's enthusiasm was contagious and Sarah felt a little better. They drove back to the Wenzel farm.

Later, after dinner with her relatives, Gerlinde took Sarah upstairs to a bedroom on the second floor. Gerlinde sat down onto one of the twin beds. "Did you know this room was my and your Oma's room when they were children? You're safe with us. I'm sleeping here tonight."

"I'm so homesick and ... I miss Oma."

"I understand," Gerlinde said in a quiet voice. She reached over and patted Sarah's leg and went to the door. "Oh... one last thing. My Oma wants to talk to you in the morning. She'd like to take a look at the book."

The next morning after breakfast, Sarah, Marie and Gerlinde sat in the dining room finishing up their coffee. The rest of the family was in the kitchen or outside on chores around the farm. Marie, who was reading the book, suddenly looked up and cried out in German. Gerlinde translated. "We're descendants from Elisabeth von Galler! She says; it's written right here that she gave up her illegitimate child to our ancestor, Farmer Wenzel. The girl, Hildegard, was raised as their own in secrecy... a young priest was her tutor."

"My goodness, she was our ancestor." Sarah sprang up putting her hand to her mouth and grabbing both of her cousin's hands. "Wow. That explains how Oma had it."

"Incredible. And that's probably why we have the necklace," Gerlinde said. Raising her brow, she pressed her palms against her cheeks.

"When Baumgartner called me the Faith-Keeper, I'm sure it had something to do with an older religion," Sarah said. "Maybe Elisabeth was something like a priestess. In Seattle, I Googled information about the early Celts in this area. They were called Norici and they worshipped a Mother Goddess called Noreia; the Lady of Light."

Gerlinde got up and peered over Marie's shoulder. "Really? So, you believe this book is about an ancient Goddess religion?"

"Yes, I do," Sarah answered. "Read more, please."

Marie sighed heavily and bent over to read.

"She writes there was a group of men and women who met regularly at the priest Georg Agricola's farmhouse. She tells of dancing..."

"Look at these two amulets," she said. Marie crossed herself.

Marie closed the book and muttered something in German.

"She says, 'It's devil's work to me.'" Gerlinde translated.

"No, Marie," Sarah said. She looked up at Gerlinde to convey what she was about to say back to the woman. "You know Oma was good, you said so yourself.

Marie listened to Gerlinde's translation then answered back in German. "Well, I don't know," Gerlinde said as the old woman wrung her hands together. The two aunts came from the kitchen and joined the discussion.

"What's all the commotion about?" Aunt Rosalie asked. Gerlinde explained to their surprise they were all related to Riegersburg's baroness.

"I want the true story of Elisabeth to be public. I'm letting the Hohenburgs borrow the book for research," Sarah said, picking up the book. "Light needs to be cast on the witch burnings."

"It's for Sarah to decide," Gerlinde said, ending the discussion. The aunts went back to the kitchen where Sarah could hear them arguing.

"Let's go for a walk," Gerlinde said, taking Sarah's hand.

Sarah followed Gerlinde along a pathway next to the apple orchard. Large red apples hung on the trees supported by horizontal wires very different than what Sarah was used to in America. All were barely five feet tall and evenly spaced. On the other side of the orchard, the green corn stalks were dense and stood higher than the young women.

Stepping in pace with her cousin on the grass footpath, Sarah watched grasshoppers jumping in front of their sandaled feet. Gerlinde caught one and held it out to Sarah to see. "I love nature," she said and stopped to face Sarah glowing happily.

"Me, too," Sarah said, feeling vindicated for her effort for traveling here.

Gerlinde was truly the sister Sarah always dreamed of. Sarah studied her cousin's heart-shaped face and sparkly blue eyes. "You must come and visit me in Seattle. The Pacific Northwest is great, the ocean and the Olympic National Park."

"I'm actually an America fan. Not all my friends here are, but I am," Gerlinde said in an excited tone. Clapping her hands together, she bounced around on the grass. "Now I have a reason to fly there."

Sarah reached into her pocket and handed one of the silver pentagrams to Gerlinde. The woman took it, smiled and hugged her.

"Really? You want me to keep it?"

For the first time she could remember, Sarah felt better. "Yes. I have the other one and every time we look at them, we'll be reminded of each other and our connection to Elisabeth,"

"I'll keep it close to my heart," Gerlinde said, and kissed the amulet before putting it in her shirt pocket. "Thank-you ever so much. Let's walk some more. What's it like living in America?"

Sarah picked up her step, and as she walked, told her of life in the big city, and all the little political and social quirks that went along with it. In the end though, she said, American people weren't all that much different than those who lived in Germany and Austria. Afterward, she shared her future plans, her love of photography and her life.

"I feel embarrassed to tell you, but I slept with Felix." Sarah observed her cousin, who didn't seem fazed.

Gerlinde shrugged and said, "We live in the 20th century. I wouldn't tell Oma but it doesn't bother me."

"I feel like I should visit him in the hospital, but I'm very hurt and mad. He betrayed me! What do you think I should do?" Sarah asked, torn inside.

"Oma; Marie always says to me, life will show us the way if we just keep our hearts and minds open for the signs," Gerlinde said. She took Sarah's hand, placing it on Sarah's heart. "Let your heart decide."

Chapter Thirty Two

Three Days Later

Sarah opened her laptop to find an email with a copy of the contract David had faxed to the Hohenburgs' lawyer. She read through it and the prompt response from the Hohenburgs. The royals had agreed to her terms. It was done. She rubbed the back of her neck and twisted her watch around her wrist, anxious to get home. As far as her boss was concerned it was none too soon. She re-read his email.

You're needed at the magazine.

She decided she better cut the visit to her family short and leave first thing in the morning. Then she read Vanderhoost's latest email.

Sarah chuckled as she thought of Vanderhoost. Since his departure, he'd texted and emailed her several times. At first his emails were more like tirades about how could she have gotten him into this mess. 'They were going to sacrifice me!' Finally, he calmed down and the whole experience became an adventure to him. "We're a modern-day Sherlock Holmes and Watson team."

Him being Sherlock, of course.

She missed his humor. "I'm writing this piece about Riegersburg and the Boss is ecstatic about it, maybe I'll make it into a series. I can't wait to see the photographs. When are you coming back to Seattle?" Vanderhoost texted. "Soon," she texted back.

After packing, Sarah went with a heavy heart to the Wenzel family, and told them she needed to fly home, promising to come back in the future, as well as to keep in touch. She hugged

Marie and the rest of her new family, inviting them all to come visit her in the States. An important broken link in her family was reconnected. Oma's wish was fulfilled.

Had this been my true calling to come here, not the book or the castle but the connection and the promise to reunite my family?

In the afternoon, Gerlinde drove her back to Riegersburg where they parted. Later, Mr. Hammer dropped by to pick up the book at the hotel. She had a twinge of remorse as she handed it over to him. "We'll take good care of it. It'll be at home in the castle." Mr. Hammer assured her.

Sarah was to leave on the next bus to Graz then catch the train back to Vienna where she would fly out of the next day back to the States. But for the time being, she had two hours to spare, so she took the opportunity to climb up the hill to the fortress one last time.

The sky was clear, without a cloud to see. A few tourists were walking up the road to visit the castle. She passed the pool and bushes where she and Felix had hidden, then the archway and up past the vineyards.

Finally, she came to the open field that offered a full view of Riegersburg. It was magnificent. To think that the castle, which had withstood the Turkish armies and the Mongolian hordes, had belonged to an ancestor of hers left her dumbfounded and just a little proud. The idea that she stood here on the very ground Elisabeth had walked on sent a giddy shiver through her. She formed a steeple with her hands and pressed them to her lips. What would Elisabeth have done?

Her iPhone rang, as if someone had heard her question.

"Hello," she answered cheerfully, thinking it was her cousin.

"It's me. Felix."

She caught her breath and stiffened. After what felt like an eternity, she gritted her teeth and said, "Felix. Good to hear your voice. I trust you're well?"

"I'm recovering, and you?"

"Well, that depends," she said, balling her fist, "On how quickly I can forget you."

He was silent for some time. Finally, he said, "I suppose I deserved that."

"Oh, trust me, you deserve much more than that!" Sarah said as her throat tightened. "So, what do you want?"

"I…I just wanted you to know…I mean…that I'm so sorry, I hurt you. he stammered with an emotion-choked voice. "I don't suppose my telling you that I love you means anything."

Sarah closed her eyes as her heart battled with her righteous anger. She cleared her throat. "That's not what I call love," she said and put her hand over her pounding heart. An uncomfortable tingling in her stomach made her want to sit down. She looked around for a bench, but couldn't find one.

"I know you don't believe me, but it's true. Ever since the first time I saw you on the train, I felt it for you. Maybe it was fate I met you on the train before - well - I don't know, but I believe it was God's intention for me to save you. I only hope and pray you'll forgive me one day."

Sarah rolled her eyes. "You really believe God intended you to save me?"

"Yes. I do."

"Well, you hold onto that. As far as forgiving you…" She exhaled and leaned against the stone wall and saw a falcon dart up and down in the sky above. She peered over the wall and saw a bird of prey show going on down below. At last, she said, "I don't think I can. Never…maybe. I don't know. I have to go. Good-bye," she said and hung up feeling breathless. Heat radiated throughout her chest. *He said he loved me.*

She stared at the phone for a long time, lost in thought as a bald eagle rose up and made a large turn in the sky, climbing higher and higher, looping elegantly above her. Then it sailed down and glided over Sarah making three circles above her head only to disappear behind the trees. It'd been called home.

Sarah realized this was the sign she was seeking; she needed time and space from Felix and from what had occurred here. She made her way down the steep path to get her bags, then sprinted the last stretch of the road to the hotel with her camera bag slung over her shoulder.

Her heart wavered at the inn asking herself whether she should see Felix one last time. Leaning forward and putting her hands on her knees, she forced herself back up, feeling as if an oppressive burden had been lifted off her shoulders. Somehow her faith was restored, and she promised herself not to let mother's suicide rule her life any more.

It was time to reclaim her life, to push negative thoughts out of her mind. *I can love and be loved.* Deep down she found the willingness in her core to believe everything will be all right.

Her next step was to fly home to Seattle, then as soon as she could, travel to the Berkshires where she was born. She had unanswered questions only her Aunt Ursula could answer; questions about who her father was. More importantly, she needed time to mend and visit her Oma's gravesite.

As if she could hear Oma saying;

Time heals all wounds.

Epilogue

Riegersburg Castle, 2011

Gerlinde leaned over the display case under the window in her ancestor's bedroom. There it was: the book. It was opened to a page showing a hand-drawn picture of a moon spell with an ash tree in the background, signed by Elisabeth von Galler. Next to the book, in a different glass case, was Elisabeth's necklace. Her pulse increased dramatically as she stared at its beauty. The dark red stone sparkled in the sunlight. She took out her phone to take a picture of the ancient heirlooms to send to Sarah. A few minutes later, she heard footsteps, and she looked around to see Mr. Hammer approaching.

"Fräulein Geist-Wenzel. So glad you could come before we opened to the public." He reached over and held her hand a little longer than necessary. "The prince and princess are extremely indebted to you and your Oma's generosity for lending us Elisabeth's necklace. It is priceless, and I assure you it's in a high security case. I want to extend condolences for your loss of her from both myself and their Highnesses."

Gerlinde looked down at her empty hands and answered in a flat, monotone voice. "Thank you, for your kind words. She died last month peaceably at home with us around her."

Mr. Hammer dipped his head, seemingly fumbling for the right words. "They say that's the best way to pass on to heaven."

Giving a half-hearted shrug, Gerlinde drew a breath before she said, "I guess you're right." She missed her terribly.

Mr. Hammer adopted a posture of exaggerated casualness. "How is your cousin?"

Gerlinde fidgeted with her earring. "You mean Sarah?"

He sighed dejectedly and looked away. "Yes, yes."

"Actually, I'm flying to see her this week. She's doing well." Gerlinde's gaze darted back to the book then over to the Baroness' coat of arms. The white and silver family crest of two doves, two swords; crossed and painted red, hung on the wall over the cold fireplace. Unexpectedly, she felt the need to touch it and the desire to investigate its meaning. She tilted her head back to him.

He nodded, sensing her unasked question. "Doves are symbols for peace. By the way, you can tell her Baumgartner will be in jail for a long time. And also, Chief Greundlar's son is up for a parole hearing next month due to good behavior. And now, if you'll excuse me, I will leave you alone. Give Fräulien Lilienthal our regards and we hope to see her here again."

After he left, Gerlinde walked to the window and gazed out at the light green countryside surrounded by brown fields, waiting to be tilled. Spring was awakening the trees and plants. Pink apple blossoms sprinkled the landscape. She took a deep breath, filling her lungs with the fresh air.

A chill ran down her back as if something or someone brushed by her. Gerlinde peered around the room, alarmed. A curtain fluttered, but there wasn't any wind. Nothing was there.

She reached for her necklace to touch the silver pentagram. She let out a huge breath, feeling a sudden lightness. A few months ago, she began to study witchcraft, finding several books about it in the bookstore. Sarah's visit had stirred a yearning in her to discover more about the Goddess.

"You can have the book after the exhibit," were Sarah's words of encouragement.

"Elisabeth, if you can hear me, you and Katarina are not forgotten. The ways of old will come again. I promise." Gerlinde swore and kissed her pentagram. Walking to the door, she thought she heard a woman's voice whisper.

"How much longer?"

Aknowledgements

I owe special thanks to Paul Baxter and Ron Bagliere for their expertise and knowledge in editing this manuscript. I give much gratitude and appreciation to my local writer's group for their listening to the journey of this story.

I want to recognize my spiritual teachers: Gerlinde Shilcher, Lucia Francia, Angelika Aliti and Starhawk who taught me "the path" of the Goddess and awakening a deep reverence of life.

My publisher, Ananke Press, and my editor, Cate Hendrickson, for her fantastic work and energy in helping me bring this story to light.

My father, Mahlon Kriebel who taught me tenacity and the passion of story-telling; my step mother, Monika, my brother Kurt, and my three daughters: Carmen, Amrita and Katarina for taking the time to listen, giving me important advice, support and encouragement. I also thank Tracey and Margaret for their patience, friendship and inspiration.

About the Author

    Julie Anne Stratton was born in Seattle, WA and grew up in New York City and Syracuse, NY. She spent most of her childhood and teen years reading books. Julie loved to explore worlds opened up by the page of a good story. When she was a child, her family put on elaborate marionette shows of their favorite stories for the neighborhood children. Julie fell in love with the role of the wicked witch of the West from the *Wizard of Oz*.

During the summer her father, a scientist, took her and her family to Cape Cod and Friday Harbor. These trips awoke a deep passion for the ocean and nature. She spent hours on the beach writing plays, journals and poetry.

She had her first flute lesson at ten, which eventually led to her life-long career as a classical musician. Julie studied at SUNY Brockport for year before leaving the US for Europe where she attended the College of Performing Arts in Graz, Austria. Instead of coming back to the states, she married and had a family there, loving the European life style. As a professional musician she collaborated with her chamber group *Cosi von Donne* producing two shows: one performing stories about women composers, and the other a re-telling of the Medea story.

While raising her three daughters, Julie stumbled on the book, *Ich bin eine Hexe* (*I am a witch*) by Gerlinde Schilcher. She traveled to mountains of upper Austria where Gerlinde introduced her to Goddess worship. She was hooked and read as many books about witchcraft as she could find.

After living in Europe for 20 years, she returned home to the States, where she attained her masters in music education. Also, she began writing again.

Her passion is writing fiction about strong women and continuing to practice her earth-based reclaiming Goddess religion.

Author's Note

Riegersburg Castle

Riegersburg Castle is a medieval castle situated on a dormant volcano above the town of Riegersburg in the Austrian state of Styria. The peak is at 482 meters above sea level. People have been living in the area around Riegersburg for a few thousand years. A large village was founded in the 9th century B.C. with three hundred people living here.

The most important owner was the baroness Katharina Elisabeth von Wechsler, who married Galler and who was known as the *Gallerin*. Between 1637 and 1653 she finished the castle, making it one of the biggest and strongest castles in the country. It is surrounded by three kilometres (two miles) of walls with five gates and two trenches and it contains hundred and eight rooms.

In the 17th century the border with the Ottoman Empire was sometimes only twenty to twenty five kilometers away from the castle and the area was troubled by conflicts with the Turks and Hungarians. Baroness Gallerin married three times and had one daughter who married a Count Purgstall. The castle passed to the Purgstall family, who died out around 1800.

The largest Styrian witch trial in Feldbach from 1673 to 1675 and among the ninety five accused men and women including Katharina Paldauf. At the age of twenty, she entered the service of *Elisabeth Katharina Freifrau von Galler († 1672)*, the owner of the Riegersburg Castle. In the spring of 1675, when Katharina was about fifty years old she was accused of having manipulated weather and participated in witch Sabbaths, arrested and incarcerated in Feldbach. Though she initially denied the accusations, after being tortured she confessed and gave the names of other people that she said participated in witch meetings. She was found guilty and sentenced to death. She was first killed and then burnt to the stake, probably on 23 September, 1675. The priest from Hatzendorf, Georg Agricola was sentenced to death for practicing witchcraft on 16th of May, 1675.

Kristallnacht in Vienna

The pogrom of November 1938, popularly known as *Kristallnacht* (or "Night of Broken Glass"), was particularly brutal in Vienna. Members of the Nazi Party and its various paramilitary organizations (including the SA and the SS) were joined by civilians, emboldened by the lack of police interventions, to form "spontaneous" mobs that torched most of the city's synagogues and small prayer houses. Many of these burned to shells as the public and fire department personnel looked on, intervening only when the blaze threatened neighboring buildings. Jewish businesses were also vandalized and ransacked.

Dr. Kurt Lingens and his wife, Dr. Ella Lingens (née Reiner) were both physicians who lived in Vienna at the end of the 1930s. Kurt Lingens was an anti-fascist, born in 1912 in Düsseldorf, Germany. Kurt Lingens was barred by the Nazi authorities from studying in German universities because of his anti-fascist activities as a student. Kurt's wife, Ella, born in Vienna in 1908, had a doctoral degree in law and studied medicine at the local university. When the Nazis annexed Austria, she began to help the Jews, especially students that she knew through her studies. During the Kristallnacht riots, she hid ten Jews in her room.